NIGHT WORLD

NIGHT WORLD

VOLUME ONE

SECRET VAMPIRE
DAUGHTERS OF DARKNESS
ENCHANTRESS

L. J. SMITH

Hodder
Children's
Books

A division of Hachette Children's Books

The Night World . . . love was never so scary.

The Night World isn't a place. It's all around us. It's a secret society of vampires, werewolves, witches, and other creatures of darkness that live among us. They're beautiful and deadly and irresistible to humans. Your high school teacher could be one, and so could your boyfriend.

The Night World laws say it's OK to hunt humans. It's OK to toy with their hearts, it's even OK to kill them. There are only two things you can't do with them.

1) Never let them find out the Night World exists.
2) Never fall in love with one of them.

These are stories about what happens when the rules get broken.

SECRET VAMPIRE

For Marilyn Marlow, a marvel of an agent.

And with thanks to Jeanie Danek and the other
wonderful nurses like her.

CHAPTER
1

It was on the first day of summer vacation that Poppy found out she was going to die.

It happened on Monday, the first *real* day of vacation (the weekend didn't count). Poppy woke up feeling gloriously weightless and thought, No school. Sunlight was streaming in the window, turning the sheer hangings around her bed filmy gold. Poppy pushed them aside and jumped out of bed – and winced.

Ouch. That pain in her stomach again. Sort of a gnawing, as if something were eating its way toward her back. It helped a little if she bent over.

No, Poppy thought. I refuse to be sick during summer vacation. I *refuse*. A little power of positive thinking is what's needed here.

Grimly, doubled over – think positive, idiot! – she made her way down the hall to the turquoise- and gold-tiled bathroom. At first she thought she was going to throw up, but then the pain eased as suddenly as it had come. Poppy straightened and regarded her tousled reflection triumphantly.

'Stick with me, kid, and you'll be fine,' she whispered to it, and gave a conspiratorial wink. Then she leaned forward, seeing her own green eyes narrow in suspicion. There on her nose were four freckles. Four and a half, if she were completely honest, which Poppy North usually was. How childish, how – *cute!* Poppy stuck her tongue out at herself and then turned away with great dignity, without bothering to comb the wild coppery curls that clustered over her head.

She maintained the dignity until she got to the kitchen, where Phillip, her twin brother, was eating Special K. Then she narrowed her eyes again, this time at him. It was bad enough to be small, slight, and curly-haired – to look, in fact, as much like an elf as anything she'd ever seen sitting on a buttercup in a children's picture book – but to have a twin who was tall, Viking-blond, and classically handsome . . . well, that just showed a certain deliberate malice in the makeup of the universe, didn't it?

'Hello, Phillip,' she said in a voice heavy with menace.

Phillip, who was used to his sister's moods, was unimpressed. He lifted his gaze from the comic section of the *L.A. Times* for a moment. Poppy had to admit that he had nice eyes: questing green eyes with very dark lashes. They were the only thing the twins had in common.

'Hi,' Phillip said flatly, and went back to the comics. Not many kids Poppy knew read the newspaper, but that was Phil all over. Like Poppy, he'd been a junior at El Camino High last year, and unlike Poppy, he'd made straight *A*s while starring on the football team, the hockey team, and the baseball team. Also serving as class president. One of Poppy's greatest joys in life was teasing him. She thought he was too strait–laced.

Just now she giggled and shrugged, giving up the menacing look. 'Where's Cliff and Mom?' Cliff Hilgard was their stepfather of three years and even straighter-laced than Phil.

'Cliff's at work. Mom's getting dressed. You'd better eat something or she'll get on your case.'

'Yeah, yeah . . .' Poppy went on tiptoe to rummage through a cupboard. Finding a box of Frosted Flakes, she thrust a hand in and delicately pulled out one flake. She ate it dry.

It wasn't *all* bad being short and elfin. She did a few dance steps to the refrigerator, shaking the cereal box in rhythm.

'I'm a . . . sex pixie!' she sang, giving it a foot-stomping rhythm.

'No, you're not,' Phillip said with devastating calm. 'And why don't you put some clothes on?'

Holding the refrigerator door open, Poppy looked down at herself. She was wearing the oversize T-shirt she'd slept in. It covered her like a minidress. 'This *is* clothes,' she said serenely, taking a Diet Coke from the fridge.

There was a knock at the kitchen door. Poppy saw who it was through the screen.

'Hi, James! C'mon in.'

James Rasmussen came in, taking off his wrap-around Ray-Bans. Looking at him, Poppy felt a pang – as always. It didn't matter that she had seen him every day, practically, for the past ten years. She still felt a quick sharp throb in her chest, somewhere between sweetness and pain, when first confronted with him every morning.

It wasn't just his outlaw good looks, which always reminded her vaguely of James Dean. He had silky light brown hair, a subtle, intelligent face, and grey eyes that were alternately intense and cool. He was the handsomest boy at El Camino High, but that wasn't it, that wasn't what Poppy responded to. It was something *inside* him, something mysterious and compelling and always just out of reach. It made her heart beat fast and her skin tingle.

Phillip felt differently. As soon as James came in, he stiffened and his face went cold. Electric dislike flashed between the two boys.

Then James smiled faintly, as if Phillip's reaction amused him. 'Hi.'

'Hi,' Phil said, not thawing in the least. Poppy had the strong sense that he'd like to bundle her up and rush her out of the room. Phillip always overdid the protective-brother bit when James was around. 'So how's Jacklyn and Michaela?' he added nastily.

James considered. 'Well, I don't really know.'

'You don't *know*? Oh, yeah, you always drop your girlfriends just before summer vacation. Leaves you free to manoeuvre, right?'

'Of course,' James said blandly. He smiled.

Phillip glared at him with unabashed hatred.

Poppy, for her part, was seized by joy. Goodbye, Jacklyn; goodbye Michaela. Goodbye to Jacklyn's elegant long legs and Michaela's amazing pneumatic chest. This was going to be a wonderful summer.

Many people thought Poppy and James's relationship platonic. This wasn't true. Poppy had known for years that she was going to marry him. It was one of her two great ambitions, the other being to see the world. She just hadn't gotten around to informing James yet. Right now he still thought he liked long-legged girls with salon fingernails and Italian pumps.

'Is that a new CD?' she said, to distract him from his stare out with his future brother-in-law.

James hefted it. 'It's the new Ethnotechno release.'

Poppy cheered. 'More Tuva throat singers – I can't *wait*. Let's go listen to it.' But just then her mother walked in. Poppy's mother was cool, blond, and perfect, like an

Alfred Hitchcock heroine. She normally
expression of effortless efficiency. Poppy, head.
the kitchen, nearly ran into her.

'Sorry – morning!'

'Hold on a minute,' Poppy's mother said, gettin
of Poppy by the back of her T-shirt. 'Good morning
good morning, James,' she added. Phil said good mo.
and James nodded, ironically polite.

'Has everybody had breakfast?' Poppy's mother ask
and when the boys said they had, she looked at h
daughter. 'And what about you?' she asked, gazing int
Poppy's face.

Poppy rattled the Frosted Flakes box and her mother
winced. 'Why don't you at least put milk on them?'

'Better this way,' Poppy said firmly, but when her
mother gave her a little push toward the refrigerator, she
went and got a carton of low fat milk.

'What are you planning to do with your first day of
freedom?' her mother said, glancing from James to Poppy.

'Oh, I don't know.' Poppy looked at James. 'Listen
to some music; maybe go up to the hills? Or drive to
the beach?'

'Whatever you want,' James said. 'We've got all
summer.'

The summer stretched out in front of Poppy, hot an
golden and resplendent. It smelled like pool chlorine ar
sea salt; it felt like warm grass under her back. Thr
whole months, she thought. That's forever. Three mon
is forever.

It was strange that she was actually thinking this w
it happened.

'We could check out the new shops at the Village—
was beginning, when suddenly the pain struck an
breath caught in her throat.

It was bad – a deep, twisting burst of agony that made her double over. The milk carton flew from her fingers and everything went grey.

CHAPTER

2

'Poppy!'

Poppy could hear her mother's voice, but she couldn't see anything. The kitchen floor was obscured by dancing black dots.

'Poppy, are you all right?' Now Poppy felt her mother's hands grasping her upper arms, holding her anxiously. The pain was easing and her vision was coming back.

As she straightened up, she saw James in front of her. His face was almost expressionless, but Poppy knew him well enough to recognize the worry in his eyes. He was holding the milk carton, she realized. He must have caught it on the fly as she dropped it – amazing reflexes, Poppy thought vaguely. Really amazing.

Phillip was on his feet. 'Are you OK? What happened?'

'I – don't know.' Poppy looked around, then shrugged, embarrassed. Now that she felt better she wished they weren't all staring at her so hard. The way to deal with the pain was to ignore it, to not think about it.

'It's just this stupid pain – I think it's gastrowhatchmacallit. You know, something I ate.'

Poppy's mother gave her daughter the barest fraction of a shake. 'Poppy, this is not gastroenteritis. You were having some pain before – nearly a month ago, wasn't it? Is this the same kind of pain?'

Poppy squirmed uncomfortably. As a matter of fact, the pain had never really gone away. Somehow, in the excitement of end-of-the-year activities, she'd managed to disregard it, and by now she was used to working around it.

'Sort of,' she temporized. 'But—'

That was enough for Poppy's mother. She gave Poppy a little squeeze and headed for the kitchen telephone. 'I know you don't like doctors, but I'm calling Dr Franklin. I want him to take a look at you. This isn't something we can ignore.'

'Oh, Mom, it's *vacation* . . .'

Her mother covered the mouthpiece of the phone. 'Poppy, this is non-negotiable. Go get dressed.'

Poppy groaned, but she could see it was no use. She beckoned to James, who was looking thoughtfully into a middle distance.

'Let's at least listen to the CD before I have to go.'

He glanced at the CD as if he'd forgotten it, and put down the milk carton. Phillip followed them into the hallway.

'Hey, buddy, you wait out here while she gets dressed.'

James barely turned. 'Get a life, Phil,' he said almost absently.

'Just keep your hands off my sister, you deve.'

Poppy just shook her head as she went into her room. As if James cared about seeing her undressed. *If only*, she thought grimly, pulling a pair of shorts out of a drawer. She stepped into them, still shaking her head. James was her best friend, her very best friend, and she was his. But he'd never shown even the slightest desire to get his hands on her. Sometimes she wondered if he realized she was a girl.

Someday I'm going to *make* him see, she thought, and shouted out the door for him.

James came in and smiled at her. It was a smile other people rarely saw, not a taunting or ironic grin, but a nice little smile, slightly crooked.

'Sorry about the doctor thing,' Poppy said.

'No. You should go.' James gave her a keen glance. 'Your mom's right, you know. This has been going on way too long. You've lost weight; it's keeping you up at night—'

Poppy looked at him, startled. She hadn't told anybody about how the pain was worse at night, not even James. But – sometimes James just knew things. As if he could read her mind.

'I just know *you*, that's all,' he said, and then gave her a mischievous sideways glance as she stared at him. He unwrapped the CD.

Poppy shrugged and flopped on her bed, staring at the ceiling. 'Anyway, I wish Mom would let me have *one* day of vacation,' she said. She craned her neck to look at James speculatively. 'I wish I had a mom like yours. Mine's always worrying and trying to *fix* me.'

'And mine doesn't really care if I come or go. So which is worse?' James said wryly.

'Your parents let you have your own *apartment*.'

'In a building they own. Because it's cheaper than hiring a manager.' James shook his head, his eyes on the CD he was putting in the player. 'Don't knock your parents, kid. You're luckier than you know.'

Poppy thought about that as the CD started. She and James both liked trance – the underground electronic sound that had come from Europe. James liked the techno beat. Poppy loved it because it was *real* music, raw and unpasteurized, made by people who believed in it. People who had the passion, not people who had the money.

Besides, world music made her feel a part of other places. She loved the differentness of it, the alienness.

Come to think of it, maybe that was what she liked about James, too. His differentness. She tilted her head to look at him as the strange rhythms of Burundi drumming filled the air.

She knew James better than anyone, but there was always something, *something* about him that was closed off to her. Something about him that nobody could reach.

Other people took it for arrogance, or coldness, or aloofness, but it wasn't really any of those things. It was just – *differentness*. He was more different than any of the exchange students at school. Time after time, Poppy felt she had almost put her finger on the difference, but it always slipped away. And more than once, especially late at night when they were listening to music or watching the ocean, she'd felt he was about to tell her.

And she'd always felt that if he *did* tell her, it would be something important, something as shocking and lovely as having a stray cat speak to her.

Just now she looked at James, at his clean, carven profile and at the brown waves of hair on his forehead, and thought. He looks sad.

'Jamie, nothing's *wrong*, is it? I mean, at home, or anything?' She was the only person on the planet allowed to call him Jamie. Not even Jacklyn or Michaela had ever tried that.

'What could be wrong at home?' he said, with a smile that didn't reach his eyes. Then he shook his head dismissively. 'Don't worry about it, Poppy. It's nothing important – just a relative threatening to visit. An unwanted relative.' Then the smile *did* reach his eyes, glinting there. 'Or maybe I'm just worried about you,' he said.

Poppy started to say, 'Oh, *as if,*' but instead she found herself saying, oddly, 'Are you really?'

Her seriousness seemed to strike some chord. His smile disappeared, and Poppy found that they were simply looking at each other without any insulating humour between them. Just gazing into each other's eyes. James looked uncertain, almost vulnerable.

'Poppy—'

Poppy swallowed. 'Yes?'

He opened his mouth – and then he got up abruptly and went to adjust her 170-watt Tall-boy speakers. When he turned back, his grey eyes were dark and fathomless.

'Sure, if you were really sick, I'd be worried,' he said lightly. 'That's what friends are for, right?'

Poppy deflated. 'Right,' she said wistfully, and then gave him a determined smile.

'But you're not sick,' he said. 'It's just something you need to get taken care of. The doctor'll probably give you some antibiotics or something – with a big needle,' he added wickedly.

'Oh, shut up,' Poppy said. He knew she was terrified of injections. Just the thought of a needle entering her skin . . .

'Here comes your mom,' James said, glancing at the door, which was ajar. Poppy didn't see how he could hear anybody coming – the music was loud and the hallway was carpeted. But an instant later her mother pushed the door open.

'All right, sweetheart,' she said briskly. 'Dr Franklin says come right in. I'm sorry, James, but I'm going to have to take Poppy away.'

'That's OK. I can come back this afternoon.'

Poppy knew when she was defeated. She allowed her mother to tow her to the garage, ignoring James's miming of someone receiving a large injection.

An hour later she was lying on Dr Franklin's examining table, eyes politely averted as his gentle fingers probed her abdomen. Dr Franklin was tall, lean, and graying, with the air of a country doctor. Somebody you could trust absolutely.

'The pain is here?' he said.

'Yeah – but it sort of goes into my back. Or maybe I just pulled a muscle back there or something. . . .'

The gentle, probing fingers moved, then stopped. Dr Franklin's face changed. And somehow, in that moment, Poppy knew it wasn't a pulled muscle. It wasn't an upset stomach; it wasn't anything simple; and things were about to change forever.

All Dr Franklin said was, 'You know, I'd like to arrange for a test on this.'

His voice was dry and thoughtful, but panic curled through Poppy anyway. She couldn't explain what was happening inside her – some sort of dreadful premonition, like a black pit opening in the ground in front of her.

'Why?' her mother was asking the doctor.

'Well.' Dr Franklin smiled and pushed his glasses up. He tapped two fingers on the examining table. 'Just as part of a process of elimination, really. Poppy says she's been having pain in the upper abdomen, pain that radiates to her back, pain that's worse at night. She's lost her appetite recently, and she's lost weight. And her gallbladder is palpable – that means I can feel that it's enlarged. Now, those are symptoms of a lot of things, and a sonogram will help rule out some of them.'

Poppy calmed down. She couldn't remember what a gallbladder did but she was pretty sure she didn't need it. Anything involving an organ with such a silly name couldn't be serious. Dr Franklin was going on, talking about the pancreas and pancreatitis and palpable livers, and Poppy's mother was nodding as if she understood. Poppy didn't understand, but the panic was gone. It was as if a cover had been whisked neatly over the black pit, leaving no sign that it had ever been there.

'You can get the sonogram done at Children's Hospital across the street,' Dr Franklin was saying. 'Come back here after it's finished.'

Poppy's mother was nodding, calm, serious, and efficient. Like Phil. Or Cliff. OK, we'll get this taken care of.

Poppy felt just slightly important. Nobody she knew had been to a hospital for tests.

Her mother ruffled her hair as they walked out of Dr Franklin's office. 'Well, Poppet. What have you done to yourself now?'

Poppy smiled impishly. She was fully recovered from her earlier worry. 'Maybe I'll have to have an operation and I'll have an interesting scar,' she said, to amuse her mother.

'Let's hope not,' her mother said, unamused.

The Suzanne G. Monteforte Children's Hospital was a handsome grey building with sinuous curves and giant picture windows. Poppy looked thoughtfully into the gift shop as they passed. It was clearly a *kids'* gift shop, full of rainbow Slinkys and stuffed animals that a visiting adult could buy as a last-minute present.

A girl came out of the shop. She was a little older than Poppy, maybe seventeen or eighteen. She was pretty, with an expertly made-up face – and a cute bandanna which didn't quite conceal the fact that she had no hair. She looked happy, round-cheeked, with earrings dangling jauntily beneath the bandanna – but Poppy felt a stab of sympathy.

Sympathy . . . and fear. That girl was *really* sick. Which was what hospitals were for, of course – for really sick people. Suddenly Poppy wanted to get her own tests over with and get out of here.

The sonogram wasn't painful, but it was vaguely disturbing. A technician smeared some kind of jelly over Poppy's middle, then ran a cold scanner over it, shooting sound waves into her, taking pictures of her insides. Poppy found her mind returning to the pretty girl with no hair.

To distract herself, she thought about James. And for some reason what came to mind was the first time she'd seen James, the day he came to kindergarten. He'd been a pale, slight boy with big grey eyes and something subtly *weird* about him that made the bigger boys start picking on him immediately. On the playground they ganged up on him like hounds around a fox – until Poppy saw what was happening.

Even at five she'd had a great right hook. She'd burst into the group, slapping faces and kicking shins until the big boys went running. Then she'd turned to James.

'Wanna be friends?'

After a brief hesitation he'd nodded shyly. There had been something oddly sweet in his smile.

But Poppy had soon found that her new friend was strange in small ways. When the class lizard died, he'd picked up the corpse without revulsion and asked Poppy if she wanted to hold it. The teacher had been horrified.

He knew where to find dead animals, too – he'd shown her a vacant lot where several rabbit carcasses lay in the tall brown grass. He was matter-of-fact about it.

When he got older, the big kids stopped picking on him. He grew up to be as tall as any of them, and surprisingly strong and quick – and he developed a reputation for being tough and dangerous. When he got angry, something almost frightening shone in his grey eyes.

He never got angry with Poppy, though. They'd remained best friends all these years. When they'd reached junior high, he'd started having girlfriends – all the girls at school wanted him – but he never kept any of them long. And he never confided in them; to them he was a mysterious, secretive bad boy. Only Poppy saw the other side of him, the vulnerable, caring side.

'OK,' the technician said, bringing Poppy back to the present with a jerk. 'You're done; let's wipe this jelly off you.'

'So what did it show?' Poppy asked, glancing up at the monitor.

'Oh, your own doctor will tell you that. The radiologist will read the results and call them over to your doctor's office.' The technician's voice was absolutely neutral – so neutral that Poppy looked at her sharply.

Back in Dr Franklin's office, Poppy fidgeted while her mother paged through out-of-date magazines. When the nurse said 'Mrs Hilgard,' they both stood up.

'Uh – no,' the nurse said, looking flustered. 'Mrs Hilgard, the doctor just wants to see you for a minute – alone.'

Poppy and her mother looked at each other. Then, slowly, Poppy's mother put down her *People* magazine and followed the nurse.

Poppy stared after her.

Now, what on *earth* . . . Dr Franklin had never done *that* before.

Poppy realized that her heart was beating hard. Not fast, just hard. Bang . . . bang . . . bang, in the middle of her chest, shaking her insides. Making her feel unreal and giddy.

Don't think about it. It's probably nothing. Read a magazine.

But her fingers didn't seem to work properly. When she finally got the magazine open, her eyes ran over the words without delivering them to her brain.

What are they talking about in there? What's going *on?* It's been so long. . . .

It kept getting longer. As Poppy waited, she found herself vacillating between two modes of thought. 1) Nothing serious was wrong with her and her mother was going to come out and laugh at her for even imagining there was, and 2) Something awful was wrong with her and she was going to have to go through some dreadful treatment to get well. The covered pit and the open pit. When the pit was covered, it seemed laughable, and she felt embarrassed for having such melodramatic thoughts. But when it was open, she felt as if all her life before this had been a dream, and now she was hitting hard reality at last.

I wish I could call James, she thought.

At last the nurse said, 'Poppy? Come on in.'

Dr Franklin's office was wood-panelled, with certificates and diplomas hanging on the walls. Poppy sat down in a leather chair and tried not to be too obvious about scanning her mother's face.

Her mother looked . . . too calm. Calm with strain underneath. She was smiling, but it was an odd, slightly unsteady smile.

Oh, God, Poppy thought. Something *is* going on.

'Now, there's no cause for alarm,' the doctor said, and immediately Poppy became more alarmed. Her palms stuck to the leather of the chair arms.

'Something showed up in your sonogram that's a little unusual, and I'd like to do a couple of other tests,' Dr

Franklin said, his voice slow and measured, soothing. 'One of the tests requires that you fast from midnight the day before you take it. But your mom says you didn't eat breakfast today.'

Poppy said mechanically, 'I ate one Frosted Flake.'

'*One* Frosted Flake? Well, I think we can count that as fasting. We'll do the tests today, and I think it's best to admit you to the hospital for them. Now, the tests are called a CAT scan and an ERCP – that's short for something even I can't pronounce.' He smiled. Poppy just stared at him.

'There's nothing frightening about either of these tests,' he said gently. 'The CAT scan is like an X-ray. The ERCP involves passing a tube down the throat, through the stomach, and into the pancreas. Then we inject into the tube a liquid that will show up on X-rays . . .'

His mouth kept moving, but Poppy had stopped hearing the words. She was more frightened than she could remember being in a long time.

I was just joking about the interesting scar, she thought. I don't want a *real* disease. I don't want to go to the hospital, and I don't want any tubes down my throat.

She looked at her mother in mute appeal. Her mother took her hand.

'It's no big deal, sweetheart. We'll just go home and pack a few things for you; then we'll come back.'

'I have to go into the hospital *today*?'

'I think that would be best,' Dr Franklin said.

Poppy's hand tightened on her mother's. Her mind was a humming blank.

When they left the office, her mother said, 'Thank you, Owen.' Poppy had never heard her call Dr Franklin by his first name before.

Poppy didn't ask why. She didn't say anything as they

walked out of the building and got in the car. As they drove home, her mother began to chat about ordinary things in a light, calm voice, and Poppy made herself answer. Pretending that everything was normal, while all the time the terrible sick feeling raged inside her.

It was only when they were in her bedroom, packing mystery books and cotton pyjamas into a small suitcase, that she asked almost casually, 'So what exactly does he think is wrong with me?'

Her mother didn't answer immediately. She was looking down at the suitcase. Finally she said, 'Well, he's not sure *anything* is wrong.'

'But what does he *think*? He must think something. And he was talking about my pancreas – I mean, it sounds like he thinks there's something wrong with my pancreas. I thought he was looking at my *gallbladder* or whatever. I didn't even know that my pancreas was *involved* in this . . .'

'Sweetheart.' Her mother took her by the shoulders, and Poppy realized she was getting a little overwrought. She took a deep breath.

'I just want to know the truth. OK? I just want to have some idea of what's going on. It's my body, and I've got a right to know what they're looking for – don't I?'

It was a brave speech, and she didn't mean any of it. What she really wanted was reassurance, a promise that Dr Franklin was looking for something trivial. That the worst that could happen wouldn't be so bad. She didn't get it.

'Yes, you do have a right to know.' Her mother let a long breath out, then spoke slowly. 'Poppy, Dr Franklin was concerned about your pancreas all along. Apparently things can happen in the pancreas that cause changes in other organs, like the gallbladder and liver. When Dr

Franklin felt those changes, he decided to check things out with a sonogram.'

Poppy swallowed. 'And he said the sonogram was – unusual. How unusual?'

'Poppy, this is all preliminary . . .' Her mother saw her face and sighed. She went on reluctantly. 'The sonogram showed that there might be something in your pancreas. Something that shouldn't be there. That's why Dr Franklin wants the other tests; they'll tell us for sure. But—'

'Something that shouldn't be there? You mean . . . like a tumour? Like . . . cancer?' Strange, it was hard to say the words.

Her mother nodded once. 'Yes. Like cancer.'

CHAPTER 3

All Poppy could think of was the pretty bald girl in the gift shop.

Cancer.

'But – but they can do something about it, can't they?' she said, and even to her own ears her voice sounded very young. 'I mean – if they had to, they could take my pancreas out . . .'

'Oh, sweetheart, *of course*.' Poppy's mother took Poppy in her arms. 'I promise you; if there's something wrong, we'll do anything and everything to fix it. I'd go to the ends of the earth to make you well. You *know* that. And at this point we aren't even sure that there *is* something wrong. Dr Franklin said that it's extremely rare for teenagers to get a tumour in the pancreas. Extremely rare. So let's not worry about things until we have to.'

Poppy felt herself relax; the pit was covered again. But somewhere near her core she still felt cold.

'I have to call James.'

Her mother nodded. 'Just make it quick.'

Poppy kept her fingers crossed as she dialled James's apartment. Please be there, please *be* there, she thought. And for once, he was. He answered laconically, but as soon as he heard her voice, he said, 'What's wrong?'

'Nothing – well, everything. Maybe.' Poppy heard herself give a wild sort of laugh. It wasn't exactly a laugh.

'What happened?' James said sharply. 'Did you have a fight with Cliff?'

'No. Cliff's at the office. And I'm going into the hospital.'

'Why?'

'They think I might have cancer.'

It was a tremendous relief to say it, a sort of emotional release. Poppy laughed again.

Silence on the other end of the line.

'Hello?'

'I'm here,' James said. Then he said, 'I'm coming over.'

'No, there's no point. I've got to leave in a minute.' She waited for him to say that he'd come and see her in the hospital, but he didn't.

'James, would you do something for me? Would you find out whatever you can about cancer in the pancreas? Just in case.'

'Is that what they think you have?'

'They don't know for sure. They're giving me some tests. I just hope they don't have to use any needles.' Another laugh, but inside she was reeling. She wished James would say something comforting.

'I'll see what I can find on the Net.' His voice was unemotional, almost expressionless.

'And then you can tell me later – they'll probably let you call me at the hospital.'

'Yeah.'

'OK, I have to go. My mom's waiting.'

'Take care of yourself.'

Poppy hung up, feeling empty. Her mother was standing in the doorway.

'Come on, Poppet. Let's go.'

* * *

James sat very still, looking at the phone without seeing it.

She was scared, and he couldn't help her. He'd never been very good at inspirational small talk. It wasn't, he thought grimly, in his nature.

To give comfort you had to have a comfortable view of the world. And James had seen too much of the world to have any illusions.

He could deal with cold facts, though. Pushing aside a pile of assorted clutter, he turned on his laptop and dialled up the Internet.

Within minutes he was using Gopher to search the National Cancer Institute's CancerNet. The first file he found was listed as 'Pancreatic cancer – Patient'. He scanned it. Stuff about what the pancreas did, stages of the disease, treatments. Nothing too gruesome.

Then he went into 'Pancreatic cancer – Physician' – a file meant for doctors. The first line held him paralyzed.

Cancer of the exocrine pancreas is rarely curable.

His eyes skimmed down the lines. *Overall survival rate . . . metastasis . . . poor response to chemotherapy, radiation therapy and surgery . . . pain . . .*

Pain. Poppy was brave, but facing constant pain would crush anyone. Especially when the outlook for the future was so bleak.

He looked at the top of the article again. Overall survival rate less than three percent. If the cancer had spread, less than one percent.

There must be more information. James went searching again and came up with several articles from newspapers and medical journals. They were even worse than the NCI file.

The overwhelming majority of patients will die, and die swiftly, experts say . . . Pancreatic cancer is usually inoperable, rapid, and debilitatingly painful . . . The average survival if the cancer has spread can be three weeks to three months . . .

Three weeks to three months.

James stared at the laptop's screen. His chest and throat felt tight; his vision was blurry. He tried to control it, telling himself that nothing was certain yet. Poppy was being tested; that didn't mean she *had* cancer.

But the words rang hollow in his mind. He had known for some time that something was wrong with Poppy. Something was – disturbed – inside her. He'd sensed that the rhythms of her body were slightly off; he could tell she was losing sleep. And the pain – he always knew when the pain was there. He just hadn't realized how serious it was.

Poppy knows, too, he thought. Deep down, she knows that something very bad is going on, or she wouldn't have asked me to find this out. But what does she expect me to do, walk in and tell her she's going to die in a few months?

And am I supposed to stand around and watch it?

His lips pulled back from his teeth slightly. Not a nice smile, more of a savage grimace. He'd seen a lot of death in seventeen years. He knew the stages of dying, knew the difference between the moment breathing stopped and the moment the brain turned off; knew the unmistakable ghostlike pallor of a fresh corpse. The way the eyeballs flattened out about five minutes after expiration. Now, that was a detail most people weren't familiar with. Five minutes after you die, your eyes go flat and filmy grey. And then your body starts to shrink. You actually get smaller.

Poppy was so small already.

He'd always been afraid of hurting her. She looked so fragile, and he could hurt somebody much stronger if he wasn't careful. That was one reason he kept a certain distance between them.

One reason. Not the main one.

The other was something he couldn't put into words, not even to himself. It brought him right up to the edge of the forbidden. To face rules that had been ingrained in him since birth.

None of the Night People could fall in love with a human. The sentence for breaking the law was death.

It didn't matter. He knew what he had to do now. Where he had to go.

Cold and precise, James logged off the Net. He stood, picked up his sunglasses, slid them into place. Went out into the merciless June sunlight, slamming his apartment door behind him.

Poppy looked around the hospital room unhappily. There was nothing so awful about it, except that it was too cold, but . . . it was a hospital. That was the truth behind the pretty pink-and-blue curtains and the closed-circuit TV and the dinner menu decorated with cartoon characters. It was a place you didn't come unless you were pretty darn sick.

Oh, come on, she told herself. Cheer up a *little*. What happened to the power of Poppytive thinking? Where's Poppyanna when you need her? Where's Mary Poppy-ins?

God; I'm even making *myself* gag, she thought.

But she found herself smiling faintly, with self deprecating humour if nothing else. And the nurses *were* nice here, and the bed was extremely cool. It had a remote control on the side that bent it into every imaginable position.

Her mother came in while she was playing with it.

'I got hold of Cliff; he'll be here later. Meanwhile, I think you'd better change so you're ready for the tests.'

Poppy looked at the blue-and-white striped seer-sucker hospital robe and felt a painful spasm that seemed to reach from her stomach to her back. And something in the deepest part of her said *Please, not yet. I'll never be ready.*

James pulled his Integra into a parking space on Ferry Street near Stoneham. It wasn't a nice part of town. Tourists visiting Los Angeles avoided this area.

The building was sagging and decrepit. Several stores were vacant, with cardboard taped over broken windows. Graffiti covered the peeling paint on the cinder-block walls.

Even the smog seemed to hang thicker here. The air itself seemed yellow and cloying. Like a poisonous miasma, it darkened the brightest day and made everything look unreal and ominous.

James walked around to the back of the building. There, among the freight entrances of the stores in front, was one door unmarked by graffiti. The sign above it had no words. Just a picture of a black flower.

A black iris.

James knocked. The door opened two inches, and a skinny kid in a wrinkled T-shirt peered out with beady eyes.

'It's me, Ulf,' James said, resisting the temptation to kick the door in. Werewolves, he thought. Why do they have to be so territorial?

The door opened just enough to let James in. The skinny kid glanced suspiciously outside before shutting it again.

'Go mark a fire hydrant or something,' James suggested over his shoulder.

The place looked like a small café. A darkened room with little round tables crammed in side by side, surrounded by wooden chairs. There were a few scattered people sitting down, all of them looking like teenagers. Two guys were playing pool in the back.

James went over to one of the round tables where a girl was sitting. He took off his sunglasses and sat down.

'Hi, Gisèle.'

The girl looked up. She had dark hair and blue eyes. Slanted, mysterious eyes which seemed to have been outlined in black eyeliner – ancient-Egyptian style.

She looked like a witch, which was no coincidence.

'James. I've missed you.' Her voice was soft and husky. 'How's it going these days?' She cupped her hands around the unlit candle on the table and made a quick motion as if releasing a captive bird. As her hands moved away, the candle wick burst into flame.

'Still as gorgeous as ever,' she said, smiling at him in the dancing golden light.

'That goes for you, too. But the truth is, I'm here on business.'

She arched an eyebrow. 'Aren't you always?'

'This is different. I want to ask your . . . professional opinion on something.'

She spread her slender hands, silver fingernails glowing in the candle's flame. On her index finger was a ring with a black dahlia. 'My powers are at your disposal. Is there someone you want cursed? Or maybe you want to attract good luck or prosperity. I know you can't need a love charm.'

'I want a spell – to cure a disease. I don't know if it needs to be specific to the disease, or if something more general would work. A – general health spell . . .'

'James.' She chuckled lazily and put a hand on his, stroking lightly. 'You're really worked up, aren't you? I've never seen you like this.'

It was true; he was experiencing a major loss of control. He worked against it, disciplining himself into perfect stillness.

'What particular disease are we talking about?' Gisèle asked, when he didn't speak again.

'Cancer.'

Gisèle threw back her head and laughed. 'You're telling me your kind can get cancer? I don't believe it. Eat and breathe all you want, but don't try to convince me the lamia get human diseases.'

This was the hard part. James said quietly, 'The person with the disease isn't my kind. She's not your kind, either. She's human.'

Gisèle's smile disappeared. Her voice was no longer husky or lazy as she said, 'An outsider? *Vermin?* Are you crazy, James?'

'She doesn't know anything about me or the Night World. I don't want to break any laws. I just want her well.'

The slanted blue eyes were searching his face. 'Are you sure you haven't broken the laws already?' And when James looked determined not to understand this, she added in a lowered voice, 'Are you sure you're not in love with her?'

James made himself meet the probing gaze directly. He spoke softly and dangerously. 'Don't say that unless you want a fight.'

Gisèle looked away. She played with her ring. The candle flame dwindled and died.

'James, I've known you for a long time,' she said without looking up. 'I don't want to get you in trouble. I believe you when you say you haven't broken any laws – but I think we'd both better forget this conversation. Just walk out now and I'll pretend it never happened.'

'And the spell?'

'There's no such thing. And if there was, I wouldn't help you. Just go.'

James went.

There was one other possibility that he could think of. He drove to Brentwood, to an area that was as different from the last as a diamond is from coal. He parked in a covered carport by a quaint adobe building with a fountain. Red and purple bougainvillaea climbed up the walls to the Spanish tile on the roof.

Walking through an archway into a courtyard, he came to an office with gold letters on the door. *Jasper R. Rasmussen, Ph.D.* His father was a psychologist.

Before he could reach for the handle, the door opened and a woman came out. She was like most of his father's clients, forty-something, obviously rich, wearing a designer jogging suit and high-heeled sandals.

She looked a little dazed and dreamy, and there were two small, rapidly healing puncture wounds on her neck.

James went into the office. There was a waiting room, but no receptionist. Strains of Mozart came from the inner office. James knocked on the door.

'Dad?'

The door opened to reveal a handsome man with dark hair. He was wearing a perfectly tailored grey suit and a shirt with French cuffs. He had an aura of power and purpose.

But not of warmth. He said, 'What is it, James?' in the same voice he used for his clients: thoughtful, deliberate, confident.

'Do you have a minute?'

His father glanced at his Rolex. 'As a matter of fact, my next patient won't be here for half an hour.'

'There's something I need to talk about.'

His father looked at him keenly, then gestured to an overstuffed chair. James eased into it, but found himself pulling forward to sit on the edge.

'What's on your mind?'

James searched for the right words. Everything depended on whether he could make his father understand. But what were the right words? At last he settled for bluntness.

'It's Poppy. She's been sick for a while, and now they think she has cancer.'

Dr Rasmussen looked surprised. 'I'm sorry to hear that.' But there was no sorrow in his voice.

'And it's a bad cancer. It's incredibly painful and just about one hundred percent incurable.'

'That's a pity.' Again there was nothing but mild surprise in his father's voice. And suddenly James knew where *that* came from. It wasn't surprise that Poppy was sick; it was surprise that James had made a trip just to tell him this.

'Dad, if she's got this cancer, she's *dying*. Doesn't that mean anything to you?'

Dr Rasmussen steepled his fingers and stared into the ruddy gloss of his mahogany desk. He spoke slowly and steadily. 'James, we've been through this before. You know that your mother and I are worried about you getting too close to Poppy. Too . . . attached . . . to her.'

James felt a surge of cold rage. 'Like I got too attached to Miss Emma?'

His father didn't blink. 'Something like that.'

James fought the pictures that wanted to form in his mind. He couldn't think about Miss Emma now; he needed to be detached. That was the only way to convince his father.

'Dad, what I'm trying to say is that I've known Poppy just about all my life. She's useful to me.'

'How? Not in the obvious way. You've never fed on her, have you?'

James swallowed, feeling nauseated. Feed on Poppy?

Use her like that? Even the thought of it made him sick.

'Dad, she's my friend,' he said, abandoning any pretense of objectivity. 'I can't just watch her suffer. I can't. I have to do something about it.'

His father's face cleared. 'I see.'

James felt dizzy with astonished relief. 'You understand?'

'James, at times one can't help a certain feeling of . . . compassion for humans. In general, I wouldn't encourage it – but you *have* known Poppy a long while. You feel pity for her suffering. If you want to make that suffering shorter, then, yes, I understand.'

The relief crashed down around James. He stared at his father for a few seconds, then said softly, 'Mercy killing? I thought the Elders had put a ban on deaths in this area.'

'Just be reasonably discreet about it. As long as it seems to be natural, we'll all look the other way. There won't be any reason to call in the Elders.'

There was a metallic taste in James's mouth. He stood and laughed shortly. 'Thanks, Dad. You've really helped a lot.'

His father didn't seem to hear the sarcasm. 'Glad to do it, James. By the way, how are things at the apartments?'

'Fine,' James said emptily.

'And at school?'

'School's over, Dad,' James said, and let himself out.

In the courtyard he leaned against an adobe wall and stared at the splashing water of the fountain.

He was out of options. Out of hope. The laws of the Night World said so.

If Poppy had the disease, she would die from it.

CHAPTER 4

Poppy was staring without appetite at a dinner tray of chicken nuggets and french fries when Dr Franklin came in the room.

The tests were over. The CAT scan had been all right, if claustrophobic, but the ERCP had been awful. Poppy could still feel the ghost of the tube in her throat every time she swallowed.

'You're leaving all this great hospital food,' Dr Franklin said with gentle humour. Poppy managed a smile for him.

He went on talking about innocuous things. He didn't say anything about the test results, and Poppy had no idea when they were supposed to come in. She was suspicious of Dr Franklin, though. Something about him, the gentle way he patted her foot under the blanket or the shadows around his eyes . . .

When he casually suggested that Poppy's mother might want to 'come for a little walk down the hall,' Poppy's suspicion crystallized.

He's going to tell her. He's got the results, but he doesn't want me to know.

Her plan was made in the same instant. She yawned

and said, 'Go on, Mom; I'm a little bit sleepy.' Then she lay back and shut her eyes.

As soon as they were gone, she got off the bed. She watched their retreating backs as they went down the hall into another doorway. Then, in her stocking feet, she quietly followed them.

She was delayed for several minutes at the nursing station. 'Just stretching my legs,' she said to a nurse who looked inquiringly at her, and she pretended to be walking at random. When the nurse picked up a clipboard and went into one of the patient's rooms, Poppy hurried on down the corridor.

The room at the end was the waiting room – she'd seen it earlier. It had a TV and a complete kitchen setup so relatives could hang out in comfort. The door was ajar and Poppy approached it stealthily. She could hear the low rumble of Dr Franklin's voice, but she couldn't hear what he was saying.

Very cautiously Poppy edged closer. She chanced one look around the door.

She saw at once that there was no need for caution. Everyone in that room was completely occupied.

Dr Franklin was sitting on one of the couches. Beside him was an African-American woman with glasses on a chain around her neck. She was wearing the white coat of a doctor.

On the other couch was Poppy's stepfather. Cliff. His normally perfect dark hair was slightly mussed, his rock-steady jaw was working. He had his arm around her mother. Dr Franklin was talking to both of them, his hand on her mother's shoulder.

And Poppy's mother was sobbing.

Poppy pulled back from the doorway.

Oh, my God. I've got it.

She'd never seen her mother cry before. Not when Poppy's grandmother had died, not during the divorce from Poppy's father. Her mother's specialty was coping with things; she was the best coper Poppy had ever known.

But now . . .

I've got it. I've definitely got it.

Still, maybe it wasn't so bad. Her mom was shocked, OK, that was natural. But it didn't mean that Poppy was going to *die* or anything. Poppy had all of modern medicine on her side.

She kept telling herself this as she edged away from the waiting room.

She didn't edge fast enough, though. Before she got out of earshot, she heard her mother's voice, raised in something like anguish.

'My baby. Oh, my little girl.'

Poppy froze.

And then Cliff, loud and angry: 'You're trying to tell me there's *nothing?'*

Poppy couldn't feel her own breathing. Against her will, she moved back to the door.

'Dr Loftus is an oncologist; an expert on this sort of cancer. She can explain better than I can,' Dr Franklin was saying.

Then a new voice came – the other doctor. At first Poppy could only catch scattered phrases that didn't seem to *mean* anything: adenocarcinoma, splenic venous occlusion, Stage Three. Medical jargon. Then Dr Loftus said, 'To put it simply, the problem is that the tumour has spread. It's spread to the liver and the lymph nodes around the pancreas. That means it's unresectable – we can't operate.'

Cliff said, 'But chemotherapy . . .'

'We might try a combination of radiation and

chemotherapy with something called 5-fluorouracil. We've had some results with that. But I won't mislead you. At best it may improve her survival time by a few weeks. At this point, we're looking at palliative measures – ways to reduce her pain and improve the *quality* of the time she has left. Do you understand?'

Poppy could hear choking sobs from her mother, but she couldn't seem to move. She felt as if she were listening to some play on the radio. As if it had nothing to do with her.

Dr Franklin said, 'There are some research protocols right here in southern California. They're experimenting with immunotherapy and cryogenic surgery. Again, we're talking about palliation rather than a cure—'

'Damn it!' Cliff's voice was explosive. 'You're talking about a *little girl*! How did this get to – to Stage Three – without anybody noticing? This kid was dancing all night two days ago.'

'Mr Hilgard, I'm sorry,' Dr Loftus said so softly that Poppy could barely pick up the words. 'This kind of cancer is called a silent disease, because there are very few symptoms until it's very far advanced. That's why the survival rate is so low. And I have to tell you that Poppy is only the second teenager I've seen with this kind of tumour. Dr Franklin made an extremely acute diagnosis when he decided to send her in for testing.'

'*I* should have known,' Poppy's mother said in a thick voice. 'I should have made her come in sooner. I should have – I should have—'

There was a banging sound. Poppy looked around the door, forgetting to be inconspicuous. Her mother was hitting the Formica table over and over. Cliff was trying to stop her.

Poppy reeled back.

Oh, God, I've got to get out of here. I can't see this. I can't look at this.

She turned and walked back down the hall. Her legs moved. Just like always. Amazing that they still worked.

And everything around her was just like always. The nursing station was still decorated for the Fourth of July. Her suitcase was still on the padded window seat in her room. The hardwood floor was still solid underneath her.

Everything was the same – but how could it be? How could the walls be still standing? How could the TV be blaring in the next room?

I'm going to die, Poppy thought.

Strangely enough, she didn't feel frightened. What she felt was vastly surprised. And the surprise kept coming, over and over, with every thought being interrupted by those four words.

It's my fault because (I'm going to die) I didn't go to the doctor's sooner.

Cliff said 'damn' for me (I'm going to die). I didn't know he liked me enough to swear.

Her mind was racing wildly.

Something *in* me, she thought. I'm going to die because of something that's *inside* me, like that alien in the movie. It's in me right now. Right now.

She put both hands to her stomach, then pulled up her T-shirt to stare at her abdomen. The skin was smooth, unblemished. She didn't feel any pain.

But it's in there and I'm going to die because of it. Die soon. I wonder how soon? I didn't hear them talk about that.

I need James.

Poppy reached for the phone with a feeling that her hand was detached from her body. She dialled, thinking *Please be there*.

But this time it didn't work. The phone rang and rang. When the answering machine came on, Poppy said, 'Call me at the hospital.' Then she hung up and stared at the plastic pitcher of ice water by her bedside.

He'll get in later, she thought. And then he'll call me. I just have to hang on until then.

Poppy wasn't sure why she thought this, but suddenly it was her goal. To hang on until she could talk to James. She didn't need to think about anything until then; she just had to survive. Once she talked to James, she could figure out what she was supposed to be feeling, what she was supposed to *do* now.

There was a light knock at the door. Startled, Poppy looked up to see her mother and Cliff. For a moment all she could focus on was their faces, which gave her the strange illusion that the faces were floating in mid-air.

Her mother had red and swollen eyes. Cliff was pale, like a piece of crumpled white paper, and his jaw looked stubbly and dark in contrast.

Oh, my God, are they going to *tell* me? They *can't;* they can't make me listen to it.

Poppy had the wild impulse to run. She was on the verge of panic.

But her mother said, 'Sweetie, some of your friends are here to see you. Phil called them this afternoon to let them know you were in the hospital, and they just arrived.'

James, Poppy thought, something springing free in her chest. But James wasn't part of the group that came crowding through the doorway. It was mostly girls from school.

It doesn't matter. He'll call later. I don't have to think now.

As a matter of fact, it was impossible to think with so

many visitors in the room. And that was good. It was incredible that Poppy could sit there and talk to them when part of her was farther away than Neptune, but she *did* talk and that kept her brain turned off.

None of them had any idea that something serious was wrong with her. Not even Phil, who was at his brotherly best, very kind and considerate. They talked about ordinary things, about parties and rollerblading and music and books. Things from Poppy's old life, which suddenly seemed to have been a hundred years ago.

Cliff talked, too, nicer than he had been since the days when he was courting Poppy's mother.

But finally the visitors left, and Poppy's mother stayed. She touched Poppy every so often with hands that shook slightly. If I didn't know, I'd know, Poppy thought. She isn't acting like Mom at all.

'I think I'll stay here tonight,' her mother said. Not quite managing to sound offhand. 'The nurse said I can sleep on the window seat; it's really a couch for parents. I'm just trying to decide whether I should run back to the house and get some things.'

'Yes, go,' Poppy said. There was nothing else she could say and still pretend that she didn't know. Besides, her mom undoubtedly needed some time by herself, away from this.

Just as her mother left, a nurse in a flowered blouse and green scrub pants came in to take Poppy's temperature and blood pressure. And then Poppy was alone.

It was late. She could still hear a TV, but it was far away. The door was ajar, but the hallway outside was dim. A hush seemed to have fallen over the ward.

She felt *very* alone, and the pain was gnawing deep inside her. Beneath the smooth skin of her abdomen, the tumour was making itself known.

Worst of all, James hadn't called. How could he not call? Didn't he know she needed him?

She wasn't sure how long she could go on not thinking about It.

Maybe the best thing would be to try to sleep. Get unconscious. Then she *couldn't* think.

But as soon as she turned out the light and closed her eyes, phantoms swirled around her. Not images of pretty bald girls; skeletons. Coffins. And worst of all, an endless darkness.

If I die, I won't *be* here. Will I be anywhere? Or will I just Not Be at all?

It was the scariest thing she'd ever imagined, NotBeing. And she was definitely thinking now, she couldn't help it. She'd lost control. A galloping fear consumed her, made her shiver under the rough sheet and thin blankets. *I'm going to die, I'm going to die, I'm going to—*

'Poppy.'

Her eyes flew open. For a second she couldn't identify the black silhouette in the darkened room. She had a wild idea that it was Death itself coming to get her.

Then she said, *'James?'*

'I wasn't sure if you were asleep.'

Poppy reached for the bedside button that turned on the light, but James said, 'No, leave it off. I had to sneak past the nurses, and I don't want them to throw me out.'

Poppy swallowed, her hands clenched on a fold of blanket. 'I'm glad you came,' she said. 'I thought you weren't going to come.' What she really wanted was to throw herself into his arms and sob and scream.

But she didn't. It wasn't just that she'd never done anything like that with him before; it was something about *him* that stopped her. Something she couldn't put her finger on, but that made her feel almost . . . frightened.

The way he was standing? The fact that she couldn't see his face? All she knew was that James suddenly seemed like a stranger.

He turned around and very slowly closed the heavy door.

Darkness. Now the only light came in through the window. Poppy felt curiously isolated from the rest of the hospital, from the rest of the world.

And that should have been good, to be alone with James, protected from everything else. If only she weren't having this weird feeling of not recognizing him.

'You know the test results,' he said quietly. It wasn't a question.

'My mom doesn't know I know,' Poppy said. How could she be talking coherently when all she wanted to do was scream? 'I overheard the doctors telling her . . . James, I've got it. And . . . it's bad; it's a bad kind of cancer. They said it's already spread. They said I'm going to . . .' She couldn't get the last word out, even though it was shrieking through her mind.

'You're going to die,' James said. He still seemed quiet and centred. Detached.

'I read up on it,' James went on, walking over to the window and looking out. 'I know how bad it is. The articles said there was a lot of pain. Serious pain.'

'James,' Poppy gasped.

'Sometimes they have to do surgery just to try to stop the pain. But whatever they do, it won't save you. They can fill you full of chemicals and irradiate you, and you'll still die. Probably before the end of summer.'

'James—'

'It will be your last summer—'

'*James, for God's sake!*' It was almost a scream. Poppy was breathing in great shaking gulps, clinging to the blankets. 'Why are you doing this to me?'

He turned and in one movement seized her wrist, his fingers closing over the plastic hospital bracelet. 'I want you to understand that they can't help you,' he said, ragged and intense. 'Do you understand that?'

'*Yes*, I understand,' Poppy said. She could hear the mounting hysteria in her own voice. 'But is that what you came here to say? Do you want to *kill* me?'

His fingers tightened painfully. 'No! I want to save you.' Then he let out a breath and repeated it more quietly, but with no less intensity. 'I want to save you, Poppy.'

Poppy spent a few moments just getting air in and out of her lungs. It was hard to do it without dissolving into sobs. 'Well, you can't,' she said at last. 'Nobody can.'

'That's where you're wrong.' Slowly he released her wrist and gripped the bed rail instead. 'Poppy, there's something I've got to tell you. Something about me.'

'James . . .' Poppy could breathe now, but she didn't know what to say. As far as she could tell, James had gone crazy. In a way, if everything else hadn't been so awful, she might have been flattered. James had lost his consummate cool – over her. He was upset enough about her situation to go completely non-linear.

'You really do care,' she said softly, with a laugh that was half a sob. She put a hand on his where it rested on the bed rail.

He laughed shortly in turn. His hand flipped over to grasp hers roughly; then he pulled away. 'You have no idea,' he said in a terse, strained voice.

Looking out the window, he added, 'You think you know everything about me, but you don't. There's something very important that you don't know.'

By now Poppy just felt numb. She couldn't understand why James kept harping on himself, when *she* was the one about to die. But she tried to conjure up some sort of gentleness for him as she said, 'You can tell me anything. You know that.'

'But this is something you won't believe. Not to mention that it's breaking the laws.'

'The law?'

'The laws. I go by different laws than you. Human laws don't mean much to us, but our own are supposed to be unbreakable.'

'James,' Poppy said, with blank terror. He really *was* losing his mind.

'I don't know the right way to say it. I feel like somebody in a bad horror movie.' He shrugged, and said without turning, 'I know how this sounds, but . . . Poppy, I'm a vampire.'

Poppy sat still on the bed for a moment. Then she groped out wildly toward the bedside table. Her fingers closed on a stack of little crescent-shaped plastic basins and she threw the whole stack at him.

'You *bastard*!' she screamed, and reached for something else to throw.

CHAPTER

5

James dodged as Poppy lobbed a paperback book at him. 'Poppy—'

'You jerk! You snake! How can you *do* this to me? You spoiled, selfish, immature—'

'Shhh! They're going to hear you—'

'Let them! Here I am, and I've just found out that I'm going to *die*, and all you can think of is playing a joke on me. A stupid, sick joke. I can't *believe* this. Do you think that's *funny*?' She ran out of breath to rave with. James, who had been making quieting motions with his hands, now gave up and looked toward the door.

'Here comes the nurse,' he said.

'Good, and I'm going to ask her to throw you *out*,' Poppy said. Her anger had collapsed, leaving her near tears. She had never felt so utterly betrayed and abandoned. 'I hate you, you know,' she said.

The door opened. It was the nurse with the flowered blouse and green scrub pants. 'Is anything the matter here?' she said, turning on the light. Then she saw James. 'Now, let's see; you don't look like family,' she said. She was smiling, but her voice had the ring of authority about to be enforced.

'He's not, and I want him out of here,' Poppy said.

The nurse fluffed up Poppy's pillows, put a gentle hand on her forehead. 'Only family members are allowed to stay overnight,' she said to James.

Poppy stared at the TV and waited for James to go. He didn't. He walked around the bed to stand by the nurse, who looked up at him while she continued straightening Poppy's blankets. Then her hands slowed and stopped moving.

Poppy glanced at her sideways in surprise.

The nurse was just staring at James. Hands limp on the blankets, she gazed at him as if she were mesmerized.

And James was just staring back. With the light on, Poppy could see James's face – and again she had that odd feeling of not recognizing him. He was very pale and almost stern looking, as if he were doing something that required an effort. His jaw was tight and his eyes – his eyes were the colour of silver. Real silver, shining in the light.

For some reason, Poppy thought of a starving panther.

'So you see there's nothing wrong here,' James said to the nurse, as if continuing a conversation they'd been having.

The nurse blinked once, then looked around the room as if she'd just awakened from a doze. 'No, no; everything's fine,' she said. 'Call me if . . .' She looked briefly distracted again, then murmured, 'If, um, you need anything.'

She walked out. Poppy watched her, forgetting to breathe. Then, slowly, moving only her eyes, she looked at James.

'I know it's a cliché,' James said. 'An overused demonstration of power. But it gets the job done.'

'You set this up with her,' Poppy said in a bare whisper.

'No.'

'Or else it's some kind of psychic trick. The Amazing Whatshisname.'

'No,' James said, and sat down on an orange plastic chair.

'Then I'm going *crazy*.' For the first time that evening Poppy wasn't thinking about her illness. She couldn't think properly about anything; her mind was a whirling, crashing jumble of confusion. She felt like Dorothy's house after it had been picked up by the tornado.

'You're not crazy. I probably did this the wrong way; I said I didn't know how to explain it. Look, I know how hard it is for you to believe. My people *arrange* it that way; they do everything they can to keep humans not believing. Their lives depend on it.'

'James, I'm sorry; I just—' Poppy found that her hands were trembling. She shut her eyes. 'Maybe you'd better just—'

'Poppy, *look at me*. I'm telling you the truth. I swear it.' He stared at her face a moment, then let out a breath. 'OK. I didn't want to have to do this, but . . .'

He stood, leaning close to Poppy. She refused to flinch, but she could feel her eyes widening.

'Now, look,' he said, and his lips skinned back from his teeth.

A simple action – but the effect was astonishing. Transforming. In that instant he changed from the pale but fairly ordinary James of a moment ago – into something Poppy had never seen before. A different species of human being.

His eyes flared silver and his entire face took on a predatory look. But Poppy scarcely noticed that; she was staring at his teeth.

Not teeth. Fangs. He had canines like a cat's. Elongated and curving, ending in delicate, piercing points.

They were nothing like the fake vampire fangs sold at novelty stores. They looked very strong and very sharp and very real.

Poppy screamed.

James clapped a hand over her mouth. 'We don't want that nurse back in here.'

When he lifted the hand, Poppy said, 'Oh, my God; oh, my *God* . . .'

'All those times when you said I could read your mind,' James said. 'Remember? And the times when I heard things you didn't hear, or moved faster than you could move?'

'Oh, my God.'

'It's true, Poppy.' He picked up the orange chair and twisted one of the metal legs out of shape. He did it easily, gracefully. 'We're stronger than humans,' he said. He twisted the leg back and put the chair down. 'We see better in the dark. We're built for hunting.'

Poppy finally managed to capture an entire thought. 'I don't care *what* you can do,' she said shrilly. 'You can't be a vampire. I've known you since you were five years *old*. And you've gotten older every year, just like me. Explain *that*.'

'Everything you know is wrong.' When she just stared at him, he sighed again and said, 'Everything you think you know about vampires, you've picked up from books or TV. And it's all written by humans, I'll guarantee that. Nobody in the Night World would break the code of secrecy.'

'The Night World. Where's the Night World?'

'It's not a place. It's like a secret society – for vampires and witches and werewolves. All the best people. And I'll explain about it later,' James said grimly. 'For now – look, it's simple. I'm a vampire because my parents are vampires. I was *born* that way. We're the lamia.'

All Poppy could think of was Mr and Mrs Rasmussen with their luxury ranch-style house and their gold Mercedes. 'Your *parents*?'

'*Lamia* is just an old word for vampires, but for us it means the ones who're born that way,' James said, ignoring her. 'We're born and we age like humans – except that we can stop aging whenever we want. We breathe. We walk around in the daylight. We can even eat regular food.'

'Your parents,' Poppy said again faintly.

He looked at her. 'Yeah. My parents. Look, why do you think my mom does interior decorating? Not because they need the money. She meets a lot of people that way, and so does my dad, the society shrink. It only takes a few minutes alone with somebody, and the human never remembers it afterward.'

Poppy shifted uncomfortably. 'So you, um, drink people's blood, huh?' Even after everything she'd seen, she couldn't say it without half laughing.

James looked at the laces of his Adidas. 'Yes. Yes, I sure do,' he said softly. Then he looked up and met her gaze directly.

His eyes were pure silver.

Poppy leaned back against the pile of pillows on her bed. Maybe it was easier to believe him because the unbelievable had already happened to her earlier today. Reality had already been turned upside down – so, honestly, what did one more impossibility matter?

I'm going to die and my best friend is a bloodsucking monster, she thought.

The argument was over, and she was out of energy. She and James looked at each other in silence.

'OK,' she said finally, and it meant everything she'd just realized.

'I didn't tell you this just to get it off my chest,' James said, his voice still muted. 'I said I could save you, remember?'

'Vaguely.' Poppy blinked slowly, then said more sharply, 'Save me how?'

His gaze shifted to empty air. 'The way you're thinking.'

'Jamie, I *can't* think anymore.'

Gently, without looking at her, he put a hand on her shin under the blanket. He shook her leg slightly, a gesture of affection. 'I'm gonna turn you into a vampire, kid.'

Poppy put both fists to her face and began to cry.

'Hey.' He let go of her shin and put an awkward arm around her, pulling her to sit up. 'Don't do that. It's OK. It's better than the alternative.'

'You're . . . freaking . . . crazy,' Poppy sobbed. Once the tears had started, they flowed too easily – she couldn't stop them. There was comfort in crying, and in being held by James. He felt strong and reliable and he smelled good.

'You said you had to be born one,' she added blurrily, between sobs.

'No, I didn't. I said *I* was born one. There are plenty of the other kind around. Made vampires. There would be more, but there's a law against just making any jerk off the street into one.'

'But I *can't*. I'm just what I am; I'm *me*. I can't be – like that.'

He put her gently away so he could look into her face. 'Then you're going to die. You don't have any other choice. I checked around – even asked a witch. There's nothing else in the Night World to help you. What it comes down to is: Do you want to live or not?'

Poppy's mind, which had been swamped in confusion again, suddenly fixed on this question. It was like a flashlight beam in a pitch-black room.

Did she want to live?

Oh, God, of *course* she did.

Until today she'd assumed it was her unconditional *right* to live. She hadn't even been grateful for the privilege. But now she knew it wasn't something to take for granted – and she also knew it was something she'd fight for.

Wake up, Poppy! This is the voice of reason calling. He says he can save your life.

'Wait a minute. I've got to think,' Poppy said tightly to James. Her tears had stopped. She pushed him away completely and stared fiercely at the white hospital blanket.

OK. OK. Now get your head straight, girl.

You knew James had a secret. So you never imagined it was anything like this, so what? He's still James. He may be some godawful undead fiend, but he still cares about you. *And there's nobody else to help you.*

She found herself clutching at James's hand without looking at him. 'What's it like?' she said through clenched teeth.

Steady and matter-of-fact, he said, 'It's different. It's not something I'd recommend if there was another choice, but . . . it's OK. You'll be sick while your body's changing, but afterward you'll never get any kind of disease again. You'll be strong and quick – and immortal.'

'I'd live forever? But would I be able to stop aging?' She had visions of herself as an immortal crone.

He grimaced. 'Poppy – you'd stop aging *now*. That's what happens to made vampires. Essentially, you're *dying* as a mortal. You'll look dead and be unconscious for a while. And then . . . you'll wake up.'

'I see.' Sort of like Juliet in the tomb, Poppy thought. And then she thought, Oh, God . . . Mom and Phil.

'There's another thing you should know,' James was

saying. 'A certain percentage of people don't make it.'

'Don't make it?'

'Through the change. People over twenty almost never do. They don't *ever* wake up. Their bodies can't adjust to the new form and they burn out. Teenagers usually live through it, but not always.'

Oddly enough, this was comforting to Poppy. A qualified hope seemed more believable than an absolute one. To live, she would have to take a chance.

She looked at James. 'How do you do it?'

'The traditional way,' he said with the ghost of a smile. Then, gravely: 'We exchange blood.'

Oh, great, Poppy thought. And I was afraid of a simple shot. Now I'm going to have my blood drawn by fangs. She swallowed and blinked, staring at nothing.

'It's your choice, Poppy. It's up to you.'

There was a long pause, and then she said, 'I want to live, Jamie.'

He nodded. 'It'll mean going away from here. Leaving your parents. They can't know.'

'Yeah, I was just realizing that. Sort of like getting a new identity from the FBI, huh?'

'More than that. You'll be living in a new world, the Night World. And it's a lonely world, full of secrets. But you'll be walking around in it, instead of lying in the ground.' He squeezed her hand. Then he said very quietly and seriously, 'Do you want to start now?'

All Poppy could think of to do was shut her eyes and brace herself the way she did for an injection. 'I'm ready,' she said through stiff lips.

James laughed again – this time as if he couldn't help it. Then he folded the bed rail down and settled beside her. 'I'm used to people being hypnotized when I do this. It's weird to have you awake.'

'Yeah, well, if I scream you can hypnotize me,' Poppy said, not opening her eyes.

Relax, she told herself firmly. No matter how much it hurts, no matter how awful it is, you can deal with it. You *have* to. Your life depends on it.

Her heart was thumping hard enough to shake her body.

'Right here,' James said, touching her throat with cool fingers as if feeling for a pulse.

Just do it, Poppy thought. Get it over with.

She could feel warmth as James leaned close to her, taking her carefully by the shoulders. Every nerve ending in her skin was aware of him. Then she felt cool breath on her throat, and quickly, before she could recoil, a double sting.

Those fangs, burying themselves in her flesh. Making two little wounds so he could drink her blood . . .

Now it's *really* going to hurt, Poppy thought. She couldn't brace herself anymore. Her life was in the hands of a hunter. She was a rabbit trapped in the coils of a snake, a mouse under the claws of a cat. She didn't feel like James's best friend, she felt like *lunch* . . .

Poppy, what are you doing? Don't fight it. It hurts when you resist.

James was speaking to her – but the warm mouth on her throat hadn't moved. The voice was in her head.

I'm not resisting, Poppy thought. I'm just ready for it to hurt, that's all.

There was a burning where his teeth pierced her. She waited for it to get worse – but it didn't. It changed.

Oh, Poppy thought.

The feeling of heat was actually pleasant. A sensation of release, of giving.

And closeness. She and James were getting closer and closer, like two drops of water moving together until they merged.

She could sense James's mind. His thoughts – and his feelings. His emotions flowed into her, through her.

Tenderness . . . concern . . . caring. A cold black rage at the disease that was threatening her. Despair that there was no other way to help her. And longing – longing to share with her, to make her happy.

Yes, Poppy thought.

A wave of sweetness made her dizzy. She found herself groping for James's hand, their fingers intertwining.

James, she thought with wonder and joy. Her communication to him a tentative caress.

Poppy. She could feel his own surprise and delight.

And all the time the dreamy pleasure was building. Making Poppy shiver with its intensity.

How could I have been so *stupid*? Poppy thought. To be afraid of this. It isn't terrible. It's . . . right.

She had never been so close to anybody. It was as if they were one being, together, not predator and prey, but partners in a dance. Poppy-and-James.

She could touch his soul.

Strangely enough, *he* was afraid of that. She could sense it. *Poppy, don't – so many dark things – I don't want you to see . . .*

Dark, yes, Poppy thought. But not dark and terrible. Dark and lonely. Such utter loneliness. A feeling of not belonging in either of the two worlds he knew. Not belonging anywhere. Except . . .

Suddenly Poppy was seeing an image of herself. In his mind she was fragile and graceful, an emerald-eyed spirit of the air. A sylph – with a core of pure – steel.

I'm not really like that, she thought. I'm not tall and

beautiful like Jacklyn or Michaela . . .

The words she heard in answer didn't seem directed toward her – she had the feeling they were something James was thinking to himself, or remembering from some long-forgotten book.

You don't love a girl because of beauty. You love her because she sings a song only you can understand . . .

With the thought came a strong feeling of protectiveness. So this was how James felt about her – she knew at last. As if she were something precious, something to be protected at all costs . . .

At all costs. No matter what happened to him. Poppy tried to follow the thought deeper into his mind, to find out what it meant. She got an impression of rules – no, *laws* . . .

Poppy, it's bad manners to search somebody's mind when you're not invited. The words were tinged with desperation.

Poppy pulled back mentally. She hadn't meant to pry. She just wanted to help . . .

I know, James's thought came to her, and with it a rush of warmth and gratitude. Poppy relaxed and simply enjoyed the feeling of oneness with him.

I wish it could last forever, she thought – and just then it stopped. The warmth at her neck disappeared, and James pulled away, straightening.

Poppy made a sound of protest and tried to drag him back. He wouldn't let her.

'No – there's something else we have to do,' he whispered. But he didn't do anything else. He just held her, his lips against her forehead. Poppy felt peaceful and languid.

'You didn't tell me it would be like that,' she said.

'I didn't know,' James said simply. 'It never has been before.'

They sat together quietly, with James gently stroking her hair.

So strange, Poppy thought. Everything is the same – but everything's different. It was as if she'd pulled herself up on dry land after almost drowning in the ocean. The terror that had been pounding inside her all day was gone, and for the first time in her life she felt completely safe.

After another minute or so James shook his head, rousing himself.

'What else do we have to do?' Poppy asked.

For an answer, James lifted his own wrist to his mouth. He made a quick jerking motion with his head, as if tearing a strip of cloth held in his teeth.

When he lowered the wrist, Poppy saw blood.

It was running in a little stream down his arm. So red it almost didn't look real.

Poppy gulped and shook her head.

'It's not that bad,' James said softly. 'And you have to do it. Without my blood in you, you won't become a vampire when you die, you'll just *die*. Like any other human victim.'

And I want to live, Poppy thought. All right, then. Shutting her eyes, she allowed James to guide her head to his wrist.

It didn't taste like blood, or at least not like the blood she'd tasted when she bit her tongue or put a cut finger in her mouth. It tasted – strange. Rich and potent.

Like some magic elixir, Poppy thought dizzily. And once again she felt the touch of James's mind. Intoxicated with the closeness, she kept drinking.

That's right. You've got to take a lot, James told her. But his mental voice was weaker than it had been. Instantly Poppy felt a surge of alarm.

But what will it do to you?

'I'll be all right,' James said aloud. 'It's you I'm worried about. If you don't get enough, you'll be in danger.'

Well, he was the expert. And Poppy was happy to let the strange, heady potion keep flowing into her. She basked in the glow that seemed to be lighting her from the inside out. She felt so tranquil, so calm . . .

And then, without warning, the calm was shattered. A voice broke into it, a voice full of harsh surprise.

'What are you *doing?*' the voice said, and Poppy looked up to see Phillip in the doorway.

CHAPTER
6

James moved fast. He picked up the plastic tumbler on the bedside table and handed it to Poppy. She understood. Feeling giddy and uncoordinated, she took a healthy swig of water and licked her lips to wash any traces of blood away.

'What are you *doing?*' Phillip repeated, striding into the room. His eyes were fixed on James, which was good, because Poppy was trying to position herself to hide the side of her neck that James had bitten.

'None of your business,' she said, and in the same instant she knew it was a mistake. Phillip, whose middle name was Stability, was looking distinctly unstable tonight.

Mom told him, Poppy thought.

'I mean, we aren't doing *anything*,' she amended. It didn't help. Phil was clearly in a mood to see everything in the world as a threat to his sister. And Poppy couldn't really blame him – he'd walked in on the two of them in a strange embrace on a rumpled hospital bed.

'James was comforting me because I was scared,' she said. She didn't even try to explain why James had been cradling her head to his arm. But she glanced at James's arm surreptitiously and saw that the wound there was already closed, the mark fading.

'Everything's all right, you know,' James said, standing to fix a mesmerizing silver gaze on Phillip. But Phil hardly gave him a glance. He was staring at Poppy.

It's not working, Poppy thought. Maybe Phil's too mad to be hypnotized. Or too *stubborn*.

She looked a question at James, which he answered with a barely discernable shake of his head. He didn't know what the problem was, either.

But they both knew what it meant. James was going to have to leave. Poppy felt cheated and frustrated. All she wanted was to talk with James, to revel in their new discovery of each other – and she couldn't. Not with Phil here.

'How come you're here, anyway?' she asked him irritably.

'I drove Mom here. You know she doesn't like driving at night. And I brought this.' He swung her boom box up onto the bedside table. 'And these.' He put a black CD case beside it. 'All your favourite music.'

Poppy felt her anger draining away. 'That was sweet,' she said. She was touched, especially since Phil hadn't said 'All your favourite *weird* music,' which was usually how he referred to it. 'Thank you.'

Phil shrugged, shooting a glare at James.

Poor Phil, Poppy thought. Her brother actually looked dishevelled. And his eyes were swollen.

'Where's Mom?' she was starting to say, when her mother walked in.

'I'm back, sweetie,' her mother said, with a very creditable cheery smile. Then she looked surprised. 'James – it was nice of you to come.'

'Yeah, but he was just leaving,' Phil said significantly.

'I'll show him the way out.'

James didn't waste energy on a fight he couldn't win. He turned to Poppy and said, 'I'll see you tomorrow.'

There was a look in his grey eyes – grey, not silver now – that was just for her. A look that had never been there before in all the years she'd known him.

'Goodbye, James,' she said softly. 'And – thank you.' She knew he understood what she meant.

It wasn't until he was out the door, with Phillip on his heels like a bouncer after a rowdy customer, that a thought occurred to her.

James had said that she would be in danger if she didn't get enough of his blood. But they'd gotten interrupted almost immediately after that. Had Poppy gotten enough? And what would happen if she *hadn't*?

She herself had no idea, and there was no way to ask James.

Phil stayed right behind James all the way out of the hospital.

Not tonight, James thought. He just couldn't deal with Phillip North tonight. His patience was gone, and his mind was occupied in calculating whether Poppy had taken enough of his blood to be safe. He *thought* she had – but the sooner she got more, the better.

'You'll "see her tomorrow" – well, you're *not* going to see her tomorrow,' Phil said abruptly as they walked into the garage.

'Phil, give me a break.'

Instead, Phillip stepped in front of him and stopped dead, forcing James to stop, too. Phillip was breathing quickly, his green eyes burning.

'OK, *bud*,' he said. 'I don't know what you think you're doing with Poppy – but it's all over now. From now on you stay away from her. *Understand?'*

Visions of breaking Phillip's neck like a new pencil danced in James's head. But Phil was Poppy's brother, and his green eyes were surprisingly like hers.

'I would never hurt Poppy,' he said wearily.

'Give *me* a break. Are you going to stand there and tell me you don't want to move in on her?'

James couldn't come up with an answer immediately. Yesterday he could have truthfully said no, he didn't want to move in on Poppy. Because it would have meant a death sentence for him and Poppy both. It was only when Poppy had received a death sentence of her own that he'd allowed himself to look at his feelings.

And now . . . now he'd been close to Poppy. He'd touched her mind, and had found that she was even braver and more gallant than he'd thought; even more compassionate – and more vulnerable.

He wanted to be that close to Poppy again. He cared about her in a way that made his throat ache. He *belonged* with Poppy.

He also realized that that might not be enough.

Sharing blood forged a powerful bond between two people. It would be wrong of him to take advantage of that bond – or of Poppy's gratitude to him. Until he was sure that Poppy's mind was clear and her decisions were her own, he should keep a little distance. It was the only honorable thing to do.

'The last thing I want to do is hurt her,' he repeated. 'Why can't you believe that?' He made a half-hearted attempt to capture Phil's gaze as he said it. It failed, just as it had in the hospital. Phillip seemed to be one of those rare humans who couldn't be influenced by mind control.

'Why can't I believe it? Because I *know* you. You and your – girlfriends.' Phil managed to make the word sound like a curse. 'You go through six or seven a year – and when you're through with them, you dump them like trash.'

James was distracted briefly by amusement, because Phil was dead on. He *needed* six girlfriends a year. After two months the bond between them became dangerously strong.

'Poppy's not my girlfriend and I'm not going to dump her,' he said, pleased at his own cleverness. He'd avoided an outright lie – Poppy *wasn't* his girlfriend in any normal sense. They'd merged their souls, that was all – they hadn't talked about dating or anything.

'So you *are* telling me you're not gonna try to put the moves on her. Is that it? Because you'd better be *sure*.' As he spoke, Phil did what was probably the most dangerous thing he'd ever done in his life. He grabbed James by the front of the shirt.

You stupid *human*, James thought. He briefly considered breaking every bone in Phil's hand. Or picking Phil up and throwing him across the garage into somebody's windshield. Or . . .

'You're Poppy's brother,' he said through his teeth. 'So I'm going to give you a chance to let go.'

Phil stared into his face a moment, then let go, looking slightly shaken. But not shaken enough to keep quiet.

'You have to leave her alone,' he said. 'You don't understand. This disease she's got – it's serious. She doesn't need anything messing up her life right now. She just needs . . .' He stopped and swallowed.

Suddenly James felt very tired. He couldn't blame Phil for being upset – Phil's mind was full of crystal-clear pictures of Poppy dying. Usually James got only general images about what humans were thinking, but Phillip was broadcasting so loud it nearly deafened him.

Half-truths and evasions hadn't worked. It was time for Outright Lies. Anything to satisfy Phil and get James away from this.

'I know that what Poppy has is serious,' he said. 'I found an article about it on the Net. That's why I was *here*, OK? I feel sorry for her. I'm not interested in Poppy except as a friend, but it makes her feel better if I pretend that I like her.'

Phillip hesitated, looking at him hard and suspiciously. Then he shook his head slowly. 'Being friends is one thing, but it's wrong to mix her up. In the end, pretending isn't going to do her any good. I don't even think it makes her feel better *now* – she looked pretty bad in there.'

'Bad?'

'Pale and shaky. You know Poppy; you know how she gets overexcited about things. You shouldn't be fooling around with her emotions.' He narrowed his eyes and said, 'So maybe you'd better stay away from her for a while. Just to make sure she hasn't got the wrong idea.'

'Whatever,' James said. He wasn't really listening. 'OK,' Phillip said. 'We have a deal. But I'm warning you, if you break it, you're in trouble.'

James wasn't listening to that, either. Which was a mistake.

In the darkened hospital room Poppy lay and listened to her mother's breathing.

You're not asleep, she thought, and I'm not asleep. And you know I'm not, and I know you're not . . .

But they couldn't talk. Poppy wanted desperately to let her mother know that everything was going to be all right – but *how*? She couldn't betray James's secret. And even if she could, her mother wouldn't believe her.

I have to find a way, Poppy thought. *I have to*. And then

a great wave of drowsiness overtook her. It had been the longest day in her life, and she was full of alien blood already working its strange magic in her. She couldn't . . . she just couldn't . . . keep her eyes open.

Several times during the night a nurse came in to take her vital signs, but Poppy never really woke up. For the first time in weeks, no pain interrupted her dreams.

She opened her eyes the next morning feeling confused and weak. Black dots swarmed through her vision when she sat up.

'Hungry?' her mother asked. 'They left this breakfast tray for you.'

The smell of hospital eggs made Poppy feel nauseated. But because her mother was watching her anxiously, she played with the food on the tray before she went to wash up. In the bathroom mirror she examined the side of her neck. Amazing – there was no trace of a mark.

When she came out of the bathroom, her mother was crying.

Not floods of tears, not sobbing. Just dabbing her eyes on a Kleenex. But Poppy couldn't stand it.

'Mom, if you're worried about telling me . . . I know.'

The whole sentence was out before Poppy could even think about it.

Her mother's head jerked up in horror. She stared at Poppy with more tears spilling. 'Sweetheart – you know . . . ?'

'I know what I've got and I know how bad it is,' Poppy said. If this was the wrong strategy, it was too late now. 'I listened when you and Cliff were talking to the doctors.'

'Oh, my *Lord*.'

What can I *say?* Poppy wondered. It's OK, Mom, because I'm not going to die; I'm going to become a vampire. I hope. I can't be sure, because sometimes you don't make it through the transformation. But with any luck, I should be sucking blood in a few weeks.

Come to think of it, she hadn't asked James exactly how long it would take to change her.

Her mother was taking deep, calming breaths. 'Poppy, I want you to know how much I love you. Cliff and I will do anything – *anything* – we can to help you. Right now he's looking into some clinical protocols – those are experimental studies where they test new ways of treating people. If we can just . . . buy time . . . until a cure . . .'

Poppy couldn't stand it. She could *feel* her mother's pain. Literally. It came in palpable waves that seemed to echo through her bloodstream, making her dizzy.

It's that blood, she thought. It's doing something to me – changing me.

Even as she thought it, she went to her mother. She wanted to hug her, and she needed help standing up.

'Mom, I'm not scared,' she said, muffled against her mother's shoulder. 'I can't explain, but I'm not scared. And I don't want you to be unhappy over me.'

Her mother just held on fiercely, as if Death might try to snatch Poppy out of her arms that minute. She was crying.

Poppy cried, too. Real tears, because even if she wasn't going to die truly, she was going to lose so much. Her old life, her family, everything familiar. It felt good to cry over it; it was something she needed to do.

But when it was done, she tried again.

'The *one* thing I don't want is for you to be unhappy or worry,' she said, and looked up at her mother. 'So could you just try not to? For my sake?'

Oh, God, I'm coming off like Beth in *Little Women*, she thought. Saint Poppy. And the truth is, if I were really dying, I'd go kicking and screaming all the way.

Still, she'd managed to comfort her mother, who drew back looking tearstained but quietly proud. 'You're really something, Poppet,' was all she said, but her lips trembled.

Saint Poppy looked away, horribly embarrassed – until another wave of dizziness saved her. She allowed her mother to help her back into bed.

And it was then that she finally found a way to pose the question she needed to ask.

'Mom,' she said slowly, 'what if there was a cure for me somewhere – like in some other country or something – and I could go there and get better, but they wouldn't ever let me come back? I mean, you'd know I was OK, but you wouldn't ever be able to see me again.' She looked at her mother intently. 'Would you want me to do it?'

Her mother answered instantly. 'Sweetheart, I'd want you cured if you had to go to the moon. As long as you were happy.' She had to pause a moment, then resumed steadily. 'But, honey, there isn't such a place. I wish there were.'

'I know.' Poppy patted her arm gently. 'I was just asking. I love you, Mom.'

Later that morning Dr Franklin and Dr Loftus came by. Facing them wasn't as horrible as Poppy expected, but she felt like a hypocrite when they marvelled over her 'wonderful attitude'. They talked about quality time, and the fact that no two cases of cancer were the same, and about people they'd known who'd beaten the percentages. Saint Poppy squirmed inside, but she listened and nodded – until they began to talk about more tests.

'We'd like to do an angiogram and a laparotomy,' Dr Loftus said. 'Now an angiogram is—'

'Tubes stuck in my *veins*?' Poppy said before she could help herself.

Everyone looked startled. Then Dr Loftus gave a rueful

smile. 'Sounds like you've been reading up on it.'

'No, I just – I guess I remember it from somewhere,' Poppy said. She knew where she was getting the images – from Dr Loftus's head. And she probably should cover her tracks instead of talking anymore, but she was too distressed. 'And a laparotomy's an operation, right?'

Dr Loftus and Dr Franklin exchanged glances. 'An exploratory operation, yes,' Dr Franklin said.

'But I don't *need* those tests, do I? I mean, you already know what I've got. And the tests *hurt*.'

'Poppy,' her mother said gently. But Dr Loftus was answering slowly.

'Well, sometimes we need the tests to confirm a diagnosis. But in your case . . . no, Poppy. We don't really need them. We're already sure.'

'Then I don't see why I have to have them,' Poppy said simply. 'I'd rather go home.'

The doctors looked at each other, then at Poppy's mother. Then, without even trying to be subtle about it, the three adults went out into the corridor to deliberate.

When they came back, Poppy knew she'd won.

'You can go home, Poppy,' Dr Franklin said quietly. 'At least until you develop any further symptoms. The nurse will tell your mother what to look out for.'

The first thing Poppy did was call James. He answered on the first ring and said, 'How do you feel?'

'Dizzy. But pretty good,' Poppy said, whispering because her mother was outside talking to a nurse. 'I'm coming home.'

'I'll come over this afternoon,' James said. 'Call me when you think you'll have an hour or so alone. And, Poppy . . . don't tell Phil I'm coming.'

'Why not?'

'I'll explain later.'

* * *

When she actually got home, it was strange. Cliff and Phil were there. Everybody was unusually nice to her, while still trying to pretend that nothing unusual was going on. (Poppy had heard the nurse tell her mother that it was good to try and maintain a normal routine.)

It's like my birthday, Poppy thought dazedly. Like some terribly important birthday and graduation rolled into one. Every few minutes the doorbell would ring as another flower arrangement arrived. Poppy's bedroom looked like a garden.

She felt badly for Phil. He looked so stricken – and so brave. She wanted to comfort him the way she'd comforted her mother – but *how?*

'Come here,' she ordered, opting for direct action. And when he obeyed, she hugged him tightly.

'You'll beat this thing,' he whispered. 'I know you will. Nobody's ever had as much will to live as you do. And nobody's ever, *ever* been as stubborn.'

It was then that Poppy realized just how terribly she was going to miss him.

When she let go, she felt light-headed.

'Maybe you'd better lie down,' Cliff said gently. And Poppy's mother helped her to the bedroom.

'Does Dad know?' she asked as her mother moved around the bedroom, straightening things.

'I tried to get hold of him yesterday, but the people at the station said he'd moved to somewhere in Vermont. They don't know where.'

Poppy nodded. It sounded like her dad – always on the move. He was a DJ – when he wasn't being an artist or a stage magician. He'd split up with her mom because he wasn't very good at being any of those things – or at least not good enough to get paid much.

Cliff was everything Poppy's father wasn't: responsible, disciplined, hardworking. He fit in perfectly with Poppy's mom and Phil. So perfectly that sometimes Poppy felt like the odd one out in her own family.

'I miss Dad,' Poppy said softly.

'I know. Sometimes I do, too,' her mother said, surprising her. Then she said firmly, 'We'll find him, Poppy. As soon as he hears, he'll want to come.'

Poppy hoped so. She didn't suppose she'd get a chance to see him – after.

It wasn't until an hour or so before dinnertime, when Phil and Cliff were out doing errands, and her mother was taking a nap, that Poppy got the chance to call James.

'I'll come right over,' he said. 'I'll let myself in.' Ten minutes later he walked into Poppy's bedroom.

Poppy felt strangely shy. Things had changed between her and James. They weren't simply best friends anymore.

They didn't even say 'Hi' to each other. As soon as he came in, their eyes caught and met. And then, for an endless moment, they just looked at each other.

This time, when Poppy felt the quick pang in her chest that always came when she saw James, it was a throb of pure sweetness. He cared about her. She could see it in his eyes.

Wait a minute, hang on, her mind whispered. Don't jump the gun here. He *cares* about you, yes, but he didn't say he was *in love* with you. There's a difference.

Shut up, Poppy told her brain soberly. Aloud, she said, 'How come you didn't want Phil to know you were here?'

James threw his light windbreaker over a chair and sat down on Poppy's bed. 'Well – I just didn't want to be interrupted,' he said with a gesture of dismissal. 'How's the pain?'

'It's *gone*,' Poppy said. 'Isn't that weird? It didn't wake me up at all last night. And there's something else. I think I'm starting to – well, read people's thoughts.'

James smiled slightly, just one corner of his mouth up. 'That's good. I was worried . . .' He broke off and went to turn Poppy's CD player on. Plaintive Bantu wailings emerged.

'I was worried you didn't get enough blood last night,' James said quietly, resuming his seat. 'You'll have to take more this time – and so will I.'

Poppy felt something tremble inside her. Her revulsion was gone. She was still afraid, but that was only because of the consequences of what they were going to do. It wasn't just a way to get closer or to feed James. They were doing it to *change* Poppy.

'The only thing I don't understand is why you never bit me before.' Her tone was light, but as she spoke the words, she realized that there was a serious question behind them.

'I mean,' she said slowly, 'you did it with Michaela and Jacklyn, didn't you? And with other girls?'

He looked away but answered steadily. 'I didn't exchange blood with them. But I fed on them, yes.'

'But not me.'

'No. How can I explain?' He looked up at her. 'Poppy, taking blood can be a lot of different things – and the Elders don't want it to be anything but feeding. They say all you should feel is the joy of the hunt. And that's all I ever *have* felt – before.'

Poppy nodded, trying to feel satisfied with this. She didn't ask who the Elders were.

'Besides, it can be *dangerous*,' James said. 'It can be done with hatred, and it can kill. Kill permanently, I mean.'

Poppy was almost amused by this. '*You* wouldn't kill.'

James stared at her. Outside, it was cloudy and the light

in Poppy's bedroom was pale. It made James's face look pale, too, and his eyes silver.

'But I have,' James said. His voice was flat and bleak. 'I've killed without exchanging enough blood, so the person didn't come back as a vampire.'

CHAPTER
7

'Then you must have had a reason,' Poppy said flatly. When he looked at her, she shrugged. 'I know you.' She knew him in a way she'd never known anyone.

James looked away. 'I didn't have a reason, but there were some . . . extenuating circumstances. You could say I was set up. But I still have nightmares.'

He sounded so tired – so sad. *It's a lonely world, full of secrets*, Poppy thought. And he'd had to keep the biggest secret of all from everyone, including her.

'It must have been awful for you,' she said, hardly aware that she was speaking out loud. 'I mean, all your life – holding this in. Not telling anybody. Pretending . . .'

'Poppy.' He gave a shiver of repressed emotion. 'Don't.'

'Don't sympathize with you?'

He shook his head. 'Nobody's ever understood before.' After a pause he said, 'How can you worry about *me*? With what you're facing?'

'I guess because – I care about you.'

'And I guess that's why I didn't treat you like Michaela or Jacklyn,' he said.

Poppy looked at the sculpted planes of his face, at the wave of brown hair falling over his forehead like silk . . .

and held her breath. Say 'I love you,' she ordered mentally. *Say it*, you thickheaded male.

But they weren't connected, and James didn't give the slightest sign of having heard. Instead he turned brisk and businesslike. 'We'd better get started.' He got up and drew the window curtains shut. 'Sunlight inhibits all vampire powers,' he said in a guest lecturer voice.

Poppy took advantage of the pause to go to the CD player. The music had changed to a Dutch club song, which was fine for doing the Netherlands skippy dance to, but not very romantic. She punched a button and a velvety Portuguese lament began.

Then she twitched the sheer hangings around the bed closed. When she sat down again, she and James were in their own little world, dim and secluded, enclosed in misty eggshell white.

'I'm ready,' she said softly, and James leaned in close to her. Even in the semi-darkness Poppy felt mesmerized by his eyes. They were like windows to some other place, someplace distant and magical.

The Night World, she thought, and tilted her chin back as James took her in his arms.

This time the double sting at her neck hurt good.

But best was when James's mind touched hers. The feeling of oneness, of suddenly being whole – it spread through her like starshine.

Once again she had the sense that they were melting together, dissolving and merging everywhere they touched. She could feel her own pulse echoing through him.

Closer, closer . . . and then she felt a pulling-back.

James? What's wrong?

Nothing, he told her, but Poppy could sense that it wasn't quite true. He was trying to weaken the growing bond between them . . . but why?

Poppy, I just don't want to force you into anything. What we're feeling is – artificial . . .

Artificial? It was the realest thing that she'd ever experienced. Realer than real. In the midst of joy, Poppy felt a surge of hurt anger at James.

I don't mean it like that, he said, and there was desperation in the thought. *It's just that you can't resist the blood-bond. You couldn't resist it if you hated me. It isn't fair. . . .*

Poppy didn't care about fair. *If you can't resist it, why are you trying?* she asked him triumphantly.

She heard something like mental laughter, and then they were both clinging together as a wave of pure emotion swept them.

The blood-bond, Poppy thought when James raised his head at last. It doesn't matter if he won't say he loves me – we're bonded now. Nothing can change that.

And in a moment or so she would seal that bond by taking his blood. Try and resist *that*, she thought, and was startled when James laughed softly.

'Reading my mind again?'

'Not exactly. You're projecting – and you're very good at it. You're going to be a strong telepath.'

Interesting . . . but right now Poppy didn't feel strong. She suddenly felt kitten-weak. Limp as a wilting flower. She needed . . .

'I know,' James whispered. Still supporting her, he started to lift one wrist to his mouth.

Poppy stopped him with a restraining hand. 'James? How many times do we have to do this before I – change?'

'Once more, I think,' James said quietly. 'I took a lot this time, and I want you to do the same. And the next time we do it . . .'

I'll die, Poppy thought. Well, at least I know how long I have left as a human.

James's lips slid back to reveal long, delicate fangs, and he struck at his own wrist. There was something snakelike in the motion. Blood welled up, the colour of syrup in a can of cherry preserves.

Just as Poppy was leaning forward, lips parted, there was a knock at the door.

Poppy and James froze guiltily.

The knock came again. In her muddled and weakened state, Poppy couldn't seem to make herself move. The only thought that resounded in her brain was *Oh, please. Please don't let it be . . .*

The door opened.

. . . Phil.

Phillip was already speaking as he poked his head in. 'Poppy, are you awake? Mom says—'

He broke off abruptly, then lunged for the lightswitch on the wall. Suddenly the room was illuminated.

Oh, *terrific,* Poppy thought in frustration. Phil was peering through the filmy draperies around the bed. Poppy peered back at him.

'What – is going – *on*?' he said in a voice that would have gotten him the lead role in *The Ten Commandments.* And then, before Poppy could gather enough wits to answer, he leaned in and grabbed James by the arm.

'Phil, *don't,*' Poppy said. 'Phil, you idiot . . .'

'We had a deal,' Phil snarled at James. 'And you broke it.'

James was gripping Phil's arms now, as ungently as Phil was grasping him. Poppy had the dismayed feeling that they were going to start head-butting each other.

Oh, Lord, if she could only *think* straight. She felt so brainless.

'You've got the wrong idea,' James said to Phil through clenched teeth.

'The wrong *idea*? I come in here and find the two of you in bed, with all the curtains drawn, and you're telling me I've got the wrong *idea*?'

'*On* the bed,' Poppy interjected. Phil ignored her.

James shook Phil. He did it quite easily and with an economy of movement, but Phil's head snapped back and forth. Poppy realized that James was not at his most rational right now. She remembered the metal chair leg and decided it was time to intervene.

'Let *go*,' she said, reaching in between the two boys to grab for hands. Anybody's hands. 'Come on, you guys!' And then, desperately, 'Phil, I know you don't understand, but James is trying to *help* me—'

'Help you? I don't think so.' And then to James: 'Look at her. Can't you see that this stupid pretending is making her *sicker*? Every time I find her with you, she's white as a sheet. You're just making things worse.'

'You don't know anything about it,' James snarled in Phil's face. But Poppy was still processing something several sentences back.

'Stupid? Pretending?' she said. Her voice wasn't very loud but everything stopped.

Both boys looked at her.

Everyone made mistakes then. Later, Poppy would realize that if any of them had kept their heads, what happened next could have been avoided. But none of them did.

'I'm sorry,' Phil said to Poppy. 'I didn't want to tell you—'

'*Shut up*,' James said savagely.

'But I have to. This – jerk – is just playing with you. He admitted it to me. He said he felt sorry for you, and he thinks that pretending he likes you makes you feel better. He's got an ego that would fill Dodger Stadium.'

'Pretending?' Poppy said again, sitting back. There was a buzzing in her head and an eruption gathering in her chest.

'Poppy, he's crazy,' James said. 'Listen—'

But Poppy wasn't listening. The problem was that she could *feel* how sorry Phil was. It was much more convincing than anger. And Phillip, honest, straightforward, trustworthy Phillip, almost never lied.

He wasn't lying now. Which meant . . . that James must be.

Eruption time.

'You . . .' she whispered to James. 'You . . .' She couldn't think of a swear word bad enough. Somehow she felt more hurt, more betrayed than she had ever felt before. She had thought she *knew* James; she had trusted him absolutely. Which made the betrayal all the worse. 'So it was all pretending? Is that it?'

Some inner voice was telling her to hold on and *think*. That she was in no state to make crucial decisions. But she was also in no state to listen to inner voices. Her own anger kept her from deciding if she had any good reason to be angry.

'You just felt *sorry* for me?' she whispered, and suddenly all the fury and grief that she'd been suppressing for the last day and a half flooded out. She was blind with pain, and nothing mattered except making James hurt as much as she hurt.

James was breathing hard, speaking rapidly. 'Poppy – this is why I didn't want Phil to know—'

'And no *wonder*,' Poppy raged. 'And no wonder you wouldn't say you loved me,' she went on, not even caring that Phillip was listening. 'And no wonder you would do all that other stuff, but you never even kissed me. Well, I don't want your *pity*—'

'*What other stuff? All what other stuff?*' Phil shouted. '*I'm gonna kill you, Rasmussen!*'

He tore free of James and swung at him. James ducked so that the fist just grazed his hair. Phil swung again and James twisted sideways and grabbed him from behind in a headlock.

Poppy heard running footsteps in the hall. 'What's happening?' her mother gasped in dismay, regarding the scene in Poppy's bedroom.

At almost the same instant Cliff appeared behind Poppy's mother. 'What's all the shouting?' he asked, his jaw particularly square.

'*You're* the one who's putting her in danger,' James was snarling in Phillip's ear. 'Right now.' He looked feral. Savage.

Inhuman.

'Let go of my *brother*!' Poppy yelled. All at once her eyes were swimming with tears.

'Oh, my God – darling,' her mother said. In two steps she was beside the bed and holding Poppy. 'You boys get *out* of here.'

The savagery drained out of James's expression, and he loosened his hold on Phillip. 'Look, I'm sorry. I have to stay. Poppy . . .'

Phillip slammed an elbow into his stomach.

It might not have hurt James as much as it would a human, but Poppy saw the fury sweep over his face as he straightened from doubling up. He lifted Phil off his feet and threw him headfirst in the general direction of Poppy's dresser.

Poppy's mother let out a cry. Cliff jumped in between Phil and James.

'That's enough!' he roared. Then, to Phil: 'Are you all right?' And to James: 'What's this all about?'

Phil was rubbing his head dazedly. James said nothing. Poppy couldn't speak.

'All right, it doesn't matter,' Cliff said. 'I guess everybody's a little jumpy right now. But you'd better go on home, James.'

James looked at Poppy.

Poppy, throbbing all over like an aching tooth, turned her back on him. She burrowed into her mother's embrace.

'I'll be back,' James said quietly. It might have been meant as a promise, but it sounded like a threat.

'Not for a while, you won't,' Cliff said in a military command voice. Gazing over her mother's arm, Poppy could see that there was blood on Phillip's blond hair. 'I think everybody needs a cooling-off period. Now, come on, move.'

He led James out. Poppy sniffled and shivered, trying to ignore both the waves of giddiness that swept over her and the agitated murmuring of all the voices in her head. The stereo went on blasting out madcore stomping music from England.

In the next two days James called eight times.

Poppy actually picked up the phone the first time. It was after midnight when her private line rang, and she responded automatically, still half asleep.

'Poppy, don't hang up,' James said.

Poppy hung up. A moment later the phone rang again.

'Poppy, if you don't want to die, you've got to listen to me.'

'That's blackmail. You're *sick*,' Poppy said, clutching the handset. Her tongue felt thick and her head ached.

'It's just the truth. Poppy, listen. You didn't take any

blood today. I weakened you, and you didn't get anything in exchange. And that could *kill* you.'

Poppy heard the words, but they didn't seem real. She found herself ignoring them, retreating into a foggy state where thought was impossible. 'I don't care.'

'You *do* care, and if you could think, you'd know that. It's the change that's doing this. You're completely messed up mentally. You're too paranoid and illogical and crazy to *know* you're paranoid and illogical and crazy.'

It was suspiciously like what Poppy had realized earlier. She was aware, dimly, that she was acting the way Marissa Schaffer had after drinking a six-pack of beer at Jan Nedjar's New Year's party. Making a ranting fool of herself. But she couldn't seem to stop.

'I just want to know one thing,' she said. 'Is it true that you said that stuff to Phillip?'

She heard James let his breath out. 'It's true that I said it. But what I *said* wasn't true. It was just to get him off my back.'

By now Poppy was too upset to even want to calm down.

'Why should I believe somebody whose whole life is a lie?' she said, and hung up again as the first tears spilled.

All the next day she stayed in her state of foggy denial. Nothing seemed real, not the fight with James, not James's warning, and not her illness. Especially not her illness. Her mind found a way to accept the special treatment she was getting from everyone without dwelling on the reason for the treatment.

She even managed to disregard her mother's whispered comments to Phil about how she was going downhill so fast. How poor Poppy was getting pale, getting weak, getting worse. And only Poppy knew that she could now hear conversations held in the hallway as clearly as if they were in her own room.

All her senses were sharpened, even as her mind was dulled. When she looked at herself in the mirror, she was startled by how white she was, her skin translucent as candle wax. Her eyes so green and fierce that they burned.

The other six times James called, Poppy's mother told him Poppy was resting.

Cliff fixed the broken trim on Poppy's dresser. 'Who would have thought the kid was that strong?' he said.

James flipped his cellular phone shut and banged a fist on the Integra's dashboard. It was Thursday afternoon.

I love you. That's what he should have said to Poppy. And now it was too late – she wouldn't even talk to him.

Why *hadn't* he said it? His reasons seemed stupid now. So he hadn't taken advantage of Poppy's innocence and gratitude . . . well, bravo. All he'd done was tap her veins and break her heart.

All he'd done was hasten her death.

But there wasn't time to think about it now. Right now he had a masquerade to attend.

He got out of the car and gave his windbreaker a twitch as he walked toward the sprawling ranchstyle house.

He unlocked and opened the door without calling to announce his presence. He didn't need to announce it; his mother would sense him.

Inside, it was all cathedral ceilings and fashionably bare walls. The one oddity was that every one of the many skylights was covered with elegant custommade drapes. This made the interior seem spacious but dim. Almost – cavernous.

'James,' his mother said, coming from the back wing. She had jet-black hair with a sheen like lacquer and a perfect figure that was emphasized rather than disguised by her silver-and-gold embroidered wrap. Her eyes were cool grey and heavily lashed, like James's. She kissed the air beside his cheek.

'I got your message,' James said. 'What do you want?'

'I'd really rather wait until your father gets home . . .'

'Mom, I'm sorry, but I'm in a hurry. I've got things to do – I haven't even fed today.'

'It shows,' his mother said. She regarded him for a moment without blinking. Then she sighed, turning toward the living room. 'At least, let's sit down . . . You've been a little agitated, haven't you, these last few days?'

James sat on the crimson-dyed suede couch. Now was the test of his acting ability. If he could get through the next minute without his mother sensing the truth, he'd be home free.

'I'm sure Dad told you why,' he said evenly.

'Yes. Little Poppy. It's very sad, isn't it?' the shade of the single treelike floor lamp was deep red, and ruby light fell across half his mother's face.

'I was upset at first, but I'm pretty much over it now,' James said. He kept his voice dull and concentrated on sending nothing – *nothing* – through his aura. He could feel his mother lightly probing the edges of his mind. Like an insect gently caressing with an antenna, or a snake tasting the air with its black forked tongue.

'I'm surprised,' his mother said. 'I thought you liked her.'

'I did. But, after all, they're not really *people*, are they?' He considered a moment, then said, 'It's sort of like losing a pet. I guess I'll just have to find another one.'

It was a bold move, quoting the party line. James willed every muscle to stay relaxed as he felt the thought-tendrils tighten suddenly, coiling around him, looking for a chink in his armour. He thought very hard – about Michaela Vasquez. Trying to project just the right amount of negligent fondness.

It worked. The probing tendrils slipped away from his mind, and his mother settled back gracefully and smiled.

'I'm glad you're taking it so well. But if you ever feel that you'd like to talk to someone . . . your father knows some very good therapists.'

Vampire therapists, she meant. To screw his head on straight about how humans were just for feeding on.

'I know you want to avoid trouble as much as I do,' she added. 'It reflects on the family, you see.'

'Sure,' James said, and shrugged. 'I've got to go now. Tell Dad I said hi, OK?'

He kissed the air beside her cheek.

'Oh, by the way,' she said as he turned toward the door. 'Your cousin Ash *will* be coming next week. I think he'd like to stay with you at the apartment – and I'm sure you'd like some company there.'

Over my unbreathing body, James thought. He'd forgotten all about Ash's threat to visit. But now wasn't the time to argue. He walked out feeling like a juggler with too many balls in the air.

Back in his car he picked up the cellular phone, hesitated, then snapped it shut without turning it on. Calling wasn't any good. It was time to change his strategy.

All right, then. No more half measures. A serious offensive – aimed where it would do the most good.

He thought for a few minutes, then drove to McDonnell Drive, parking just a few houses away from where Poppy lived.

And then he waited.

He was prepared to sit there all night if necessary, but

he didn't have to. Just around sunset the garage door opened and a white Volkswagen Jetta backed out. James saw a blond head in the driver's seat.

Hi, Phil. Nice to see you.

When the Jetta pulled away, he followed it.

CHAPTER

8

When the Jetta turned into the parking lot of a 7-Eleven, James smiled. There was a nice isolated area behind the store, and it was getting dark.

He drove his own car around back, then got out to watch the store entrance. When Phil came out with a bag, he sprang on him from behind.

Phil yelled and fought, dropping the bag. It didn't matter. The sun had gone down and James's power was at full strength.

He dragged Phil to the back of the store and put him facing the wall beside a Dumpster. The classic police frisking position.

'I'm going to let go now,' he said. 'Don't try to run away. That would be a mistake.'

Phil went tense and motionless at the sound of his voice. 'I don't *want* to run away. I want to smash your face in, Rasmussen.'

'Go ahead and try.' James was going to add, *Make my night*, but he reconsidered. He let go of Phil, who turned around and regarded him with utter loathing.

'What's the matter? Run out of girls to jump?' he said, breathing hard.

James gritted his teeth. Trading insults wasn't going to do any good, but he could already tell it was going to be hard to keep his temper. Phil had that effect on him. 'I didn't bring you out here to fight. I brought you to ask you something. Do you care about Poppy?'

Phil said, 'I'll take stupid questions for five hundred, Alex,' and loosened his shoulder as if getting ready for a punch.

'Because if you do, you'll get her to talk to me. You were the one who convinced her not to see me, and now you've got to convince her that she *has* to see me.'

Phil looked around the parking lot, as if calling for somebody to witness this insanity.

James spoke slowly and clearly, enunciating each word. 'There is something I can do to help her.'

'Because you're Don Juan, right? You're gonna heal her with your love.' The words were flippant, but Phil's voice was shaky with sheer hatred. Not just hatred for James, but for a universe that would give Poppy cancer.

'No. You've got it completely wrong. Look, you think I was making out with her, or trifling with her affections or whatever. That's not what was going on at all. I let you think that because I was tired of getting the third degree from you – and because I didn't want you to know what we *were* doing.'

'Sure, sure,' Phil said in a voice filled with equal measures of sarcasm and contempt. 'So what *were* you doing? Drugs?'

'This.'

James had learned something from his first encounter with Poppy in the hospital. Show and tell should be done in that order. This time he didn't say anything; he just grabbed Phil by the hair and jerked his head back.

There was only a single light behind the store, but it

was enough to give Phil a good view of the bared fangs looming over him. And it was more than enough for James, with his night vision, to see Phillip's green eyes dilate as he stared.

Phillip yelled, then went limp.

Not with fear, James knew. He wasn't a coward. With the shock of disbelief turning to belief.

Phillip swore. 'You're a . . .'

'Right.' James let him go.

Phil almost lost his balance. He grabbed at the Dumpster for support. 'I don't believe it.'

'Yes, you do,' James said. He hadn't retracted his fangs, and he knew that his eyes were shining silver. Phil *had* to believe it with James standing right in front of him.

Phil apparently had the same idea. He was staring at James as if he wanted to look away, but couldn't. The colour had drained out of his face, and he kept swallowing as if he were going to be sick.

'God,' he said finally. 'I knew there was something wrong with you. Weird wrong. I could never figure out why you gave me the creeps. So this is it.'

I disgust him, James realized. It's not just hatred anymore. He thinks I'm less than human.

It didn't augur well for the rest of James's plan.

'Now do you understand how I can help Poppy?'

Phil shook his head slowly. He was leaning against the wall, one hand still on the Dumpster.

James felt impatience rise in his chest. 'Poppy has a disease. Vampires don't get diseases. Do you need a road map?'

Phillip's expression said he did.

'If,' James said through his teeth, 'I exchange enough blood with Poppy to turn her into a vampire, she won't have cancer anymore. Every cell in her body will change and she'll end up a perfect specimen: flawless, disease-free. She'll have powers that humans don't even dream of. And, incidentally, she'll be immortal.'

There was a long, long silence as James watched this sink in with Phillip. Phil's thoughts were too jumbled and kaleidoscopic for James to make anything of them, but Phil's eyes got wider and his face more ashen.

At last Phil said, 'You can't do that to her.'

It was the *way* he said it. Not as if he were protesting an idea because it was too radical, too new. Not the knee-jerk overreaction that Poppy had had.

He said it with absolute conviction and utmost horror. As if James were threatening to steal Poppy's soul.

'It's the only way to save her *life*,' James said.

Phil shook his head slowly again, eyes huge and trancelike. 'No. No. She wouldn't want it. Not at that cost.'

'What cost?' James was more than impatient now, he was defensive and exasperated. If he'd realized that this was going to turn into a philosophical debate, he would have picked somewhere less public. As it was, he had to keep all his senses on the alert for possible intruders.

Phil let go of the Dumpster and stood on his own two feet. There was fear mixed with the horror in his eyes, but he faced James squarely.

'It's just – there are some things that humans think are more important than just staying alive,' he said. 'You'll find that out.'

I don't believe this, James thought. He sounds like a junior space captain talking to the alien invaders in a B movie. *You won't find Earth people quite the easy mark you imagine.*

Aloud, he said, 'Are you nuts? Look, Phil, I was born in San Francisco. I'm not some bug-eyed monster from Alpha Centauri. I eat Wheaties for breakfast.'

'And what do you eat for a midnight snack?' Phil asked, his green eyes somber and almost childlike. 'Or are the fangs just for decoration?'

Walked right into that one, James's brain told him.

He looked away. 'OK. Touché. There are some differences. I never said I was a human. But I'm not some kind of—'

'If you're not a monster, then I don't know what is.'

Don't kill him, James counselled himself frantically. You have to *convince* him. 'Phil, we're not like what you see at the movies. We're not all-powerful. We can't dematerialize through walls or travel through time, and we don't need to kill to feed. We're not evil, at least not all of us. We're not damned.'

'You're unnatural,' Phillip said softly, and James could feel that he meant it from his heart. 'You're *wrong*. You shouldn't exist.'

'Because we're higher up on the food chain than you?'

'Because people weren't meant to . . . feed . . . on other people.'

James didn't say that his people didn't think of Phillip's people as people. He said, 'We only do what we have to do to survive. And Poppy's already agreed.'

Phillip froze. 'No. She wouldn't want to become like you.'

'She wants to stay alive – or at least, she did, before she got mad at me. Now she's just irrational because she hasn't got enough of my blood in her to finish changing her. Thanks to you.' He paused, then said deliberately, 'Have you ever seen a three-week-old corpse, Phil? Because *that's* what she's going to become if I don't get to her.'

Phil's face twisted. He whirled around and slammed a fist into the metal side of the Dumpster. *'Don't you think I know that?* I've been living with that since Monday night.'

James stood still, heart pounding. Feeling the anguish Phil was giving off and the pain of Phil's injured hand. It was several seconds before he was able to say calmly. 'And you think that's better than what I can give her?'

'It's lousy. It stinks. But, yes, it's better than turning into something that hunts people. That *uses* people. That's why all the girlfriends, isn't it?'

Once again, James couldn't answer right away. Phil's problem, he was realizing, was that Phil was far too smart for his own good. He thought too much. 'Yeah. That's why all the girlfriends,' he said at last, tiredly. Trying not to see this from Phil's point of view.

'Just tell me one thing. Rasmussen.' Phillip straightened and looked him dead in the eye. 'Did you' – he stopped and swallowed – 'feed on Poppy – before she got sick?'

'No.'

Phil let out his breath. 'That's good. Because if you *had*, I'd have killed you.'

James believed him. He was much stronger than Phil, much faster, and he'd never been afraid of a human before. But just at that moment he had no doubt that Phil would somehow have found a way to do it.

'Look, there's something you don't understand,' he said. 'Poppy *did* want this, and it's something we've already started. She's only just beginning to change; if she dies now, she won't become a vampire. But she might not die all the way, either. She could end up a walking corpse. A zombie, you know? Mindless. Body rotting, but immortal.'

Phil's mouth quivered with revulsion. 'You're just saying that to scare me.'

James looked away. 'I've seen it happen.'

'I don't believe you.'

'I've seen it *firsthand*!' Dimly James realized he was yelling and that he'd grabbed Phil by the shirt-front. He was out of control – and he didn't care. 'I've seen it happen to somebody I *cared* about, all right?'

And then, because Phil was still shaking his head: 'I was only four years old and I had a nanny. All the rich kids in San Francisco have nannies. She was human.'

'Let go,' Phil muttered, pulling at James's wrist. He was breathing hard – he didn't want to hear this.

'I was crazy about her. She gave me everything my mom didn't. Love, attention – she was never too busy. I called her Miss Emma.'

'*Let go.*'

'But my parents thought I was too attached to her. So they took me on a little vacation – and they didn't let me feed. Not for three days. By the time they brought me back, I was starving. Then they sent Miss Emma up to put me to bed.'

Phil had stopped fighting now. He stood with his head bowed and turned to one side so he wouldn't have to look at James. James threw his words at the averted face.

'I was only four. I couldn't stop myself. And the thing is, I wanted to. If you'd asked me who I'd rather have die, me or Miss Emma, I'd've said me. But when you're starving, you lose control. So I fed on her, and all the time I was crying and trying to stop. And when I finally could stop, I knew it was too late.'

There was a pause. James suddenly realized that his fingers were locked in an agonizing cramp. He let go of Phil's shirt slowly. Phil said nothing.

'She was just lying there on the floor. I thought, wait, if I give her my own blood she'll be a vampire, and everything will be OK.' He wasn't yelling anymore. He wasn't even really speaking to Phillip, but staring out into the dark parking lot. 'So I cut myself and let the blood run into her mouth. She swallowed some of it before my parents came up and stopped me. But not enough.'

A longer pause – and James remembered why he was telling the story. He looked at Phillip.

'She died that night – but not all the way. The two different kinds of blood were fighting inside her. So by morning she was walking around again – but she wasn't Miss Emma anymore. She drooled and her skin was grey and her eyes were flat like a corpse's. And when she started to – rot – my dad took her out to Inverness and buried her. He killed her first.' Bile rose in James's throat and he added almost in a whisper, 'I hope he killed her first.'

Phil slowly turned around to look at him. For the first time that evening, there was something other than horror and fear in his face. Something like pity, James thought.

James took a deep breath. After thirteen years of silence he'd finally told the story – to Phillip North, of all people. But it was no good wondering about the absurdity. He had a point to drive home.

'So take my advice. If you don't convince Poppy to see me, make sure they don't do an autopsy on her. You don't want her walking around without her internal organs. And have a wooden stake ready for the time when you can't stand to look at her anymore.'

The pity was gone from Phil's eyes. His mouth was a hard, trembling line.

'We won't let her turn into . . . some kind of half-alive abomination,' he said. 'Or a vampire, either. I'm sorry about what happened to your Miss Emma, but it doesn't change anything.'

'*Poppy* should be the one to decide—'

But Phillip had reached his limit, and now he was simply shaking his head. 'Just keep away from my sister,' he said. 'That's all I want. If you do, I'll leave you alone. And if you don't—'

'What?'

'I'm going to tell everybody in El Camino what you are. I'm going to call the police and the mayor and I'm going to stand in the middle of the street and yell it.'

James felt his hands go icy cold. What Phil didn't realize was that he'd just made it James's duty to kill him. It wasn't just that any human who stumbled on Night World secrets had to die, but that one actively threatening to *tell* about the Night World had to die immediately, no questions asked, no mercy given.

Suddenly James was so tired he couldn't see straight.

'Get out of here, Phil,' he said in a voice drained of emotion and vitality both. 'Now. And if you really want to protect Poppy, you won't tell anybody anything. Because they'll trace it back and find out that Poppy knows the secrets, too. And then they'll kill her – after bringing her in for questioning. It won't be fun.'

'Who're "they"? Your parents?'

'The Night People. We're all around you, Phil. Anybody you know could be one – including the mayor. So keep your mouth shut.'

Phillip looked at him through narrowed eyes. Then he turned and walked to the front of the store.

James couldn't remember when he'd felt so empty. Everything he'd done had turned out wrong. Poppy was now in more kinds of danger than he could count.

And Phillip North thought he was unnatural and evil. What Phil didn't know was that most of the time James thought the same thing.

* * *

Phillip got halfway home before he remembered that he'd dropped the bag with Poppy's cranberry juice and wild cherry Popsicles. Poppy had hardly eaten in the last two days, and when she did get hungry, it was for something weird.

No – something *red*, he realized as he paid for a second time at the 7-Eleven. He felt a sick lurch in his stomach. Everything she wanted lately was red and at least semiliquid.

Did Poppy realize that herself?

He studied her when he went into her bedroom to give her a Popsicle. Poppy spent most of the time in bed now.

And she was so pale and still. Her green eyes were the only alive thing about her. They dominated her face, glittering with an almost savage awareness.

Cliff and Phil's mother were talking about getting round-the-clock nurses to be with her.

'Don't like the Popsicle?' Phil asked, dragging a chair to sit beside her bed.

Poppy was eyeing the thing with distaste. She took a tiny lick and grimaced.

Phillip watched her.

Another lick. Then she put the Popsicle into an empty plastic cup on her nightstand. 'I don't know . . . I just don't feel hungry,' she said, leaning back against the pillows. 'Sorry you had to go out for nothing.'

'No problem.' God, she looks sick, Phil thought. 'Is there anything else I can do for you?'

Eyes shut, Poppy shook her head. A very small motion. 'You're a good brother,' she said distantly.

She used to be so alive, Phil thought. Dad called her Kilowatt or Eveready. She used to *radiate* energy.

Without in the least meaning to, he found himself saying, 'I saw James Rasmussen today.'

9 1

Poppy stiffened. Her hands on the bedspread formed not fists, but claws. 'He'd better keep away from here!'

There was something subtly wrong about her reaction. Something not-Poppy. Poppy could get fierce, sure, but Phil had never heard that animal tone in her voice before.

A picture flashed through Phil's mind. A creature from *Night of the Living Dead*, walking even though its intestines were spilling out. A living corpse like James's Miss Emma.

Was that really what would happen if Poppy died right now? Was she that much changed already?

'I'll scratch his eyes out if he comes around here,' Poppy said, her fingers working on the spread like a cat kneading.

'Poppy – he told me the truth about what he really is.'

Strangely, Poppy had no reaction. 'He's scum,' she said. 'He's a reptile.'

Something about her voice made Phillip's flesh creep. 'And I told him you would never want to become something like that.'

'I wouldn't,' Poppy said shortly. 'Not if it meant hanging around with *him* for eternity. I don't want to see him ever again.'

Phil stared at her for a long moment. Then he leaned back and shut his eyes, one thumb jammed against his temple where the ache was worst.

Not just subtly wrong. He didn't want to believe it, but Poppy was *strange*. Irrational. And now that he thought about it, she'd been getting stranger every hour since James had been thrown out.

So maybe she *was* in some eerie in-between state. Not a human and not a vampire. And not able to think clearly. Just as James had said.

Poppy should be the one to decide.

There was something he had to ask her.

'Poppy?' He waited until she looked at him, her green eyes large and unblinking. 'When we talked, James said that you'd agreed to let him – change you. Before you got mad at him. Is that right?'

Poppy's eyebrows lifted. 'I'm mad at him,' she confirmed, as if this was the only part of the question she'd processed. 'And you know why I like you? Because you've always hated him. Now we both hate him.'

Phil thought for a moment, then spoke carefully. 'OK. But when you *weren't* mad at him, back then, did you want to turn into – what he is?'

Suddenly a gleam of rationality showed in Poppy's eyes. 'I just didn't want to *die*,' she said. 'I was so scared – and I wanted to live. If the doctors could do anything for me, I'd try that. But they can't.' She was sitting up now, staring into space as if she saw something terrible there. 'You don't know what it feels like to know you're going to die,' she whispered.

Waves of chills washed over Phillip. No, he didn't know that, but he did know – he could suddenly picture vividly – what it was going to be like for *him* after Poppy died. How empty the world was going to be without her.

For a long time they both sat in silence.

Then Poppy fell back onto the pillows again. Phillip could see pastel blue smudges under her eyes, as if the conversation had exhausted her. 'I don't think it matters,' she said in a faint but frighteningly cheerful voice. 'I'm not going to die anyway. Doctors don't know everything.'

So that's how she's dealing with it, Phillip thought. Total denial.

He had all the information he needed, though. He had a clear view of the situation. And he knew what he had to do now.

'I'll leave so you can get some rest,' he said to Poppy,

and patted her hand. It felt very cool and fragile, full of tiny bones like a bird's wing. 'See you later.'

He slipped out of the house without telling anyone where he was going. Once on the road, he drove very fast. It only took ten minutes to reach the apartment building.

He'd never been to James's apartment before.

James answered the door with a cold. 'What are you doing here?'

'Can I come in? I've got something to say.'

James stood back expressionlessly to let him in.

The place was roomy and bare. There was a single chair beside a very cluttered table, an equally cluttered desk, and a square unbeautiful couch. Cardboard boxes full of books and CDs were stacked in the corners. A door led to a spartan bedroom.

'What do you want?'

'First of all, I have to explain something. I know you can't help being what you are – but I can't help how I feel about it, either. You can't change, and neither can I. I need you to understand that from the beginning.'

James crossed his arms over his chest, wary and defiant. 'You can skip the lecture.'

'I just need to make sure you understand, OK?'

'What do you *want*, Phil?'

Phil swallowed. It took two or three tries before he could get the words out past the blockage of his pride.

'I want you to help my sister.'

CHAPTER
9

Poppy shifted on her bed.

She was unhappy. It was a hot, restless unhappiness that seemed to swarm underneath her skin. Coming from her body instead of from her mind. If she hadn't been so weak, she would have gotten up and tried to run the feeling off. But she had spaghetti for muscles now and she wasn't running anywhere.

Her mind was simply cloudy. She didn't try to think much anymore. She was happiest when she was asleep.

But tonight she couldn't sleep. She could still taste the wild cherry Popsicle in the corners of her mouth. She would have tried to wash the taste away, but the thought of water made her feel vaguely nauseated.

Water's no good. Not what I need.

Poppy turned over and pressed her face into the pillow. She didn't know what she needed, but she knew she wasn't getting it.

A soft sound came from the hallway. Footsteps. The footsteps of at least two people. It didn't sound like her mother and Cliff, and anyway they'd gone to bed.

There was the lightest of knocks at her door, then a fan of light opened on the floor as the door cracked. Phil whispered, 'Poppy, you asleep? Can I come in?'

To Poppy's slowly rising indignation, he *was* coming in, without waiting for an answer. And someone was with him.

Not just someone. *The* one. The one who had hurt Poppy worst of all. The betrayer. James.

Anger gave Poppy the strength to sit up. 'Go away! I'll hurt you!' The most primitive and basic of warning-off messages. An animal reaction.

'Poppy, please let me talk to you,' James said. And then something amazing happened. Even Poppy, in her befuddled state, recognized that it was amazing.

Phil said, 'Please do it, Poppy. Just listen to him.'

Phil siding with James?

Poppy was too confused to protest as James came and knelt by her bedside.

'Poppy, I know you're upset. And it's my fault; I made a mistake. I didn't want Phil to know what was really going on, and I told him I was just pretending to care for you. But it wasn't true.'

Poppy frowned.

'If you search your feelings, you'll *know* it's not true. You're turning into a telepath, and I think you already have enough power to read me.'

Behind James, Phil stirred as if uneasy at the mention of telepathy. '*I* can tell you it's not true,' he said, causing both Poppy and James to look at him in surprise. 'That's one thing I found out from talking to you,' he added, speaking to James without looking at him. 'You may be some kind of monster, but you really do care about Poppy. You're not trying to hurt her.'

'*Now* you finally get it? After causing all this—?' James broke off and shook his head, turning back to Poppy. 'Poppy, concentrate. Feel what I'm feeling. Find the truth for yourself.'

I won't and you can't make me, Poppy thought. But the part of her that wanted to find out the truth was stronger than the irrational, angry part. Tentatively she *reached* for James – not with her hand, but with her mind. She couldn't have described to anyone how she did it. She just did it.

And she found James's mind, diamond-bright and burning with intensity. It wasn't the same as being one with him, the way she had been when they shared blood. It was like looking at him from the outside, sensing his emotions from a distance. But it was enough. The warmth and longing and protectiveness he had for her were all clear. So was the anguish: the pain he felt to know that she was hurting – and that she hated him.

Poppy's eyes filled. 'You really do care,' she whispered.

James's grey eyes met hers, and there was a look in them Poppy couldn't remember seeing before. 'There are two cardinal rules in the Night World,' he said steadily. 'One is not to tell humans that it exists. The other is not to fall in love with a human. I've broken both of them.'

Poppy was aware, vaguely, that Phillip was walking out of the room. The fan of light contracted as he half shut the door behind him. James's face was partly in shadow.

'I could never tell you how I felt about you,' James said. 'I couldn't even admit it to myself. Because it puts you in terrible danger. You can't imagine what kind of danger.'

'And you, too,' Poppy said. It was the first time she'd really thought about this. Now the idea emerged from her muddled consciousness like a bubble in a pot of stew. 'I mean,' she said slowly, puzzling it out, 'if it's against the rules to tell a human or love a human, and you break the rules, then there must be some punishment for *you* . . .' Even as she said it, she sensed what the punishment was.

More of James's face went into shadow. 'Don't you worry about that,' he said in his old voice, his cool-guy voice.

Poppy never took advice, not even from James. A surge of irritation and anger swept through her – an animal surge, like the feverish restlessness. She could feel her eyes narrow and her fingers claw.

'Don't you tell me what to worry about!'

He frowned. 'Don't you tell me not to tell you—' he began, and then broke off. 'What am I doing? You're still sick with the change and I'm just sitting here.' He rolled up a sleeve of his windbreaker and drew a fingernail along his wrist. Where the nail cut, blood welled up.

It looked black in the darkness. But Poppy found her eyes fixing on its liquid beading in fascination. Her lips parted and her breath came faster.

'Come on,' James said, and held his wrist in front of her. The next second Poppy had pounced and fixed her mouth on it as if she were trying to save him from a snakebite.

It was so natural, so easy. *This* is what she'd needed when she was dispatching Phil to get Popsicles and cranberry juice. This sweet, heady stuff was the real thing and nothing else was like it. Poppy sucked avidly.

It was all good: the closeness, the rich, dark-red taste; the strength and vitality that flooded through her, warming her to her fingertips. But best, better than any mere sensation, was the touch of James's mind. It made her giddy with pleasure.

How could she ever have mistrusted him? It seemed ridiculous now that she could *feel*, directly, how he felt about her. She would never know anyone the way she knew James.

I'm sorry, she thought to him, and felt her thought

accepted, forgiven, cherished. Held gently by the cradling of James's mind.

It wasn't your fault, he told her.

Poppy's mind seemed to be clearing with every second that went by. It was like waking up out of a deep and uncomfortable sleep. *I don't ever want this to end*, she thought, not really directing it at James, just thinking it.

But she felt a reaction in him – and then felt him bury the reaction quickly. Not quickly enough. Poppy had sensed it.

Vampires don't do this to each other.

Poppy was shocked. They would never have this glory again after she changed? She wouldn't believe that; she refused. There must be a way . . .

Again, she felt the beginning of a reaction in James, but just as she was chasing it, he gently pulled his wrist back. 'You'd better not take any more tonight,' he said, and his real-world voice sounded strange to Poppy's ears. It wasn't as much *James* as his mental voice, and now she couldn't really feel him properly. They were two separate beings. The isolation was awful.

How could she survive if she could never touch his mind again? If she had to use *words*, which suddenly seemed as clumsy as smoke signals for communication? If she could never feel him fully, his whole being open to her?

It was cruel and unfair and all vampires must be idiots if they settled for anything less.

Before she could open her mouth to begin the clumsy process of verbally explaining this to James, the door moved. Phillip looked around it.

'Come on in,' James said. 'We've got a lot to talk about.'

Phil was staring at Poppy. 'Are you . . .' He stopped and

swallowed before finishing in a husky whisper. 'Better?'

It didn't take telepathy to sense his disgust. He glanced at her mouth, and then quickly away. Poppy realized what he must be seeing. A stain as if she'd been eating berries. She rubbed at her lips with the back of her hand.

What she wanted to say was, it isn't disgusting. It's part of Nature. It's a way of giving life, pure life. It's secret and beautiful. It's *all right*.

What she said was, 'Don't knock it till you've tried it.'

Phillip's face convulsed in horror. And the weird thing was that on this subject James was in perfect agreement with him. Poppy could sense it – James thought sharing blood was dark and evil, too. He was filled with guilt. Poppy heaved a long, exasperated sigh, and added, '*Boys.*'

'You're better,' Phil said, cracking a faint smile.

'I guess I was pretty bizarre before,' Poppy said. 'Sorry.'

'*Pretty* is not the word.'

'It wasn't her fault,' James said shortly to Phil. 'She was dying – and hallucinating, sort of. Not enough blood to the brain.'

Poppy shook her head. 'I don't get it. You didn't take that much blood from me the last time. How could I not have enough blood to the brain?'

'It's not that,' James said. 'The two kinds of blood react against each other – they fight each other. Look, if you want a scientific explanation, it's something like this. Vampire blood destroys the haemoglobin – the red cells – in human blood. Once it destroys enough of the red cells, you stop getting the oxygen you need to think straight. And when it destroys more, you don't have the oxygen you need to live.'

'So vampire blood is like poison,' Phil said, in the tones of someone who knew it all along.

James shrugged. He wasn't looking at either Poppy or

Phil. 'In some ways. But in other ways it's like a universal cure. It makes wounds heal fast, makes flesh regenerate. Vampires can live on very little oxygen because their cells are so resilient. Vampire blood does everything – except carry oxygen.'

A light went on in Poppy's brain. Dawning revelation – the mystery of Count Dracula explained. 'Wait a minute,' she said. 'Is *that* why you need human blood?'

'That's one of the reasons,' James said. 'There are some . . . some more mystical things human blood does for us, but keeping us alive is the most basic one. We take a little and that carries oxygen through our system until our own blood destroys it. Then we take a little more.'

Poppy settled back. 'So that's it. And it *is* natural . . .'

'Nothing about this is natural,' Phil said, his disgust surfacing again.

'Yes, it is; it's like whatdoyoucallit, from biology class. Symbiosis—'

'It doesn't *matter* what it's like,' James said. 'We can't sit here and talk about it. We've got to make plans.'

There was an abrupt silence as Poppy realized what kind of plans he was talking about. She could tell Phil was realizing it, too.

'You're not out of danger yet,' James said softly, his eyes holding Poppy's. 'It's going to take one more exchange of blood, and you should have it as soon as possible. Otherwise, you might relapse again. But we're going to have to plan the next exchange carefully.'

'Why?' Phil said, at his most deliberately obstructive.

'Because it's going to kill me,' Poppy said flatly before James could answer. And when Phil flinched, she went on ruthlessly, 'That's what this is all *about*, Phil. It's not some little game James and I are playing. We have to deal with the reality, and the reality is that one way or another I'm going to die soon. And I'd rather die and wake up a vampire than die and not wake up at all.'

There was another silence, during which James put his hand on hers. It was only then that Poppy realized she was shaking.

Phil looked up. Poppy could see that his face was drawn, his eyes dark. 'We're twins. So how'd you get so much older than me?' he said in a muted voice.

A little hush, and then James said, 'I think tomorrow night would be a good time to do it. It's Friday – do you think you can get your mom and Cliff out of the house for the night?'

Phil blinked. 'I guess – if Poppy seems better, they might go out for a little while. If I said I'd stay with her.'

'Convince them they need a break. I don't want them around.'

'Can't you just make them not notice anything? Like you did with that nurse at the hospital?' Poppy asked.

'Not if I'm going to be concentrating on *you*,' James said. 'And there are certain people who can't be influenced by mind control at all – your brother, here, is one of them. Your mom could be another.'

'All right; I'll get them to go out,' Phillip said. He gulped, obviously uncomfortable and trying to hide it. 'And once they're gone . . . then what?'

James looked at him inscrutably. 'Then Poppy and I do what we have to do. And then *you* and I watch TV.'

'Watch TV,' Phil repeated, sounding numb.

'I've got to be here when the doctor comes – and the people from the funeral home.'

Phil looked utterly horrified at the mention of the funeral home. For that matter, Poppy didn't feel too cheerful about it herself. If it weren't for the rich, strange blood coursing inside her, calming her . . .

'*Why?*' Phillip was demanding of James.

James shook his head, very slightly. His face was expressionless. 'I just do,' he said. 'You'll understand later. For now, just trust me.'

Poppy decided not to pursue it.

'So you guys are going to have to make up tomorrow,' she said. 'In front of Mom and Cliff. Otherwise it'll be too weird for you to hang out together.'

'It'll be too weird no matter what,' Phil said under his breath. 'All right. Come over tomorrow afternoon and we'll make up. And I'll get them to leave us with Poppy.'

James nodded. 'I'd better go now.' He stood. Phil stepped back to let him out the door, but James hesitated by Poppy.

'You gonna be all right?' he asked in a low voice.

Poppy nodded staunchly.

'Tomorrow, then.' He touched her cheek with his fingertips. The briefest contact, but it made Poppy's heart leap and it turned her words into the truth. She *would* be all right.

They looked at each other a moment, then James turned away.

Tomorrow, Poppy thought, watching the door close behind him. Tomorrow is the day I die.

One thing about it, Poppy thought – not many people were privileged to *know* exactly when they were going to die. So not many people had the chance to say goodbye the way she planned to.

It didn't matter that she wasn't *really* dying. When a caterpillar changes into a butterfly it loses its caterpillar life. No more shinnying up twigs, no more eating leaves.

No more El Camino High School, Poppy thought. No more sleeping in this bed.

She was going to have to leave it all behind. Her family, her hometown. Her entire human life. She was starting out into a strange new future with no idea of what was ahead. All she could do was trust James – and trust her own ability to adapt.

It was like looking at a pale and curving road stretching in front of her, and not being able to see where it went as it disappeared into the darkness.

No more rollerblading down the boardwalk at Venice Beach, Poppy thought. No more slap of wet feet on concrete at the Tamashaw public pool. No more shopping at the Village.

To say goodbye, she looked at every corner of her room. Goodbye white-painted dresser. Goodbye desk where she had sat writing hundreds of letters – as proven by the stains where she'd dropped sealing wax on the wood. Goodbye bed, goodbye misty white bed curtains that had made her feel like an Arabian princess in a fairy tale. Goodbye stereo.

Ouch, she thought. My stereo. And my *CDs*. I can't leave them; I can't . . .

But of course she could. She would have to.

It was probably just as well that she had to deal with the stereo before she walked out of her room. It built her up to start dealing with the loss of *people*.

'Hi, Mom,' she said shakily, in the kitchen.

'Poppy! I didn't know you were up.'

She hugged her mother hard, in that one moment aware of so many little sensations: the kitchen tile under her bare feet, the faint coconut smell that clung to her mother's hair from her shampoo. Her mother's arms around her, and the warmth of her mother's body.

'Are you hungry, sweetie? You look so much better.'

Poppy couldn't stand to look into her mother's

anxiously hopeful face, and the thought of food made her nauseated. She burrowed back into her mother's shoulder.

'Just hold me a minute,' she said.

It came to her, then, that she wasn't going to be able to say goodbye to everything after all. She couldn't tie up all the loose ends of her life in one afternoon. She might be privileged to know that this was her last day here, but she was going out just like everyone else – unprepared.

'Just remember I love you,' she muttered into her mother's shoulder, blinking back tears.

She let her mother put her back to bed, then. She spent the rest of the day making phone calls. Trying to learn a *little* bit about the life she was about to exit, the people she was supposed to know. Trying to appreciate it all, *fast*, before she had to leave it.

'So, Elaine, I miss you,' she said into the mouthpiece, her eyes fixed on the sunlight coming in her window.

'So, Brady, how's it going?'

'So, Laura, thanks for the flowers.'

'Poppy, are you OK?' they all said. 'When are we going to see you again?'

Poppy couldn't answer. She wished she could call her dad, but nobody knew where he was.

She also wished she had actually *read* the play *Our Town* when she'd been assigned it last year, instead of using Cliff Notes and quick thinking to fake it. All she could remember now was that it was about a dead girl who got the chance to look at one ordinary day in her life and really appreciate it. It might have helped her sort out her own feelings now – but it was too late.

I wasted a lot of high school, Poppy realized. I used my brains to outsmart the teachers – and that really wasn't very smart at all.

She discovered in herself a new respect for Phil, who

actually used his brain to learn things. Maybe her brother wasn't just a pitiful strait-laced grind after all. Maybe – oh, God – *he'd* been right all along.

I'm changing so much, Poppy thought, and she shivered. Whether it was the strange alien blood in her or the cancer itself or just part of growing up, she didn't know. But she was changing.

The doorbell rang. Poppy knew who it was without leaving the room. She could sense James.

He's here to start the play, Poppy thought, and looked at her clock. Incredible. It was almost four o'clock already.

Time literally seemed to be flying by.

Don't panic. You have hours yet, she told herself, and picked up the phone again. But it seemed only minutes later that her mother came knocking on the bedroom door.

'Sweetie, Phil thinks we should go out – and James has come over – but I told him I don't think you want to see him – and I don't really want to leave you at night . . .' Her mother was uncharacteristically flustered.

'No, I'm happy to see James. Really. And I think you *should* take a break. Really.'

'Well – I'm glad you and James have made up. But I still don't know . . .'

It took time to convince her, to persuade her that Poppy was so much better, that Poppy had weeks or months ahead of her to live. That there was no reason to stick around on this particular Friday night.

But at last Poppy's mother kissed her and agreed. And then there was nothing to do but say goodbye to Cliff. Poppy got a hug from him and finally forgave him for not being her dad.

You did your best, she thought as she disengaged from his crisp dark suit and looked at his boyishly square jaw.

And you're going to be the one to take care of Mom –
afterward. So I forgive you. You're all right, really.

And then Cliff and her mom were walking out, and it
was the last time, the very last time to say goodbye. Poppy
called it after them and they both turned and smiled.

When they were gone, James and Phil came into
Poppy's room. Poppy looked at James. His grey eyes were
opaque, revealing nothing of his feelings.

'Now?' she said, and her voice trembled slightly.

'Now.'

CHAPTER
10

'Things have to be right,' Poppy said. 'Things have to be just right for this. Get some candles, Phil.'

Phil was looking ashen and haggard. 'Candles?'

'As many as you can find. And some pillows. I need lots of pillows.' She knelt by the stereo to examine a haphazard pile of CDs. Phil stared at her briefly, then went out.

'*Structures from Silence* . . . no. Too repetitious,' Poppy said, rummaging through the pile. '*Deep Forest* – no. Too hyper. I need something *ambient*.'

'How about this?' James picked a CD up. Poppy looked at the label.

Music to Disappear In.

Of course. It was perfect. Poppy took the CD and met James's gaze. Usually he referred to the haunting soft strains of ambient music as 'New Age mush'.

'You understand,' she said quietly.

'Yes. But you're not dying, Poppy. This isn't a death scene you're setting up.'

'But I'm going away. I'm changing.' Poppy couldn't explain exactly, but something in her said she was doing the right thing. She was dying to her old life. It was a solemn occasion, a Passage.

And of course, although neither of them mentioned it, they both knew she *might* die for good. James had been very frank about that – some people didn't make it through the transition.

Phil came back with candles, Christmas candles, emergency candles, scented votive candles. Poppy directed him to place them around the room and light them. She herself went to the bathroom to change into her best nightgown. It was flannel, with a pattern of little strawberries.

Just imagine, she thought as she left the bathroom. This is the last time I'll ever walk down this hall, the last time I'll push open my bedroom door.

The bedroom was beautiful. The soft glow of candlelight gave it an aura of sanctity, of mystery. The music was unearthly and sweet, and Poppy felt she could fall into it forever, the way she fell in her dreams.

Poppy opened the closet and used a hanger to bat a tawny stuffed lion and a floppy grey Eeyore down from the top shelf. She took them to her bed and put them beside the mounded pillows. Maybe it was stupid, maybe it was childish, but she wanted them with her.

She sat on the bed and looked at James and Phillip.

They were both looking at her. Phil was clearly upset, touching his mouth to stop its trembling. James was upset, too, although only someone who knew him as well as Poppy did would have been able to tell.

'It's all right,' Poppy told them. 'Don't you see? *I'm* all right, so there's no excuse for you not to be.'

And the strange thing was, it was the truth. She was all right. She felt calm and clear now, as if everything had become very simple. She saw the road ahead of her, and all she had to do was follow it, step by step.

Phil came over to squeeze her hand. 'How does this –
how does this work?' he asked James huskily.

'First we'll exchange blood,' James said – speaking to
Poppy. Looking only at her. 'It doesn't have to be a lot;
you're right on the border of changing already. Then the
two kinds of blood fight it out – sort of the last battle, if
you see what I mean.' He smiled faintly and painfully, and
Poppy nodded.

'While that's happening you'll feel weaker and weaker.
And then you'll just – go to sleep. The change happens
while you're asleep.'

'And when do I wake up?' Poppy asked.

'I'll give you a kind of posthypnotic suggestion about
that. Tell you to wake up when I come to get you. Don't
worry about it; I've got all the details figured out. All you
need to do is rest.'

Phil was running nervous hands through his hair, as if
he was just now thinking about what kind of details he
and James were going to have to deal with.

'Wait a minute,' he said in almost a croak. 'When –
when you say "sleep" – she's going to look . . .'

'Dead,' Poppy supplied, when his voice ran out.

James gave Phil a cold look. 'Yes. We've been over this.'

'And then – we're really going to – what's going to
happen to her?'

James glared.

'It's OK,' Poppy said softly. 'Tell him.'

'You know what's going to happen,' James said
through clenched teeth to Phillip. 'She can't just
disappear. We'd have the police *and* the Night People after
us, looking for her. No, it's got to seem that she died from
the cancer, and that means everything's got to happen
exactly the way it would if she *had* died.'

Phil's sick expression said he wasn't at his most

rational. 'You're sure there isn't any other way?'

'No,' James said.

Phil wet his lips. 'Oh, God.'

Poppy herself didn't want to dwell on it too much. She said fiercely, '*Deal* with it, Phil. You've got to. And remember, if it doesn't happen now it's going to happen in a few weeks – for real.'

Phil was holding on to one of the brass bedposts so hard that his knuckles were pale. But he'd gotten the point, and there was no one better than Phil at bracing himself. 'You're right,' he said thinly, with the ghost of his old efficient manner. 'OK, I'm dealing with it.'

'Then let's get started,' Poppy said, making her voice calm and steady. As if she were dealing with everything effortlessly herself.

James said to Phil, 'You don't want to see this part. Go out and watch TV for a few minutes.'

Phil hesitated, then nodded and left.

'One thing,' Poppy said to James as she scooted to the middle of the bed. She was still trying desperately to sound casual. 'After the funeral – well, I'll be asleep, won't I? I won't wake up . . . you know. In my nice little coffin.' She looked up at him. 'It's just that I'm claustrophobic, a little.'

'You won't wake up there,' James said. 'Poppy, I wouldn't let that happen to you. Trust me; I've thought of everything.'

Poppy nodded. I do trust you, she thought.

Then she held her arms out to him.

He touched her neck, so she tilted her chin back. As the blood was drawn from her, she felt her mind drawn into his.

Don't worry, Poppy. Don't be afraid. All his thoughts were ferociously protective. And even though it only confirmed that there was something to be afraid *of*, that this could go wrong, Poppy felt peaceful. The direct sense of his love made her calm, flooded her with light.

She suddenly felt distance and height and depth – spaciousness. As if her horizons had expanded almost to infinity in an instant. As if she'd discovered a new dimension. As if there were no limits or obstacles to what she and James could do together.

She felt . . . free.

I'm getting light-headed, she realized. She could feel herself going limp in James's arms. Swooning like a wilting flower.

I've taken enough, James said in her mind. The warm animal mouth on her throat pulled back. 'Now it's your turn.'

This time, though, he didn't make the cut at his wrist. He took off his T-shirt and, with a quick, impulsive gesture, ran a fingernail along the base of his throat.

Oh, Poppy thought. Slowly, almost reverently, she leaned forward. James's hand supported the back of her head. Poppy put her arms around him, feeling his bare skin under the flannel of her nightgown.

It was better this way. But if James was right, it was another last time. She and James could never exchange blood again.

I can't accept that, Poppy thought, but she couldn't concentrate on anything for very long. This time, instead of clearing her brain, the wild, intoxicating vampire blood was making her more confused. More heavy and sleepy.

James?

It's all right. It's the beginning of the change.

Heavy . . . sleepy . . . warm. Lapped in salty ocean waves. She could almost picture the vampire blood trickling through her veins, conquering everything in its path. It was ancient blood, primeval. It was changing her into something old, something that had been around since the dawn of time. Something primitive and basic.

Every molecule in her body, changing . . .

Poppy, can you hear me? James was shaking her slightly. Poppy had been so engrossed in the sensations that she hadn't even realized she wasn't drinking any longer. James was cradling her.

'Poppy.'

It was an effort to open her eyes. 'I'm all right. Just . . . sleepy.'

His arms tightened around her, then he laid her gently on the mounded pillows. 'You can rest now. I'll get Phil.'

But before he went, he kissed her on the forehead.

My first kiss, Poppy thought, her eyes drifting shut again. And I'm comatose. Great.

She felt the bed give under weight and looked up to see Phil. Phil looked very nervous, sitting gingerly, staring at Poppy. 'So what's happening now?' he asked.

'The vampire blood's taking over,' James said.

Poppy said, 'I'm really sleepy.'

There was no pain. Just a feeling of wanting to glide away. Her body now felt warm and numb, as if she were insulated by a soft, thick aura.

'Phil? I forgot to say – thank you. For helping out. And everything. You're a good brother, Phil.'

'You don't have to say that now,' Phil said tersely. 'You can say it later. I'm still going to be here later, you know.'

But I might not be, Poppy thought. This is all a gamble. And I'd never take it, except that the only alternative was to give up without even trying to fight.

I fought, didn't I? At least I fought.

'Yes, you did,' Phil said, his voice trembling. Poppy hadn't been aware she was speaking aloud. 'You've always been a fighter,' Phil said. 'I've learned so much from you.'

Which was funny, because she'd learned so much from *him*, even if most of it was in the last twenty-four hours. She wanted to tell him that, but there was so much to say, and she was so tired. Her tongue felt thick; her whole body weak and languorous.

'Just . . . hold my hand,' she said, and she could hear that her voice was no louder than a breath. Phillip took one of her hands and James the other.

That was good. This was the way to do it, with Eeyore and her lion on the pillows beside her and Phil and James holding her hands, keeping her safe and anchored.

One of the candles was scented with vanilla, a warm and homey smell. A smell that reminded her of being a kid. Nilla wafers and naptime. That was what this was like. Just a nap in Miss Spurgeon's kindergarten, with the sun slanting across the floor and James on a mat beside her.

So safe, so serene . . .

'Oh, Poppy,' Phil whispered.

James said, 'You're doing great, kiddo. Everything's just right.'

That was what Poppy needed to hear. She let herself fall backward into the music, and it *was* like falling in a dream, without fear. It was like being a raindrop falling into the ocean that had started you.

At the last moment she thought, I'm not ready. But she already knew the answer to that. Nobody was ever ready.

But she'd been stupid – she'd forgotten the most important thing. She'd never told James she loved him. Not even when he'd said he loved her.

She tried to get enough air, enough strength to say it. But it was too late. The outside world was gone and she couldn't feel her body any longer. She was floating in the darkness and the music, and all she could do now was sleep.

'Sleep,' James said, leaning close to Poppy. 'Don't wake up until I call you. Just sleep.'

Every muscle in Phil's body was rigid. Poppy looked so peaceful – pale, with her hair spread out in coppery curls on the pillow, and her eyelashes black on her cheeks and her lips parted as she breathed gently. She looked like a porcelain baby doll. But the more peaceful she got, the more terrified Phil felt.

I can deal with this, he told himself. I *have* to.

Poppy gave a soft exhalation, and then suddenly she was moving. Her chest heaved once, twice. Her hand tightened on Phil's and her eyes flew open – but she didn't seem to be seeing anything. She simply looked astonished.

'Poppy!' Phil grabbed at her, getting a handful of flannel nightgown. She was so small and fragile inside it. 'Poppy!'

The heaving gasps stopped. For one moment Poppy was suspended in air, then her eyes closed and she fell back on the pillows. Her hand was limp in Phil's.

Phil lost all rationality.

'Poppy,' he said, hearing the dangerous, unbalanced tone in his own voice. 'Poppy, come on. Poppy, wake up!' – on a rising note. His hands were shaking violently, scrabbling at Poppy's shoulders.

Other hands pushed his away. 'What the hell are you doing?' James said quietly.

'Poppy? Poppy?' Phil kept staring at her. Her chest wasn't moving. Her face had a look of – innocent release. The kind of newness you only see in babies.

And it was – changing. Taking on a white, transparent look. It was uncanny, ghostlike, and even though Phil had never seen a corpse, he knew instinctively that this was the death pallor.

Poppy's essence had left her. Her body was flat and toneless, no longer inflated by the vital spirit. Her hand in Phil's was slack, not like the hand of a sleeping person. Her skin had lost its shine, as if somebody had breathed on it softly.

Phil threw back his head and let out an animal sound. It wasn't human. It was a howl.

'You killed her!' He tumbled off the bed and lurched toward James. 'You said she was just going to sleep, but you killed her! She's dead!'

James didn't back away from the attack. Instead, he grabbed Phil and dragged him out into the hallway.

'Hearing is the last sense to go,' he snarled in Phillip's ear. 'She may be able to *hear* you.'

Phil wrenched free and ran toward the living room. He didn't know what he was doing, he only knew that he needed to destroy things. Poppy was dead. She was gone. He grabbed the couch and flipped it over, then kicked the coffee table over, too. He snatched up a lamp, yanked its cord out of the socket, and threw it toward the fireplace.

'Stop it!' James shouted over the crash. Phil saw him and ran at him. The sheer force of his charge knocked James backward into the wall. They fell to the floor together in a heap.

'You – killed her!' Phil gasped, trying to get his hands around James's throat.

Silver. James's eyes blazed like the molten lava. He grabbed Phil's wrists in a painful grip.

'Stop it *now*, Phillip,' he hissed.

Something about the way he said it made Phil stop. Almost sobbing, he struggled to get air into his lungs.

'I'll kill *you* if I have to, to keep Poppy safe,' James said, his voice still savage and menacing. 'And she's only safe if you stop this and do exactly what I tell you to. *Exactly* what I tell you. Understand?' He shook Phil hard, nearly banging Phil's head into the wall.

Strangely enough, it was the right thing to say. James was saying he cared about Poppy. And weird as it might sound, Phil had come to trust James to tell the truth.

The raging red insanity in Phil's brain died away. He took a long breath.

'OK. I understand,' he said hoarsely. He was used to being in charge – both of himself and of other people. He didn't like James giving him orders. But in this case there was no help for it. 'But – she is dead, isn't she?'

'It depends on your definition,' James said, letting go and slowly pushing himself off the floor. He scanned the living room, his mouth grim. 'Nothing went wrong, Phil. Everything went just the way it was supposed to – except for this. I was going to let your parents come back and find her, but we don't have that option now. There isn't any way to explain this mess, except the truth.'

'The truth being?'

'That you went in there and found her dead and went berserk. And then I called your parents – you know what restaurant they're at, don't you?'

'It's Valentino's. My mom said they were lucky to get in.'

'OK. That'll work. But first we have to clean up the bedroom. Get all the candles and stuff out. It's got to look as if she just went to sleep, like any other night.'

Phil glanced at the sliding glass door. It was just getting dark. But then Poppy had been sleeping a lot these last few days. 'We'll say she got tired and told us to go watch TV,' he said slowly, trying to conquer his dazed feeling and be clearheaded. 'And then I went in after a while and checked on her.'

'Right,' James said, with a faint smile that didn't reach his eyes.

It didn't take long to clear out the bedroom. The hardest thing was that Phil had to keep looking at Poppy, and every time he looked, his heart lurched. She looked so tiny, so delicate-limbed. A Christmas angel in June.

He hated to take the stuffed animals away from her.

'She is going to wake up, isn't she?' he said, without looking at James.

'God, I hope so,' James said, and his voice was very tired. It sounded more like a prayer than a wish. 'If she doesn't you won't have to come after me with a stake, Phil. I'll take care of it myself.'

Phil was shocked – and angry. 'Don't be stupid,' he said brutally. 'If Poppy stood for anything – if she *stands* for anything – it's for life. Throwing your life away would be like a slap in her face. Besides, even if it goes wrong now, you did your best. Blaming yourself is just stupid.'

James looked at him blankly, and Phil realized they'd managed to surprise each other. Then James nodded slowly. 'Thanks.'

It was a milestone, the first time they'd ever been on precisely the same wavelength. Phillip felt an odd connection between them.

He looked away and said briskly, 'Is it time to call the restaurant?'

James glanced at his watch. 'In just a few minutes.'

'If we wait too long they're going to have left by the time we call.'

'That doesn't matter. What matters is that we don't have any paramedics trying to resuscitate her, or taking her to the hospital. Which means she's got to be cold by the time anybody gets here.'

Phil felt a wave of dizzy horror. 'You're a coldblooded snake after all.'

'I'm just practical,' James said wearily, as if speaking to a child. He touched one of Poppy's marblewhite hands where it lay on the bedspread. 'All right. It's time. I'm going to call. You can go berserk again if you want to.'

Phil shook his head. He didn't have the energy anymore. But he did feel like crying, which was almost as good. Crying and crying like a kid who was lost and hurt.

'Get my mom,' he said thickly.

He knelt on the floor beside Poppy's bed and waited. Poppy's music was off and he could hear the TV in the family room. He had no sense of time passing until he also heard a car in the driveway.

Then he leaned his forehead against Poppy's mattress. His tears were absolutely genuine. At that moment he was sure he'd lost her forever.

'Brace yourself,' James said from behind him. 'They're here.'

CHAPTER

11

The next few hours were the worst of Phil's life.

First and foremost was his mother. As soon as she walked in, Phil's priorities changed from wanting her to comfort him to wanting to comfort her. And of course there wasn't any comfort. All he could do was hold on to her.

It's too cruel, he thought dimly. There ought to be a way to tell her. But she would never believe it, and if she did, she'd be in danger, too . . .

Eventually the paramedics did come, but only after Dr Franklin had arrived.

'I called him,' James said to Phil during one of the interludes when Phil's mom was crying on Cliff.

'Why?'

'To keep things simple. In this state, doctors can issue a death certificate if they've seen you within the last twenty days and they know the cause of death. We don't want any hospitals or coroners.'

Phil shook his head. 'Why? What's your problem with hospitals?'

'My problem,' James said in a clipped, distinct voice. 'is that in hospitals they do autopsies.'

Phil froze. He opened his mouth but no sound came out.

'And in funeral homes they do embalming. Which is why I need to be around when they come to pick up the body. I need to influence their minds not to embalm her, or sew her lips shut, or—'

Phil bolted for the bathroom and was sick. He hated James again.

But nobody took Poppy to the hospital, and Dr Franklin didn't mention an autopsy. He just held Phil's mother's hand and spoke quietly about how these things could happen suddenly, and how at least Poppy had been spared any pain.

'But she was so much better today,' Phil's mother whispered through tears. 'Oh, my baby, my baby. She'd been getting worse, but today she was *better*.'

'It happens like that sometimes,' Dr Franklin said. 'It's almost as if they rally for a last burst of life.'

'But I wasn't *there* for her,' Phil's mom said, and now there weren't any tears, just the terrible grating sound of guilt. 'She was alone when she died.'

Phil said, 'She was asleep. She just went to sleep and never woke up. If you look at her, you can see how peaceful it was.'

He kept saying things like that, and so did Cliff and so did the doctor, and eventually the paramedics went away. And sometime after that, while his mother was sitting on Poppy's bed and stroking her hair, the people from the mortuary came.

'Just give me a few minutes,' Phil's mother said, dry-eyed and pale. 'I need a few minutes alone with her.'

The mortuary men sat awkwardly in the family room, and James stared at them. Phil knew what was going on.

James was fixing in their minds the fact that there was to be no embalming.

'Religious reasons, is that it?' one of the men said to Cliff, breaking a long silence.

Cliff stared at him, eyebrows coming together. 'What are you talking about?'

The man nodded. 'I understand. It's no problem.'

Phil understood, too. Whatever the man was hearing, it wasn't what Cliff was saying.

'The only thing is, you'll want to have the viewing right away,' the other man said to Cliff. 'Or else a closed casket.'

'Yes, it was unexpected,' Cliff said, his face straightening out. 'It's been a very short illness.'

So now *he* wasn't hearing what the men were saying. Phil looked at James and saw sweat trickling down his face. Clearly it was a struggle to control three minds at once.

At last Cliff went in and got Phil's mother. He led her to the master bedroom to keep her from seeing what happened next.

What happened was that the two men went into Poppy's room with a body bag and a gurney. When they came out, there was a small, delicate hump in the bag.

Phil felt himself losing rationality again. He wanted to knock things down. He wanted to run a marathon to get away.

Instead, his knees started to buckle and his vision greyed out.

Hard arms held him up, led him to a chair. 'Hang on,' James said. 'Just a few more minutes. It's almost over.'

Right then Phil could almost forgive him for being a bloodsucking monster.

It was very late that night when everyone finally went to bed. To bed, not to sleep. Phil was one solid ache of misery from his throat down to his feet, and he lay awake with the light on until the sun came up.

The funeral home was like a Victorian mansion, and the room Poppy was in was filled with flowers and people. Poppy herself was in a white casket with gold fittings, and from far away she looked as if she were sleeping.

Phil didn't like to look at her. He looked instead at the visitors who kept coming in and filling the viewing room and the dozens of wooden pews. He'd never realized how many people loved Poppy.

'She was so full of life,' her English teacher said.

'I can't believe she's gone,' a guy from Phil's football team said.

'I'll never forget her,' one of her friends said, crying.

Phil wore a dark suit and stood with his mother and Cliff. It was like a receiving line for a wedding. His mother kept saying, 'Thank you for coming,' and hugging people. The people went over and touched the casket gently and cried.

And in the process of greeting so many mourners, something strange happened. Phil got drawn in. The reality of Poppy's death was *so* real that all the vampire stuff began to seem like a dream. Bit by bit, he started to believe the story he was acting out.

After all, everybody else was so sure. Poppy had gotten cancer, and now she was dead. Vampires were just superstition.

James didn't come to the viewing.

Poppy was dreaming.

She was walking by the ocean with James. It was warm and she could smell salt and her feet were wet and sandy. She was wearing a new bathing suit, the kind that changes colour when it gets wet. She hoped James would notice the suit, but he didn't say anything about it.

Then she realized he was wearing a mask. That was strange, because he was going to get a very weird tan with most of his face covered up.

'Shouldn't you take that off?' she said, thinking he might need help.

'I wear it for my health,' James said – only it wasn't James's voice.

Poppy was shocked. She reached out and pulled the mask away.

It wasn't James. It was a boy with ash blond hair, even lighter than Phil's. Why hadn't she noticed his hair earlier? His eyes were green – and then they were blue.

'Who are you?' Poppy demanded. She was afraid.

'That would be telling.' He smiled. His eyes were violet. Then he lifted his hand, and she saw that he was holding a poppy. At least, it was shaped like a poppy, but it was black. He caressed her cheek with the flower.

'Just remember,' he said, still smiling whimsically. 'Bad magic happens.'

'*What?*'

'Bad magic happens,' he said and turned and walked away. She found herself holding the poppy. He didn't leave any footprints in the sand.

Poppy was alone and the ocean was roaring. Clouds were gathering overhead. She wanted to wake up now, but she couldn't, and she was alone and scared. She dropped the flower as anguish surged through her.

'*James!*'

Phil sat up in bed, heart pounding.

God, what had that been? Something like a shout – in Poppy's voice.

I'm hallucinating.

Which wasn't surprising. It was Monday, the day of Poppy's funeral. In – Phil glanced at the clock – about four hours he had to be at the church. No wonder he was dreaming about her.

But she had sounded so scared . . .

Phil put the thought out of his mind. It wasn't even hard. He'd convinced himself that Poppy was dead, and dead people didn't shout.

At the funeral, though, Phil got a shock. His father was there. He was even wearing something resembling a suit, although the jacket didn't match the trousers and his tie was askew.

'I came as soon as I heard . . .'

'Well, where *were* you?' Phil's mother said, the fine lines of strain showing around her eyes, the way they always did when she had to deal with Phil's father.

'Backpacking in the Blue Ridge Mountains. Next time, I swear, I'll leave an address. I'll check my messages . . .' He began to cry. Phil's mom didn't say anything else. She just reached for him, and Phil's heart twisted at the way they clung to each other.

He knew his dad was irresponsible and hopelessly behind in child support and flaky and a failure. But nobody had ever loved Poppy more. Right then, Phil couldn't disapprove of him, not even with Cliff standing there for comparison.

The shock came when his dad turned to Phil before the service. 'You know, she came to me last night,' he said in a low voice. 'Her spirit, I mean. She visited me.'

Phil looked at him. This was the kind of weird statement that had brought on the divorce. His father had always talked about peculiar dreams and seeing things that weren't there. Not to mention collecting articles about astrology, numerology, and UFOs.

'I didn't see her, but I heard her calling. I just wish she hadn't sounded so frightened. Don't tell your mother, but I got the feeling she's not at rest.' He put his hands over his face.

Phil felt every hair on the back of his neck stand up.

But the spooky feeling was drowned almost immediately in the sheer grief of the funeral. In hearing things like 'Poppy will live on forever in our hearts and memories.' A silver hearse led the way to Forest Park cemetery, and everyone stood in the June sunshine as the minister said some last words over Poppy's casket. By the time Phil had to put a rose on the casket, he was shaking.

It was a terrible time. Two of Poppy's girlfriends collapsed in near-hysterical sobs. Phillip's mother doubled over and had to be led away from the casket. There was no time to think – then or at the potluck at Phil's house afterward.

But it was at the house that Phil's two worlds collided. In the middle of all the milling confusion, he saw James.

He didn't know what to do. James didn't fit into what was going on here. Phil had half a mind to go over and tell him to get out, that the sick joke was over.

Before he could do anything, James walked up and said under his breath, 'Be ready at eleven o'clock tonight.'

Phil was jolted. 'For what?'

'Just be ready, OK? And have some of Poppy's clothes with you. Whatever won't be missed.' Phil didn't say anything, and James gave him an exasperated sideways look.

'We have to get her *out*, stupid. Or did you want to leave her there?'

Crash. That was the sound of worlds colliding. For a

moment Phil was spinning in space with his feet on neither one.

Then with the normal world in shards around him, he leaned against a wall and whispered, 'I can't. I can't do it. You're crazy.'

'You're the one who's crazy. You're acting like it never happened. And you have to help, because I can't do it alone. She's going to be disoriented at first, like a sleepwalker. She'll *need* you.'

That galvanized Phil. He jerked to stand up straight and whispered, 'Did you hear her last night?'

James looked away. 'She wasn't awake. She was just dreaming.'

'How could we hear her from so far away? Even my *dad* heard it. Listen.' He grabbed James by the lapel of his jacket. 'Are you sure she's OK?'

'A minute ago you were convinced she was dead and gone. Now you want guarantees that she's fine. Well, I can't give you any.' He stared Phil down with eyes as cold as grey ice. 'I've never done this before, all right? I'm just going by the book. And there are always things that can go wrong. *But*,' he said tersely when Phil opened his mouth, 'the one thing I *do* know is that if we leave her where she is, she's going to have a very unpleasant awakening. Get it?'

Phil's hand unclenched slowly and he let go of the jacket. 'Yeah. I'm sorry. I just can't believe any of this.' He looked up to see that James's expression had softened slightly. 'But if she was yelling last night, then she was alive then, right?'

'And strong,' James said. 'I've never known a stronger telepath. She's really going to be something.'

Phil tried not to picture what. Of course, James was a vampire, and he looked perfectly normal – most of the time. But Phil's mind kept throwing out pictures of Poppy as a Hollywood monster. Red eyes, chalky skin, and dripping teeth.

If she came out like that, he'd try to love her. But part of him might want to get a stake.

Forest Park cemetery was completely different at night. The darkness seemed very thick. There was a sign on the iron gate that said, 'No visitors after sunset,' but the gate itself was open.

I don't want to be here, Phil thought.

James dróve down the single lane road that curved around the cemetery and parked underneath a huge and ancient gingko tree.

'What if somebody sees us? Don't they have a guard or something?'

'They have a night watchman. He's asleep. I took care of it before I picked you up.' James got out and began unloading an amazing amount of equipment from the backseat of the Integra.

Two heavy duty flashlights. A crowbar. Some old boards. A couple of tarps. And two brand-new shovels.

'Help me carry this stuff.'

'What's it all *for*?' But Phil helped. Gravel crunched under his feet as he followed James on one of the little winding paths. They went up some weathered wooden stairs and down the other side and then they were in Toyland.

That was what somebody at the funeral had called it. Phil had overheard two business friends of Cliff's talking about it. It was a section of the cemetery where mostly kids were buried. You could tell without even looking at the headstones because there were teddy bears and things on the graves.

Poppy's grave was right on the edge of Toyland. It didn't have a headstone yet, of course. There was only a green plastic marker.

James dumped his armload on the grass and then knelt to examine the ground with a flashlight.

Phil stood silently, looking around the cemetery. He was still scared, partly with the normal fear that they'd get caught before they got finished, and partly with the supernatural fear that they *wouldn't*. The only sounds were crickets and distant traffic. Tree branches and bushes moved gently in the wind.

'OK,' James said. 'First we've got to peel this sod off.'

'Huh?' Phil hadn't even thought about why there was already grass on the new grave. But of course it was sod. James had found the edge of one strip and was rolling it up like a carpet.

Phil found another edge. The strips were about six feet long by one and a half feet wide. They were heavy, but it wasn't too hard to roll them up and off the foot of the grave.

'Leave 'em there. We've got to put them on again afterward,' James grunted. 'We don't want it to look as if this place has been disturbed.'

A light went on for Phil. *'That's* why the tarps and stuff.'

'Yeah. A little mess won't be suspicious. But if we leave dirt scattered everywhere, somebody's going to wonder.' James laid the boards around the perimeter of the grave, then spread the tarps on either side. Phil helped him straighten them.

What was left where the sod had been was fresh, loamy soil. Phil positioned a flashlight and picked up a shovel.

I don't believe I'm doing this, he thought.

But he was doing it. And as long as all he thought

about was the physical work, the job of digging a hole in the ground, he was OK. He concentrated on that and stepped on the shovel.

It went straight into the dirt, with no resistance. It was easy to spade up one shovelful of dirt and drop it onto the tarp. But by about the thirtieth shovelful, he was getting tired.

'This is insane. We need a backhoe,' he said, wiping his forehead.

'You can rest if you want,' James said coolly.

Phil understood. James was the backhoe. He was stronger than anyone Phil had ever seen. He pitched up shovelful after shovelful of dirt without even straining. He made it look like fun.

'*Why* don't we have you on any of the teams at school?' Phil said, leaning heavily on his shovel.

'I prefer individual sports. Like wrestling,' James said and grinned, just for a moment, up at Phil. It was the kind of locker-room remark that couldn't be misunderstood from one guy to another. He meant wrestling with, for instance, Jacklyn and Michaela.

And, just at that particular moment, Phil couldn't help grinning back. He couldn't summon up any righteous disapproval.

Even with James, it took a long time to dig the hole. It was wider than Phil would have thought necessary. When his shovel finally *chunked* on something solid, he found out why.

'It's the vault,' James said.

'*What* vault?'

'The burial vault. They put the coffin inside it so it doesn't get crushed if the ground collapses. Get out and hand me the crowbar.'

Phil climbed out of the hole and gave him the crowbar.

He could see the vault now. It was made of unfinished concrete and he guessed that it was just a rectangular box with a lid. James was prying the lid off with the crowbar.

'There,' James said, with an explosive grunt as he lifted the lid and slid it, by degrees, behind the concrete box. That was why the hole was so wide, to accommodate the lid on one side and James on the other.

And now, looking straight down into the hole, Phil could see the casket. A huge spray of slightly crushed yellow roses was on top.

James was breathing hard, but Phil didn't think it was with exertion. His own lungs felt as if they were being squeezed flat, and his heart was thudding hard enough to shake his body.

'Oh, God,' he said quietly and with no particular emphasis.

James looked up. 'Yeah. This is it.' He pushed the roses down toward the foot of the casket. Then, in what seemed like slow motion to Phillip, he began unfastening latches on the casket's side.

When they were unfastened, he paused for just an instant, both hands flat on the smooth surface of the casket. Then he lifted the upper panel, and Phillip could see what was inside.

CHAPTER
12

Poppy was lying there on the white velvet lining, eyes shut. She looked very pale and strangely beautiful – but was she dead?

'Wake up,' James said. He put his hand on hers. Phillip had the feeling that he was calling with his mind as well as his voice.

There was an agonizingly long minute while nothing happened. James put his other hand under Poppy's neck, lifting her just slightly. 'Poppy, it's time. Wake up. Wake up.'

Poppy's eyelashes fluttered.

Something jarred violently in Phillip. He wanted to give a yell of victory and pound the grass. He also wanted to run away. Finally he just collapsed by the graveside, his knees giving out altogether.

'Come on, Poppy. Get up. We have to go.' James was speaking in a gentle, insistent voice, as if he were talking to someone coming out of anesthesia.

Which was exactly how Poppy looked. As Phil watched with fascination and awe and dread, she blinked and rolled her head a little, then opened her eyes. She shut them again almost immediately, but James went on talking to her, and the next time she opened them they stayed open.

Then, with James urging her gently, she sat up.

'*Poppy*,' Phil said. An involuntary outburst. His chest was swelling, burning.

Poppy looked up, then squinted and turned immediately from the beam of the flashlight. She looked annoyed.

'Come on,' James said, helping her out of the open half of the casket. It wasn't hard; Poppy was small. With James holding her arm, she stood on the closed half of the casket, and Phil reached into the hole and pulled her up.

Then, with something like a convulsion, he hugged her.

When he pulled back, she blinked at him. A slight frown puckered her forehead. She licked her index finger and drew the wet finger across his cheek.

'You're filthy,' she said.

She could talk. She didn't have red eyes and a chalky face. She was really alive.

Weak with relief, Phil hugged her again. 'Oh, God, Poppy, you're OK. You're OK.'

He barely noticed that she wasn't hugging him back.

James scrambled out of the hole. 'How do you feel, Poppy?' he said. Not a politeness. A quiet, probing question.

Poppy looked at him, and then at Phillip. 'I feel . . . fine.'

'That's good,' James said, still watching her as if she were a six-hundred-pound schizophrenic gorilla.

'I feel . . . hungry,' Poppy said, in the same pleasant, musical voice she'd used before.

Phil blinked.

'Why don't you come over here, Phil?' James said, making a gesture behind him.

Phil was beginning to feel very uneasy. Poppy was . . . could she be *smelling* him? Not loud, wet sniffs, but the delicate little sniffs of a cat. She was nosing around his shoulder.

'Phil, I think you should come around over here,' James said, with more emphasis. But what happened next happened too quickly for Phil even to start moving.

Delicate hands clenched like steel around his biceps. Poppy smiled at him with very sharp teeth, then darted like a striking cobra for his throat.

I'm going to die, Phil thought with a curious calm. He couldn't fight her. But her first strike missed. The sharp teeth grazed his throat like two burning pokers.

'No, you don't,' James said. He looped an arm around Poppy's waist, lifting her off Phil.

Poppy gave a disappointed wail. As Phil struggled to his feet, she watched him the way a cat watches an interesting insect. Never taking her eyes off him, not even when James spoke to her.

'That's your brother, Phil. Your twin brother. Remember?'

Poppy just stared at Phil with hugely dilated pupils. Phil realized that she looked not only pale and beautiful but dazed and starving.

'My brother? One of our kind?' Poppy said, sounding puzzled. Her nostrils quivered and her lips parted. 'He doesn't smell like it.'

'No, he's not one of our kind, but he's not for biting, either. You're going to have to wait just a little while to feed.' To Phillip, he said, 'Let's get this hole filled in, fast.'

Phillip couldn't move at first. Poppy was still watching him in that dreamy but intense way. She stood there in the darkness in her best white dress, supple as a lily, with her hair falling around her face. And she looked at him with the eyes of a jaguar.

She wasn't human anymore. She was something *other*.

She'd said it herself, she and James were of one kind and Phil was something different. She belonged to the Night World now.

Oh, God, maybe we should just have let her die, Phil thought, and picked up a shovel with loose and trembling hands. James had already gotten the lid back on the vault. Phil shovelled dirt on it without looking at where it landed. His head wobbled as if his neck were a pipe cleaner.

'Don't be an *idiot*,' a voice said, and hard fingers closed on Phil's wrist briefly. Through a blur, Phil saw James.

'She's not better off dead. She's just confused right now. This is *temporary*, all right?'

The words were brusque, but Phil felt a tiny surge of comfort. Maybe James was right. Life was good, in whatever form. And Poppy had chosen this.

Still, she'd changed, and only time would tell how much.

One thing – Phil had made the mistake of thinking that vampires were like humans. He'd gotten so comfortable with James that he'd almost forgotten their differences.

He wouldn't make that mistake again.

Poppy felt wonderful – in almost every way.

She felt secret and strong. She felt poetic and full of possibility. She felt as if she'd sloughed off her old body like a snake shedding its skin, to reveal a fresh new body underneath.

And she knew, without being quite sure how she knew, that she didn't have cancer.

It was gone, the terrible thing that had been running wild inside her. Her new body had killed it and absorbed it somehow. Or maybe it was just that every cell that made up Poppy North, every molecule, had changed.

However it was, she felt vibrant and healthy. Not just

better than she had before she'd gotten the cancer, but better than she could remember feeling in her life. She was strangely aware of her own body, and her muscles and joints all seemed to be working in a way that was sweet and almost magical.

The only problem was that she was hungry. It was taking all her willpower not to pounce on the blond guy in the hole. Phillip. Her brother.

She *knew* he was her brother, but he was also human and she could sense the rich stuff, lush with life, that was coursing through his veins. The electrifying fluid she needed to survive.

So jump him, part of her mind whispered. Poppy frowned and tried to wiggle away from the thought. She felt something in her mouth nudging her lower lip, and she poked her thumb at it instinctively.

It was a tooth. A delicate curving tooth. Both her canine teeth were long and pointed and very sensitive.

How weird. She rubbed at the new teeth gently, then cautiously explored them with her tongue. She pressed them against her lip.

After a moment they shrank to normal size. If she thought about humans full of blood like berries, they grew again.

Hey, look what I can do!

But she didn't bother the two grimy boys who were filling in the hole. She glanced around and tried to distract herself instead.

Strange – it didn't really seem to be either day or night. Maybe there was an eclipse. It was too dim to be daytime, but far too bright for nighttime. She could see the leaves on the maple trees and the grey Spanish moss hanging from the oak trees. Tiny moths were fluttering around the moss, and she could see their pale wings.

When she looked at the sky, she got a shock. There was something floating there, a giant round thing that blazed with silvery light. Poppy thought of spaceships, of alien worlds, before she realized the truth.

It was the *moon*. Just an ordinary full moon. And the reason it looked so big and throbbing with light was that she had night vision. That was why she could see the moths, too.

All her senses were keen. Delicious smells wafted by her, the smells of small burrowing animals and fluttering dainty birds. On the wind came a tantalizing hint of rabbit.

And she could *hear* things. Once she whipped her head around as a dog barked right beside her. Then she realized that it was far away, outside the cemetery. It only sounded close.

I'll bet I can run fast, too, she thought. Her legs felt tingly. She wanted to go running out into the lovely, gloriously-scented night, to be one with it. She was *part* of it now.

James, she said. And the strange thing was that she said it without saying it out loud. It was something she knew how to do without thinking.

James looked up from his shovelling. *Hang on*, he said the same way. *We're almost done, kiddo.*

Then you'll teach me to hunt?

He nodded, just slightly. His hair was falling over his forehead and he looked adorably grubby. Poppy felt as if she'd never really seen him before – because now she was seeing him with new senses. James wasn't just silky brown hair and enigmatic grey eyes and a lithe-muscled body. He was the smell of winter rain and the sound of his predator's heartbeat and the silvery aura of power she could feel around him. She could sense his mind, lean and tiger-tough but somehow gentle and almost wistful at the same time.

We're hunting partners now, she told him eagerly, and he smiled an acknowledgment. But underneath she felt that he was worried. He was either sad or anxious about something, something he was keeping from her.

She couldn't think about it. She didn't feel hungry anymore . . . she felt strange. As if she was having trouble getting enough air.

James and Phillip were shaking out the tarps, unrolling strips of fresh sod to cover the grave. Her grave. Funny she hadn't really thought about that before. She'd been lying in a grave – she ought to feel repulsed or scared.

She didn't. She didn't remember being in there at all – didn't remember anything from the time she'd fallen asleep in her bedroom until she'd woken up with James calling her.

Except a dream . . .

'OK,' James said. He was folding up a tarp. 'We can go. How're you feeling?'

'Ummm . . . a little weird. I can't get a deep breath.'

'Neither can I,' Phil said. He was breathing hard and wiping his forehead. 'I didn't know grave digging was such hard work.'

James gave Poppy a searching look. 'Do you think you can make it back to my apartment?'

'Hmm? I guess.' Poppy didn't actually know what he was talking about. Make it how? And why should going to his apartment help her to breathe?

'I've got a couple of safe donors there in the building,' James said. 'I don't really want you out on the streets, and I think you'll make it there OK.'

Poppy didn't ask what he meant. She was having trouble thinking clearly.

James wanted her to hide in the backseat of his car. Poppy refused. She needed to sit up front and to feel the night air on her face.

'OK,' James said at last. 'But at least sort of cover your face with your arm. I'll drive on back roads. You *can't* be seen, Poppy.'

There didn't seem to be anyone on the streets to see her. The air whipping her cheeks was cool and good, but it didn't help her breathing. No matter how she tried, she couldn't seem to get a proper breath.

I'm hyperventilating, she thought. Her heart was racing, her lips and tongue felt parchment-dry. And still she had the feeling of being air-starved.

What's *happening* to me?

Then the pain started.

Agonizing seizures in her muscles – like the cramps she used to get when she went out for track in junior high. Vaguely, through the pain, she remembered something the P.E. teacher had said. *'The cramps come when your muscles don't get enough blood. A charley horse is a clump of muscles starving to death.'*

Oh, it *hurt*. It *hurt*. She couldn't even call to James for help, now; all she could do was hang on to the car door and try to breathe. She was whooping and wheezing, but it wasn't any good.

Cramps everywhere – and now she was so dizzy that she saw the world through sparkling lights.

She was dying. Something had gone terribly wrong. She felt as if she were underwater, trying desperately to claw her way to oxygen – only there *was* no oxygen.

And then she saw the way.

Or smelled it, actually. The car was stopped at a red light. Poppy's head and shoulders were out the window by now – and suddenly she caught a whiff of life.

Life. What she needed. She didn't think, she simply acted. With one motion she threw the car door open and plunged out.

She heard Phil's shout behind her and James's shout in her head. She ignored both of them. Nothing mattered except stopping the pain.

She grabbed for the man on the sidewalk the way a drowning swimmer grabs at a rescuer. Instinctively. He was tall and strong for a human. He was wearing a dark sweatsuit and a bomber jacket. His face was stubbly and his skin wasn't exactly clean, but that wasn't important. She wasn't interested in the container, only in the lovely sticky red stuff inside.

This time her strike was perfectly accurate. Her wonderful teeth extended like claws and stabbed into the man's throat. Puncturing him like one of those old-fashioned bottle openers. He struggled a little and then went limp.

And then she was drinking, her throat drenched in copper-sweetness. Sheer animal hunger took over as she tapped his veins. The liquid filling her mouth was wild and raw and primal and every swallow gave her new life.

She drank and drank, and felt the pain disappear. In its place was a euphoric lightness. When she paused to breathe, she could feel her lungs swell with cool, blessed air.

She bent to drink again, to suck, lap, tipple. The man had a clear bubbling stream inside him, and she wanted it all.

That was when James pulled her head back.

He spoke both aloud and in her mind and his voice was collected but intense. 'Poppy, I'm sorry. I'm sorry. It was my fault. I shouldn't have made you wait so long. But you've had enough now. You can stop.'

Oh . . . confusion. Poppy was peripherally aware of Phillip, her brother Phillip, looking on in horror. James said she *could* stop, but that didn't mean she had to. She didn't *want* to. The man wasn't fighting at all now. He seemed to be unconscious.

She bent down again. James pulled her back up almost roughly.

'Listen,' he said. His eyes were level, but his voice was hard. 'This is the time you can choose, Poppy. Do you *really* want to kill?'

The words shocked her back to awareness. To kill . . . that was the way to get power, she knew. Blood was power and life and energy and food and drink. If she drained this man like squeezing an orange, she would have the power of his very essence. Who knew what she might be able to do then?

But . . . he was a man, not an orange. A human being. She'd been one of those once.

Slowly, reluctantly, she lifted herself off the man. James let out a long breath. He patted her shoulder and sat down on the sidewalk as if too tired to stand up right then.

Phil was slumped against the wall of the nearest building.

He was appalled, and Poppy could feel it. She could even pick up words he was thinking – words like *ghastly* and *amoral*. A whole sentence that went something like 'Is it worth it to save her life if she's lost her soul?'

James jerked around to look at him, and Poppy could feel the silver flare of his anger. 'You just don't get it, do you?' he said savagely. 'She could have attacked *you* anytime, but she didn't, even though she was dying. You don't know what the bloodlust feels like. It's not like being thirsty – it's like suffocating. Your cells start to die from oxygen starvation, because your own blood can't carry oxygen to them. It's the worst pain there is, but she didn't go after you to make it stop.'

Phillip looked staggered. He stared at Poppy, then held out a hand uncertainly.

'I'm sorry . . .'

'Forget it,' James said shortly. He turned his back on Phil and examined the man. Poppy could feel him extend his mind. 'I'm telling him to forget this,' he said to Poppy. 'All he needs is some rest, and he might as well do that right here. See, the wounds are already healing.'

Poppy saw, but she couldn't feel happy. She knew Phil still disapproved of her. Not just for something she'd done, but for what she *was*.

What's happened to me? she asked James, throwing herself into his arms. *Have I turned into something awful?*

He held her fiercely. *You're just different. Not awful. Phil's a jerk.*

She wanted to laugh at that. But she could feel a tremor of sadness behind his protective love. It was the same anxious sadness she'd sensed in him earlier. James didn't like being a predator, and now he'd made Poppy one, too. Their plan had succeeded brilliantly – and Poppy would never be the old Poppy North again.

And although she could hear his thoughts, it wasn't exactly like the total immersion when they'd exchanged blood. They might not ever have that togetherness again.

'There wasn't any other choice,' Poppy said stoutly, and she said it aloud. 'We did what we had to do. Now we have to make the best of it.'

You're a brave girl. Did I ever tell you that?

No. And if you did, I don't mind hearing it again.

But they drove to James's apartment building in silence, with Phil's depression weighing heavily in the backseat.

'Look, you can take the car back to your house,' James

said as he unloaded the equipment and Poppy's clothes into his carport. 'I don't want to bring Poppy anywhere near there, and I don't want to leave her alone.'

Phil glanced up at the dark two-storey building as if something had just struck him. Then he cleared his throat. Poppy knew why – James's apartment was a notorious place, and she'd never been allowed to visit it at night. Apparently Phil still had some brotherly concern for his vampire sister. 'You, uh, can't just take her to your parents' house?'

'How many times do I have to explain? No, I can't take her to my parents, because my parents don't know she's a vampire. Right at the moment she's an illegal vampire, a renegade, which means she's got to be kept a secret until I can straighten things out – somehow.'

'How—' Phil stopped and shook his head. 'OK. Not tonight. We'll talk about it later.'

'No, "we" won't,' James said harshly. 'You're not a part of this anymore. It's up to Poppy and me. All you need to do is go back and live your normal life and keep your mouth shut.'

Phil started to say something else, then caught himself. He took the keys from James. Then he looked at Poppy.

'I'm glad you're alive. I love you,' he said.

Poppy knew that he wanted to hug her, but something kept both of them back. There was an emptiness in Poppy's chest.

'Bye, Phil,' she said, and he got in the car and left.

CHAPTER

13

'He doesn't understand,' Poppy said softly as James unlocked the door to his apartment. 'He just hasn't grasped that you're risking your life, too.'

The apartment was very bare and utilitarian. High ceilings and spacious rooms announced that it was expensive, but there wasn't much furniture. In the living room there was a low, square couch, a desk with a computer, and a couple of Oriental-looking pictures on the wall. And books. Cardboard boxes of books stacked in the corners.

Poppy turned to face James directly. 'Jamie ... *I* understand.'

James smiled at her. He was sweaty and dirty and tired-looking. But his expression said Poppy made it all worthwhile.

'Don't blame Phil,' he said, with a gesture of dismissal. 'He's actually handling things pretty well. I've never broken cover to a human before, but I think most of them would run screaming and never come back. He's *trying* to cope, at least.'

Poppy nodded and dropped the subject. James was tired, which meant they should go to sleep. She picked up the duffel bag that Phil had packed with her clothes and headed for the bathroom.

She didn't change right away, though. She was too fascinated by her own reflection in the mirror. So this was what a vampire Poppy looked like.

She was prettier, she noted with absent satisfaction. The four freckles on her nose were gone. Her skin was creamy-pale, like an advertisement for face cream. Her eyes were green as jewels. Her hair was wind-blown into riotous curls, metallic-copper.

I don't look like something that sits on a buttercup anymore, she thought. I look wild and dangerous and exotic. Like a model. Like a rock star. Like James.

She leaned forward to examine her teeth, poking at the canines to make them grow. Then she jerked back, gasping.

Her eyes. She hadn't realized. Oh, God, no wonder Phil had been scared. When she did that, when her teeth extended, her eyes went silvery-green, uncanny. Like the eyes of a hunting cat.

All at once she was overcome by terror. She had to cling to the sink to stay on her feet.

I don't want it, I don't want it . . .

Oh, *deal* with it, girl. Stop whining. So what did you expect to look like, Shirley Temple? You're a hunter now. And your eyes go silver and blood tastes like cherry preserves. And that's all there is to it, and the other choice was resting in peace. So *deal*.

Gradually her breathing slowed. In the next few minutes something happened inside her; she *did* deal. She found . . . acceptance. It felt like something giving way in her throat and her stomach. She wasn't weird and dreamy now, as she'd been when she had first awakened in the cemetery; she could think clearly about her situation. And she could accept it.

And I did it without running to James, she thought suddenly, startled. I don't need him to comfort me or tell me it's OK. I can *make* it OK, myself.

Maybe that was what happened when you faced the very worst thing in the world. She'd lost her family and her old life and maybe even her childhood, but she'd found herself. And that would have to do.

She pulled the white dress over her head and changed into a T-shirt and sweatpants. Then she walked out to James, head high.

He was in the bedroom, lying on a full-sized bed made up with light brown sheets. He was still wearing his dirty clothes, and he had one arm crooked over his eyes. When Poppy came in, he stirred.

'I'll go sleep on the couch,' he said.

'No, you won't,' Poppy said firmly. She flopped on the bed beside him. 'You're dead tired. And I know I'm safe with you.'

James grinned without moving his arm. 'Because I'm dead tired?'

'Because I've always been safe with you.' She knew that. Even when she'd been a human and her blood must have tempted him, she'd been safe.

She looked at him as he lay there, brown hair ruffled, body lax, Adidas unlaced and caked with soil. She found his elbows endearing.

'I forgot to mention something before,' she said. 'I only realized I forgot when I was . . . going to sleep. I forgot to mention that I love you.'

James sat up. 'You only forgot to say it with words.'

Poppy felt a smile tugging at her lips. That was the amazing thing, the only purely good thing about what had happened to her. She and James had come together. Their relationship had changed – but it still had everything she'd valued in their old relationship. The understanding, the camaraderie. Now on top of that was the new excitement of discovering each other as more than best friends.

And she'd found the part of him that she had never been able to reach before. She knew his secrets, knew him inside out. Humans could never know each other that way. They could never really get into another person's head. All the talking in the world couldn't even prove that you and the other person both saw the same colour red.

And if she and James never merged like two drops of water again, she would always be able to touch his mind.

A little shy, she leaned against him, resting on his shoulder. In all the times they'd been close, they'd never kissed or been romantic. For now, just sitting here like this was enough, just feeling James breathe and hearing his heart and absorbing his warmth. And his arm around her shoulders was almost *too* much, almost too intense to bear, but at the same time it was safe and peaceful.

It was like a song, one of those sweet, wrenching songs that makes the hair on your arms stand up. That makes you want to throw yourself on the floor and just bawl. Or fall backward and surrender to the music utterly. One of *those* songs.

James cupped her hand, brought it to his lips, and kissed the palm.

I told you. You don't love somebody because of their looks or their clothes or their car. You love them because they sing a song that nobody but you can understand.

Poppy's heart swelled until it hurt.

Aloud she said, 'We always understood the same song, even when we were little.'

'In the Night World there's this idea called the soulmate principle. It says that every person has one soulmate out there, just one. And that person is perfect for you and is your destiny. The problem being that almost nobody ever *finds* their soulmate, just because of distance. So most people go through their whole lives feeling not complete.'

'I think it's the truth. I *always* knew you were perfect for me.'

'Not *always*.'

'Oh, yes. Since I was five. I knew.'

'I'd have known you were perfect for me – except that everything I'd been taught said it was hopeless.' He cleared his throat and added, 'That *is* why I went out with Michaela and those other girls, you know. I didn't care about them. I could get close to them without breaking the law.'

'I know,' Poppy said. 'I mean – I think I always knew it was something like that, underneath.' She added, 'James? What am I now?' Some things she could tell instinctively; she could feel them in her blood. But she wanted to know more, and she knew James understood why. This was her life now. She had to learn the rules.

'Well.' He settled against the headboard, head tilted back as she rested under his chin. 'You're pretty much like me. Except for not being able to age or have families, made vampires are basically like the lamia.' He shifted. 'Let's see. You already know about being able to see and hear better than humans. And you're a whiz at reading minds.'

'Not everybody's mind.'

'No vampire can read everybody's mind. Lots of times all I get is a sort of general feeling for what people are thinking. The only certain way to make a connection is to—' James opened his mouth and clicked his teeth. Poppy giggled as the sound travelled through her skull.

'And how often do I have to—?' She clicked her own teeth.

'Feed.' She felt James getting serious. 'About once a day on average. Otherwise you'll go into the bloodlust. You can eat human food if you want, but there's no nutrition in it. Blood is everything for us.'

'And the more blood, the more power.'

'Basically, yes.'

'Tell me about power. Can we – well, what can we do?'

'We have more control over our bodies than humans. We can heal from almost any kind of injury – except from wood. Wood can hurt us, even kill us.' He snorted. 'So there's one thing the movies have right – a wooden stake through the heart will, in fact, kill a vampire. So will burning.'

'Can we change into animals?'

'I've never met any vampire that powerful. But theoretically it's possible for us, and shapeshifters and werewolves do it all the time.'

'Change into mist?'

'I've never even met a shapeshifter who could do that.'

Poppy thumped the bed with her heel. 'And obviously we don't have to sleep in coffins.'

'No, and we don't need native earth, either. Myself, I prefer a Sealy Posturepedic, but if you'd like some dirt . . .'

Poppy elbowed him. 'Um, can we cross running water?'

'Sure. And we can walk into people's homes without being invited, and roll in garlic if we don't mind losing friends. Anything else?'

'Yes. Tell me about the Night World.' It was her home now.

'Did I tell you about the clubs? We have clubs in every big city. In a lot of small ones, too.'

'What kind of clubs?'

'Well, some are just dives, and some are like cafés, and some are like nightclubs, and some are like lodges – those are mostly for adults. I know one for kids that's just a big old warehouse with skate ramps built in. You can hang out and skateboard. And there are poetry slams every week at the Black Iris.'

Black iris, Poppy thought. That reminded her of something. Something unpleasant . . .

What she said was, 'That's a funny name.'

'All the clubs are named for flowers. Black flowers are the symbols of the Night People.' He rotated his wrist to show her his watch. An analog watch, with a black iris in the centre of the face. 'See?'

'Yeah. You know, I noticed that black thing, but I never really looked at it before. I think I assumed it was Mickey Mouse.'

He rapped her lightly on the nose in reproof. 'This is serious business, kid. One of these will identify you to other Night People – even if they're as stupid as a werewolf.'

'You don't like werewolves?'

'They're great if you like double-digit IQs.'

'But you let them in the clubs.'

'Some clubs. Night People may not marry out of their own kind, but they all mix: lamia, made vampires, werewolves, both kinds of witches . . .'

Poppy, who had been playing at intertwining their fingers in different ways, shifted curiously. 'What's both kinds of witches?'

'Oh . . . there's the kind that know about their heritage and have been trained, and the kind that don't. That second kind are what humans call psychics. Sometimes they just have latent powers, and some of them aren't even psychic enough to *find* the Night World, so they don't get in.'

Poppy nodded. 'OK. Got it. But what if a human walks into one of those clubs?'

'Nobody would let them. The clubs aren't what you'd call conspicuous, and they're always guarded.'

'But if they *did* . . .'

James shrugged. His voice was suddenly bleak. 'They'd be killed. Unless somebody wanted to pick them up as a toy or pawn. That means a human who's basically brainwashed – who lives with vampires but doesn't know it because of the mind control. Sort of like a sleepwalker. I had a nanny once . . .' His voice trailed off, and Poppy could feel his distress.

'You can tell me about it later.' She didn't want him ever to be hurt again.

'M'm.' He sounded sleepy. Poppy settled herself more comfortably against him.

It was amazing, considering her last experience going to sleep, that she could even shut her eyes. But she could. She was with her soulmate, so what could go wrong? Nothing could hurt her here.

Phil was having trouble shutting his eyes.

Every time he did, he saw Poppy. Poppy asleep in the casket, Poppy watching him with a hungry cat's gaze. Poppy lifting her head from that guy's throat to show a mouth stained as if she'd been eating berries.

She wasn't human anymore.

And just because he'd known all along that she wouldn't be didn't make it any easier to accept.

He couldn't – he *couldn't* – condone jumping on people and tearing up their throats for dinner. And he wasn't sure that it was any better to charm people and bite them and then hypnotize them to forget it. The whole system was scary on some deep level.

Maybe James had been right – humans just couldn't deal with the idea that there was somebody higher on the food chain. They'd lost touch with their caveman ancestors, who knew what it was like to be hunted. They thought all that primal stuff was behind them.

Could Phillip tell them a thing or two.

The bottom line was that he couldn't accept, and Poppy couldn't change. And the only thing that made it bearable was that somehow he loved her anyway.

Poppy woke in the dim, curtained bedroom the next day to find the other half of the bed empty. She wasn't alarmed, though. Instinctively she reached out with her mind, and . . . there. James was in the kitchenette.

She felt . . . energetic. Like a puppy straining to be let loose in a field. But as soon as she walked into the living room, she felt that her powers were weaker. And her eyes hurt. She squinted toward the painful brightness of a window.

'It's the sun,' James said. 'Inhibits all vampire powers, remember?' He went over to the window and closed the curtains – they were the blackout type, like the ones in the bedroom. The mid-afternoon sunshine was cut off. 'That should help a little – but you'd better stay inside today until it gets dark. New vampires are more sensitive.'

Poppy caught something behind his words. 'You're going out?'

'I have to.' He grimaced. 'There's something I forgot – my cousin Ash is supposed to show up this week. I've got to get my parents to head him off.'

'I didn't know you had a cousin.'

He winced again. 'I've got lots, actually. They're back East in a safe town – a whole town that's controlled by the Night World. Most of them are OK, but not Ash.'

'What's wrong with him?'

'He's crazy. Also cold-blooded, ruthless—'

'You sound like Phil describing you.'

'No, Ash is the real thing. The ultimate vampire. He doesn't care about anybody but himself, and he loves to make trouble.'

Poppy was prepared to love all James's cousins for his sake, but she had to agree that Ash sounded dangerous.

'I wouldn't trust anyone to know about you just now,' James said, 'and Ash is out of the question. I'm going to tell my parents he can't come here, that's all.'

And then what do we do? Poppy thought. She couldn't stay hidden forever. She belonged to the Night World – but the Night World wouldn't accept her.

There had to be some solution – and she could only hope that she and James would find it.

'Don't be gone too long,' she said, and he kissed her on the forehead, which was nice. As if it was getting to be a habit.

When he was gone, she took a shower and put on clean clothes. Good old Phil – he'd slipped in her favourite jeans. Then she made herself putter around the apartment, because she didn't want to sit and *think*. Nobody should have to think on the day after their own funeral.

The phone sat beside the square couch and mocked her. She found herself resisting the impulse to pick it up so often that her arm ached.

But who could she call? Nobody. Not even Phil, because what if somebody overheard him? What if her mother answered?

No, no, don't think about Mom, you idiot.

But it was too late. She was overwhelmed, suddenly, by a desperate *need* to hear her mother's voice. Just to hear a 'hello'. She knew she couldn't say anything herself. She just needed to establish that her mom still existed.

She punched the phone number in without giving herself time to think. She counted rings. One, two, three . . .

'Hello?'

It was her mother's voice. And it was already over, and it wasn't enough. Poppy sat trying to breathe, with tears running down her face. She hung there, wringing the phone cord, listening to the faint buzz on the other end. Like a prisoner in court waiting to hear her sentence.

'Hello? Hello.' Her mother's voice was flat and tired. Not acerbic. Prank phone calls were no big deal when you'd just lost your daughter.

Then a click signalled disconnection.

Poppy clutched the earpiece to her chest and cried, rocking slightly. At last she put it back on the cradle.

Well, she wouldn't do *that* again. It was worse than not being able to hear her mother at all. And it didn't help her with reality, either. It gave her a dizzy Twilight Zone feeling to think that her mom was at home, and everybody was at home, and *Poppy wasn't there*. Life was going on in that house, but she wasn't part of it anymore. She couldn't just walk in, any more than she could walk into some strange family's house.

You're really a glutton for punishment, aren't you? Why don't you stop thinking about this and *do* something distracting?

She was snooping through James's file cabinet when the apartment door opened.

Because she heard the metallic jingle of a key, she assumed it was James. But then, even before she turned, she knew it *wasn't* James. It wasn't James's mind.

She turned and saw a boy with ash blond hair.

He was very good looking, built about like James, but a little taller, and maybe a year older. His hair was longish.

His face had a nice shape, clean-cut features, and wicked slightly tilted eyes.

But that wasn't why she was staring at him.

He gave her a flashing smile.

'I'm Ash,' he said. 'Hi.'

Poppy was still staring. 'You were in my dream,' she said. 'You said, "Bad magic happens".'

'So you're a psychic?'

'What?'

'Your dreams come true?'

'Not usually.' Poppy suddenly got hold of herself. 'Listen, um, I don't know how you got in—'

He jingled a key ring at her. 'Aunt Maddy gave me these. James told you to keep me out, I bet.'

Poppy decided that the best defense was a good offense. 'Now, why would he tell me that?' she said, and folded her arms over her chest.

He gave her a wicked, laughing glance. His eyes looked hazel in this light, almost golden. 'I'm bad,' he said simply.

Poppy tried to plaster a look of righteous disapproval – like Phil's – on her face. It didn't work very well. 'Does James know you're here? Where *is* he?'

'I have no idea. Aunt Maddy gave me the keys at lunch, and then she went out on some interior decorating job. What did you dream about?'

Poppy just shook her head. She was trying to think. Presumably, James was wandering around in search of his mother right now. Once he found her he'd find out that Ash was over here, and then he'd come back fast. Which meant . . . well, Poppy supposed it meant she should keep Ash occupied until James arrived.

But how? She'd never really practiced being winsome and adorable with guys. And she was worried about talking too much. She might give herself away as a new vampire.

Oh, well. When in doubt, shut your eyes and jump right in.

'Know any good werewolf jokes?' she said.

He laughed. He had a nice laugh, and his eyes weren't hazel after all. They were grey, like James's.

'You haven't told me your name yet, little dreamer,' he said.

'Poppy,' Poppy said and immediately wished she hadn't. What if Mrs Rasmussen had mentioned that one of James's little friends called Poppy had just died? To conceal her nervousness, she got up to close the door.

'Good lamia name,' he said. 'I don't like this yuppy thing of taking on human names, do you? I've got three sisters, and they all have regular old-fashioned names. Rowan, Kestrel, Jade. My dad would burst a blood vessel if one of them suddenly wanted to call herself "Susan".'

'Or "Maddy?" ' Poppy asked, intrigued despite herself.

'Huh? It's short for Madder.'

Poppy wasn't sure what madder was. A plant, she thought.

'Of course I'm not saying anything against James,' Ash said, and it was perfectly clear from his voice that he *was* saying something against James. 'Things are different for you guys in California. You have to mix more with humans; you have to be more careful. So if naming yourself after vermin makes it easier . . .' He shrugged.

'Oh, yeah, they're vermin all right,' Poppy said at random. She was thinking, he's playing with me. Isn't he playing with me?

She had the sinking feeling that he knew everything. Agitation made her need to move. She headed for James's stereo centre.

'So you like any vermin music?' she said. 'Techno? Acid jazz? Trip-hop? Jungle?' She waved a vinyl record at him. 'This is some serious jump-up jungle.' He blinked. 'Oh, and this is great industrial noise. And this is a real good acid house stomper with a sort of madcore edge to it . . .'

She had him on the defensive now. Nobody could stop Poppy when she got going like this. She widened her eyes at him and blathered on, looking as fey as she knew how.

'And I say freestyle's coming *back*. Completely underground, so far, but on the *rise*. Now, Euro-dance, on the other hand . . .'

Ash was sitting on the square couch, long legs stretched out in front of him. His eyes were deep blue and slightly glazed.

'Sweetheart,' he said finally, 'I hate to interrupt. But you and I need to talk.'

Poppy was too clever to ask him what about. '. . . these sort of eternal void keys and troll groaning sounds that make you want to ask, "Is anybody out there?" ' she finished, and then she had to breathe. Ash jumped in.

'We *really* have to talk,' he said. 'Before James gets back.'

There was no way to evade him now. Poppy's mouth was dry. He leaned forward, his eyes a clear blue-green like tropical waters. And, yes, they really *do* change colour, Poppy thought.

'It's not your fault,' he said.

'What?'

It's not your fault. That you can't shield your mind. You'll learn how to do it, he said, and Poppy only realized halfway through that he wasn't saying it out loud.

Oh . . . *spit*. She should have thought of that. Should

have been concentrating on veiling her thoughts. She tried to do it now.

'Listen, don't bother. I know that you're not lamia. You're made, and you're illegal. James has been a bad boy.'

Since there was no point in denying it, Poppy lifted her chin and narrowed her eyes at him. 'So you know. So what are you going to do about it?'

'That depends.'

'On what?'

He smiled. 'On you.'

CHAPTER

14

'**Y**ou see, I like James,' Ash said. 'I think he's a little soft on vermin, but I don't want to see him in trouble. I certainly don't want to see him *dead*.'

Poppy felt the way she had last night when her body was starving for air. She was frozen, too still to breathe.

'I mean, do *you* want him dead?' Ash asked, as if it were the most reasonable question in the world.

Poppy shook her head.

'Well, then,' Ash said.

Poppy got a breath at last. 'What are you *saying*?' Then, without waiting for him to answer, she said, 'You're saying that they're going to kill him if they find out about me. But they don't *have* to find out about me. Unless you tell them.'

Ash glanced at his fingernails thoughtfully. He made a face to show that this was as painful for him as it was for her.

'Let's go over the facts,' he said. 'You are, in fact, a former human.'

'Oh, yeah, I was a vermin, all right.'

He gave her a droll look. 'Don't take that so seriously. It's what you are now that counts. But James did, in fact, change you without clearing it with *anybody*. Right? And he did, in fact, break cover and tell you about the Night World before you were changed. Right?'

'How do you know? Maybe he just changed me without telling me a thing.'

He shook a finger. 'Ah, but James wouldn't do that. He's got these radical permissive ideas about humans having free will.'

'If you know all about it, why ask me?' Poppy said tensely. 'And if you've got a point—'

'The point is that he's committed at least two capital offences. Three, I bet.' He flashed the wild, handsome smile again. 'He must have been in love with you to have done the rest.'

Something swelled in Poppy like a bird trapped in her rib cage and trying to get out. She blurted, 'I don't see how you people can make laws about not falling in love! It's insane.'

'But don't you see *why*? You're the perfect example. Because of love, James told you and then he changed you. If he'd had the sense to squash his feelings for you in the beginning, the whole thing would have been nipped in the bud.'

'But what if you *can't* squash it? You can't *force* people to stop feeling.'

'Of course not,' Ash said, and Poppy stopped dead. She stared at him.

His lips curved and he beckoned to her. 'I'll tell you a secret. The Elders know they can't really legislate how you *feel*. What they can do is terrorize you so that you don't dare show your feelings – ideally, so you can't even admit them to yourself.'

Poppy settled back. She'd seldom felt so at a loss. Talking to Ash made her head whirl, made her feel as if she were too young and stupid to be sure of *anything*.

She made a forlorn and helpless gesture. 'But what do I do now? I can't change the past . . .'

'No, but you can act in the present.' He jumped to his feet in a lovely, graceful motion and began pacing. 'Now. We have to think fast. Presumably everyone here thinks you're dead.'

'Yes, but—'

'So the answer is simple. You have to get out of the area and stay out. Go someplace where you won't be recognized, where nobody will care if you're new or illegal. Witches. That's it! I've got some cross-cousins in Las Vegas that will put you up. The main thing is to leave *now*.'

Poppy's head wasn't just whirling, it was *reeling*. She felt dizzy and physically sick, as if she'd just stepped off Space Mountain at Disneyland. 'What? I don't even understand what you're talking about,' she said feebly.

'I'll explain on the way. Come on, hurry! Do you have some clothes you want to take?'

Poppy planted her feet solidly on the floor. She shook her head to try and clear it. 'Look, I don't know what you're saying, but I can't go *anywhere* right now. I have to wait for James.'

'But don't you see?' Ash stopped his whirlwind pacing and rounded on her. His eyes were green and hypnotically brilliant. 'That's just what you *can't* do. James can't even know where you're going.'

'*What?*'

'Don't you *see*?' Ash said again. He spread his hands and spoke almost pityingly. '*You're* the only thing putting James in danger. As long as you're here, anybody can look at you and put the pieces together. You're circumstantial evidence that he's committed a crime.'

Poppy understood that. 'But I can just wait and James can go away with me. He would *want* that.'

'But it wouldn't work,' Ash said softly. 'It doesn't matter where you go; whenever you're together, you're a danger to him. One look at you and any decent vampire can sense the truth.'

Poppy's knees felt weak.

Ash spoke soberly. 'I'm not saying that you'll be much safer yourself if you leave. You bring your own danger with you, because of what you are. But as long as you're away from James, nobody can connect you with *him*. It's the only way to keep him safe. Do you see?'

'Yes. Yes, I see that now.' The ground seemed to have disappeared beneath Poppy. She was falling, not into music, but into an icy dark void. There was nothing to hold on to.

'But, of course, it's a lot to expect, to ask you to give him up. You may not want to make that kind of sacrifice—'

Poppy's chin came up. She was blind and empty and giddy, but she spoke to Ash with utter contempt, spitting out the words. 'After everything he sacrificed for me? What do you think I am?'

Ash bowed his head. 'You're a brave one, little dreamer. I can't believe you were ever human.' Then he looked up and spoke briskly. 'So do you want to pack?'

'I don't have much,' Poppy said, slowly, because moving and speaking hurt her. She walked toward the bedroom as if the floor was covered with broken glass. 'Hardly anything. But I have to write a note for James.'

'No, no,' Ash said. 'That's the last thing you want to do. Well, after all,' he added as she swivelled slowly to look at him, 'James being so noble and lovestruck and everything

– if you let him know where you're going, he'll come right after you. And then where will you be?'

Poppy shook her head. 'I . . . OK.' Still shaking her head, she stumbled into the bedroom.

She wasn't going to argue with him anymore, but she wasn't going to take his advice, either. She shut the bedroom door and tried as hard as she could to shield her mind. She visualized a stone wall around her thoughts.

Stuffing her sweat pants and T-shirt and white dress into the duffel bag took thirty seconds. Then she found a book under the nightstand and a felt-tip pen in the drawer. She tore the flyleaf out of the book and scribbled rapidly.

Dear James,

I'm so sorry, but if I stay to explain this to you, I know you'll try to stop me. Ash has made me understand the truth – that as long as I stick around I'm putting your life in danger. And I just can't do that. If something happened to you because of me, I would die. I really would.

I'm going away now. Ash is taking me somewhere far away where you won't find me. Where they won't care what I am. I'll be safe there. You'll be safe here. And even if we're not together, we'll never really be apart.

I love you. I'll love you forever. But I have to do this.

Please tell Phil goodbye.

Your soulmate, Poppy.

She was dripping tears onto the paper as she signed it.

She put the flyleaf on the pillow and went out to Ash.

'Oh, there, there,' he said. 'Don't cry. You're doing the right thing.' He put an arm around her shoulders. Poppy was too miserable to shrug it off.

She looked at him. 'One thing. Won't I be putting *you*

in danger if I go with you? I mean, somebody might think *you* were the one who made me an illegal vampire.'

He looked at her with wide, earnest eyes. They happened to be blue-violet at the moment.

'I'm willing to take that risk,' he said. 'I have a lot of respect for you.'

James took the stairs two at a time, sending probing thoughts ahead of him and then refusing to believe what his own senses told him.

She had to be there. She *had* to be . . .

He pounded on the door at the same time as he was thrusting the key into the lock. At the same time as he was shouting mentally.

Poppy! Poppy, answer me! Poppy!

And then, even with the door flung open and his own thoughts ricocheting off the emptiness in the apartment, he *still* didn't want to believe. He ran around, looking in every room, his heart thudding louder and louder in his chest. Her duffel bag was gone. Her clothes were gone. She was gone.

He ended up leaning against the glass of the living room window. He could see the street below, and there was no sign of Poppy.

No sign of Ash, either.

It was James's fault. He'd been following his mother's trail all afternoon, from decorating job to decorating job, trying to catch up with her. Only to find, once he did catch up, that Ash was already in El Camino, and had, in fact, been sent over to James's apartment hours ago. With a key.

Putting him alone with Poppy.

James had called the apartment immediately. No answer. He'd broken all speed limits getting back here.

But he was too late.

Ash, you snake, he thought. If you hurt her, if you put one finger on her . . .

He found himself roving over the apartment again, looking for clues as to what had happened. Then, in the bedroom, he noticed something pale against the light brown of the pillowcase.

A note. He snatched it up and read it. And got colder and colder with every line. By the time he reached the end, he was made of ice and ready to kill.

There were little round splashes where the felt-tip pen had run. Tears. He was going to break one of Ash's bones for each one.

He folded the note carefully and put it in his pocket. Then he took a few things from his closet and made a call on his cellular phone as he was walking down the stairs of the apartment building.

'Mom, it's me,' he said at the beep of an answering machine. 'I'm going to be gone for a few days. Something's come up. If you see Ash, leave me a message. I want to talk with him.'

He didn't say please. He knew his voice was clipped and sharp. And he didn't care. He hoped his tone would scare her.

Just at the moment he felt ready to take on his mother and father and all the vampire Elders in the Night World. One stake for all of them.

He wasn't a child anymore. In the last week he'd been through the crucible. He'd faced death and found love. He was an adult.

And filled with a quiet fury that would destroy everything in its path. Everything necessary to get to Poppy.

He made other phone calls as he guided the Integra swiftly and expertly through the streets of El Camino. He called the Black Iris and made sure that Ash hadn't turned up there. He called several other black flower clubs, even though he didn't expect to find anything. Poppy had said Ash was going to take her far away.

But where?

Damn you, Ash, he thought. *Where?*

Phil was staring at the TV without really seeing it. How could he be interested in talk shows or infomercials when all he could think about was his sister? His sister who was maybe watching the same shows and maybe out biting people?

He heard the car screech to a stop outside and was on his feet before he knew it. Weird how he was absolutely certain of who it was. He must have come to recognize the Integra's engine.

He opened the door as James reached the porch. 'What's up?'

'Come on.' James was already heading for the car. There was a deadly energy in his movements, a barely controlled power, that Phil had never seen before. White-hot fury, leashed but straining.

'What's *wrong*?'

James turned at the driver's side door. 'Poppy's missing!'

Phil threw a wild glance around. There was nobody on the street, but the door to the house was open. And James was shouting as if he didn't care who heard.

Then the words sank in. 'What do you mean, she's—' Phil broke off and jerked the door to the house shut. Then he went to the Integra. James already had the passenger door open.

'What do you mean, she's missing?' Phil said as soon as he was in the car.

James gunned the engine. 'My cousin Ash has taken her someplace.'

'*Who's Ash?*'

'He's dead,' James said, and somehow Phillip knew he didn't mean Ash was one of the walking dead. He meant Ash was going to *be* dead, completely dead, at some point very soon.

'Well, where's he taken her?'

'I don't know,' James said through his teeth. 'I have no idea.'

Phil stared a moment, then said, 'OK. OK.' He didn't understand what was going on, but he could see one thing. James was too angry and too intent on revenge to think logically. He might *seem* rational, but it was stupid to drive around at fifty-five miles an hour through a residential zone with no idea of where to go.

It was strange that Phil felt comparatively calm – it seemed as if he'd spent the last week being wacko while James played the cool part. But having someone else be hysterical always made Phil go levelheaded.

'OK, look,' he said. 'Let's take this one step at a time. Slow down, OK? We might be going in exactly the wrong direction.' At that, James eased up on the gas pedal slightly.

'OK, now tell me about Ash. Why's he taking Poppy somewhere? Did he kidnap her?'

'No. He talked her into it. He convinced her that it was dangerous for me if she stuck around here. It was the one thing guaranteed to make her go with him.' One hand on the wheel, James fished in his pocket and handed a folded piece of paper to Phil.

It was a page torn out of a book. Phillip read the note and swallowed. He glanced at James, who was staring straight ahead at the road.

Phil shifted, embarrassed at having intruded on private territory, embarrassed at the sting in his eyes. *Your soulmate, Poppy?* Well. Well.

'She loves you a lot,' he said finally, awkwardly. 'And I'm glad she said goodbye to me.' He folded the note carefully and tucked it under the emergency brake handle. James picked it up and put it in his pocket again.

'Ash used her feelings to get her away. Nobody can push buttons and pull strings like he can.'

'But why would he want to?'

'First because he likes girls. He's a *real* Don Juan.' James glanced at Phil caustically. 'And now he's got her alone. And second because he likes to play with things. Like a cat with a mouse. He'll fool around with her for a while, and then when he gets tired of her, he'll hand her over.'

Phillip went still. 'Who *to*?'

'The Elders. Somebody in charge somewhere who'll realize she's a renegade vampire.'

'And then what?'

'And then they kill her.'

Phil grabbed the dashboard. 'Wait a minute. You're telling me that a cousin of yours is going to hand Poppy over to be killed?'

'It's the law. Any good vampire would do the same. My own mother would do it, without a second thought.' His voice was bitter.

'And he's a vampire. Ash,' Phil said stupidly.

James gave him a look. '*All* my cousins are vampires,' he said with a short laugh. Then his expression changed, and he took his foot off the gas.

'What's the – hey, that was a stop sign!' Phil yelped.

James slammed on the brakes and swung into a U-turn in the middle of the street. He ran over somebody's lawn.

'What is it?' Phil said tightly, still braced against the dashboard.

James was looking almost dreamy. 'I've just realized where they've gone. Where he'd take her. He told her someplace safe, where people wouldn't care what she was. But vampires *would* care.'

'So they're with humans?'

'No. Ash hates humans. He'd want to take her someplace in the Night World, someplace where he's a big man. And the nearest city that's controlled by the Night World is Las Vegas.'

Phil felt his jaw drop. *Las Vegas?* Controlled by the Night World? He had the sudden impulse to laugh. Sure, of course it would be. 'And I always thought it was the Mafia,' he said.

'It is,' James said seriously, swerving onto a freeway on-ramp. 'Just a different mafia.'

'But, look, wait. Las Vegas is a big city.'

'It's not, actually. But it doesn't matter anyway. I know where they are. Because all my cousins *aren't* vampires. Some of them are witches.'

Phil's forehead puckered. 'Oh, yeah? And how did you arrange that?'

'I didn't. My great-grandparents did, about four hundred years ago. They did a blood-tie ceremony with a witch family. The witches aren't my *real* cousins; they're not related. They're cross-cousins. Adopted family. It probably won't even occur to them that Poppy might not be legal. And that's where Ash would go.'

'They're cross-kin,' Ash told Poppy. They were driving in the Rasmussen's gold Mercedes, which Ash insisted his Aunt Maddy would want him to take. 'They won't be suspicious of you. And witches don't know the signs of being a new vampire the way vampires do.'

Poppy just stared at the far horizon. It was evening now, and a lowering red sun was setting behind them. All around them was a weird alien landscape: not as brown as Poppy would have expected a desert to be. More grey-green, with clumps of green-grey. The Joshua trees were strangely beautiful, but also the closest thing to a plant made up of tentacles as she'd ever seen.

Most everything growing had spikes.

It was oddly fitting as a place to go into exile. Poppy felt as if she were leaving behind not only her old life, but everything she'd ever found familiar about the earth.

'I'll take care of you,' Ash said caressingly.

Poppy didn't even blink.

Phillip first saw Nevada as a line of lights in the darkness ahead. As they got closer to the state line, the lights resolved into signs with blinking, swarming, flashing neon messages. Whiskey Pete's, they announced. Buffalo Bill's. The Prima Donna.

Some guy with a reputation for being a Don Juan was taking Poppy in *this* direction?

'Go faster,' he told James as they left the lights behind and entered a dark and featureless desert. 'Come on. This car can do ninety.'

'Here we are. Las Vegas,' Ash said as if making Poppy a present of the whole city. But Poppy didn't see a city, only a light in the clouds ahead like the rising moon. Then, as the freeway curved, she saw that it wasn't the moon, it was the reflection of city lights. Las Vegas was a glittering pool in a flat basin between the mountains.

Something stirred in Poppy despite herself. She'd always wanted to see the world. Faraway places. Exotic lands. And this would have been perfect – if only James had been with her.

Up close, though, the city wasn't quite the gem it looked from a distance. Ash got off the freeway, and Poppy was thrown into a world of colour and light and movement – and of tawdry cheapness.

'The Strip,' Ash announced. 'You know, where all the casinos are. There's no place like it.'

'I bet,' Poppy said, staring. On one side of her was a towering black pyramid hotel with a huge sphinx in front. Lasers were flashing out of the sphinx's eyes. On the other side was a sleazy motor inn with a sign saying 'Rooms $18.'

'So this is the Night World,' she said, with a twinge of cynical amusement that made her feel very adult.

'Nah, this is for the tourists,' Ash said. 'But it's good business and you can do some fairly serious partying. I'll show you the real Night World, though. First, I want to check in with my cousins.'

Poppy considered telling him that she didn't really care to have *him* show her the Night World. Something about Ash's manner was beginning to bother her. He was acting more as if they were out on a date than as if he were escorting her into exile.

But he's the only person I know here, she realized with a dismayed sinking in her stomach. And it's not as if I have any money or anything – not even eighteen dollars for that crummy motel.

There was something worse. She'd been hungry for some time now, and now she was starting to feel breathless. But she wasn't the dazed, unthinking animal she'd been last night. She didn't *want* to attack some human on the street.

'This is the place,' Ash said. It was a side street, dark

and not crowded like the Strip. He pulled into an alley. 'OK, just let me see if they're in.'

On either side of them were high buildings with cinder-block walls. Above, tiers of power lines obscured the sky. Ash knocked at a door set in the cinder block – a door with no knob on the outside. There was no sign on the door, either, just some crudely spray-painted graffiti. It was a picture of a black dahlia.

Poppy stared at a Dumpster and tried to control her breathing. In, out. Slow and deep. It's OK, there's air. It may not feel like it, but there's air.

The door opened and Ash beckoned to her.

'This is Poppy,' Ash said, putting an arm around her as Poppy stumbled inside. The place looked like a shop – a shop with herbs and candles and crystals. And lots of other weird things that Poppy didn't recognize. Witchy-looking supplies.

'And these are my cousins. That's Blaise, and that's Thea.' Blaise was a striking girl with masses of dark hair and lots of curves. Thea was slimmer and blond. They both kept going out of focus as Poppy's vision blurred.

'Hi,' she said, the longest greeting she could manage.

'Ash, what's wrong with you? She's sick. What have you been doing to her?' Thea was looking at Poppy with sympathetic brown eyes.

'Huh? Nothing,' Ash said, looking surprised, as if noticing Poppy's state for the first time. Poppy guessed he wasn't the type to worry about other people's discomfort. 'She's hungry, I guess. We'll have to run out and feed—'

'Oh, no, you don't. Not around here. Besides, she's not going to make it,' Thea said. 'Come on, Poppy, I'll be a donor this once.'

She took Poppy by the arm and led her through a bead curtain into another room. Poppy let herself be towed.

She couldn't think anymore – and her whole upper jaw was aching. Even the word *feed* sharpened her teeth.

I need . . . I have to . . .

But she didn't know how. She had a vision of her own face in the mirror, silvery eyes and savage canines. She didn't *want* to be an animal again and jump on Thea and rip her throat. And she couldn't ask how – that would give her away as a new vampire for sure. She stood, trembling, unable to move.

CHAPTER

15

'Come on, it's OK,' Thea said. She seemed to be about Poppy's age, but she had a gentle, sensible air that gave her authority. 'Sit down. Here.' She set Poppy on a shabby couch and extended her wrist. Poppy stared at the wrist for an instant and then remembered.

James, giving her blood from his arm. *That* was how to do it. Friendly and civilized.

She could see pale blue veins under the skin. And that sight blasted away the last of her hesitation. Instinct took over and she grabbed Thea's arm. The next thing she knew she was drinking.

Warm salty-sweetness. Life. Relief from pain. It was so good that Poppy could almost cry. No wonder vampires hated humans, she thought dimly. Humans didn't have to hunt for this marvellous stuff; they were full of it already.

But, another part of her mind pointed out, Thea wasn't a human. She was a witch. Strange, because her blood tasted exactly the same. Poppy's every sense confirmed it.

So witches are just humans, but humans with special powers, Poppy thought. Interesting.

It took an effort to control herself, to know when to stop. But she did stop. She let go of Thea's wrist and sat back, a little embarrassed, licking her lips and teeth. She didn't want to meet Thea's brown eyes.

It was only then that she realized she'd been keeping her thoughts shielded during the entire process. There had been no mental connection as there had been when she shared blood with James. So she'd mastered one vampire power already. Faster than James or Ash had expected.

And she felt good now. Energetic enough to do the Netherlands skippy dance. Confident enough to smile at Thea.

'Thank you,' she said.

Thea smiled back, as if she found Poppy odd or quaint, but nice. She didn't seem suspicious. 'It's OK,' she said, flexing her wrist and grimacing gently.

For the first time Poppy was able to look around her. This room was more like a living room than part of a shop. Besides the couch there was a TV and several chairs. At the far end was a large table with candles and incense burning.

'This is the teaching room,' Thea said. 'Grandma does spells here and lets the students hang out.'

'And the other part is a store,' Poppy said, cautiously because she didn't know what she was supposed to know.

Thea didn't look surprised. 'Yes. I know you wouldn't think there'd be enough witches around here to keep us in business, but actually they come from all over the country. Grandma's famous. And her students buy a lot.'

Poppy nodded, looking properly impressed. She didn't dare ask more questions, but her chilly heart had warmed just a tiny bit. All Night People weren't harsh and evil. She had the feeling she could be friends with this girl if given the chance. Maybe she could make it in the Night World after all.

'Well, thanks again,' she murmured softly.

'Don't mention it. But don't let Ash get you run down like that, either. He's so *irresponsible*.'

'You wound me, Thea. You really do,' Ash said. He was standing in the doorway, holding the bead curtain open with one hand. 'But come to think of it, I'm feeling a little run down myself . . .' He raised his eyebrows insinuatingly.

'Go jump in Lake Mead, Ash,' Thea said sweetly.

Ash looked innocent and yearning. 'Just a little bite. A nibble. A nip,' he said. 'You have such a pretty white throat . . .'

'Who does?' Blaise said, pushing her way through the other half of the bead curtain. Poppy had the feeling she was only speaking to focus attention on herself. She stood in the centre of the room and shook back her long black hair with the air of a girl used to attention.

'You both do,' Ash said gallantly. Then he seemed to remember Poppy. 'And, of course, this little dreamer has a pretty white everything.'

Blaise, who had been smiling, now looked sour. She stared at Poppy long and hard. With dislike – and something else.

Suspicion. Dawning suspicion.

Poppy could *feel* it. Blaise's thoughts were bright and sharp and malicious, like jagged glass.

Then suddenly Blaise smiled again. She looked at Ash. 'I suppose you've come for the party,' she said.

'No. What party?'

Blaise sighed in a way that emphasized her low-cut blouse. 'The Solstice party, of course. Thierry's giving a big one. *Everybody* will be there.'

Ash looked tempted. In the dim light of the teaching room his eyes gleamed dark. Then he shook his head.

'No, can't make it. Sorry. I'm going to show Poppy the town.'

'Well, you can do that and still come to the party later. It won't really get going until after midnight.' Blaise was staring at Ash with an odd insistence. Ash bit his lip, then shook his head again, smiling.

'Well, maybe,' he said. 'I'll see how things go.'

Poppy knew he was saying more than that. Some unspoken message seemed to be passing between him and Blaise. But it wasn't telepathic, and Poppy couldn't pick it up.

'Well, have a good time,' Thea said, and gave Poppy a quick smile as Ash piloted her away.

Ash peered ahead at the Strip. 'If we hurry we can watch the volcano erupting,' he said. Poppy gave him a look, but didn't ask.

Instead, she said, 'What's a Solstice party?'

'Summer solstice. The longest day of the year. It's a holiday for the Night People. Like Groundhog Day for humans.'

'Why?'

'Oh, it always has been. It's very magical, you know. I'd take you to the party, but it would be too dangerous. Thierry's a vampire Elder.' Then he said, 'Here's the volcano.'

It was a volcano. In front of a hotel. Waterfalls crashed down its sides, and red lights shone from the cone. Ash double-parked across the street.

'You see, we've got a great view right here,' he said. 'All the comforts of home.'

The volcano was emitting rumbling sounds. As Poppy watched in disbelief, a pillar of fire shot out of the top. Real fire. Then the waterfalls caught fire. Red and gold flames spread down the sides of the black rock until the entire lake around the volcano was ablaze.

'Inspiring, isn't it?' Ash asked, very close to her ear.

'Well – it's . . .'

'Thrilling?' Ash inquired. 'Stimulating? Rousing?' His arm was creeping around her, and his voice was sweetly hypnotic.

Poppy didn't say anything.

'You know,' Ash murmured, 'you can see a lot better if you get over here. I don't mind crowding.' His arm was urging her gently but inevitably closer. His breath ruffled her hair.

Poppy slammed an elbow into his stomach.

'*Hey!*' Ash yelped – in genuine pain, Poppy thought. Good.

He'd dropped his arm and now he was looking at her with aggrieved brown eyes. 'What did you do that for?'

'Because I *felt* like it,' Poppy said smartly. She was tingling with new blood and ready for a fight. 'Look, Ash, I don't know what gave you the idea that I'm your date here. But I'm telling you right now that I'm *not*.'

Ash tilted his head and smiled painfully. 'You just don't know me well enough,' he offered. 'When we get to know each other—'

'*No*. Never. I'm not interested in other guys. If I can't have James . . .' Poppy had to stop and steady her voice. 'There's nobody else I want,' she said finally, flatly. 'Nobody.'

'Well, not now, maybe, but—'

'*Never*.' She didn't know how to explain. Then she had an idea. 'You know the soulmate principle?'

Ash opened his mouth and then shut it. Opened it again. 'Oh, no. Not *that* garbage.'

'Yes. James is my soulmate. I'm sorry if it sounds stupid, but it's true.'

Ash put a hand to his forehead. Then he started to laugh. 'You're serious.'

'Yes.'

'And that's your final word.'

'Yes.'

Ash laughed again, sighed, and cast his eyes upward. 'OK. OK. I should have known.' He chuckled in what seemed like self-derision.

Poppy was relieved. She'd been afraid he'd be disgruntled and huffy – or *mean*. Despite his charm, she could always feel something cold runing below the surface in Ash, like an icy river.

But now he seemed perfectly good-humoured. 'OK,' he said. 'So if romance isn't on the menu, let's go to the party.'

'I thought you said it was too dangerous.'

He waved a hand. 'That was a little fib. To get you alone, you know.' He glanced sideways at her. 'Sorry.'

Poppy hesitated. She didn't care about a party. But she didn't want to be alone with Ash, either.

'Maybe you should just take me back to your cousins' place.'

'They won't *be* there,' Ash said. 'I'm sure they've gone to the party by now. Oh, come on, it'll be fun. Give me a chance to make things up to you.'

Thin curls of uneasiness were roiling inside Poppy. But Ash looked so penitent and persuasive . . . and what other choice did she have?

'OK,' she said finally. 'For just a little while.'

Ash gave a dazzling smile. 'Just a very little while,' he said.

'So they could be anywhere on the Strip,' James said.

Thea sighed. 'I'm sorry. I should have known Ash was

up to something. But hijacking your girlfriend . . .' She lifted her hands in a what-next gesture. 'For what it's worth, she didn't seem very interested in him. If he's planning to put the moves on her, he's going to get a surprise.'

Yes, James thought, and so is she. Poppy was only useful to Ash as long as Ash thought he could play with her. Once he realized he couldn't . . .

He didn't want to think about what would happen then. A quick visit to the nearest Elder, he supposed.

His heart was pounding, and there was a ringing in his ears.

'Did Blaise go with them?' he asked.

'No, she went to the Solstice party. She tried to get Ash to go, but he said he wanted to show Poppy the town.' Thea paused, raising a finger. 'Wait – you might check at the party. Ash said he might stop in later.'

James spent a moment forcing himself to breathe. Then he said, very gently, 'And just who is giving this party?'

'Thierry Descouedres. He always has a big one.'

'And he's an Elder.'

'What?'

'Nothing. Never mind.' James backed out of the shop. 'Thanks for the help. I'll be in touch.'

'James . . .' She looked at him helplessly. 'Do you want to come in and sit down? You don't look very well . . .'

'I'm fine,' James said, already out the door.

In the car he said, 'You can get up now.'

Phillip emerged from the floor of the backseat where he'd been hiding. 'What's happening? You were gone a long time.'

'I think I know where Poppy is.'

'You just *think*?'

'Shut up, Phil.' He didn't have energy for exchanging insults. He was entirely focused on Poppy.

'OK, so where is she?'

James spoke precisely. 'She is either now, or she will be later, at a party. A very large party, filled with vampires. And at least one Elder. The perfect place to expose her.'

Phil gulped. 'And you think that's what Ash is going to do?'

'I know that's what Ash is going to do.'

'Then we've got to stop him.'

'We may be too late.'

The party was strange. Poppy was amazed at how young most of the people were. There were a few scattered adults, but far more teenagers.

'Made vampires,' Ash explained obligingly. Poppy remembered what James had said – made vampires remained forever the age of their death, but lamia could stop aging anytime. She supposed that meant that James could get as old as he wanted, while she would be stuck at sixteen eternally. Not that it mattered. If she and James were going to be together, they could both stay young – but apart, maybe he'd want to age.

But it *was* odd to see a guy who looked about nineteen talking earnestly with a little kid who looked about four. The kid was cute, with shiny black hair and tilted eyes, but there was something at once innocent and cruel in his expression.

'Let's see, now that's Circe. A witch of renown. And that's Sekhmet, a shapeshifter. You don't want to get *her* mad,' Ash said genially. He and Poppy were standing in a little anteroom, looking down a level into the main room of the house. Of the mansion, rather. It was the most opulent private residence Poppy had ever seen – and she'd seen Bel Air and Beverly Hills.

'OK,' Poppy said, looking in the general direction he was pointing. She saw two tall and lovely girls, but she had no idea which was which.

'And that's Thierry, our host. He's an Elder.'

An Elder? The guy Ash was indicating didn't seem older than nineteen. He was beautiful, like all the vampires, tall and blond and pensive. Almost sad-looking.

'How old *is* he?'

'Oh, I forget. He got bitten by an ancestress of mine a long time ago. Back when people lived in caves.'

Poppy thought he was joking. But maybe not.

'What do the Elders do, exactly?'

'They just make rules. And see that people keep them.' An odd smile was playing around Ash's lips. He turned to look directly at Poppy.

With the black eyes of a snake.

That was when Poppy knew.

She backed away rapidly. But Ash came after her, just as rapidly. She saw a door on the other side of the anteroom and headed for it. Got through it. Only to find herself on a balcony.

With her eyes, she measured the distance to the ground. But before she could make another move, Ash had her arm.

Don't fight yet, her mind counselled desperately. He's strong. Wait for an opportunity.

She made herself relax a fraction and met Ash's dark gaze. 'You brought me here.'

'Yes.'

'To hand me over.'

He smiled.

'But *why*?'

Ash threw back his head and laughed. It was lovely,

melodious laughter, and it made Poppy sick.

'You're a *human*,' he said. 'Or you should be. James should never have done what he did.'

Poppy's heart was racing, but her mind was oddly clear. Maybe she'd known all along that this was what he was going to do. Maybe it was even the *right* thing to do. If she couldn't be with James and she couldn't be with her family, did the rest really matter? Did she *want* to live in the Night World if it was full of people like Blaise and Ash?

'So you don't care about James, either,' she said. 'You're willing to put him in danger to get rid of me.'

Ash considered, then grinned. 'James can take care of himself,' he said.

Which was obviously Ash's entire philosophy. Everybody took care of themselves, and nobody helped anybody else.

'And Blaise knew, too,' Poppy said. 'She knew what you were going to do and she didn't care.'

'Not much gets past Blaise,' Ash said. He started to say something else – and Poppy saw her chance.

She kicked – *hard*. And twisted at the same time. Trying to get over the balcony rail.

'Stay here,' James said to Phil before the car had even stopped. They were in front of a huge white mansion fringed with palm trees. James threw the door open, but took the time to say again, 'Stay *here*. No matter what happens, don't go in that house. And if somebody besides me comes up to the car, drive away.'

'But—'

'Just do it, Phil! Unless you want to find out about death firsthand – tonight.'

James set out at a dead run for the mansion. He was too intent to really notice the sound of a car door opening behind him.

* * *

'And you looked like such a nice girl,' Ash gasped. He had both of Poppy's arms behind her back and was trying to get out of the range of her feet. 'No – no, quit that, now.'

He was too strong. There was nothing Poppy could do. Inch by inch he was dragging her back into the anteroom.

You might as well give up, Poppy's mind told her. It's useless. You're done.

She could picture the whole thing: herself being dragged out in front of all of those sleek and handsome Night People and revealed. She could picture their pitiless eyes. That pensive-looking guy would walk up to her and his face would change and he wouldn't look pensive anymore. He'd look savage. His teeth would grow. His eyes would go silvery. Then he'd snarl – and strike.

And that would be the end of Poppy.

Maybe that wasn't the way they did it, maybe they executed criminals some other way in the Night World. But it wouldn't be pleasant, whatever it was.

And I won't make it easy for you! Poppy thought. She thought it directly at Ash, throwing all of her anger and grief and betrayal at him. Instinctively. Like a kid shouting in a temper tantrum.

Except it had an effect shouting usually didn't.

Ash flinched. He almost lost his grip on her arms.

It was only a momentary weakening, but it was enough for Poppy's eyes to widen.

I hurt him. *I hurt him!*

She stopped struggling physically in that same instant. She put all her concentration, all her energy, into a mental explosion. A thought-bomb.

LET GO OF ME, YOU ROTTEN VAMPIRE CREEP!

Ash staggered. Poppy did it again, this time making her thought a fire hose, a high-power jetstream bombardment.

LET GOOOOOOOOOOOO!

Ash let go. Then, as Poppy ran out of steam, he tried in a fumbling way to reach her again.

'I don't think so,' a voice as cold as steel said. Poppy looked into the anteroom and saw James.

Her heart lurched violently. And then, without consciously being aware of moving, she was in his arms.

Oh, James, how did you find *me?*

All he kept saying was *Are you all right?*

'Yes,' Poppy said finally, aloud. It was indescribably good to be with him again, to be held by him. Like waking up from a nightmare to see your mother smiling. She buried her face in his neck.

'You're sure you're all right?'

'Yes. Yes.'

'Good. Then just hang on a moment while I kill this guy and we'll go.'

He was absolutely serious. Poppy could feel it in his thoughts, in every muscle and sinew of his body. He wanted to murder Ash.

She lifted her head at the sound of Ash's laugh.

'Well, it ought to be a good fight, anyway,' Ash said.

No, Poppy thought. Ash was looking silky and dangerous and in a very bad mood. And even if James could beat him, James was going to get hurt. Even if she and James fought him together, there was going to be some damage.

'Let's just go,' she said to James. 'Quick.' She added silently, *I think he wants to keep us around until somebody from the party gets here.*

'No, no,' Ash said, in gloatingly enthusiastic tones. 'Let's settle this like vampires.'

'Let's not,' said a breathless familiar voice. Poppy's head jerked around. Climbing over the railing of the balcony, dusty but triumphant, was Phil.

'Don't you *ever* listen?' James said to him.

'Well, well,' Ash said. 'A human in an Elder's house. What *are* we going to do about that?'

'Look, buddy,' Phil said, still breathless, brushing off his hands. 'I don't know who you are or what horse you rode in on. But that's my *sister* there you're messing with, and I figure I've got the first right to knock your head off.'

There was a pause while Poppy, James, and Ash all looked at him. The pause stretched. Poppy was aware of a sudden, completely inappropriate impulse to laugh. Then she realized that James was fighting desperately not to crack a smile.

Ash just looked Phil up and down, then looked at James sideways.

'Does this guy *understand* about vampires?' he said.

'Oh, yeah,' James said blandly.

'And he's going to knock my head in?'

'Yeah,' Phil said, and cracked his knuckles. 'What's so surprising about that?'

There was another pause. Poppy could feel minute tremors going through James. Choked-back laughter. At last James said, admirably sober, 'Phil really feels strongly about his sister.'

Ash looked at Phil once more, then at James, and finally at Poppy. 'Well . . . there *are* three of you,' he said.

'Yes, there are,' James said, genuinely sober now. Grim.

'So I guess you do have me at a disadvantage. All right, I give up.' He lifted his hands and then dropped them. 'Go on, scram. I won't fight.'

'And you won't tell on us, either,' James said. It wasn't a request.

'I wasn't going to anyway,' Ash said. He had on his most innocent and guileless expression. 'I know you think

I brought Poppy here to expose her, but I really wasn't going to go through with it. I was just having fun. The whole thing was just a joke.'

'Oh, sure,' Phil said.

'Don't even bother lying,' James said.

But Poppy, oddly, wasn't as certain as they were. She looked at Ash's wide eyes – his wide violet eyes – and felt doubt slosh back and forth inside her.

It was hard to read him, as it had been hard all along. Maybe because he always meant everything he said at the time he said it – or maybe because he *never* meant anything he said. No matter which, he was the most irritating, frustrating, impossible person she'd ever met.

'OK, we're going now,' James said. 'We're going to walk very quietly and calmly right through that little room and down the hall, and we're not going to stop for *anything* – Phillip. Unless you'd rather go back down the way you came up,' he added.

Phil shook his head. James gathered Poppy in his arm again, but he paused and looked back at Ash.

'You know, you've never really cared about anyone,' he said. 'But someday you will, and it's going to hurt. It's going to hurt – a lot.'

Ash looked back at him, and Poppy could read nothing in his ever-changing eyes. But just as James turned again, he said, 'I think you're a lousy prophet. But your girlfriend's a good one. You might want to ask her about her dreams sometime.'

James stopped. He frowned. 'What?'

'And you, little dreamer, you might want to check out your family tree. You have a very loud yell.' He smiled at Poppy engagingly. 'Bye now.'

James stayed for another minute or so, just staring at his cousin. Ash gazed serenely back. Poppy counted heartbeats while the two of them stood motionless.

Then James shook himself slightly and turned Poppy toward the anteroom. Phil followed right on their heels.

They walked out of the house very quietly and very calmly. No one tried to stop them.

But Poppy didn't feel safe until they were on the road.

'What did he mean with that crack about the family tree?' Phil asked from the backseat.

James gave him an odd look, but answered with a question. 'Phil, how did you know where to find Poppy in that house? Did you see her on the balcony?'

'No, I just followed the shouting.'

Poppy turned around to look at him.

James said, 'What shouting?'

'*The* shouting. Poppy shouting. "Let go of me you rotten vampire creep." '

Poppy turned to James. 'Should *he* have been able to hear it? I thought I was just yelling at Ash. Did everybody at the party hear?'

'No.'

'But, then—'

James cut her off. 'What dream was Ash talking about?'

'Just a dream I had,' Poppy said, bewildered. 'I dreamed about him before I actually met him.'

James's expression was now *very* peculiar. 'Oh, did you?'

'Yes. James, what's this all about? What did he mean, I should check my family tree?'

'He meant that you – and Phil – aren't human after all. Somewhere among your ancestors there's a witch.'

CHAPTER
16

'**Y**ou have *got* to be kidding,' Poppy said.

Phil just gaped.

'No. I'm perfectly serious. You're witches of the second kind. Remember what I told you?'

'There are the kind of witches that know their heritage and get trained – and the kind that don't. Who just have powers. And humans call that kind—'

'Psychics!' James chorused with her. 'Telepaths. Clairvoyants,' he went on alone. There was something in his voice between laughing and crying. 'Poppy, that's what *you* are. That's why you picked up on telepathy so quickly. That's why you had clairvoyant dreams.'

'And that's why Phil heard me,' Poppy said.

'Oh, no,' Phil said. 'Not me. Come on.'

'Phil, you're twins,' James said. 'You have the same ancestors. Face it, you're a witch. That's why I couldn't control your mind.'

'Oh, *no*,' Phil said. 'No.' He flopped back in his seat. 'No,' he said again, but more weakly.

'But whose side do we get it from?' Poppy wondered.

'Dad's. Of course.' The voice from the backseat was very faint.

'Well, that would *seem* logical, but—'

'It's the truth. Don't you remember how Dad was always talking about seeing weird things? Having dreams about things before they happened? And, Poppy, he heard you yell in *your* dream. When you were calling for James. James heard it, and I heard it, and Dad heard it, too.'

'Then that settles it. Oh, and it explains other things about all of us – all those times we've had *feelings* about things – hunches, whatever. Even you have hunches, Phil.'

'I had one that James was creepy, and I was right.'

'Phil—'

'And maybe a few others,' Phil said fatalistically. 'I knew it was James driving up this afternoon. I thought I just had a fine ear for car engines.'

Poppy was shivering with delight and astonishment, but she couldn't quite understand James. James was absolutely beaming. Filled with unbelieving elation that she could feel like streamers and fireworks in the air.

'What, James?'

'Poppy, don't you see?' James actually pounded the steering wheel in joy. 'It means that even before you became a vampire, *you were a Night Person*. A secret witch. You have every right to know about the Night World. You belong there.'

The world turned upside down and Poppy couldn't breathe. At last she whispered. 'Oh . . .'

'And *we* belong together. Nobody can separate us. We don't have to hide.'

'Oh . . .' Poppy whispered again. Then she said, 'James, pull the car over. I want to kiss you.'

When they were in motion once more, Phil said, 'But where are you two going to go now? Poppy can't come home.'

'I know,' Poppy said softly. She had accepted that.

There was no going back for her; the old life was over. Nothing to do but build a new one.

'And you can't just wander around from place to place,' Phil said, doggedly persistent.

'We won't,' Poppy said calmly. 'We'll go to Dad.'

It was perfect. Poppy could feel James think, *Of course*.

They would go to her father, the always-late, always-impractical, always-affectionate parent. Her father the witch who didn't know he was a witch. Who probably thought he was crazy when his powers acted up.

He'd give them a place to stay, and that was all they needed, really. That and each other. The whole Night World would be open to them, whenever they wanted to explore it. Maybe they could come back and visit Thea sometime. Maybe they could dance at one of Thierry's parties.

'If we can *find* Dad, that is,' Poppy said, struck by sudden alarm.

'You can,' Phil said. 'He flew out last night, but he left an address. For the first time.'

'Maybe somehow he knew,' James said.

They rode for a while, and then Phil cleared his throat and said, 'You know, I just had a thought. I don't want any part of the Night World, you understand – I don't *care* what my heritage is. I just want to live like a human – and I want everybody to be clear on that . . .'

'We're clear, Phil,' James interrupted. 'Believe me. Nobody in the Night World is going to force you in. You can live like a human all you want as long as you avoid Night People and keep your mouth shut.'

'OK. Good. But here's my thought. I still don't approve of vampires, but it occurs to me that maybe they're not as completely bad as they seem. I mean, vampires don't treat their food any worse than humans do. When you think of what we do to cows . . . at least they don't breed humans in pens.'

'I wouldn't bet on it,' James said, suddenly grim. 'I've heard rumours about the old days . . .'

'You always have to argue, don't you? But my other thought was that you're part of Nature, and Nature just is what it is. It's not always pretty, but . . . well, it's Nature, and there it is.' He wound up glumly, 'Maybe that doesn't make any sense.'

'It makes sense to me,' James said, entirely serious. 'And – thanks.' He paused to look back at Phil in acknowledgment. Poppy felt a sting behind her eyes. If he admits we're part of Nature, she thought, then he doesn't believe we're unnatural anymore.

It meant a lot.

She said, 'Well, you know, *I've* been thinking, too. And it occurs to me that maybe there are other choices for feeding besides just jumping on humans when they don't expect it. Like animals. I mean, is there any reason their blood won't work?'

'It's not the same as human blood,' James said. 'But it's a possibility. I've fed on animals. Deer are good. Rabbits are OK. Possums stink.'

'And then there must be *some* people who'd be willing donors. Thea was a donor for me. We could ask other witches.'

'Maybe,' James said. He grinned suddenly. 'I knew a witch back home who was *very* willing. Name of Gisèle. But you couldn't ask them to do it every day, you know. You'd have to give them time to recover.'

'I know, but maybe we could alternate. Animals one day and witches the next. Hey, maybe even werewolves on weekends!'

'I'd rather bite a possum,' James said.

Poppy socked him in the arm. 'The point is, maybe we don't have to be horrible bloodsucking monsters. Maybe we can be *decent* bloodsucking monsters.'

'Maybe,' James said quietly, almost wistfully.

'Hear, hear,' Phil said very seriously from the back.

'And we can do it together,' Poppy said to James.

He took his eyes off the road to smile at her. And there was nothing wistful about his gaze. Nothing cool or mysterious or secretive, either.

'Together,' he said out loud. And mentally he added, *I can't wait. With that telepathy of yours – you realize what we can do, don't you?*

Poppy stared, then felt an effervescent rush that almost shot her out of the car. *Oh, James – do you think?*

I'm certain. The only thing that makes exchanging blood so special is that it enhances telepathy. But you *don't need any enhancement – you little dreamer.*

Poppy sat back to try and still her heart.

They would be able to join their minds again. Anytime they wanted. She could imagine it, being swept into James's mind, feeling him surrender his thoughts to hers.

Merging like two drops of water. Together in a way that humans could never know.

I can't wait, either, she told him. *I think I'm going to like being a witch.*

Phil cleared his throat. 'If you guys want some privacy . . .'

'We can't have any,' James said. 'Not with you around. Obviously.'

'I can't help it,' Phil said through his teeth. 'You're the ones who're yelling.'

'We're not yelling. You're snooping.'

'Both of you give it a rest,' Poppy said. But she felt warm and glowing all over. She couldn't resist adding to

Phil, 'So, if you're willing to give us some privacy, that means you trust James alone with your sister . . .'

'I didn't *say* that.'

'You didn't have to,' Poppy said.

She was happy.

It was very late the next day. Almost midnight, in fact. The witching hour. Poppy was standing in a place she'd thought she'd never see again, her mother's bedroom.

James was waiting outside with a carload of stuff, including one large suitcase of Poppy's CDs, smuggled for them by Phil. In a few minutes James and Poppy would be heading for the East Coast and Poppy's father.

But first, there was something Poppy had to do.

She glided quietly toward the king-size bed, making no more noise than a shadow, not disturbing either of the sleepers. She stopped by her mother's still form.

She stood looking down, and then she spoke with her mind.

I know you think this is a dream, Mom. I know you don't believe in spirits. But I had to tell you that I'm all right. I'm all right, and I'm happy, and even if you don't understand, please try to believe. Just this once, believe in what you can't see.

She paused, then added, *I love you, Mom. I always will.*

When she left the room, her mother was still asleep – and smiling.

Outside, Phil was standing by the Integra. Poppy hugged him and he hugged back, hard.

'Goodbye,' she whispered. She got into the car.

James stuck his hand out the window toward Phil. Phil took it without hesitation.

'Thank you,' James said. 'For everything.'

'No, thank *you*.' Phil said. His smile and his voice were

both shaky. 'Take care of her ... and of yourself.' He stepped back, blinking.

Poppy blew him a kiss. Then she and James drove off together into the night.

DAUGHTERS OF DARKNESS

In Memory of John Manford Divola

And for Julie Ann Divola, still the best
of best friends

CHAPTER
1

'**R**owan, Kestrel, and Jade,' Mary-Lynnette said as she and Mark passed the old Victorian farmhouse.

'Huh?'

'Rowan. And Kestrel. And Jade. The names of the girls who're moving in.' Mary-Lynnette tilted her head toward the farmhouse – her hands were full of lawn chair. 'They're Mrs Burdock's nieces. Don't you remember I told you they were coming to live with her?'

'Vaguely,' Mark said, readjusting the weight of the telescope he was carrying as they trudged up the manzanita-covered hill. He spoke shortly, which Mary-Lynnette knew meant he was feeling shy.

'They're pretty names,' she said. 'And they must be sweet girls, because Mrs Burdock said so.'

'Mrs Burdock is crazy.'

'She's just eccentric. And yesterday she told me her nieces are all beautiful. I mean, I'm sure she's prejudiced and everything, but she was pretty definite. Each one of them gorgeous, each one a completely different type.'

'So they should be going to California,' Mark said in an almost-inaudible mutter. 'They should be posing for *Vogue*. Where do you want this thing?' he added as they reached the top of the hill.

'Right here.' Mary-Lynnette put the lawn chair down. She scraped some dirt away with her foot so the telescope would sit evenly. Then she said casually, 'You know, I thought maybe we could go over there tomorrow and introduce ourselves – sort of welcome them, you know . . .'

'Will you cut it *out*?' Mark said tersely. 'I can organize my own life. If I want to meet a girl, I'll meet a girl. I don't need help.'

'OK, OK. You don't need help. Be careful with that focuser tube—'

'And besides, what are we going to say?' Mark said, on a roll now. 'Welcome to Briar Creek, where nothing ever happens. Where there are more coyotes than people. Where if you *really* want some excitement you can ride into town and watch the Saturday night mouse racing at the Gold Creek Bar . . .'

'OK. OK.' Mary-Lynnette sighed. She looked at her younger brother, who just at the moment was illuminated by the last rays of sunset. To see him now, you'd think he'd never been sick a day in his life. His hair was as dark and shiny as Mary-Lynnette's, his eyes were as blue and clear and snapping. He had the same healthy tan as she did; the same glow of colour in his cheeks.

But when he'd been a baby, he'd been thin and scrawny and every breath had been a challenge. His asthma had been so bad he'd spent most of his second year in an oxygen tent, fighting to stay alive. Mary-Lynnette, a year and a half older, had wondered every day if her baby brother would ever come home.

It had changed him, being alone in that tent where even their mother couldn't touch him. When he came out he was shy and clingy – holding on to their mother's arm all the time. And for years he hadn't been able to go out for sports like the other kids. That was all a long time ago – Mark was going to be a junior in high school this year – but he was still shy. And when he got defensive, he bit people's heads off.

Mary-Lynnette wished one of the new girls *would* be right for him, draw him out a bit, give him confidence. Maybe she could arrange it somehow . . .

'What are you thinking about?' Mark asked suspiciously.

Mary-Lynnette realized he was staring at her.

'About how the seeing's going to be really good tonight,' she said blandly. 'August's the best month for star-watching; the air's so warm and still. Hey, there's the first star – you can make a wish.'

She pointed to a bright point of light above the southern horizon. It worked; Mark was distracted and looked, too.

Mary-Lynnette stared at the back of his dark head. If it would do any good. I'd wish for romance for you, she thought.

I'd wish it for myself, too – but what would be the point? There's nobody around here to be romantic *with*.

None of the guys at school – except maybe Jeremy Lovett – understood why she was interested in astronomy, or what she felt about the stars. Most of the time Mary-Lynnette didn't care – but occasionally she felt a vague ache in her chest. A longing to . . . share. If she *had* wished, it would have been for that, for someone to share the night with.

Oh, well. It didn't help to dwell on it. And besides, although she didn't want to tell Mark, what they were wishing on was the planet Jupiter, and not a star at all.

* * *

Mark shook his head as he tramped down the path that wound through buckbrush and poison hemlock. He should have apologized to Mary-Lynnette before leaving – he didn't *like* being nasty to her. In fact, she was the one person he usually tried to be decent to.

But why was she always trying to *fix* him? To the point of wishing on stars. And Mark hadn't really made a wish, anyway. He'd thought, if I was making a wish, which I'm not because it's hokey and stupid, it would be for some excitement around here.

Something wild, Mark thought – and felt an inner – shiver as he hiked downhill in the gathering darkness.

Jade stared at the steady, brilliant point of light above the southern horizon. It was a planet, she knew. For the last two nights she'd seen it moving across the sky, accompanied by tiny pinpricks of light that must be its moons. Where she came from, nobody was in the habit of wishing on stars, but this planet seemed like a friend – a traveller, just like her. As Jade watched it tonight, she felt a sort of concentration of hope rise inside her. *Almost* a wish.

Jade had to admit that they weren't off to a very promising start. The night air was too quiet; there wasn't the faintest sound of a car coming. She was tired and worried and beginning to be very, very hungry.

Jade turned to look at her sisters.

'Well, where *is* she?'

'I don't know,' Rowan said in her most doggedly gentle voice. 'Be patient.'

'Well, maybe we should scan for her.'

'No,' Rowan said. 'Absolutely not. Remember what we decided.'

'She's probably forgotten we were coming,' Kestrel

said. 'I told you she was getting senile.'

'Don't *say* things like that. It's not *polite*,' Rowan said, still gentle, but through her teeth.

Rowan was always gentle when she could manage it. She was nineteen, tall, slim, and stately. She had cinnamon-brown eyes and warm brown hair that cascaded down her back in waves.

Kestrel was seventeen and had hair the colour of old gold sweeping back from her face like a bird's wings. Her eyes were amber and hawklike, and she was never gentle.

Jade was the youngest, just turned sixteen, and she didn't look like either of her sisters. She had white-blond hair that she used as a veil to hide behind, and green eyes. People said she looked serene, but she almost never felt serene. Usually she was either madly excited or madly anxious and confused.

Right now it was anxious. She was worried about her battered, half-century-old Morocco leather suitcase. She couldn't hear a thing from inside it.

'Hey, why don't you two go down the road a little way and see if she's coming?'

Her sisters looked back at her. There were few things that Rowan and Kestrel agreed on, but Jade was one of them. She could see that they were about to team up against her.

'Now what?' Kestrel said, her teeth showing just briefly.

And Rowan said, 'You're up to something. What are you up to, Jade?'

Jade smoothed her thoughts and her face out and just looked at them artlessly. She hoped.

They stared back for a few minutes, then looked at each other, giving up. 'We're going to have to walk, you know,' Kestrel said to Rowan.

'There are worse things than walking,' Rowan said. She

pushed a stray wisp of chestnut-coloured hair off her forehead and looked around the bus station – which consisted of a three-sided, glass-walled cubicle, and the splintering wooden bench. 'I wish there was a telephone.'

'Well, there isn't. And it's twenty miles to Briar Creek,' Kestrel said, golden eyes glinting with a kind of grim enjoyment. 'We should probably leave our bags here.'

Alarm tingled through Jade. 'No, *no*. I've got all my – all my clothes in there. Come on, twenty miles isn't so far.' With one hand she picked up her cat carrier – it was homemade, just boards and wires – and with the other she picked up the suitcase. She got quite a distance down the road before she heard the crunch of gravel behind her. They were following: Rowan sighing patiently, Kestrel chuckling softly, her hair shining like old gold in the starlight.

The one-lane road was dark and deserted. But not entirely silent – there were dozens of tiny night sounds, all adding up to one intricate, harmonizing night stillness. It would have been pleasant, except that Jade's suitcase seemed to get heavier with every step, and she was hungrier than she had ever been before. She knew better than to mention it to Rowan, but it made her feel confused and weak.

Just when she was beginning to think she would have to put the suitcase down and rest, she heard a new sound.

It was a car, coming from behind them. The engine was so loud that it seemed to take a long time to get close to them, but when it passed, Jade saw that it was actually going very fast. Then there was a rattling of gravel and the car stopped. It backed up and Jade saw a boy looking through the window at her.

There was another boy in the passenger seat. Jade looked at them curiously.

They seemed to be about Rowan's age, and they were both deeply tanned. The one in the driver's seat had blond hair and looked as if he hadn't washed in a while. The other one had brown hair. He was wearing a vest with no shirt underneath. He had a toothpick in his mouth.

They both looked back at Jade, seeming just as curious as she was. Then the driver's window slid down. Jade was fascinated by how quickly it went.

'Need a ride?' the driver said, with an oddly bright smile. His teeth shone in contrast to his dingy face.

Jade looked at Rowan and Kestrel, who were just catching up. Kestrel said nothing, but looked at the car through narrow, heavy-lashed amber eyes. Rowan's brown eyes were very warm.

'We sure would,' she said, smiling. Then, doubtfully, 'But we're going to Burdock Farm. It may be out of your way . . .'

'Oh, hey, I know that place. It's not far,' the one in the vest said around his toothpick. 'Anyway, anything for a lady,' he said, with what seemed to be an attempt at gallantry. He opened his door and got out of the car. 'One of you can sit up front, and I can sit in back with the other two. Lucky me, huh?' he said to the driver.

'Lucky you,' the driver said, smiling largely again. He opened his door, too. 'You go on and put that cat carrier in front, and the suitcases can go in the trunk,' he said.

Rowan smiled at Jade, and Jade knew what she was thinking. *I wonder if everybody out here is so friendly?* They distributed their belongings and then piled in the car, Jade in the front with the driver, Rowan and Kestrel in the back on either side of the vested guy. A minute later they were flying down the road at what Jade found a delightful speed, gravel crunching beneath the tyres.

'I'm Vic,' the driver said.

'I'm Todd,' the vested guy said.

Rowan said, 'I'm Rowan, and this is Kestrel. That's Jade up there.'

'You girls friends?'

'We're sisters,' Jade said.

'You don't look like sisters.'

'Everybody says that.' Jade meant everybody they had met since they'd run away. Back home, everybody *knew* they were sisters, so nobody said it.

'What are you doing out here so late?' Vic asked. 'It's not the place for nice girls.'

'We're not nice girls,' Kestrel explained absently.

'We're *trying* to be,' Rowan said reprovingly through her teeth. To Vic, she said, 'We were waiting for our Great-aunt Opal to pick us up at the bus stop, but she didn't come. We're going to live at Burdock Farm.'

'Old lady Burdock is your aunt?' Todd said, removing his toothpick. 'That crazy old bat?' Vic turned around to look at him, and they both laughed and shook their heads.

Jade looked away from Vic. She stared down at the cat carrier, listening for the little squeaking noises that meant Tiggy was awake.

She felt just slightly . . . uneasy. She sensed something. Even though these guys seemed friendly, there was something beneath the surface. But she was too sleepy – and too light-headed from hunger – to figure out exactly what it was.

They seemed to drive a long time before Vic spoke again.

'You girls ever been to Oregon before?'

Jade blinked and murmured a negative.

'It's got some pretty lonely places,' Vic said. 'Out here, for example. Briar Creek was a gold rush town, but when the gold ran out and the railroad passed it by, it just died.

Now the wilderness is taking it back.'

His tone was significant, but Jade didn't understand what he was trying to convey.

'It does seem peaceful,' Rowan said politely from the backseat.

Vic made a brief snorting sound. 'Yeah, well, peaceful wasn't exactly what I meant. I meant, take this road. These farmhouses are miles apart, right? If you screamed, there wouldn't be anyone to hear you.'

Jade blinked. What a strange thing to say.

Rowan, still politely making conversation, said, 'Well, you and Todd would.'

'I mean, nobody *else*,' Vic said, and Jade could feel his impatience. He had been driving more and more slowly. Now he pulled the car off to the side of the road and stopped. Parked.

'Nobody out *there* is going to hear,' he clarified, turning around to look into the backseat. Jade looked, too, and saw Todd grinning, a wide bright grin with teeth clenched on his toothpick.

'That's right,' Todd said. 'You're out here alone with us, so maybe you'd better listen to us, huh?'

Jade saw that he was gripping Rowan's arm with one hand and Kestrel's wrist with the other.

Rowan was still looking polite and puzzled, but Kestrel looked at the car door on her side thoughtfully. Jade knew what she was looking for – a handle. There wasn't one.

'Too bad,' Vic said. 'This car's a real junkheap; you can't even open the back doors from inside.'

He grabbed Jade's upper arm so hard she could feel pressure on the bone. 'Now, you girls just be nice and nobody's going to get hurt.'

CHAPTER

2

'You see, we're both lonely guys,' Todd said from the back. 'There aren't any girls our age around here, so we're lonely. And then when we come across three nice girls like you – well, we just naturally want to get to know you better. Understand?'

'So if you girls play along, we can all have fun,' Vic put in.

'Fun – oh, no,' Rowan said, dismayed. Jade knew she had caught part of Vic's thought and was trying very hard not to pry further. 'Kestrel and Jade are much too young for anything like that. I'm sorry, but we have to say no.'

'I won't do it even when I *am* old enough,' Jade said. 'But that isn't what these guys mean anyway – they mean this.' She projected some of the images she was getting from Vic into Rowan's mind.

'Oh, dear,' Rowan said flatly. 'Jade, you know we agreed not to spy on people like that.'

Yeah, but look what they're thinking, Jade said soundlessly, figuring that if she had broken one rule, she might as well break them all.

'Now, look,' Vic said in a tone that showed he knew he was losing control of the situation. He reached out and grabbed Jade's other arm, forcing her to face him. 'We're not here to talk. See?' He gave her a little shake. Jade studied his features a moment, then turned her head to look inquiringly into the backseat.

Rowan's face was creamy-pale against her brown hair. Jade could feel that she was sad and disappointed. Kestrel's hair was dim gold and she was frowning.

Well? Kestrel said silently to Rowan.

Well? Jade said the same way. She wriggled as Vic tried to pull her closer. *Come on, Rowan, he's pinching me.*

I guess we don't have any choice, Rowan said.

Immediately Jade turned back to Vic. He was still trying to pull her, looking surprised that she didn't seem to be coming. Jade stopped resisting and let him drag her in close – and then smoothly detached one arm from his grip and slammed her hand upward. The heel of her hand made contact just under his chin. His teeth clicked and his head was knocked backward, exposing his throat.

Jade darted in and bit.

She was feeling guilty and excited. She wasn't used to doing it like this, to taking down prey that was awake and struggling instead of hypnotized and docile. But she knew her instincts were as good as any hunter who'd grown up stalking humans in alleys. It was part of her genetic programming to evaluate anything she saw in terms of 'Is it food? Can I get it? What are its weaknesses?'

The only problem was that she shouldn't be enjoying this feeding, because it was exactly the opposite of what she and Rowan and Kestrel had come to Briar Creek to do.

She was tangentially aware of activity in the backseat. Rowan had lifted the arm Todd had been using to restrain her. On the other side Kestrel had done the same.

Todd was fighting, his voice thunderstruck. 'Hey – hey what are you—'

Rowan bit.

'What are you doing?'

Kestrel bit.

'What the freak are you doing? Who are you? What the freak are you?'

He thrashed wildly for a minute or so, and then subsided as Rowan and Kestrel mentally urged him into a trance.

It was only another minute or so before Rowan said, 'That's enough.'

Jade said, *Aw, Rowan . . .*

'That's *enough*. Tell him not to remember anything about this – and find out if he knows where Burdock Farm is.'

Still feeding, Jade reached out with her mind, touching lightly with a tentacle of thought. Then she pulled back, her mouth closing as if in a kiss as it left Vic's skin. Vic was just a big rag doll at this point, and he flopped bonelessly against the steering wheel and the car door when she let him go.

'The farm's back that way – we have to go back to the fork in the road,' she said. 'It's weird,' she added, puzzled. 'He was thinking that he wouldn't get in trouble for attacking us because – because of something about Aunt Opal. I couldn't get what.'

'Probably that she was crazy,' Kestrel said unemotionally. 'Todd was thinking that he wouldn't get in trouble because his dad's an Elder.'

'They don't have Elders,' Jade said, vaguely smug. 'You mean a governor or a police officer or something.'

Rowan was frowning, not looking at them. 'All right,' she said. 'This was an emergency; we had to do it. But now we're going back to what we agreed.'

'Until the next emergency,' Kestrel said, smiling out the car window into the night.

To forestall Rowan, Jade said, 'You think we should just leave them here?'

'Why not?' Kestrel said carelessly. 'They'll wake up in a few hours.'

Jade looked at Vic's neck. The two little wounds where her teeth had pierced him were already almost closed. By tomorrow they would be faint red marks like old bee stings.

Five minutes later they were on the road again with their suitcases. This time, though, Jade was cheerful. The difference was food – she felt as full of blood as a tick, charged with energy and ready to skip up mountains. She swung the cat carrier and her suitcase alternately, and Tiggy growled.

It was wonderful being out like this, walking alone in the warm night air, with nobody to frown in disapproval. Wonderful to listen to the deer and rabbits and rats feeding in the meadows around her. Happiness bubbled up inside Jade. She'd never felt so free.

'It is nice, isn't it?' Rowan said softly, looking around as they reached the fork in the road. 'It's the real world. And we have as much right to it as anybody else.'

'I think it's the blood,' Kestrel said. 'Free-range humans are so much better than the kept ones. Why didn't our dear brother ever mention that?'

Ash, Jade thought, and felt a cold wind. She glanced behind her, not looking for a car but for something much more silent and deadly. She realized suddenly how fragile her bubble of happiness was.

'Are we going to get caught?' she asked Rowan. Reverting, in the space of one second, to a six-year-old turning to her big sister for help.

And Rowan, the best big sister in the world, said immediately and positively, '*No.*'

'But if Ash figures it out – he's the only one who might realize—'

'We are not going to get caught,' Rowan said. 'Nobody will figure out that we're here.'

Jade felt better. She put down her suitcase and held out a hand to Rowan, who took it. 'Together forever,' she said.

Kestrel, who'd been a few steps ahead, glanced over her shoulder. Then she came back and put her hand on theirs.

'Together forever.'

Rowan said it solemnly; Kestrel said it with a quick narrowing of her yellow eyes. Jade said it with utter determination.

As they walked on, Jade felt buoyant and cheerful again, enjoying the velvet-dark night.

The road was just dirt here, not paved. They passed meadows and stands of Douglas fir. A farmhouse on the left, set back on a long driveway. And finally, dead ahead at the end of the road, another house.

'That's it,' Rowan said. Jade recognized it, too, from the pictures Aunt Opal had sent them. It had two storeys, a wraparound porch, and a steeply pitched roof with lots of gables. A cupola sprouted out of the rooftop, and there was a weather vane on the barn.

A real weather vane, Jade thought, stopping to stare. Her happiness flooded back full force. 'I love it,' she said solemnly.

Rowan and Kestrel had stopped, too, but their expressions were far from awed. Rowan looked a hairsbreadth away from horrified.

'It's a wreck,' she gasped. 'Look at that barn – the paint's completely gone. The pictures didn't show that.'

'And the porch,' Kestrel said helpfully. 'It's falling to pieces. Might go any minute.'

'The work,' Rowan whispered. 'The work it would take to fix this place up . . .'

'And the money,' Kestrel said.

Jade gave them a cold look. 'Why fix it? I like it. It's different.' Rigid with superiority, she picked up her luggage and walked to the end of the road. There was a ramshackle, mostly fallen-down fence around the property, and a dangerous-looking gate. Beyond, on a weed-covered path, was a pile of white pickets – as if somebody had been planning to fix the fence but had never got around to it.

Jade put down the suitcase and cat carrier and pulled at the gate. To her surprise, it moved easily.

'See, it may not look good, but it still works—' She didn't get to finish the sentence properly. The gate fell on her.

'Well, it may not work, but it's still ours,' she said as Rowan and Kestrel pulled it off her.

'No, it's Aunt Opal's,' Kestrel said.

Rowan just smoothed her hair back and said, 'Come on.'

There was a board missing from the porch steps, and several boards gone from the porch itself. Jade limped around them with dignity. The gate had given her a good whack in the shin, and since it was wood, it still hurt. In fact, everything seemed to be made of wood here, which gave Jade a pleasantly alarmed feeling. Back home, wood was revered – and kept out of the way.

You have to be awfully careful to live in this kind of world, Jade thought. Or you're going to get hurt.

Rowan and Kestrel were knocking on the door, Rowan politely, with her knuckles, Kestrel loudly, with the side of her hand. There wasn't any answer.

'She doesn't seem to be here,' Rowan said.

'She's decided she doesn't want us,' Kestrel said, golden eyes gleaming.

'Maybe she went to the wrong bus station,' Jade said.

'Oh – that's it. I bet that's it,' Rowan said. 'Poor old thing, she's waiting for us somewhere, and she's going to be thinking that we didn't show up.'

'Sometimes you're not completely stupid,' Kestrel informed Jade. High praise from Kestrel.

'Well, let's go in,' Jade said, to conceal how pleased she was. 'She'll come back here sometime.'

'Human houses have locks,' Rowan began, but this house wasn't locked. The doorknob turned in Jade's hand. The three of them stepped inside.

It was dark, even darker than the moonless night outside, but Jade's eyes adjusted in a few seconds.

'Hey, it's not bad,' she said. They were in a shabby but handsome living room filled with huge, ponderous furniture. Wood furniture, of course – dark and highly polished. The tables were topped with marble.

Rowan found a light switch, and suddenly the room was too bright. Blinking, Jade saw that the walls were pale apple green, with fancy woodwork and muldings in a darker shade of the same green. It made Jade feel oddly peaceful. And anchored, somehow, as if she belonged here. Maybe it was all the heavy furniture.

She looked at Rowan, who was looking around, tall graceful body slowly relaxing.

Rowan smiled and met her eyes. She nodded, once. 'Yes.'

Jade basked for a moment in the glory of having been right twice in five minutes – and then she remembered her suitcase.

'Let's see what the rest of the place is like,' she said hastily. 'I'll take the upstairs; you guys look around here.'

'You just want the best bedroom,' Kestrel said.

Jade ignored her, hurrying up a wide, carpeted flight of stairs. There were lots of bedrooms, and each one had lots of room. She didn't want the best, though, just the farthest away.

At the very end of the hall was a room painted sea-blue. Jade slammed the door behind her and put her suitcase on the bed. Holding her breath, she opened the suitcase.

Oh. Oh, *no*. Oh, *no* . . .

Three minutes later she heard the click of the door behind her, but didn't care enough to turn.

'What are you *doing*?' Kestrel's voice said.

Jade looked up from her frantic efforts to resuscitate the two kittens she held. 'They're *dead*!' she wailed.

'Well, what did you expect? They need to breathe, idiot. How did you expect them to make it through two days of travelling?'

Jade sniffled.

'Rowan told you that you could take only one.'

Jade sniffled harder and glared. 'I *know*. That's why I put these two in the suitcase.' She hiccuped. 'At least Tiggy's all right.' She dropped to her knees and peered in the cat carrier to make sure he *was* all right. His ears were laid back, his golden eyes gleaming out of a mass of black fur. He hissed, and Jade sat up. He was fine.

'For five dollars I'll take care of the dead ones,' Kestrel said.

'No!' Jade jumped up and moved protectively in front of them, fingers clawed.

'Not like *that*,' Kestrel said, offended. 'I don't eat carrion. Look, if you don't get rid of them somehow, Rowan's going to find out. For God's sake, girl, you're a vampire,' she added as Jade cradled the limp bodies to her chest. 'Act like one.'

'I want to bury them,' Jade said. 'They should have a funeral.'

Kestrel rolled her eyes and left. Jade wrapped the small

corpses in her jacket and tiptoed out after her.

A shovel, she thought. Now, where would that be?

Keeping her ears open for Rowan, she sidled around the first floor. All the rooms looked like the living room: imposing and in a state of genteel decay. The kitchen was huge. It had an open fireplace and a shed off the back door for washing laundry. It also had a door to the cellar.

Jade made her way down the steps cautiously. She couldn't turn on a light because she needed both hands for the kittens. And, because of the kittens, she couldn't see her feet. She had to feel with her toe for the next step.

At the bottom of the stairs her toe found something yielding, slightly resilient. It was blocking her path.

Slowly Jade craned her neck over the bundle of jacket and looked down.

It was dim here. She herself was blocking the light that filtered down from the kitchen. But she could make out what looked like a pile of old clothes. A lumpy pile.

Jade was getting a very, very bad feeling.

She nudged the pile of clothes with one toe. It moved slightly. Jade took a deep breath and nudged it hard.

It was all one piece. It rolled over. Jade looked down, breathed quickly for a moment, and screamed.

A good, shrill, attention-getting scream. She added a non-verbal thought, the telepathic equivalent of a siren.

Rowan! Kestrel! You guys get down here!

Twenty seconds later the cellar light went on and Rowan and Kestrel came clattering down the stairs.

'I have told you and *told* you,' Rowan was saying through her teeth. 'We don't use our—' She stopped, staring.

'I think it's Aunt Opal,' Jade said.

CHAPTER
3

'She's not looking so good,' Kestrel said, peering over Rowan's shoulder.

Rowan said, 'Oh, *dear*,' and sat down.

Great-aunt Opal was a mummy. Her skin was like leather: yellow-brown, hard, and smooth. Almost shiny. And the skin was all there was to her, just a leathery frame stretched over bones. She didn't have any hair. Her eye sockets were dark holes with dry tissue inside. Her nose was collapsed.

'Poor auntie,' Rowan said. Her own brown eyes were wet.

'We're going to look like that when we die,' Kestrel said musingly.

Jade stamped her foot. 'No, *look*, you guys! You're both missing it completely. Look at *that*!' She swung a wild toe at the mummy's midsection. There, protruding from the blue-flowered housedress and the leathery skin, was a gigantic splinter of wood. It was almost as long as an arrow, thick at the base and tapered where it disappeared into Aunt Opal's chest. Flakes of white paint still clung to one side.

Several other pickets were lying on the cellar floor.

'Poor old thing,' Rowan said. 'She must have been carrying them when she fell.'

Jade looked at Kestrel. Kestrel looked back with exasperated golden eyes. There were few things they agreed on, but Rowan was one of them.

'Rowan,' Kestrel said distinctly, 'she was *staked*.'

'Oh, no.'

'Oh, yes,' Jade said. 'Somebody killed her. And somebody who knew she was a vampire.'

Rowan was shaking her head. 'But who would know that?'

'Well . . .' Jade thought. 'Another vampire.'

'Or a vampire *hunter*,' Kestrel said.

Rowan looked up, shocked. 'Those aren't real. They're just stories to frighten kids – aren't they?'

Kestrel shrugged, but her golden eyes were dark.

Jade shifted uneasily. The freedom she'd felt on the road, the peace in the living room – and now *this*. Suddenly she felt empty and isolated.

Rowan sat down on the stairs, looking too tired and preoccupied to push back the lock of hair plastered to her forehead. 'Maybe I shouldn't have brought you here,' she said softly. 'Maybe it's worse here.' She didn't say it, but Jade could sense her next thought. *Maybe we should go back.*

'*Nothing* could be worse,' Jade said fiercely. 'And I'd *die* before I'd go back.' She meant it. Back to waiting on every man in sight? Back to arranged marriages and endless restrictions? Back to all those disapproving faces, so quick to condemn anything different, anything that wasn't done the way it had been done four hundred years ago?

'We *can't* go back,' she said.

'No, we can't,' Kestrel said dryly. 'Literally. Unless we want to end up like Great-aunt Opal. Or—' she paused significantly – 'like Great-uncle Hodge.'

Rowan looked up. 'Don't even say that!'

Jade's stomach felt like a clenched fist. 'They wouldn't,' she said, shoving back at the memory that was trying to emerge. 'Not to their own grandkids. Not to us.'

'The point,' Kestrel said, 'is that we can't go back, so we have to go forward. We've got to figure out what we're going to do here without Aunt Opal to help us – especially if there's a vampire hunter around. But first, what are we going to do with *that*?' She nodded toward the body.

Rowan just shook her head helplessly. She looked around the cellar as if she might find an answer in a corner. Her gaze fell on Jade. It stopped there, and Jade could see the sisterly radar system turn on.

'Jade. What's that in your jacket?'

Jade was too wrung-out to lie. She opened the jacket and showed Rowan the kittens. 'I didn't know my suitcase would kill them.'

Rowan looked too wrung-out to be angry. She glanced heavenward, sighing. Then, looking back at Jade sharply: 'But why were you bringing them down *here*?'

'I wasn't. I was just looking for a shovel. I was going to bury them in the backyard.'

There was a pause. Jade looked at her sisters and they looked at each other. Then all three of them looked at the kittens.

Then they looked at Great-aunt Opal.

Mary-Lynnette was crying.

It was a beautiful night, a perfect night. An inversion layer was keeping the air overhead still and warm, and the seeing was excellent. There was very little light pollution and no direct light. The Victorian farmhouse just below Mary-Lynnette's hill was mostly dark. Mrs Burdock was always very considerate about that.

Above, the Milky Way cut diagonally across the sky like a river. To the south, where Mary-Lynnette had just directed her telescope, was the constellation Sagittarius, which always looked more like a teapot than like an archer to her. And just above the spout of the teapot was a faintly pink patch of what looked like steam.

It wasn't steam. It was clouds of stars. A star factory called the Lagoon Nebula. The dust and gas of dead stars was being recycled into hot young stars, just being born.

It was four thousand and five hundred light-years away. And she was looking at it, right this minute. A seventeen-year-old kid with a second-hand Newtonian reflector telescope was watching the light of stars being born.

Sometimes she was filled with so much awe and – and – and – and *longing* – that she thought she might break to pieces.

Since there was nobody else around, she could let the tears roll down her cheeks without pretending it was an allergy. After a while she had to sit back and wipe her nose and eyes on the shoulder of her T-shirt.

Oh, come on, give it a rest now, she told herself. You're *crazy*, you know.

She wished she hadn't thought of Jeremy earlier. Because now, for some reason, she kept picturing him the way he'd looked that night when he came to watch the eclipse with her. His level brown eyes had held a spark of excitement, as if he really cared about what he was seeing. As if, for that moment, anyway, he understood.

I have been one acquainted with the night, a maudlin little voice inside her chanted romantically, trying to get her to cry again.

Yeah, right, Mary-Lynnette told the voice cynically. She

reached for the bag of Cheetos she kept under her lawn chair. It was impossible to feel romantic and overwhelmed by grandeur while eating Cheetos.

Saturn next, she thought, and wiped sticky orange crumbs off her fingers. It was a good night for Saturn because its rings were just passing through their edgewise position.

She had to hurry because the moon was rising at 11:16. But before she turned her telescope toward Saturn, she took one last look at the Lagoon. Actually just to the east of the Lagoon, trying to make out the open cluster of fainter stars she knew was there.

She couldn't see it. Her eyes just weren't good enough. If she had a bigger telescope – if she lived in Chile where the air was dry – if she could get above the earth's atmosphere . . . then she might have a chance. But for now . . . she was limited by the human eye. Human pupils just didn't open farther than nine millimetres.

Nothing to be done about *that*.

She was just centring Saturn in the field of view when a light went on behind the farmhouse below. Not a little porch light. A barnyard vapour lamp. It illuminated the back property of the house like a searchlight.

Mary-Lynnette sat back, annoyed. It didn't really matter – she could see Saturn anyway, see the rings that tonight were just a delicate silver line cutting across the centre of the planet. But it was strange. Mrs Burdock never turned the back light on at night.

The girls, Mary-Lynnette thought. The nieces. They must have gotten there and she must be giving them a tour. Absently she reached for her binoculars. She was curious.

They were good binoculars, Celestron Ultimas, sleek and lightweight. She used them for looking at everything from deep sky objects to the craters on the moon. Right now, they magnified the back of Mrs Burdock's house ten times.

She didn't see Mrs Burdock, though. She could see the garden. She could see the shed and the fenced-in area where Mrs Burdock kept her goats. And she could see three girls, all well illuminated by the vapour lamp. One had brown hair, one had golden hair, and one had hair the colour of Jupiter's rings. That silvery. Like starlight. They were carrying something wrapped in plastic between them. Black plastic. Hefty garbage bags, if Mary-Lynnette wasn't mistaken.

Now, what on earth were they doing with that?

Burying it.

The short one with the silvery hair had a shovel. She was a good little digger, too. In a few minutes she had rooted up most of Mrs Burdock's irises. Then the medium-sized one with the golden hair took a turn, and last of all the tall one with the brown hair.

Then they picked up the garbage-bagged object – even though it was probably over five feet long, it seemed very light – and put it in the hole they'd just made.

They began to shovel dirt back into the hole.

No, Mary-Lynnette told herself. No, don't be ridiculous. Don't be *insane*. There's some mundane, perfectly commonplace explanation for this.

The problem was, she couldn't think of any.

No, no, no. This is not *Rear Window*, we are not in the Twilight Zone. They're just burying – something. Some sort of . . . ordinary . . .

What else besides a dead body was five-feet-and-some-odd-inches long, rigid, and needed to be wrapped in garbage bags before burial?

And, Mary-Lynnette thought, feeling a rush of

adrenaline that made her heart beat hard. And. *And . . .*

Where was Mrs Burdock?

The adrenalin was tingling painfully in her palms and feet. It made her feel out of control, which she hated. Her hands were shaking so badly she had to lower the binoculars.

Mrs B's OK. She's all right. Things like this don't *happen* in real life.

What would Nancy Drew do?

Suddenly, in the middle of her panic, Mary-Lynnette felt a tiny giggle try to escape like a burp. Nancy Drew, of course, would hike right down there and investigate. She'd eavesdrop on the girls from behind a bush and then dig up the garden once they went back inside the house.

But things like that *didn't* happen. Mary-Lynnette couldn't even imagine trying to dig up a neighbour's garden in the dead of night. She would get caught and it would be a humiliating farce. Mrs Burdock would walk out of the house alive and alarmed, and Mary-Lynnette would *die* of embarrassment trying to explain.

In a book that might be amusing. In real life – she didn't even want to think about it.

One good thing, it made her realize how absurd her paranoia was. Deep down, she obviously knew Mrs B. was just fine. Otherwise, she wouldn't be sitting here; she'd be calling the police, like any sensible person.

Somehow, though, she suddenly felt tired. Not up to more starwatching. She checked her watch by the ruby glow of a red-filtered flashlight. Almost eleven – well, it was all over in sixteen minutes anyway. When the moon rose it would bleach out the sky.

But before she broke down her telescope for the trip back, she picked up the binoculars again. Just one last look.

The garden was empty. A rectangle of fresh dark soil showed where it had been violated. Even as Mary-Lynnette watched, the vapour lamp went out.

It wouldn't do any harm to go over there tomorrow, Mary-Lynnette thought. Actually, I was going to, anyway. I should welcome those girls to the neighbourhood. I should return those pruning shears Dad borrowed and the knife Mrs B gave me to get my gas cap off. And of course I'll see Mrs B there, and then I'll know everything's OK.

Ash reached the top of the winding road and stopped to admire the blazing point of light in the south. You really could see more from these isolated country towns. From here Jupiter, the king of the planets, looked like a UFO.

'Where have you been?' a voice nearby said. 'I've been waiting for you for hours.'

Ash answered without turning around. 'Where have *I* been? Where have *you* been? We were supposed to meet on *that* hill, Quinn.' Hands in his pockets, he pointed with an elbow.

'Wrong. It was this hill and I've been sitting right here waiting for you the entire time. But forget it. Are they here or aren't they?'

Ash turned and walked unhurriedly to the open convertible that was parked just beside the road, its lights off. He leaned one elbow on the door, looking down. 'They're here. I told you they would be. It was the only place for them to go.'

'All three of them?'

'Of course, all three of them. My sisters always stick together.'

Quinn's lip curled. 'Lamia are so wonderfully family oriented.'

'And made vampires are so wonderfully . . . short,' Ash

said serenely, looking at the sky again.

Quinn gave him a look like black ice. His small, compact body was utterly still inside the car. 'Well, now, I never got to finish growing, did I?' he said very softly. 'One of your ancestors took care of that.'

Ash boosted himself to sit on the hood of the car, long legs dangling. 'I think I may stop aging this year myself,' he said blandly, still looking down the slope. 'Eighteen's not such a bad age.'

'Maybe not if you have a choice,' Quinn said, his voice still as soft as dead leaves falling. 'Try being eighteen for four centuries – with no end in sight.'

Ash turned to smile at him again. 'Sorry. On my family's behalf.'

'And I'm sorry for your family. The Redferns have been having a little trouble lately, haven't they? Let's see if I've got it right. First your Uncle Hodge breaks Night World law and is appropriately punished—'

'My great-uncle by marriage,' Ash interrupted in polite tones, holding one finger up. 'He was a Burdock, not a Redfern. And that was over ten years ago.'

'And then your Aunt Opal—'

'My *Great*-aunt Opal—'

'Disappears completely. Breaks off all contact with the Night World. Apparently because she prefers living in the middle of nowhere with humans.'

Ash shrugged, eyes fixed on the southern horizon. 'It must be good hunting in the middle of nowhere with humans. No competition. And no Night World enforcement – no Elders putting a limit on how many you can bag.'

'And no supervision,' Quinn said sourly. 'It doesn't matter so much that *she's* been living here, but she's obviously been encouraging your sisters to join her. You should have informed on them when you found out they were writing to each other secretly.'

Ash shrugged, uncomfortable. 'It wasn't against the law. I didn't know what they had in mind.'

'It's not just them,' Quinn said in his disturbingly soft voice. 'You know there are rumours about that cousin of yours – James Rasmussen. People are saying that he fell in love with a human girl. That she was dying and he decided to change her without permission . . .'

Ash slid off the hood and straightened. 'I never listen to rumours,' he said, briskly and untruthfully. 'Besides, that's not the problem right now, is it?'

'No. The problem is your sisters and the mess they're in. And whether you can really do what's necessary to clean it up.'

'Don't worry, Quinn. I can handle it.'

'But I *do* worry, Ash. I don't know how I let you talk me into this.'

'You didn't. You lost that game of poker.'

'And you cheated.' Quinn was looking off into a middle distance, his dark eyes narrowed, his mouth a straight line. 'I still think we should tell the Elders,' he said abruptly. 'It's the only way to guarantee a really *thorough* investigation.'

'I don't see why it needs to be so thorough. They've only been here a few hours.'

'Your sisters have only been here a few hours. Your aunt has been here – how long? Ten years?'

'What have you got against my aunt, Quinn?'

'Her husband was a traitor. *She's* a traitor now for encouraging those girls to run away. And who knows what she's been doing here in the last ten years? Who knows how many humans she's told about the Night World?'

Ash shrugged, examining his nails. 'Maybe she hasn't told any.'

'And maybe she's told the whole town.'

'Quinn,' Ash said patiently, speaking as if to a very young child, 'if my aunt has broken the laws of the Night World, she has to die. For the family honour. Any blotch on that reflects on *me*.'

'That's one thing I can count on,' Quinn said half under his breath. 'Your self-interest. You always look after Number One, don't you?'

'Doesn't everybody?'

'Not everybody is quite so blatant about it.' There was a pause, then Quinn said, 'And what about your sisters?'

'What about them?'

'Can you kill them if it's necessary?'

Ash didn't blink. 'Of course. If it's necessary. For the family honour.'

'If they've let something slip about the Night World—'

'They're not stupid.'

'They're innocent. They might get tricked. That's what happens when you live on an island completely isolated from normal humans. You never learn how cunning vermin can be.'

'Well, *we* know how cunning they can be,' Ash said, smiling. 'And what to do about them.'

For the first time Quinn himself smiled, a charming, almost dreamy smile. 'Yes, I know your views on that. All right. I'll leave you here to take care of it. I don't need to tell you to check out every human those girls have had contact with. Do a good job and maybe you can save your family honour.'

'Not to mention the embarrassment of a public trial.'

'I'll come back in a week. And if you haven't got things under control, I go to the Elders. I don't mean your

Redfern family Elders, either. I'm taking it all the way up to the joint Council.'

'Oh, fine,' Ash said. 'You know, you really ought to get a hobby, Quinn. Go hunting yourself. You're too repressed.'

Quinn ignored that and said shortly, 'Do you know where to start?'

'Sure. The girls are right ... down ... there.' Ash turned east. With one eye shut, he zeroed in with his finger on a patch of light in the valley below. 'At Burdock Farm. I'll check things out in town, then I'll go look up the nearest vermin.'

CHAPTER
4

What a difference a day made.

Somehow, in the hot, hazy August sunlight the next morning, Mary-Lynnette couldn't get serious about checking on whether Mrs Burdock was dead. It was just too ridiculous. Besides, she had a lot to do – school started in just over two weeks. At the beginning of June she had been sure summer would last forever, sure that she would *never* say, 'Wow, this summer has gone by so fast.' And now here she stood in mid-August, and she was saying, 'Wow, it's gone by so fast.'

I need clothes, Mary-Lynnette thought. And a new backpack, and notebooks, and some of those little purple felt-tip pens. And I need to make Mark get all those things, too, because he won't do it by himself and Claudine will never make him.

Claudine was their stepmother. She was Belgian and very pretty, with curly dark hair and sparkling dark eyes. She was only ten years older than Mary-Lynnette, and she looked even younger. She'd been the family's housecleaning helper when Mary-Lynnette's mom first got sick five years ago. Mary-Lynnette liked her, but she was hopeless as a substitute mother, and Mary-Lynnette usually ended up taking charge of Mark.

So I don't have time to go over to Mrs B's.

She spent the day shopping. It wasn't until after dinner that she thought about Mrs Burdock again.

She was helping to clear dishes out of the family room, where dinner was traditionally eaten in front of the TV, when her father said, 'I heard something today about Todd Akers and Vic Kimble.'

'Those losers,' Mark muttered.

Mary-Lynnette said, 'What?'

'They had some kind of accident over on Chiloquin Road – over between Hazel Green Creek and Beavercreek.'

'A car accident?' Mary-Lynnette said.

'Well, this is the thing,' her father said. 'Apparently there wasn't any damage to their car, but they both *thought* they'd been in an accident. They showed up at home after midnight and said that something had happened to them out there – but they didn't know what. They were missing a few hours.' He looked at Mark and Mary-Lynnette. 'How about that, guys?'

'It's the UFOs!' Mark shouted immediately, dropping into discus-throwing position and wiggling his plate.

'UFOs are a crock,' Mary-Lynnette said. 'Do you know how far the little green men would have to travel – and there's no such *thing* as warp speed. Why do people have to make things up when the universe is just – just *blazing* with incredible things that are *real*—' She stopped. Her family was looking at her oddly.

'Actually Todd and Vic probably just got smashed,' she said, and put her plate and glass in the sink. Her father grimaced slightly. Claudine pursed her lips. Mark grinned.

'In a very real and literal sense,' he said. 'We hope.'

It was as Mary-Lynnette was walking back to the family room that a thought struck her.

Chiloquin Road was right off Kahneta, the road her own house was on. The road Mrs B's house was on. It was only two miles from Burdock Farm to Chiloquin.

There couldn't be any connection. Unless the girls were burying the little green man who'd abducted Vic and Todd.

But it bothered her. Two really strange things happening in the same night, in the same area. In a tiny, sleepy area that never saw any kind of excitement.

I know, I'll call Mrs B. And she'll be fine, and that'll prove everything's OK, and I'll be able to laugh about all this.

But nobody answered at the Burdock house. The phone rang and rang. Nobody picked it up and the answering machine never came on. Mary-Lynnette hung up feeling grim but oddly calm. She knew what she had to do now.

She snagged Mark as he was going up the stairs.

'I need to talk to you.'

'Look, if this is about your iPod—'

'Huh? It's about something we have to do tonight.' Mary-Lynnette looked at him. 'What about my iPod?'

'Uh, nothing. Nothing at all.'

Mary-Lynnette groaned but let it go. 'Listen, I need you to help me out. Last night I saw something weird when I was on the hill . . .' She explained as succinctly as possible. 'And now more weird stuff with Todd and Vic,' she said.

Mark was shaking his head, looking at her in something like pity. 'Mare, Mare,' he said kindly. 'You really are crazy, you know.'

'Yes,' Mary-Lynnette said. 'It doesn't matter. I'm still going over there tonight.'

'To do *what*?'

'To check things out. I just want to *see* Mrs B. If I can

talk to her, I'll feel better. And if I can find out what's buried in that garden, I'll feel a whole *lot* better.'

'Maybe they were burying Sasquatch. That government study in the Klamaths never did find him, you know.'

'Mark, you owe me for the Walkman. For whatever happened to the Walkman.'

'Uh . . .' Mark sighed, then muttered resignedly. 'OK, I owe you. But I'm telling you right now, I'm not going to talk to those girls.'

'You don't have to talk to them. You don't even have to see them. There's something else I want you to do.'

The sun was just setting. They'd walked this road a hundred times to get to Mary-Lynnette's hill – the only difference tonight was that Mark was carrying a pair of pruning shears and Mary-Lynnette had pulled the Rubylith filter off her flashlight.

'You don't *really* think they offed the old lady.'

'No,' Mary-Lynnette said candidly. 'I just want to put the world back where it belongs.'

'You want *what*?'

'You know how you have a view of the way the world is, but every so often you wonder, "Oh, my God, what if it's really *different*?" Like, "What if I'm really adopted and the people I think are my parents aren't my parents at all?" And if it were true, it would change everything, and for a minute you don't know what's real. Well, that's how I feel right now, and I want to get rid of it. I want my old world back.'

'You know what's scary?' Mark said. 'I think I understand.'

By the time they got to Burdock Farm, it was full dark. Ahead of them, in the west, the star Arcturus seemed to hang over the farmhouse, glittering faintly red.

Mary-Lynnette didn't bother trying to deal with the rickety gate. She went to the place behind the blackberry bushes where the picket fence had fallen flat.

The farmhouse was like her own family's, but with lots of Victorian-style gingerbread added. Mary-Lynnette thought the spindles and scallops and fret-work gave it a whimsical air – eccentric, like Mrs Burdock. Just now, as she was looking at one of the second-storey windows, the shadow of a moving figure fell on the roller blind.

Good, Mary-Lynnette thought. At least I know somebody's home.

Mark began hanging back as they walked down the weedy path to the house.

'You said I could hide.'

'OK. Right. Look, why don't you take those shears and sort of go around back—'

'And look at the Sasquatch grave while I'm there? Maybe do a little digging? I don't *think* so.'

'Fine,' Mary-Lynnette said calmly. 'Then hide somewhere out here and hope they don't see you when they come to the door. At least with the shears you have an excuse to be in the back.'

Mark threw her a bitter glance and she knew she'd won. As he started off, Mary-Lynnette said suddenly, 'Mark, be careful.'

Mark just waved a dismissive hand at her without turning around.

When he was out of sight, Mary-Lynnette knocked on the front door. Then she rang the doorbell – it wasn't a button but an actual bellpull. She could hear chimes inside, but nobody answered.

She knocked and rang with greater authority. Every minute she kept expecting the door to open to reveal Mrs

B, petite, gravelly-voiced, blue-haired, dressed in an old cotton housedress. But it didn't happen. Nobody came.

Mary-Lynnette stopped being polite and began knocking with one hand and ringing with the other. It was somewhere in the middle of this frenzy of knocks and rings that she realized she was frightened. Really frightened. Her world view was wobbling. Mrs Burdock hardly ever left the house. She always answered the door. And Mary-Lynnette had seen with her own eyes that *somebody* was home here.

So why weren't they answering?

Mary-Lynnette's heart was beating very hard. She had an uncomfortable falling sensation in her stomach.

I should get out of here and call Sheriff Akers. It's his *job* to know what to do about things like this. But it was hard to work up any feeling of confidence in Todd's father. She took her alarm and frustration out on the door.

Which opened. Suddenly. Mary-Lynnette's fist hit air and for an instant she felt sheer panic, fear of the unknown.

'What can I do for you?'

The voice was soft and beautifully modulated. The girl was just plain beautiful. What Mary-Lynnette hadn't been able to see from the top of her hill was that the brown hair was aglow with rich chestnut highlights, the features were classically moulded, the tall figure was graceful and willowy.

'You're Rowan,' she said.

'How did you know?'

You couldn't be anything else; I've never seen anybody who looked so much like a tree spirit. 'Your aunt told me about you. I'm Mary-Lynnette Carter; I live just up Kahneta Road. You probably saw my house on your way here.'

Rowan looked noncommittal. She had such a sweet, grave face – and skin that looked like white orchid petals, Mary-Lynnette thought abstractedly. She said, 'So, I just wanted to welcome you to the neighbourhood, say hello, see if there's anything you need.'

Rowan looked less grave; she almost smiled and her brown eyes grew warm. 'How nice of you. Really. I almost wish we did need something . . . but actually we're fine.'

Mary-Lynnette realized that, with the utmost civility and good manners, Rowan was winding up the conversation. Hastily she threw a new subject into the pool. 'There are three of you girls, right? Are you going to school here?'

'My sisters are.'

'That's great. I can help show them around. I'll be a senior this year.' Another subject, quick, Mary-Lynnette thought. 'So, how do you like Briar Creek? It's probably quieter than you're used to.'

'Oh, it was pretty quiet where we came from,' Rowan said. 'But we love it here; it's such a wonderful place. The trees, the little animals . . .' She broke off.

'Yeah, those cute little animals,' Mary-Lynnette said. Get to the *point*, her inner voices were telling her. Her tongue and the roof of her mouth felt like Velcro. Finally she blurted, 'So – so, um, how is your aunt right now?'

'She's – fine.'

That instant's hesitation was all Mary-Lynnette needed. Her old suspicions, her old panic, surged up immediately. Making her feel bright and cold, like a knife made of ice.

She found herself saying in a confident, almost chirpy voice, 'Well, could I just talk to her for a minute? Would you mind? It's just that I have something sort of important to tell her . . .' She made a move as if to step over the threshold.

Rowan kept on blocking the door. 'Oh, I'm so sorry. But – well, that's not really possible right now.'

'Oh, is it one of her headaches? I've seen her in bed before.' Mary-Lynnette gave a little tinkly laugh.

'No, it's not a headache.' Rowan spoke gently, deliberately. 'The truth is that she's gone for a few days.'

'*Gone?*'

'I know.' Rowan made a little grimace acknowledging that this was odd. 'She just decided to take a few days off. A little vacation.'

'But – gosh, with you girls just getting here . . .' Mary-Lynnette's voice was brittle.

'Well, you see, she knew we'd take care of the house for her. That's why she waited until we came.'

'But – gosh,' Mary-Lynnette said again. She felt a spasm in her throat. 'Where – just where did she go?'

'Up north, somewhere on the coast. I'm not sure of the name of the town.'

'But . . .' Mary-Lynnette's voice trailed off. Back off, her inner voices warned. *Now* was the time to be polite, to be cautious. Pushing it meant showing this girl that Mary-Lynnette knew something was wrong with this story. And since something *was* wrong, this girl might be dangerous . . .

It was hard to believe that while looking at Rowan's sweet, grave face. She didn't *look* dangerous. But then Mary-Lynnette noticed something else. Rowan was barefoot. Her feet were as creamy-pale as the rest of her, but sinewy. Something about them, the way they were placed or the clean definition of the toes, made Mary-Lynnette think of those feet running. Of savage, primal speed.

When she looked up, there was another girl walking up behind Rowan. The one with dark golden hair. Her skin was milky instead of blossomy, and her eyes were yellow.

'This is Kestrel,' Rowan said.

'Yes,' Mary-Lynnette said. She realized she was staring. And realized, the moment after that, that she was scared. *Everything* about Kestrel made her think of savage, primal movement. The girl walked as if she were flying.

'What's going on?' Kestrel said.

'This is Mary-Lynnette,' Rowan said, her voice still pleasant. 'She lives down the road. She came to see Aunt Opal.'

'Really just to see if you needed anything,' Mary-Lynnette interjected quickly. 'We're sort of your only neighbours.' Strategy change, she was thinking. About-face. Looking at Kestrel, she believed in danger. Now all she wanted was to keep these girls from guessing what she knew.

'You're a friend of Aunt Opal's?' Kestrel asked silkily. Her yellow eyes swept Mary-Lynnette, first up, then down.

'Yeah, I come over sometimes, help her with the' – oh, God, don't say gardening – 'goats. Um, I guess she told you that they need to be milked every twelve hours.'

Rowan's expression changed fractionally. Mary-Lynnette's heart gave a violent thud. Mrs B would never, *ever* leave without giving instructions about the goats.

'Of course she told us,' Rowan said smoothly, just an instant too late.

Mary-Lynnette's palms were sweating. Kestrel hadn't taken that keen, dispassionate, unblinking gaze off her for a moment. Like the proverbial bird of prey staring down the proverbial rabbit. 'Well, it's getting late and I bet you guys have things to do. I should let you go.'

Rowan and Kestrel looked at each other. Then they both looked at Mary-Lynnette, cinnamon-brown eyes and golden eyes fixed intently on her face. Mary-Lynnette had the falling feeling in her stomach again.

'Oh, don't go yet,' Kestrel said silkily. 'Why don't you come inside?'

CHAPTER

5

Mark was still muttering as he rounded the back corner of the house. What was he even *doing* here?

It wasn't easy to get into the garden area from outside. He had to bushwhack through the overgrown rhododendron bushes and blackberry canes that formed a dense hedge all around it. And even when he emerged from a tunnel of leathery green leaves, the scene in front of him didn't immediately register. His momentum kept him going for a few steps before his brain caught up.

Hey, wait. There's a *girl* here.

A pretty girl. An *extremely* pretty girl. He could see her clearly by the back porch light. She had hip-length white-blond hair, the colour that normally only preschoolers have, and it was as fine as a child's hair, too, whipping around her like pale silk when she moved. She was smallish. Little bones. Her hands and feet were delicate.

She was wearing what looked like an old-fashioned nightshirt and dancing to what sounded like a rent-to-own commercial. There was a battered clock radio on the porch steps. There was also a black kitten that took one look at Mark and darted away into the shadows.

'*Baaad* cred-it, *nooo* cred-it, *doon't* wor-ry, *weee'll* take you . . .' the radio warbled. The girl danced with her arms above her head – light as thistledown, Mark thought, staring in astonishment. Really, actually that light, and so what if it was a cliché?

As the commercial ended and a country western song began, she did a twirl and saw him. She stopped, frozen, arms still above her head, wrists crossed. Her eyes got big and her mouth sagged open.

She's scared, Mark thought. Of me. The girl didn't look graceful now; she was scrambling to seize the clock radio, fumbling with it, shaking it. Trying to find an off switch, Mark realized. Her desperation was contagious. Before he thought, Mark dropped the pruning shears and swooped in to grab the radio from her. He twisted the top dial, cutting the song short. Then he stared at the girl, who stared back with wide silvery-green eyes. They were both breathing quickly, as if they'd just disarmed a bomb.

'Hey, I hate country western, too,' Mark said after a minute, shrugging.

He'd never talked to a girl this way before. But then he'd never had a girl look scared of him before. And *so* scared – he imagined he could see her heart beating in the pale blue veins beneath the translucent skin of her throat.

Then, suddenly, she stopped looking terrified. She bit her lip and chortled. Then, still grinning, she blinked and sniffed.

'I forgot,' she said, dabbing at the corner of her eye. 'You don't have the same rules we do.'

'Rules about country western music?' Mark hazarded. He liked her voice. It was ordinary, not celestial. It made her seem more human.

'Rules about *any* music from outside,' she said. 'And any TV, too.'

Outside what? Mark thought. He said, 'Uh, hi. I'm Mark Carter.'

'I'm Jade Redfern.'

'You're one of Mrs Burdock's nieces.'

'Yes. We just came last night. We're going to live here.'

Mark snorted and muttered, 'You have my condolences.'

'Condolences? Why?' Jade cast a darting glance around the garden.

'Because living in Briar Creek is just slightly more exciting than living in a cemetery.'

She gave him a long, fascinated look. 'You've . . . lived in a cemetery?'

He gave *her* a long look. 'Uh, actually, I just meant it's boring here.'

'Oh.' She thought, then smiled. 'Well, it's interesting to us,' she said. 'It's different from where we come from.'

'And just where *do* you come from?'

'An island. It's sort of near . . .' She considered. 'The State of Maine.'

' "The State of Maine." '

'Yeah.'

'Does this island have a name?'

She stared at him with wide green eyes. 'Well, I can't tell you *that*.'

'Uh – OK.' Was she making fun of him? But there was nothing like mockery or sly teasing in her face. She looked mysterious . . . and innocent. Maybe she had some kind of mental problem. The kids at Dewitt High School would have a field day with that. They weren't very tolerant of differences.

'Look,' he said abruptly. 'If there's ever anything I can do for you – you know, if you ever get in trouble or something – then just tell me. OK?'

She tilted her head sideways. Her eyelashes actually

cast shadows in the porch light, but her expression wasn't coy. It was straightforward and assessing, and she was looking him over carefully; as if she needed to figure him out. She took her time doing it. Then she smiled, making little dimples in her cheeks, and Mark's heart jumped unexpectedly.

'OK,' she said softly. 'Mark. You're not silly, even though you're a boy. You're a good guy, aren't you?'

'Well . . .' Mark had never been called upon to be a good guy, not in the TV sense. He wasn't sure how he'd measure up if he were. 'I, um, hope I am.'

Jade was looking at him steadily. 'You know, I just decided. I'm going to like it here.' She smiled again, and Mark found it hard to breathe – and then her expression changed.

Mark heard it, too. A wild crashing in the overgrown tangle of rhododendrons and blackberry bushes at the back of the garden. It was a weird, frenzied sound, but Jade's reaction was out of all proportion. She had frozen, body tense and trembling, eyes fixed on the underbrush. She looked terrified.

'Hey.' Mark spoke gently, then touched her shoulder. 'Hey. It's all right. It's probably one of the goats that got loose; goats can jump over any kind of fence.' She was shaking her head. 'Or a deer. When they're relaxed they sound just like people walking.'

'It's not a deer,' she hissed.

'They come down and eat people's gardens at night. You probably don't have deer roaming around where you come from—'

'I can't *smell* anything,' she said in a kind of whispered wail. 'It's that stupid pen. Everything smells like *goat*.'

She couldn't smell . . . ? Mark did the only thing he could think of in response to a statement like that.

He put his arms around the girl.

'Everything's OK,' he said softly. He couldn't help but notice that she was cool and warm at the same time, supple, wonderfully alive underneath the nightshirt. 'Why don't I take you inside now? You'll be safe there.'

'Leggo,' Jade said ungratefully, squirming. 'I may have to fight.' She wriggled out of his arms and faced the bushes again. 'Stay behind me.'

OK, so she *is* crazy. I don't care. I think I love her.

He stood beside her. 'Look, I'll fight, too. What do you think it is? Bear, coyote . . . ?'

'My brother.'

'Your . . .' Dismay pooled in Mark. She'd just stepped over the line of acceptable craziness. 'Oh.'

Another thrashing sound from the bushes. It was definitely something big, not a goat. Mark was just wondering vaguely if a Roosevelt elk could have wandered down the hundred or so miles from Waldo Lake, when a scream ripped through the air.

A human scream – or, worse, *almost* human. As it died, there was a wail that was definitely inhuman – it started out faint, and then suddenly sounded shrill and close. Mark was stunned. When the drawn-out wail finally stopped, there was a sobbing, moaning sound, then silence.

Mark got his breath and swore. 'What in the – what *was* that?'

'Shh. Keep still.' Jade was in a half-crouch, eyes on the bushes.

'Jade – Jade, listen. We've got to get inside.' Desperate, he looped an arm around her waist, trying to pick her up. She was light, but she flowed like water out of his arms. Like a cat that doesn't want to be petted. 'Jade, whatever that thing is, we need a *gun*.'

'I don't.' She seemed to be speaking through her teeth – anyway there was something odd about her diction. She had her back to him and he couldn't see her face, but her hands were clawed.

'*Jade*,' Mark said urgently. He was scared enough to run, but he couldn't leave her. He *couldn't*. No good guy would do that.

Too late. The blackberry bushes to the south quivered. Parted. Something was coming through.

Mark's heart seemed to freeze solid, but then he found himself moving. Pushing Jade roughly aside. Standing in front of her to face whatever the thing in the dark was.

Mary-Lynnette kicked her way through the blackberry canes. Her arms and legs were scratched, and she could feel ripe, bright-black berries squishing against her. She'd probably picked a bad place to get through the hedge, but she hadn't been thinking about that. She'd been thinking about Mark, about finding him as fast as possible and getting away from here.

Just please let him be here, she thought. Let him be here and be OK and I'll never ask for anything else.

She struggled through the last of the canes into the backyard – and then things happened very fast. The first thing she saw was Mark, and she felt a rush of relief. Then a flash of surprise. Mark was standing in front of a girl, his arms lifted like a basketball guard. As if to protect her from Mary-Lynnette.

And then, so quickly that Mary-Lynnette could barely follow the motion, the girl was rushing at her. And Mary-Lynnette was throwing her arms up and Mark was shouting, 'No, that's my sister!'

The girl stopped a foot away from Mary-Lynnette. It was the little silvery-haired one, of course. This close

Mary-Lynnette could see that she had green eyes and skin so translucent it almost looked like quartz crystal.

'Jade, it's my sister,' Mark said again, as if anxious to get this established. 'Her name's Mary-Lynnette. She won't hurt you. Mare, tell her you won't hurt her.'

Hurt her? Mary-Lynnette didn't know what he was talking about, and didn't want to. This girl was as weirdly beautiful as the others, and something about her eyes – they weren't ordinary green, but almost silvery – made Mary-Lynnette's skin rise in goose pimples.

'Hello,' Jade said.

'Hello. OK, Mark, c'mon. We've got to go. Like right now.'

She expected him to agree immediately. He was the one who hadn't wanted to come, and now here he was with his most dreaded phobia, a girl. But instead he said, 'Did you hear that yelling? Could you tell where it came from?'

'What yelling? I was inside. Come on.' Mary-Lynnette took Mark's arm, but since he was as strong as she was, it didn't do any good. 'Maybe I heard something. I wasn't paying attention.' She'd been looking desperately around the Victorian living room, babbling out lies about how her family knew where she'd gone tonight and expected her back soon. How her father and stepmother were such good friends of Mrs Burdock's and how they were just waiting at home to hear about Mrs B.'s nieces. She still wasn't sure if that was why they'd let her go. But for some reason, Rowan had finally stood up, given Mary-Lynnette a grave, sweet smile, and opened the front door.

'You know, I bet it was a wolverine,' Mark was saying to Jade excitedly. 'A wolverine that came down from Willamette Forest.'

Jade was frowning. 'A wolverine?' She considered.

'Yeah, I guess that could have been it. I've never heard one before.' She looked at Mary-Lynnette. 'Is that what you think it was?'

'Oh, sure,' Mary-Lynnette said at random. 'Definitely a wolverine.' *I should ask where her aunt is*, she thought suddenly. *It's the perfect opportunity to catch her in a lie. I'll ask and then she'll say something – anything, but not that her aunt's gone up north for a little vacation on the coast. And then I'll* know.

She didn't do it. She simply didn't have the courage. She didn't want to catch anyone in a lie anymore; she just wanted to get out.

'Mark, please . . .'

He looked at her and for the first time seemed to see how upset she was. 'Uh – OK,' he said. And to Jade: 'Look, why don't you go back inside now? You'll be safe there. And maybe – maybe I could come over again sometime?'

Mary-Lynnette was still tugging at him, and now, to her relief, he began to move. Mary-Lynnette headed for the blackberry bushes that she'd trampled coming in.

'Why don't you go through there? It's like a path,' Jade said, pointing. Mark immediately swerved, taking Mary-Lynnette with him, and she saw a comfortable gap between two rhododendron bushes at the back of the garden. She would never have seen it unless she knew what to look for.

As they reached the hedge, Mark turned to glance behind him. Mary-Lynnette turned, too.

From here, Jade was just a dark silhouette against the porch light – but her hair, lit from behind, looked like a silver halo. It shimmered around her. Mary-Lynnette heard Mark draw in his breath.

'You both come back sometime,' Jade said cordially.

'Help us milk the goats like Aunt Opal said. She gave us *very* strict orders before she went on vacation.'

Mary-Lynnette was dumbfounded.

She turned back and reeled through the gap, her head spinning. When they got to the road, she said, 'Mark, what happened when you got into the garden?'

Mark was looking preoccupied. 'What do you mean what happened? Nothing happened.'

'Did you look at the place that was dug up?'

'No,' Mark said shortly. 'Jade was in the garden when I got there. I didn't get a chance to look at anything.'

'Mark . . . was she there the whole time? Jade? Did she ever go in the house? Or did either of the other girls ever come out?'

Mark grunted. 'I don't even know what the other girls look like. The only one I saw was Jade, and she was there the whole time.' He looked at her darkly. 'You're not still on this *Rear Window* thing, are you?'

Mary-Lynnette didn't answer. She was trying to gather her scattered thoughts.

I don't believe it. But she *said* it. Orders about the goats. Before her aunt went on vacation.

But Rowan didn't know about the goats before I told her. I'd *swear* she didn't know. And I was so sure she was winging it with the vacation business . . .

OK, maybe I was wrong. But that doesn't mean Rowan was telling the truth. Maybe they *did* figure the story out before tonight, and Rowan's just a lousy actress. Or maybe . . .

'Mark, this is going to sound crazy . . . but Jade didn't have, like, a cellular phone or anything, did she?'

Mark stopped dead and gave Mary-Lynnette a long, slow look that said more clearly than words what he thought of this. 'Mary-Lynnette, what's *wrong* with you?'

'Rowan and Kestrel told me that Mrs B. is on vacation. That she suddenly *decided* to take a vacation just when they arrived in town.'

'So? Jade said the same thing.'

'Mark, Mrs B. has lived there for ten years, and she's *never* taken a vacation. Never. How could she take one starting the same day her nieces come to live with her?'

'Maybe because they can house-sit for her,' Mark said with devastating logic.

It was exactly what Rowan had said. Mary-Lynnette had a sudden feeling of paranoia, like someone who realizes that everyone around her is a pod person, all in on the conspiracy. She had been about to tell him about the goats, but now she didn't want to.

Oh, get a *grip* on yourself, girl. Even Mark is being logical. The least you can do is think about this rationally before you run to Sheriff Akers.

The fact is, Mary-Lynnette told herself, brutally honest, that you panicked. You got a *feeling* about those girls for some reason, and then you forgot logic completely. You didn't get any kind of hard evidence. You ran away.

She could hardly go to the sheriff and say that she was suspicious because Rowan had creepy feet.

There's no evidence at all. Nothing except . . .

She groaned inwardly.

'It all comes down to what's in the garden,' she said out loud.

Mark, who had been walking beside her in frowning silence, now stopped. 'What?'

'It all comes back to that again,' Mary-Lynnette said, her eyes shut. 'I should have just looked at that dug-up place when I had the chance, even if Jade saw me. It's the only real evidence there is . . . so I've got to see what's there.'

Mark was shaking his head. 'Now, look—'

'I have to go back. Not tonight. I'm dead tired. But tomorrow. Mark, I *have* to check it out before I go to Sheriff Akers.'

Mark exploded.

'Before you *what*?' he shouted, loud enough to raise echoes. 'What are you *talking* about, going to the sheriff?'

Mary-Lynnette stared. She hadn't realized how different Mark's point of view was from hers. Why, she thought, why he's . . .

'You wanted to check out where Mrs B was – so we checked where Mrs B was,' Mark said. 'They *told* us where. And you *saw* Jade. I know she's a little different – it's like you said about Mrs B; she's eccentric. But did she look like the kind of person who could hurt somebody? Well, *did* she?'

Why, he's in love with her, Mary-Lynnette thought. Or at least seriously in like. Mark likes a girl.

Now she was *really* confused.

This could be so good for him – if only the girl weren't crazy. Well, maybe even if the girl was crazy – if it wasn't a homicidal craziness. Either way, Mary-Lynnette couldn't call the police on Mark's new girlfriend unless she had some evidence.

I wonder if she likes him, too? she thought. They certainly seemed to be protecting each other when I walked in.

'No, you're right,' she said aloud, glad that she'd had practice lying tonight. 'She doesn't look like the kind of person who could hurt somebody. I'll just let it drop.'

With you. And tomorrow night when you think I'm star-watching, I'll sneak over there. This time bringing my own shovel. And maybe a big stick to fend off wolverines.

'Do you really think you heard a wolverine over

there?' she asked, to change the subject.

'Um ... maybe.' Mark was slowly losing his scowl. 'It was *something* weird. Something I've never heard before. So you're going to forget all this crazy stuff about Mrs B, right?'

'Yeah, I am.' I'll be safe, Mary-Lynnette was thinking. This time I won't panic, and I'll make sure they don't see me. Besides, if they were going to kill me, they would have done it tonight, wouldn't they?

'Maybe it was Sasquatch we heard yelling,' Mark said.

CHAPTER
6

'**W**hy didn't we just kill her?' Kestrel asked.

Rowan and Jade looked at each other. There were few things they agreed on, but one of them was definitely Kestrel.

'First of all, we agreed not to do that here. We don't use our powers—'

'And we don't feed on humans. Or kill them,' Kestrel finished the chant. 'But you already used your powers tonight; you called Jade.'

'I had to let her know what story I'd just told about Aunt Opal. Actually, I should have planned for this earlier. I should have realized that people are going to come and ask where Aunt Opal is.'

'*She's* the only one who's asking. If we killed her—'

'We can't just go killing people in our new home,' Rowan said tightly. 'Besides, she said she had family waiting for her. Are we going to kill all of them?'

Kestrel shrugged.

'We are *not* going to start a blood feud,' Rowan said even more tightly.

'But what about influencing her?' Jade said. She was sitting with Tiggy in her arms, kissing the velvety black top

of the kitten's head. 'Making her forget she's suspicious –
or making her think she *saw* Aunt Opal?'

'That would be fine – if it were just her,' Rowan said
patiently. 'But it's not. Are we going to influence *everyone*
who comes to the house? What about people who call on
the phone? What about teachers? You two are supposed
to start school in a couple of weeks.'

'Maybe we'll just have to miss that,' Kestrel said
without regret.

Rowan was shaking her head. 'We need a permanent
solution. We need to find some reasonable explanation for
why Aunt Opal is gone.'

'We need to move Aunt Opal,' Kestrel said flatly. 'We
need to get rid of her.'

'No, no. We might have to produce the *body*,'
Rowan said.

'Looking like *that*?'

They began to argue about it. Jade rested her chin on
Tiggy's head and stared out the multi-paned kitchen
window. She was thinking about Mark Carter, who had
such a gallant heart. It gave her a pleasantly forbidden
thrill just to picture him. Back home there weren't any
humans wandering around free. She could never have
been tempted to break Night World law and fall in love
with one. But here . . . yes, Jade could almost imagine
falling in love with Mark Carter. Just as if she were a
human girl.

She shivered deliciously. But just as she was trying to
picture what human girls did when they were in love,
Tiggy gave a sudden heave. He twisted out of her arms and
hit the kitchen floor running. The fur on his back was up.

Jade looked at the window again. She couldn't see
anything. But . . . she *felt* . . .

She turned to her sisters. 'Something was out there in

the garden tonight,' she said. 'And I couldn't smell it.'

Rowan and Kestrel were still arguing. They didn't hear her.

Mary-Lynnette opened her eyes and sneezed. She'd overslept. Sun was shining around the edges of her dark blue curtains.

Get up and get to work, she told herself. But instead she lay rubbing sleep out of her eyes and trying to wake up. She was a night person, not a morning person.

The room was large and painted twilight blue. Mary-Lynnette had stuck the glow-in-the-dark stars and planets to the ceiling herself. Taped onto the dresser mirror was a bumper sticker saying I BRAKE FOR ASTEROIDS. On the walls were a giant relief map of the moon, a poster from the *Sky-Gazer's Almanac*, and photographic prints of the Pleiades, the Horsehead Nebula, and the total eclipse of 1995.

It was Mary-Lynnette's retreat, the place to go when people didn't understand. She always felt safe in the night.

She yawned and staggered to the bathroom, grabbing a pair of jeans and a T-shirt on the way. She was brushing her hair as she walked down the stairs when she heard voices from the living room.

Claudine's voice . . . and a male voice. Not Mark; weekdays he usually went to his friend Ben's house. A stranger.

Mary-Lynnette peeked through the kitchen. There was a guy sitting on the living room couch. She could see only the back of his head, which was ash blond. Mary-Lynnette shrugged and started to open the refrigerator, when she heard her own name.

'Mary-Lynnette is very good friends with her,' Claudine was saying in her quick, lightly accented voice. 'I remember a few years ago she helped her fix up a goat shed.'

They're talking about Mrs B!

'Why does she keep goats? I think she told Mary-Lynnette it would help since she couldn't get out that much anymore.'

'How strange,' the guy said. He had a lazy, careless-sounding voice. 'I wonder what she meant by that.'

Mary-Lynnette, who was now peering intently through the kitchen while keeping absolutely still, saw Claudine give one of her slight, charming shrugs.

'I suppose she meant the milk – every day she has fresh milk now. She doesn't have to go to the store. But I don't know. You'll have to ask her yourself.' She laughed.

Not going to be easy, Mary-Lynnette thought. Now, why would some strange guy be here asking questions about Mrs B.?

Of course. He had to be police or something. FBI. But his voice made her wonder. He sounded too young to be either, unless he was planning to infiltrate Dewitt High as a narc. Mary-Lynnette edged farther into the kitchen, getting a better view. There – she could see him in the mirror.

Disappointment coursed through her.

Definitely not old enough to be FBI. And much as Mary-Lynnette wanted him to be a keen-eyed, quick-witted, hard-driving detective, he wasn't. He was only the handsomest boy she'd ever seen in her life.

He was lanky and elegant, with long legs stretched out in front of him, ankles crossed under the coffee table. He looked like a big amiable cat. He had cleancut features, slightly tilted wicked eyes, and a disarming lazy grin.

Not just lazy, Mary-Lynnette decided. Fatuous. Bland. Maybe even stupid. She wasn't impressed by good looks unless they were the thin, brown, and interesting kind, like – well, like Jeremy Lovett for instance. Gorgeous guys

– guys who looked like big ash-blond cats – didn't have any reason to develop their minds. They were self-absorbed and vain. With IQs barely high enough to keep a seat warm.

And this guy looked as if he couldn't get awake or serious to save his life.

I don't care what he's here for. I think I'll go upstairs.

It was then that the guy on the couch lifted one hand, wiggling the fingers in the air. He half-turned. Not far enough actually to look at Mary-Lynnette, but far enough to make it clear he was talking to somebody behind him. She could now see his profile in the mirror. 'Hi, there.'

'Mary-Lynnette, is that you?' Claudine called.

'Yes.' Mary-Lynnette opened the refrigerator door and made banging noises. 'Just getting some juice. Then I'm going out.'

Her heart was beating hard – with embarrassment and annoyance. OK, so he must have seen her in the mirror. He probably thought she was staring at him because of the way he looked. He probably had people staring at him everywhere he went. So what, big deal, go away.

'Don't go yet,' Claudine called. 'Come out here and talk for a few minutes.'

No. Mary-Lynnette knew it was a childish and stupid reaction, but she couldn't help it. She banged a bottle of apricot juice against a bottle of Calistoga sparkling water.

'Come meet Mrs Burdock's nephew,' Claudine called.

Mary-Lynnette went still.

She stood in the cold air of the refrigerator, looking sightlessly at the temperature dial in the back. Then she put the bottle of apricot juice down. She twisted a Coke out of a six-pack without seeing it.

What nephew? I don't remember hearing about any nephew.

But then, she'd never heard much about Mrs B's nieces either, not until they were coming out. Mrs B just didn't talk about her family much.

So he's her nephew . . . *that's* why he's asking about her. But does he *know?* Is he in on it with those girls? Or is he after them? Or . . .

Thoroughly confused, she walked into the living room.

'Mary-Lynnette, this is Ash. He's here to visit with his aunt and his sisters,' Claudine said. 'Ash, this is Mary-Lynnette. The one who's such good friends with your aunt.'

Ash got up, all in one lovely, lazy motion. Just like a cat, including the stretch in the middle. 'Hi.'

He offered a hand. Mary-Lynnette touched it with fingers damp and cold from the Coke can, glanced up at his face, and said 'Hi.'

Except that it didn't happen that way.

It happened like this: Mary-Lynnette had her eyes on the carpet as she came in, which gave her a good view of his Nike tennis shoes and the ripped knees of his jeans. When he stood up she looked at his T-shirt, which had an obscure design – a black flower on a white background. Probably the emblem of some rock group. And then when his hand entered her field of vision, she reached for it automatically, muttering a greeting and looking up at his face just as she touched it. And—

This was the part that was hard to describe.

Contact.

Something happened.

Hey, don't I *know* you?

She didn't. That was the thing. She didn't know him – but she felt that she should. She also felt as if somebody had reached inside her and touched her spine with a live electric wire. It was extremely not-enjoyable. The room turned vaguely pink. Her throat swelled and she could feel her heart beating there. Also not-enjoyable. But somehow when you put it all together, it made a kind of trembly dizziness like . . .

Like what she felt when she looked at the Lagoon Nebula. Or imagined galaxies gathered into clusters and superclusters, bigger and bigger, until size lost any meaning and she felt herself falling.

She was falling now. She couldn't see anything except his eyes. And those eyes were strange, prism-like, changing colour like a star seen through heavy atmosphere. Now blue, now gold, now violet.

Oh, take this away. Please, I don't *want* it.

'It's so good to see a new face around here, isn't it? We're very boring out here by ourselves,' Claudine said, in completely normal and slightly flustered tones. Mary-Lynnette was snapped out of her trance, and she reacted as if Ash had just offered her a mongoose instead of his hand. She jumped backward, looking anywhere but at him. She had the feeling of being saved from falling down a mine shaft.

'O-K,' Claudine said in her cute accent. 'Hmm.' She was twisting a strand of curly dark hair, something she only did when she was extremely nervous. 'Maybe you guys know each other already?'

There was a silence.

I should say something, Mary-Lynnette thought dazedly, staring at the fieldstone fireplace. I'm acting crazy and humiliating Claudine.

But what just happened here?

Doesn't matter. Worry later. She swallowed, plastered a smile on her face, and said, 'So, how long are you here for?'

Her mistake was that then she looked at him. And it all

happened again. Not quite as vividly as before, maybe because she wasn't touching him. But the electric shock feeling was the same.

And *he* looked like a cat who's had a shock. Bristling. Unhappy. Astonished. Well, at least he was awake, Mary-Lynnette thought. He and Mary-Lynnette stared at each other while the room spun and turned pink.

'Who *are* you?' Mary-Lynnette said, abandoning any vestige of politeness.

'Who are *you*?' he said, in just about exactly the same tone.

They both glared.

Claudine was making little clicking noises with her tongue and clearing away the tomato juice. Mary-Lynnette felt distantly sorry for her, but couldn't spare her any attention. Mary-Lynnette's whole consciousness was focused on the guy in front of her; on fighting him, on blocking him out. On getting rid of this bizarre feeling that she was one of two puzzle pieces that had just been snapped together.

'Now, look,' she said tensely, at the precise moment that he began brusquely, 'Look—'

They both stopped and glared again. Then Mary-Lynnette managed to tear her eyes away. Something was tugging at her mind . . .

'Ash,' she said, getting hold of it. '*Ash*. Mrs Burdock *did* say something about you . . . about a little boy named Ash. I didn't know she was talking about her nephew.'

'Great-nephew,' Ash said, his voice not quite steady. 'What did she say?'

'She said that you were a bad little boy, and that you were probably going to grow up even worse.'

'Well, she had *that* right,' Ash said, and his expression softened a bit – as if he were on more familiar ground.

Mary-Lynnette's heart was slowing. She found that if she concentrated, she could make the strange feelings recede. It helped if she looked away from Ash.

Deep breath, she told herself. And another. OK, now let's get things straight. Let go of what just happened; forget all that; think about it later. What's important *now*?

What was important *now* was that: 1) This guy was the brother of those girls; 2) He might be in on whatever had happened to Mrs B; and, 3) If he *wasn't* in on it, he might be able to help with some information. Such as whether his aunt had left a will, and if so, who got the family jewels.

She glanced at Ash from the side of her eye. He definitely looked calmer. Hackles going down. Chest lifting more slowly. They were both switching gear.

'So Rowan and Kestrel and Jade are your sisters,' she said, with all the polite nonchalance she could muster. 'They seem – nice.'

'I didn't know you knew them,' Claudine said, and Mary-Lynnette realized her stepmother was hovering in the doorway, petite shoulder against the doorjamb, arms crossed, dishtowel in hand. 'I told him you hadn't met them.'

'Mark and I went over there yesterday,' Mary-Lynnette said. And when she said it, something flashed in Ash's face – something there and gone before she could really analyze it. But it made her feel as if she were standing on the edge of a cliff in a cold wind.

Why? What could be wrong with mentioning she'd met the girls?

'You and Mark . . . and Mark would be – your brother?'

'That's right,' Claudine said from the doorway.

'Any other brothers or sisters?'

Mary-Lynnette blinked. 'What, you're taking a census?'

Ash did a bad imitation of his former lazy smile. 'I just like to keep track of my sisters' friends.'

Why? 'To see if you approve or something?'

'Actually, yes.' He did the smile again, with more success. 'We're an old-fashioned family. Very old-fashioned.

Mary-Lynnette's jaw dropped. Then, all at once, she felt happy. Now she didn't need to think about murders or pink rooms or what this guy knew. All she needed to think about was what she was going to do to him.

'So you're an old-fashioned family,' she said, moving a step forward.

Ash nodded.

'And you're in charge,' Mary-Lynnette said.

'Well, out here. Back home, my father is.'

'And you're just going to tell your sisters which friends they can have. Maybe you get to decide your aunt's friends, too?'

'Actually, I was just discussing that . . .' He waved a hand toward Claudine.

Yes, you were, Mary-Lynnette realized. She took another step toward Ash, who was still smiling.

'Oh, no,' Claudine said. She flapped her dishtowel once. 'Don't smile.'

'I like a girl with spirit,' Ash offered, as if he'd worked hard on finding the most obnoxious thing possible to say. Then, with a sort of determined bravado, he winked, reached out, and chucked Mary-Lynnette under the chin.

Fzzz! Sparks. Mary-Lynnette sprang back. So did Ash, looking at his own hand as if it had betrayed him.

Mary-Lynnette had an inexplicable impulse to knock Ash flat and fall down on top of him. She'd never felt *that* for any boy before.

She ignored the impulse and kicked him in the shin.

He yelped and hopped backward. Once again the sleepy smugness was gone from his face. He looked alarmed.

'I think you'd better go away now,' Mary-Lynnette said pleasantly. She was amazed at herself. She'd never been the violent type. Maybe there were things hidden deep inside her that she'd never suspected.

Claudine was gasping and shaking her head. Ash was still hopping, but not going anywhere. Mary-Lynnette advanced on him again. Even though he was half a head taller, he backed up. He stared at her in something like wonder.

'Hey. Hey, look, you know, you really don't know what you're doing,' he said. 'If you knew . . .' And Mary-Lynnette saw it again – something in his face that made him suddenly look not fatuous or amiable at all. Like the glitter of a knife blade in the light. Something that said *danger* . . .

'Oh, go bother someone *else*,' Mary-Lynnette said. She drew back her foot for another kick.

He opened his mouth, then shut it. Still holding his shin, he looked at Claudine and managed a hurt and miserable flirtatious smile.

'Thanks so much for all your—'

'*Go!*'

He lost the smile. 'That's what I'm doing!' He limped to the front door. She followed him.

'What do they call you, anyway?' he asked from the front yard, as if he'd finally found the comeback he'd been looking for. 'Mary? Marylin? M'lin? ML?'

'They call me Mary-Lynnette,' Mary-Lynnette said flatly, and added under her breath, 'that do speak of me.' She'd read *The Taming of the Shrew* in honours English last year.

'Oh, yeah? How about M'lin the cursed?' He was still backing away.

Mary-Lynnette was startled. So maybe his class had read it, too. But he didn't look smart enough to quote Shakespeare.

'Have fun with your sisters,' she said, and shut the door. Then she leaned against it, trying to get her breath. Her fingers and face were prickly-numb, as if she were going to faint.

If those girls had only murdered *him*, I'd understand, she thought. But they're *all* so strange – there's something seriously weird about that whole family.

Weird in a way that scared her. If she'd believed in premonitions, she'd have been even more scared. She had a bad feeling – a feeling that *things* were going to happen . . .

Claudine was staring at her from the living room. 'Very fabulous,' she said. 'You've just kicked a guest. Now, what was that all *about*?'

'He wouldn't leave.'

'You know what I mean. Do you two know each other?'

Mary-Lynnette just shrugged vaguely. The dizziness was passing, but her mind was swimming with questions.

Cludine looked at her intently, then shook her head. 'I remember my little brother – when he was four years old he used to push a girl flat on her face in the sandbox. He did it to show he liked her.'

Mary-Lynnette ignored this. 'Claude – what was Ash *here* for? What did you talk about?'

'About nothing,' Claudine said, exasperated. 'Just ordinary conversation. Since you hate him so much, what difference does it make?' Then, as Mary-Lynnette kept looking at her, she sighed. 'He was very interested in weird facts about life in the country. All the local stories.'

Mary-Lynnette snorted. 'Did you tell him about Sasquatch?'

'I told him about Vic and Todd.'

Mary-Lynnette froze. 'You're joking. Why?'

'Because that's the kind of thing he asked about! People lost in time—'

'Losing time.'

'Whatever. We were just having a nice conversation. He was a nice boy. *Finis*.'

Mary-Lynnette's heart was beating fast.

She was right. She was sure of it now. Todd and Vic *were* connected to whatever had happened with the sisters and Mrs B. But what was the connection?

I'm going to go and find out, she thought.

CHAPTER

7

Finding Todd and Vic turned out not to be easy.

It was late afternoon by the time Mary-Lynnette walked into the Briar Creek general store, which sold everything from nails to nylons to canned peas.

'Hi, Bunny. I don't suppose you've seen Todd or Vic around?'

Bunny Marten looked up from behind the counter. She was pretty, with soft blond hair, a round, dimpled face, and a timid expression. She was in Mary-Lynnette's class at school. 'Did you check over at the Gold Creek Bar?'

Mary-Lynnette nodded. 'And at their houses, and at the other store, and at the sheriff's office.' The sheriff's office was also city hall and the public library.

'Well, if they're not playing pool, they're usually plinking.' Plinking was shooting at cans for practice.

'Yeah, but where?' Mary-Lynnette said.

Bunny shook her head, earrings glinting. 'Your guess is as good as mine.' She hesitated, staring down at her cuticles, which she was pushing back with a little blunt-pointed wooden stick. 'But, you know, I've heard they go down to Mad Dog Creek sometimes.' Her wide blue eyes lifted to Mary-Lynnette's meaningfully.

Mad Dog Creek . . . Oh, great. Mary-Lynnette grimaced.

'I know.' Bunny raised her shoulders in a shiver. '*I* wouldn't go down there. I'd be thinking about that body the whole time.'

'Yeah, me, too. Well, thanks, Bun. See you.'

Bunny examined her cuticles critically. 'Good hunting,' she said absently.

Mary-Lynnette went out of the store, squinting in the hot, hazy August sunlight. Main Street wasn't big. It had a handful of brick and stone buildings from the days when Briar Creek had been a gold rush supply town, and a few modern frame buildings with peeling paint. Todd and Vic weren't in any of them.

Well, what now? Mary-Lynnette sighed. There was no road to Mad Dog Creek, only a trail that was constantly blocked by new growth and deadfall. And everyone knew more than plinking went on there.

If they're out there, they're probably hunting, she thought. Not to mention drinking, maybe using drugs. Guns and beer. And then there's that body.

The body had been found last year around this time. A man; a hiker, from his backpack. Nobody knew who he was or how he'd died – the corpse was too desiccated and chewed by animals to tell. But people talked about ghosts floating around the creek last winter.

Mary-Lynnette sighed again and got into her station wagon.

The car was ancient, it was rusty, it made alarming sounds when forced to accelerate, but it was *hers*, and Mary-Lynnette did her best to keep it alive. She loved it because there was plenty of room in the back to store her telescope.

At Briar Creek's only gas station she fished a scrolled fruit knife from under the seat and went to work, prying at the rusty gas cap cover.

A little higher up . . . almost, almost . . . now *twist* . . .

The cover flew open.

'Ever think of going into the safecracking business?' a voice behind her said. 'You've got the touch.'

Mary-Lynnette turned. 'Hi, Jeremy.'

He smiled – a smile that showed mostly in his eyes, which were clear brown with outrageously dark lashes.

If I were going to fall for a guy – and I'm not – it would be for somebody like him. *Not* for a big blond cat who thinks he can pick his sisters' friends.

It was a moot point, anyway – Jeremy didn't go out with girls. He was a loner.

'Want me to look under the hood?' He wiped his hands on a rag.

'No, thanks. I just checked everything last week.' Mary-Lynnette started to pump gas.

He picked up a squeegee and a spray bottle and began to wash the windshield. His movements were deft and gentle and his face was utterly solemn.

Mary-Lynnette had to swallow a giggle herself, but she appreciated him not laughing at the pitted glass and corroded windshield wipers. She'd always had an odd feeling of kinship with Jeremy. He was the only person in Briar Creek who seemed even slightly interested in astronomy – he'd helped her build a model of the solar system in eighth grade, and of course he'd watched last year's lunar eclipse with her.

His parents had died in Medford when he was just a baby, and his uncle brought him to Briar Creek in a Fleetwood trailer. The uncle was strange – always wandering off to dowse for gold in the Klamath wilderness. One day he didn't come back.

After that, Jeremy lived alone in the trailer in the

woods. He did odd jobs and worked at the gas station to make money. And if his clothes weren't as nice as some of the other kids', he didn't care – or he didn't let it show.

The handle of the gas hose clicked in Mary-Lynnette's hand. She realized she had been daydreaming.

'Anything else?' Jeremy said. The windshield was clean.

'No . . . well, actually, yes. You haven't, um, seen Todd Akers or Vic Kimble today, have you?'

Jeremy paused in the middle of taking her twenty-dollar bill.

'Why?'

'I just wanted to talk to them,' Mary-Lynnette said. She could feel heat in her cheeks. Oh, God, he thinks I want to see Todd and Vic socially – and he thinks I'm crazy for asking *him*.

She hurried to explain. 'It's just that Bunny said they might be down by Mad Dog Creek, so I thought you might have seen them, maybe sometime this morning, since you live down around there . . .'

Jeremy shook his head. 'I left at noon, but I didn't hear any gunshots from the creek this morning. Actually, I don't think they've been there all summer – I keep telling them to stay away.'

He said it quietly, without emphasis, but Mary-Lynnette had the sudden feeling that maybe even Todd and Vic might listen to him. She'd never known Jeremy to get in a fight. But sometimes a look came into his level brown eyes that was . . . almost frightening. As if there was something underneath that quiet-guy exterior – something primitive and pure and deadly that could do a lot of damage if roused.

'Mary-Lynnette – I know you probably think this is none of my business, but . . . well, I think you should stay away from those guys. If you really want to go find them, let me go with you.'

Oh. Mary-Lynnette felt a warm flush of gratitude. She wouldn't take him up on the offer . . . but it was nice of him to make it.

'Thanks,' she said. 'I'll be fine, but . . . thanks.'

She watched as he went to get her change inside the station. What must it feel like to be on your own since you were twelve years old? Maybe he needed help. Maybe she should ask her dad to offer him some odd jobs around the house. He did them for everyone else. She just had to be careful – she knew Jeremy hated anything that smacked of charity.

He brought back the change. 'Here you go. And, Mary-Lynnette . . .'

She looked up.

'If you do find Todd and Vic, be careful.'

'I know.'

'I mean it.'

'I know,' Mary-Lynnette said. She had reached for the change, but he hadn't let go of it. Instead, he did something odd: He opened her curled fingers with one hand while giving her the bills and coins with the other. Then he curled her fingers back over it. In effect, he was holding her hand.

The moment of physical contact surprised her – and touched her. She found herself looking at his thin brown fingers, at their strong but delicate grip on her hand, at the gold seal ring with the black design that he wore.

She was even more surprised when she glanced up at his face again. There was open concern in his eyes – and something like respect. For an instant she had a wild and completely inexplicable impulse to tell him everything. But she could just imagine what he would think. Jeremy was very practical.

'Thanks, Jeremy,' she said, conjuring up a weak smile.
'Take care.'

'*You* take care. There are people who'd miss you if
anything happened.' He smiled, but she could feel his
worried gaze on her even as she drove away.

All right, *now* what?

Well, she'd wasted most of the day looking for Todd
and Vic. And now, with the image of Jeremy's level brown
eyes in her mind, she wondered if it had been a stupid
idea from the beginning.

Brown eyes . . . and what colour eyes did the big blond
cat have? Strange, it was hard to remember. She thought
that they had looked brown at one point – when he was
talking about his old-fashioned family. But when he'd said
he liked a girl with spirit, she remembered them being a
sort of insipid blue. And when that odd knife-glint had
flashed in them, hadn't they been icy grey?

Oh, who *cares*? Maybe they were orange. Let's just go
home now. Get ready for tonight.

How come Nancy Drew always found the people she
wanted to interrogate?

Why? Why? Why me?

Ash was staring at a yellow cedar weeping into a creek.
A squirrel too stupid to get out of the sun was staring back
at him. On a rock beside him a lizard lifted first one foot,
then another.

It wasn't fair. It wasn't right.

He didn't even believe it.

He'd always been lucky. Or at least he'd always
managed to escape a hairs breadth away from disaster.
But this time the disaster had hit and it was a total
annihilation.

Everything he was, everything he believed about himself . . . could he lose that in five minutes? For a girl who was probably deranged and certainly more dangerous than all three of his sisters put together?

No, he concluded grimly. Absolutely not. Not in five minutes. It only took five seconds.

He knew so many girls – nice girls. Witches with mysterious smiles, vampires with delicious curves, shapeshifters with cute furry tails. Even human girls with fancy sports cars who never seemed to mind when he nibbled their necks. Why couldn't it have been one of them?

Well, it wasn't. And there was no point in wondering about the injustice of it. The question was, what was he going to *do* about it? Just sit back and let fate ride over him like an eighteen-wheeler?

I'm sorry for your family, Quinn had said to him. And maybe that was the problem. Ash was a victim of his Redfern genes. Redferns never could stay out of trouble; they seemed to tangle with humans at every turn.

So was he going to wait for Quinn to come back and then offer that as an excuse? I'm sorry; I can't handle things here after all; I can't even finish the investigation.

If he did that, Quinn would call in the Elders and they would investigate for themselves.

Ash felt his expression harden. He narrowed his eyes at the squirrel, which suddenly darted for the tree in a flash of red fur. Beside him, the lizard stopped moving.

No, he wasn't just going to wait for fate to finish him off. He'd do what he could to salvage the situation – and the family honour.

He'd do it tonight.

'We'll do it tonight,' Rowan said. 'After it's fully dark; before the moon rises. We'll move her to the forest.'

Kestrel smiled magnanimously. She'd won the argument.

'We'll have to be careful,' Jade said. 'That thing I heard outside last night – it wasn't an animal. I think it was one of *us*.'

'There aren't any other Night People around here,' Rowan said gently. 'That was the whole point of coming here in the first place.'

'Maybe it was a vampire hunter,' Kestrel said. 'Maybe the one that killed Aunt Opal.'

'*If* a vampire hunter killed Aunt Opal,' Rowan said. 'We don't know that. Tomorrow we should look around town, see if we can at least get an idea who *might* have done it.'

'And when we find them, we'll take care of them,' Jade said fiercely.

'And if the thing you heard in the garden turns up, we'll take care of it, too,' Kestrel said. She smiled, a hungry smile.

Twilight, and Mary-Lynnette was watching the clock. The rest of her family was comfortably settled in for the night; her father reading a book about World War II, claudine working conscientiously on a needlepoint project, Mark trying to tune up his old guitar that had been sitting in the basement for years. He was undoubtedly trying to think of words to rhyme with *Jade*.

Mary-Lynnette's father looked up from his book. 'Going star-watching?'

'Yup. It should be a good night – no moon till after midnight. It's the last chance to see some Perseids.' She wasn't exactly lying. It *would* be a good night, and she could keep an eye out for stragglers from the Perseid meteor storm as she walked to Burdock Farm.

'OK; just be careful,' her father said.

Mary-Lynnette was surprised. He hadn't said anything like that for years. She glanced at Claudine, who jabbed with her needle, lips pursed.

'Maybe Mark should go with you,' Claudine said, without looking up.

Oh, God, she thinks I'm unstable, Mary-Lynnette thought. I don't really blame her.

'No, no. I'll be fine. I'll be careful.' She said it too quickly.

Mark's eyes narrowed. 'Don't you need any help with your stuff?'

'No, I'll take the car. I'll be fine. *Really.*' Mary-Lynnette fled to the garage before her family could come up with anything else.

She didn't pack her telescope. Instead, she put a shovel in the backseat. She looped the strap of her camera around her neck and stuck a pen flashlight in her pocket.

She parked at the foot of her hill. Before she got the shovel out, she paused a moment to look dutifully northeast, toward the constellation Perseus.

No meteors right this second. All right. Keys in hand, she turned to open the back of the station wagon – and jumped violently.

'Oh, God!'

She'd nearly walked into Ash.

'Hi.'

Mary-Lynnette's pulse was racing and her knees felt weak. From fear, she told herself. And that's *all.*

'You nearly gave me a heart attack!' she said. 'Do you always creep up behind people like that?'

She expected some smart-ass answer of either the joking-menacing or the hey-baby variety. But Ash just frowned at her moodily. 'No. What are you doing out here?'

Mary-Lynnette's heart skipped several beats. But she heard her own voice answering flatly, 'I'm star-watching. I do it every night. You might want to make a note of that for the thought police.'

He looked at her, then at the station wagon. 'Star-watching?'

'Of course. From that hill.' She gestured.

Now he was looking at the camera looped around her neck. 'No telescope,' he commented skeptically. 'Or is that what's in the car?'

Mary-Lynnette realized she was still holding the keys, ready to open the back of the wagon. 'I didn't bring a telescope tonight.' She went around to the passenger side of the car, unlocked the door, reached in to pull out her binoculars. 'You don't need a telescope to star-watch. You can see plenty with these.'

'Oh, really?'

'Yes, *really*.' Now, that was a mistake, Mary-Lynnette thought, suddenly grimly amused. Acting as if you don't believe me . . . just you *wait*.

'You want to see light from four million years ago?' she said. Then, without waiting for him to answer: 'OK. Face east.' She rotated a finger at him. 'Here, take the binoculars. Look at that line of fir trees on the horizon. Now pan up . . .' She gave him directions, rapping them out like a drill sergeant. 'Now do you see a bright disk with a kind of smudge all around it?'

'Um. Yeah.'

'That's Andromeda. Another *galaxy*. But if you tried to look at it through a telescope, you couldn't see it all at once. Looking through a telescope is like looking at the sky through a soda straw. That's all the field of view you get.'

'All right. OK. Point taken.' He started to lower the

binoculars. 'Look, could we suspend the star-watching for just a minute? I wanted to talk to you . . .'

'Want to see the centre of *our* galaxy?' Mary-Lynnette interrupted. 'Turn south.'

She did everything but physically make him turn. She didn't dare touch him. There was so much adrenalin racing through her system already – if she made contact she might go supercritical and explode.

'*Turn*,' she said. He shut his eyes briefly, then turned, bringing the binoculars up again.

'You have to look in the constellation Sagittarius.' She rattled off instructions. 'See that? That's where the centre of the Milky Way is. Where all the star clouds are.'

'How nice.'

'Yes, it is nice. OK, now go up and east – you should be able to find a little dim sort of glow . . .'

'The pink one?'

She gave him a quick look. 'Yeah, the pink one. Most people don't see that. That's the Trifid Nebula.'

'What are those dark lines in it?'

Mary-Lynnette stopped dead.

She forgot her drill sergeant manner. She stepped back. She stared at him. She could feel her breath coming quicker.

He lowered the binoculars and looked at her. 'Something wrong?'

'They're dark nebulae. Lanes of dust in front of the hot gas. But . . . you can't see them.'

'I just did.'

'No. No. You can't *see* those. It's not possible, not with binoculars. Even if you had nine-millimetre pupils . . .' She pulled the flashlight out of her pocket and trained it full in his face.

'*Hey*!' He jerked back, eyes squeezing shut, hand over them. 'That *hurt*!'

But Mary-Lynnette had already seen. She couldn't tell what colour his eyes were right now, because the coloured parts, the irises, were reduced to almost invisible rings. His eye was *all* pupil. Like a cat's at maximum dilation.

Oh, my God . . . the things he must be able to *see*. Eighth-magnitude stars, maybe ninth-magnitude stars. Imagine that, seeing a Mag 9 star with your naked eye. To see colours in the star clouds – hot hydrogen glowing pink, oxygen shining green-blue. To see thousands more stars cluttering the sky . . .

'Quick,' she said urgently. 'How many stars do you see in the sky right now?'

'I can't see *anything*,' he said in a muffled voice, hand still over his eyes. 'I'm *blind*.'

'No, I mean *seriously*,' Mary-Lynnette said. And she caught his arm.

It was a stupid thing to do. She wasn't thinking. But when she touched his skin, it was like completing a current. Shock swept over her. Ash dropped his hand and looked at her.

For just a second they were face-to-face, gazes locked. Something like lightning trembled between them. Then Mary-Lynnette pulled away.

I can't *take* any more of this. Oh, God, why am I even standing here talking to him? I've got enough ahead of me tonight. I've got a *body* to find.

'That's it for the astronomy lesson,' she said, holding out a hand for the binoculars. Her voice was just slightly unsteady. 'I'm going up the hill now.'

She didn't ask where *he* was going. She didn't care, as long as it was away.

He hesitated an instant before giving her the binoculars, and when he did he made sure not to touch her.

Fine, Mary-Lynnette thought. We both feel the same.

'Goodbye.'

'Bye,' he said limply. He started to walk away. Stopped, his head lowered. 'What I wanted to say . . .'

'Well?'

Without turning, he said in a flat and perfectly composed voice, 'Stay away from my sisters, OK?'

Mary-Lynnette was thunderstruck. So outraged and full of disbelief that she couldn't find words. Then she thought: Wait, maybe he knows they're killers and he's trying to protect me. Like Jeremy.

Around the sudden constriction in her throat she managed to say, 'Why?'

He shook his drooping head. 'I just don't think you'd be a very good influence on them. They're kind of impressionable, and I don't want them getting any ideas.'

Mary-Lynnette deflated. I should have known, she thought. She said, sweetly and evenly, 'Ash? Get bent and die.'

CHAPTER

8

She waited another hour after he set off down the road, heading east – doing what, she had no idea. There was nothing that way except two creeks and lots of trees. And her house. She hoped he was going to try to walk into town, and that he didn't realize how far it was.

All right, he's gone, now forget about him. You've got a job to do, remember? A slightly dangerous one. And he's not involved. I don't believe he knows anything about what happened to Mrs B.

She got the shovel and started down the road west. As she walked she found that she was able to put Ash out of her mind completely. Because all she could think of was what was waiting ahead.

I'm not scared to do it; I'm not scared; I'm not scared . . . Of *course* I'm scared.

But being scared was good; it would make her careful. She would do this job quickly and quietly. In through the gap in the hedge, a little fast work with the shovel, out again before anybody saw her.

She tried not to picture what she was going to find with that shovel if she was right.

She approached Burdock Farm cautiously, going north

and then doubling back southeast to come in through the back property. The farmland had gone wild here, taken over by poison oak, beargrass, and dodder, besides the inevitable blackberry bushes and gorse. Tan oaks and chinquapins were moving in. Sometime soon these pastures would be forest.

I'm not sure I believe I'm doing this, Mary-Lynnette thought as she reached the hedge that surrounded the garden. But the strange thing was that she *did* believe it. She was going to vandalize a neighbour's property and probably look at a dead body – and she was surprisingly cool about it. Scared but not panicked. Maybe there was more hidden inside her than she realized.

I may not be who I've always thought I am.

The garden was dark and fragrant. It wasn't the irises and daffodils Mrs B had planted; it wasn't the fireweed and bleeding heart that were growing wild. It was the goats.

Mary-Lynnette stuck to the perimetre of the hedge, eyes on the tall, upright silhouette of the farmhouse. There were only two windows lit.

Please don't let them see me and please don't let me make a noise.

Still looking at the house, she walked slowly, taking careful baby steps to the place where the earth was disturbed. The first couple of swipes with the shovel hardly moved the soil.

OK. Put a little conviction in it. And don't watch the house; there's no point. If they look out, they're going to see you, and there's nothing you can do about it.

Just as she put her foot on the shovel, something went *hoosh* in the rhododendrons behind her.

Crouched over her shovel, Mary-Lynnette froze.

Stop worrying, she told herself. That's not the sisters. It's not Ash coming back. That's an animal.

She listened. A mournful *maaaa* came from the goat shed.

It wasn't anything. It was a rabbit. *Dig!*

She got out a spadeful of dirt – and then she heard it again.

Hoosh.

A snuffling sound. Then a rustling. Definitely an animal. But if it was a rabbit, it was an awfully loud one.

Who cares what it is? Mary-Lynnette told herself. There aren't any *dangerous* animals out here. And I'm not afraid of the dark. It's my natural habitat. I *love* the night.

But tonight, somehow, she felt differently. Maybe it was just the scene with Ash that had shaken her, made her feel confused and discontented. But just now she felt almost as if something was trying to tell her that the dark wasn't *any* human's natural habitat. That she wasn't built for it, with her weak eyes and her insensitive ears and dull nose. That she didn't belong.

Hoosh.

I may have rotten hearing, but I can hear *that* just fine. And it's big. Something big's sniffing around in the bushes.

What kind of big animal could be out here? It wasn't a deer; deer went *snort-wheeze*. It sounded larger than a coyote, taller. A bear?

Then she heard a different sound, the vigorous shaking of dry, leathery rhododendron leaves. In the dim light from the house she could *see* the branches churning as something tried to emerge.

It's coming out.

Mary-Lynnette clutched her shovel and ran. Not toward the gap in the hedge, not toward the house – they were both too dangerous. She ran to the goat shed.

I can defend myself in here – keep it out – hit it with the shovel . . .

The problem was that she couldn't *see* from in here. There were two windows in the shed, but between the dirt on the glass and the darkness outside, Mary-Lynnette couldn't make out anything. She couldn't even see the goats, although she could hear them.

Don't turn on the penlight. It'll just give away your position.

Holding absolutely still, she strained to hear anything from outside.

Nothing.

Her nostrils were full of goat. The layers of oat straw and decomposing droppings on the floor were smelly, and they kept the shed too warm. Her palms were sweating as she gripped the shovel.

I've never hit anybody . . . not since Mark and I were kids fighting . . . but, heck, I kicked a stranger this morning . . .

She hoped the potential for violence would come out now when she needed it.

A goat nudged her shoulder. Mary-Lynnette shrugged it away. The other goat bleated suddenly and she bit her lip.

Oh, God – I heard something out there. The goat heard it, too.

She could taste her bitten lip. It was like sucking on a penny. Blood tasted like copper, which, she realized suddenly, tasted like fear.

Something opened the shed door.

What happened then was that Mary-Lynnette panicked.

Something unholy was after her. Something that sniffed like an animal but could open doors like a human. She couldn't see what it was – just a shadow of darkness against darkness. She didn't think of turning on the penlight – her only impulse was to smash out with the shovel *now*, to get It before It could get her. She was tingling with the instinct for pure, primordial violence.

Instead, she managed to hiss, 'Who is it? Who's there?'

A familiar voice said, 'I *knew* you were going to do this. I've been looking *everywhere* for you.'

'Oh, *God*, Mark.' Mary-Lynnette sagged against the wall of the shed, letting go of the shovel.

The goats were both bleating. Mary-Lynnette's ears were ringing. Mark shuffled farther in.

'Jeez, this place smells. What are you doing in here?'

'You *jerk*,' Mary-Lynnette said. 'I almost brained you!'

'You said you were forgetting all this crazy stuff. You lied to me.'

'Mark, you don't . . . We can talk later . . . Did you *hear* anything out there?' She was trying to gather her thoughts.

'Like what?' He was so calm. It made Mary-Lynnette feel vaguely foolish. Then his voice sharpened. 'Like a yowling?'

'No. Like a snuffling.' Mary-Lynnette's breath was slowing.

'I didn't hear anything. We'd better get out of here. What are we supposed to say if Jade comes out?'

Mary-Lynnette didn't know how to answer that. Mark was in a different world, a happy, shiny world where the worst that could happen tonight was embarrassment.

Finally she said, 'Mark, listen to me. I'm your sister. I don't have any reason to lie to you, or play tricks on you, or put down somebody you like. And I don't just jump to conclusions; I don't imagine things. But I'm telling you, *absolutely seriously*, that there is something *weird* going on with these girls.'

Mark opened his mouth, but she went on relentlessly.

'So now there are only two things you can believe, and one is that I'm completely out of my mind, and the other is that it's true. Do you *really* think I'm crazy?'

She was thinking of the past as she said it, of all the nights they'd held on to each other when their mother was sick, of the books she'd read out loud to him, of the times she'd put plaster on his scrapes and extra cookies in his lunch. And somehow, even though it was dark, she could sense that Mark was remembering, too. They'd shared so much. They would always be connected.

Finally Mark said quietly, 'You're not crazy.'

'Thank you.'

'But I don't know *what* to think. Jade wouldn't hurt anybody. I just *know* that. And since I met her . . .' He paused. 'Mare, it's like now I know why I'm alive. She's different from any girl I've ever known. She's – she's so brave, and so funny, and so . . . *herself.*'

And I thought it was the blond hair, Mary-Lynnette thought. Shows how shallow I am.

She was moved and surprised by the change in Mark – but mostly she was frightened. Frightened sick. Her cranky, cynical brother had found somebody to care about at last . . . and the girl was probably descended from Lucrezia Borgia.

And now, even though she couldn't see him, she could hear earnest appeal in his voice. 'Mare, can't we just go home?'

Mary-Lynnette felt sicker.

'Mark—'

She broke off and they both snapped their heads to look at the shed window. Outside a light had gone on.

'Shut the door,' Mary-Lynnette hissed, in a tone that made Mark close the door to the shed instantly.

'And be *quiet*,' she added, grabbing his arm and

pulling him next to the wall. She looked cautiously out the window.

Rowan came out of the back door first, followed by Jade, followed by Kestrel. Kestrel had a shovel.

Oh. My. God.

'What's happening?' Mark said, trying to get a look. Mary-Lynnette clamped a hand over his mouth.

What was happening was that the girls were digging up the garden again.

She didn't see anything wrapped in garbage bags this time. So what were they doing? Destroying the evidence? Were they going to take it into the house and burn it, chop it up?

Her heart was pounding madly.

Mark had scooted up and was looking out. Mary-Lynnette heard him take a breath – and then choke. Maybe he was trying to think of an innocent explanation for this. She squeezed his shoulder.

They both watched as the girls took turns with the shovel. Mary-Lynnette was impressed all over again at how strong they were. Jade looked so fragile.

Every time one of the sisters glanced around the garden, Mary-Lynnette's heart skipped a beat. Don't see us, don't hear us, don't catch us, she thought.

When a respectable mound of dirt had piled up, Rowan and Kestrel reached into the hole. They lifted out the long garbage-bagged bundle Mary-Lynnette had seen before. It seemed to be stiff – and surprisingly light.

For the first time, Mary-Lynnette wondered if it was *too* light to be a body. Or too stiff . . . how long did rigor mortis last?

Mark's breathing was irregular, almost wheezing.

The girls were carrying the bundle to the gap in the hedge.

Mark cursed.

Mary-Lynnette's brain was racing. She hissed, 'Mark, stay here. I'm going to follow them—'

'I'm going with you!'

'You have to tell Dad if anything happens to me—'

'I'm going *with* you.'

There wasn't time to argue. And something inside Mary-Lynnette was glad to have Mark's strength to back her.

She gasped, 'Come on, then. And don't make a sound.'

She was worried they might have already lost the sisters – it was such a dark night. But when she and Mark squeezed through the gap in the rhododendron bushes, she saw a light ahead. A tiny, bobbing white light. The sisters were using a flashlight.

Keep quiet, move carefully. Mary-Lynnette didn't dare say it out loud to Mark, but she kept thinking it over and over, like a mantra. Her whole consciousness was fixed on the little shaft of light that was leading them, like a comet's tail in the darkness.

The light took them south, into a stand of Douglas fir. It wasn't long before they were walking into forest.

Where are they *going*? Mary-Lynnette thought. She could feel fine tremors in her muscles as she tried to move as quickly as possible without making a sound. They were lucky – the floor of this forest was carpeted with needles from Douglas fir and Ponderosa pine. The needles were fragrant and slightly damp and they muffled footsteps. Mary-Lynnette could hardly hear Mark walking behind her except when he hurt himself.

They went on for what seemed like forever. It was pitch dark and Mary-Lynnette very quickly lost any sense of where they were. Or how they were going to get back.

Oh, God, I was crazy to do this – and to bring Mark

along, too. We're out in the middle of the woods with three crazy girls . . .

The light had stopped.

Mary-Lynnette stopped, holding out an arm that Mark immediately ran into. She was staring at the light, trying to make sure it really wasn't moving away.

No. It was steady. It was pointed at the ground.

'Let's get closer,' Mark whispered, putting his lips against Mary-Lynnette's ear. She nodded and began to creep toward the light, as slowly and silently as she knew how. Every few steps she paused and stood absolutely still, waiting to see if the light was going to turn her way.

It didn't. She got down and crawled the last ten feet to the edge of the clearing where the girls had stopped. Once there, she had a good view of what they were doing.

Digging. Kestrel had shovelled the pine needles aside and was working on a hole.

Mary-Lynnette felt Mark crawl up beside her, crushing sword fern and woodfern. She could feel his chest heaving. She knew he saw what she saw.

I'm so sorry. Oh, Mark, I'm so sorry.

There was no way to deny it now. Mary-Lynnette *knew*. She didn't even need to look in the bag.

How am I going to find this place again? When I bring the sheriff back, how am I going to remember it? It's like a maze in one of those computer fantasy games – Mixed Evergreen Forest in every direction, and nothing to distinguish any bit of it from any other bit.

She chewed her lip. The bed of moist needles she was lying on was soft and springy – actually comfortable. They could wait here for a long time, until the sisters left, and then mark the trees somehow. Take photographs. Tie their socks to branches.

In the clearing the flashlight beam showed a hand

putting down the shovel. Then Rowan and Kestrel lifted the garbage-bagged bundle – Jade must be holding the flashlight, Mary-Lynnette thought – and lowered it into the hole.

Good. Now cover it up and leave.

The beam showed Rowan bending to pick up the shovel again. She began quickly covering the hole with dirt. Mary-Lynnette was happy. Over soon, she thought, and let out a soft breath of relief.

And in that instant everything in the clearing changed.

The flashlight beam swung wildly. Mary-Lynnette flattened herself, feeling her eyes widen. She could see a silhouette against the light – golden hair haloed around the face. Kestrel. Kestrel was standing, facing Mark and Mary-Lynnette, her body tense and still. Listening. Listening.

Mary-Lynnette lay absolutely motionless, mouth open, trying to breathe without making a sound. There were things crawling in the soft, springy needle bed under her. Centipedes and millipedes. She didn't dare move even when she felt something tickle across her back under her shirt.

Her own ears rang from listening. But the forest was silent . . . eerily silent. All Mary-Lynnette could hear was her own heart pounding wildly in her chest – although it *felt* as if it were in her throat, too. It made her head bob with its rhythm.

She was afraid.

And it wasn't just fear. It was something she couldn't remember experiencing since she was nine or ten. *Ghost fear*. The fear of something you're not even sure exists.

Somehow, watching Kestrel's silhouette in the dark woods, Mary-Lynnette was afraid of monsters. She had a terrible, terrible feeling.

Oh, please – I shouldn't have brought Mark here.

It was then that she realized that Mark's breathing was making a noise. Just a faint sound, not a whistling, more like a cat purring. It was the sound he'd made as a kid when his lungs were bad.

Kestrel stiffened, her head turning, as if to locate a noise.

Oh, Mark, *no*. Don't breathe. *Hold your breath—*

Everything happened very fast.

Kestrel sprang forward. Mary-Lynnette saw her silhouette come running and jumping with unbelievable speed. *Too* fast – nobody moves *that* fast . . . nobody human . . .

What are these girls?

Her vision came in flashes, as if she were under a strobe light. Kestrel jumping. Dark trees all around. A moth caught in the beam.

Kestrel coming down.

Protect Mark . . .

A deer. Kestrel was coming down on a deer. Mary-Lynnette's mind was filled with jumbled, careening images. Images that didn't make sense. She had a wild thought that it wasn't Kestrel at all, but one of those raptor dinosaurs she'd seen at the movies. Because Kestrel moved like that.

Or maybe it wasn't a deer – but Mary-Lynnette could see the white at its throat, as pure as a lace ruffle at the throat of a young girl. She could see its liquid black eyes.

The deer screamed.

Disbelief.

I can't be seeing this . . .

The deer was on the ground, delicate legs thrashing. And Kestrel was tangled with it. Her face buried in the white of its throat. Her arms around it.

The deer screamed again. Wrenched violently. Seemed to be having convulsions.

The flashlight beam was all over the place. Then it dropped. At the very edge of the light, Mary-Lynnette could see two other figures join Kestrel. They were all holding the deer. There was one last spasm and it stopped fighting. Everything went still. Mary-Lynnette could see Jade's hair, so fine that individual strands caught the light against the background of darkness.

In the silent clearing the three figures cradled the deer. Huddling over it. Shoulders moving rhythmically. Mary-Lynnette couldn't see exactly what they were doing, but the general scene was familiar. She'd seen it on dozens of nature documentaries. About wild dogs or lionesses or wolves. The pack had hunted and now it was feeding.

I have always tried . . . to be a very good observer. And now, I have to believe my own eyes . . .

Beside her, Mark's breath was sobbing.

Oh, God, let me get him out of here. Please just let us get out.

It was as if she'd been suddenly released from paralysis. Her lip was bleeding again – she must have bitten down on it while she was watching the deer. Copperbloodfear filled her mouth.

'Come on,' she gasped almost soundlessly, wiggling backward. Twigs and needles raked her stomach as her T-shirt rode up. She grabbed Mark's arm. 'Come on!'

Instead, Mark lurched to his feet.

'Mark!' She wrenched herself to her knees and tried to drag him down.

He pulled away. He took a step toward the clearing.

No—

'Jade!'

He was heading for the clearing.

No, Mary-Lynnette thought again, and then she was moving after him. They were caught now, and it really didn't matter what he did. But she wanted to be with him.

'Jade!' Mark said and he grabbed the flashlight. He turned it directly on the little huddle at the edge of the clearing. Three faces turned toward him.

Mary-Lynnette's mind reeled. It was one thing to guess what the girls were doing; it was another thing to *see* it. Those three beautiful faces, white in the flashlight beam . . . with what looked like smeared lipstick on their mouths and chins. Cardinal red, thimbleberry colour.

But it wasn't lipstick or burst thimbleberries. It was blood, and the deer's white neck was stained with it.

Eating the deer; they're really *eating the deer*; oh, God, they're really doing it . . .

Some part of her mind – the part that had absorbed horror movies – expected the three girls to hiss and cringe away from the light. To block it out with bloodstained hands while making savage faces.

It didn't happen. There were no animal noises, no demon voices, no contortions.

Instead, as Mary-Lynnette stood frozen in an agony of horror, and Mark stood trying to get a normal breath, Jade straightened up.

And said, 'What are you guys doing out here?'

In a puzzled, vaguely annoyed voice. The way you would speak to some boy who keeps following you everywhere and asking you for a date.

Mary-Lynnette felt her mind spinning off.

There was a long silence. Then Rowan and Kestrel stood up. Mark was breathing heavily, moving the flashlight from one of the girls to another, but always coming back to Jade.

'What are *you* doing out here; that's the question!' he

said raggedly. The flashlight whipped to the hole, then back to the girls. 'What are you *doing*?'

'I asked you first,' Jade said, frowning. If it had just been her, Mary-Lynnette would have started to wonder if things were so awful after all. If maybe they weren't in terrible danger.

But Rowan and Kestrel were looking at each other, and then at Mark and Mary-Lynnette. And their expressions made Mary-Lynnette's throat close.

'You shouldn't have followed us,' Rowan said. She looked grave and sad.

'They shouldn't have been *able* to,' Kestrel said. She looked grim.

'It's because they smell like goats,' Jade said.

'*What are you doing?*' Mark shouted again, almost sobbing. Mary-Lynnette wanted to reach for him, but she couldn't move.

Jade wiped her mouth with the back of her hand. 'Well, can't you *tell*?' She turned to her sisters. 'Now what are we supposed to do?'

There was a silence. Then Kestrel said, 'We don't have a choice. We have to kill them.'

CHAPTER

9

Mary-Lynnette's hearing had gone funny. She heard Kestrel's words like a character remembering a phrase in a bad movie. Kill them, kill them, kill them.

Mark laughed in a very strange way.

This is going to be really rotten for him, Mary-Lynnette thought, curiously dispassionate. I mean, if we were going to *live* through this, which we're not, it would be really rotten for him. He was already afraid of girls, and sort of pessimistic about life in general.

'Why don't we all sit down?' Rowan said with a stifled sigh. 'We've got to figure this out.'

Mark threw back his head and gave another short bark of a laugh.

'Why not?' he said. 'Let's all sit down, why not?'

They're fast as whippets, Mary-Lynnette thought. If we run now, they'll catch us. But if we sit, and they get comfortable, and I distract them – or hit them with something . . .

'Sit!' she ordered Mark briskly. Rowan and Kestrel moved away from the deer and sat. Jade stood with her hands on her hips for a moment, then sat, too.

Sitting, Mark was still acting punch-drunk. He waved

the flashlight around. 'You girls are *something else.* You girls are really—'

'We're vampires,' Jade said sharply.

'Yeah.' Mark laughed quietly to himself. 'Yeah,' he said again.

Mary-Lynnette took the flashlight away from him. She wanted control of it. And it was heavy plastic and metal. It was a weapon.

And while one layer of her mind was thinking: *Shine the light in their eyes at just the right moment and then hit one of them*; another part was thinking: *She means they're people who think they're vampires; people with that weird disease that makes them anaemic*; and one final part was saying: *You might as well face it; they're real.*

Mary-Lynnette's world view had been knocked right out of the ballpark.

'Don't you just *hate* that,' Mark was saying. 'You meet a girl and she seems pretty nice and you tell all your friends and then before you know it she turns out to be a *vampire.* Don't you just hate it when that happens?'

Oh, God, he's hysterical, Mary-Lynnette realized.

She grabbed his shoulder and hissed in his ear, 'Get a grip, *now.*'

'I don't see what the point is in talking to them, Rowan,' Kestrel was saying. 'You know what we have to do.'

And Rowan was rubbing her forehead. 'I was thinking we might influence them,' she said in an undertone.

'You know why that won't work.' Kestrel's voice was soft and flat.

'Why?' Jade said sharply.

'They followed us for a reason,' Rowan said tiredly. She nodded toward the hole. 'So they've been suspicious for a while – for how long?' She looked at Mary-Lynnette.

'I saw you dig the hole Tuesday night,' Mary-Lynnette said. *She* nodded toward the hole. 'Is that your aunt in there?'

There was a brief silence and Rowan looked self-conscious. Then she inclined her head slightly. Gracefully.

'Oh, hell,' Mark said. His eyes were shut and his head was rolling on his neck. '*Oh*, hell. They've got Mrs B in a bag.'

'Two days,' Rowan said to Jade. 'They've suspected for two whole days. And we can't remove memories that are interlaced with other things for that long. We'd never know if we got them all.'

'Well, we could just take *everything* for the last two days,' Jade said.

Kestrel snorted. 'And have two more people wandering around with lost time?'

Mary-Lynnette's mind went click. 'Todd Akers and Vic Kimble,' she said. 'You did something to give them amnesia. I *knew* there had to be a connection.'

'There's no other choice for us,' Kestrel said quietly to Rowan. 'And you know it as well as I do.'

She's not being malicious, Mary-Lynnette realized. Just practical. If a lioness or a wolf or a falcon could talk, it would say the same thing. 'We have to either kill or die; it's as simple as that.'

Despite herself, Mary-Lynnette felt something like fascination – and respect.

Mark had his eyes open now. And Rowan was looking sad, so sad. It's awful, her expression said, but somebody here is going to have to get hurt.

Rowan bowed her head, then lifted it to face Mary-Lynnette directly. Their eyes met, held. After a moment Rowan's face changed slightly and she nodded.

Mary-Lynnette knew that in that instant they were

communicating without words. Each recognizing the other as an alpha female who was willing to fight and die for her kin.

Meaning they were both big sisters.

Yes, somebody's going to get hurt, Mary-Lynnette thought. You threaten my family, I fight back.

She knew Rowan understood. Rowan was going to really hate killing her . . .

'*No*,' a voice said passionately, and Mary-Lynnette realized it was Jade. And the next second Jade was on her feet, hands clenched, words erupting like a steam boiler exploding. 'No, you *can't* kill Mark. I won't *let* you.'

Rowan said, 'Jade, I know this is hard—'

Kestrel said, 'Jade, don't be a wimp—'

Jade was trembling, body tensed like a cat ready to fight. Her voice was louder than either of them. 'You just can't do it! I think – I think—'

'Jade—'

'*I think he's my soulmate!*'

Dead silence.

Then Rowan groaned. 'Oh, dear . . .'

Kestrel said, 'Oh, *sure*.'

They were both looking at Jade. Focused on her. Mary-Lynnette thought, *now*.

She swung the flashlight viciously at Kestrel, wanting to take her out first, betting that Rowan would stay behind if Kestrel were hurt. But the swing never connected. Mark threw himself in front of her, slamming into her arm.

'Don't hurt Jade!'

Then everything was just a mad tangle. Arms, legs, grasping fingers, kicking feet. Jade and Mark both yelling for it to stop. Mary-Lynnette felt the flashlight wrenched out of her hand. She found long hair, got hold of it, yanked. Someone kicked her, and pain blossomed in her ribs.

Then she felt herself being dragged backward. Mark was holding her, pulling her away from the fight. Jade was lying on top of Kestrel and clutching at Rowan.

Everybody was panting. Mark was almost crying.

'We just can't do this,' he said. 'This is terrible. This is all wrong.'

Meanwhile Jade was snarling, 'He's my soulmate, OK? *OK?* I can't do anything with him *dead*!'

'He's not your soulmate, idiot,' Kestrel said in a somewhat muffled voice. She was face-down on the carpet of needles. 'When you're soulmates, it hits you like lightning, and you know that's the one person in the world you were meant to be with. You don't *think* you're soulmates; you just know it's your destiny whether you like it or not.'

Somewhere, deep in Mary-Lynnette's brain, something stirred in alarm. But she had more urgent things to worry about.

'Mark, get out of here,' she said breathlessly. 'Run!'

Mark didn't even ease his grip. 'Why do we have to be enemies?'

'Mark, they're *killers*. You can't justify that. They killed their own aunt.'

Three faces turned toward her, startled. A half-full moon had risen above the trees, and Mary-Lynnette could see them clearly.

'We did *not*!' Jade said indignantly.

'What made you think that?' Rowan asked.

Mary-Lynnette felt her mouth hang open. 'Because you *buried* her, for God's sake!'

'Yes, but we found her dead.'

'Somebody staked her,' Kestrel said, brushing pine

needles out of her golden hair. 'Probably a vampire hunter. I don't suppose you'd know anything about *that*.'

Mark gulped. 'Staked her – with a stake?'

'Well, with a picket from the fence,' Kestrel said.

'She was already dead?' Mary-Lynnette said to Rowan. 'But then why on earth did you bury her in the backyard?'

'It would have been disrespectful to leave her in the cellar.'

'But why didn't you have her taken to a *cemetery*?'

Rowan looked dismayed.

Jade said, 'Um, you haven't seen Aunt Opal.'

'She's not looking so good,' Kestrel said. 'Kind of hard and stiff. You might say mummified.'

'It's what happens to us,' Rowan said almost apologetically.

Mary-Lynnette slumped back against Mark, trying to get her new world view into place. Everything was whirling.

'So . . . you were just trying to hide her. But . . . you *did* do something to Todd Akers and Vic Kim—'

'They *attacked* us,' Jade interrupted. 'They were thinking very bad things and they pinched our arms.'

'They—?' Mary-Lynnette sat up suddenly. All at once she understood. 'Oh, my God. Those jerks!'

Why hadn't she thought of that? Todd and Vic – last year there had been rumours about them jumping some girl from Westgrove. So they'd tried it on these girls, and . . .

Mary-Lynnette gasped and then snorted with half inhaled laughter. 'Oh, no. Oh, I hope you got them good . . .'

'We just bit them a little,' Rowan said.

'I wish I'd been there to *see* it.'

She was laughing. Rowan was smiling. Kestrel was grinning barbarically. And suddenly Mary-Lynnette knew that they weren't going to fight anymore.

Everybody took a deep breath and sat back and looked at one another.

They do look different from normal humans, Mary-Lynnette thought, staring at them in the moonlight. It's so obvious once you know.

They were inhumanly beautiful, of course. Rowan with her soft chestnut hair and sweet face; Kestrel with her feral sleekness and golden eyes; Jade with her delicate features and her hair like starshine. Like the Three Graces, only fiercer.

'OK,' Rowan said softly. 'We seem to have a situation here. Now we've got to figure something out.'

'We won't tell on you,' Mark said. He and Jade were gazing at each other.

'We've got Romeo and Juliet on our hands here, is what we've got,' Mary-Lynnette said to Rowan.

But Kestrel was speaking to Rowan, too. 'No matter *what* they promise, how do we know we can believe them?'

Rowan considered, eyes roving around the clearing. Then she let out a long breath and nodded.

'There's only one way,' she said. 'Blood-tie.'

Kestrel's eyebrows flew up. 'Oh, really?'

'What is it?' Mary-Lynnette asked.

'A blood-tie?' Rowan looked helpless. 'Well, it's a kinship ceremony, you know.' When Mary-Lynnette just looked at her, she went on: 'It makes our families related. It's like, one of our ancestors did it with a family of witches.'

Witches, Mary-Lynnette thought. Oh . . . gosh. So witches are real, too. I wonder how many other things are real that I don't know about?

'Vampires don't usually get along with witches,' Rowan was saying. 'And Hunter Redfern – that's our ancestor – had a real blood feud going with them back in the sixteen hundreds.'

'But then he couldn't have kids,' Jade said gleefully. 'And he needed a witch to help or the whole Redfern family would end with him. So he had to apologize and do a kinship ceremony. And then he had all *daughters*. Ha ha.'

Mary-Lynnette blinked. Ha ha?

'So, you see, we're part witch. All the Redferns are,' Rowan was explaining in her gentle teaching voice.

'Our father used to say that's why we're so disobedient,' Jade said. 'Because it's in our *genes*. Because in witch families, *women* are in charge.'

Mary-Lynnette began to like witches. 'Ha ha,' she said. Mark gave her a skittish sideways look.

'The point is that we could do a ceremony like that now,' Rowan said. 'It would make us family forever. We couldn't betray each other.'

'No problem,' Mark said, still looking at Jade.

'Fine with *me*,' Jade said, and gave him a quick, fierce smile.

But Mary-Lynnette was thinking. It was a serious thing Rowan was talking about. You couldn't do something like this on a whim. It was worse than adopting a puppy; it was more like getting married. It was a *lifetime* responsibility. And even if these girls didn't kill humans, they killed animals. With their teeth.

But so did people. And not always for food. Was it worse to drink deer blood than to make baby cows into boots?

Besides, strange as it seemed, she felt close to the three sisters already. In the last couple of minutes she'd established more of a relationship with Rowan than she ever had with any girl at school. Fascination and respect had turned into a weird kind of instinctive trust.

And beside *that*, what other real choice was there?

Mary-Lynnette looked at Mark, and then at Rowan. She nodded slowly.

'OK.'

Rowan turned to Kestrel.

'So I'm supposed to decide, am I?' Kestrel said.

'We can't do it without you,' Rowan said. 'You know that.'

Kestrel looked away. Her golden eyes were narrowed. In the moonlight her profile was absolutely perfect against the darkness of trees. 'It would mean we could never go home again. Make ourselves kin to vermin? That's what *they'd* say.'

'Who's vermin?' Mark said, jolted out of his communion with Jade.

Nobody answered. Jade said, with odd dignity, 'I can't go home, anyway. I'm in love with an Outsider. And I'm going to tell him about the Night World. So I'm dead no matter what.' Mark was opening his mouth – to protest that Jade shouldn't take such a risk for *him*, Mary-Lynnette thought – when Jade added absently, 'And so is he, of course.'

Mark shut his mouth.

Rowan said, 'Kestrel, we've come too far to go back.'

Kestrel stared at the forest for another minute or so. Then suddenly she turned back to the others, laughing. There was something wild in her eyes.

'All right, let's go the whole way,' she said. 'Tell them everything. Break every rule. We might as well.'

Mary-Lynnette felt a twinge. She hoped she wasn't going to regret this. But what she said was 'Just how do we do this – ceremony?'

'Exchange blood. I've never done it before, but it's simple.'

'It might be a *little* bit strange, though,' Jade said, 'because you'll be a little bit vampires afterward.'

'A little bit *what*?' Mary-Lynnette said, her voice rising in spite of her.

'Just a *little* bit.' Jade was measuring out tiny bits of air between her index finger and thumb. 'A drop.'

Kestrel cast a look skyward. 'It'll go away in a few days,' she said heavily, which was what Mary-Lynnette wanted to know.

'As long as you don't get yourself bitten by a vampire again in the meanwhile,' Rowan added. 'Otherwise, it's perfectly safe. Honestly.'

Mary-Lynnette and Mark exchanged glances. Not to discuss things, they'd gone beyond that now. Just to brace themselves. Then Mary-Lynnette took a deep breath and flicked a bit of fern off her knee.

'OK,' she said, feeling lightheaded but determined. 'We're ready.'

CHAPTER

10

It felt like a jellyfish sting.

Mary-Lynnette kept her eyes shut and her face turned away as Rowan bit into her neck. She was thinking of the way the deer had screamed. But the pain wasn't so bad. It went away almost immediately.

She could feel warmth at her neck as the blood flowed, and, after a minute, a slight dizziness. A weakness. But the most interesting thing was that all at once she seemed to have a new sense. She could sense Rowan's *mind*. It was like seeing, but without eyes – and using different wavelengths than visual light. Rowan's mind – her presence – was warm red, like glowing embers in a campfire. It was also fuzzy and rounded like a ball of hot gas floating in space.

Is this what psychics mean when they talk about people having an aura?

Then Rowan pulled back, and it was over. The new sense disappeared.

Mary-Lynnette's fingers went automatically to her neck. She felt wetness there. A little tenderness.

'Don't fool with it,' Rowan said, brushing at her lips with her thumb. 'It'll go away in just a minute.'

Mary-Lynnette blinked, feeling languid. She looked over at Mark, who was being released by Kestrel. He looked OK, if a little dazed. She smiled at him and he reaised his eyebrows and shook his head slightly.

I wonder what *his* mind looks like, Mary-Lynnette thought. Then she said, startled, 'What are you doing?'

Rowan had picked up a twig and was testing its end for sharpness.

'Every species has some substance that's harmful to it,' she said. 'Silver for werewolves, iron for witches . . . and wood for vampires. It's the only thing out here that will cut our skin,' she added.

'I didn't mean that. I meant *why*,' Mary-Lynnette said, but she knew why already. She watched redness bead in the wake of the twig as Rowan drew it across her wrist.

Exchange blood, Rowan had said.

Mary-Lynnette gulped. She didn't look at Mark and Kestrel.

I'll do it first and then he'll see it's not so bad, she told herself. I can do this, I can do this . . . It's so we can stay *alive*.

Rowan was looking at her, offering her wrist.

Copperbloodfear, Mary-Lynnette thought, feeling queasy.

She shut her eyes and put her mouth to Rowan's wrist.

Warmth. Well-being. And a taste not like copper, but like something rich and strange. Later, she'd always grope for ways to describe it, but she could only think of things like: well, a little bit like the way vanilla bean smells, and a little bit like the way silk feels, and a little bit like the way a waterfall looks. It was faintly sweet.

Afterward, she felt as if she could run up mountains.

'*Oh*, boy,' Mark said, sounding giddy. 'If you could bottle that stuff, you'd make millions.'

'It's been thought of before,' Kestrel said coolly. 'Humans hunting us for our blood.'

'Talk later,' Rowan said firmly. 'Blood-tie now.'

Kestrel's mind was gold. With brilliant knifelike edges sending glitters in every direction.

'OK, Jade,' Rowan said. 'Mark. Enough, you guys. Let go of each other now.'

Mary-Lynnette saw that she was physically pulling Mark and Jade apart. Mark was wearing a silly smile, and Mary-Lynnette felt the tiniest stab of envy. What would it be like to see the mind of somebody you were in love with?

Jade's mind was silver and lacy, an intricate filigreed sphere like a Christmas ornament. And by the time Mary-Lynnette sat back from drinking Jade's blood, she felt light-headed and sparkling. As if she had a mountain stream in her veins.

'All right,' Rowan said. 'Now we share the same blood.' She held out a hand, and Jade and Kestrel did the same. Mary-Lynnette glanced at Mark, then they each reached out, all their hands meeting like spokes in a wheel.

'We promise to be kin to you, to protect and defend you always,' Rowan said. She nodded to Mary-Lynnette.

'We promise to be kin to you,' Mary-Lynnette repeated slowly. 'To protect and defend you always.'

'That's it,' Rowan said simply. 'We're family.'

Jade said, 'Let's go *home*.'

They had to finish burying Aunt Opal first. Mary-Lynnette watched as Rowan scattered pine needles over the grave.

'You inherit our blood feuds, too,' Kestrel told Mary-Lynnette pleasantly. 'Meaning you have to help us find out who killed her.'

'I've been trying to do that all along.'

They left the deer where it was. Rowan said, 'There are already lots of scavengers around here. It won't be wasted.'

Yep, that's life, Mary-Lynnette thought as they left the clearing. She glanced behind her – and for just an instant she thought she saw a shadow there and a glint of greenish-orange eyes at her own eye level. It was much too big for a coyote.

She opened her mouth to tell the others . . . and the shadow was gone.

Did I imagine that? I think my eyes are going funny. Everything seems too bright.

All her senses seemed changed – sharpened. It made it easier to get out of the woods than it had been getting in. Mark and Jade didn't walk hand in hand – that would have been impractical – but Jade looked back at him frequently. And when they got to rough spots, they helped each other.

'You're happy, aren't you?' Mary-Lynnette said softly when she found herself beside Mark.

He gave a startled, sheepish grin, white in the moonlight. 'Yeah. I guess I am.' After a minute he said, 'It's like – I don't know how to describe it, but it's like I belong with Jade. She really *sees* me. I mean, not the outside stuff. She sees me *inside*, and she likes me. Nobody else has ever done that . . . except you.'

'I'm happy for you.'

'Listen,' he said. 'I think we should start looking around for you. There are lots of guys around here –'

Mary-Lynnette snorted. 'Mark. If I want to meet a guy, I'll meet a guy. I don't need any help.'

He gave the sheepish grin again. 'Sorry.'

But Mary-Lynnette was thinking. Of *course* she'd like to find somebody who would accept her completely, who would share everything with her. That was everybody's dream. But for how many people did it come true?

And there *weren't* lots of guys around here . . .

She found herself thinking of Jeremy Lovett again. His clear brown eyes . . .

But she couldn't hold the picture. It kept dissolving – to her horror – into eyes that flashed blue and gold and grey, depending on the way they caught the light.

Oh, God, *no*. Ash was the last person who would understand her. And she didn't want to share a bus seat with him, much less her life.

'What I want to know is who *made* you guys vampires,' Mark said. They were sitting on oversize, over-stuffed Victorian furniture in the living room at Burdock Farm. Rowan had a fire going in the fireplace. 'Was it the old lady? Your aunt?'

'It wasn't anybody,' Jade said, looking affronted. 'We're not *made* vampires. We're the lamia.' She pronounced it LAY-mee-uh.

Mark looked at her sideways. 'Uh-huh. And what's that?'

'It's *us*. It's vampires that can have babies, and eat, and drink, and get old if we let ourselves, and live in families. The *best* kind of vampires.'

'It's a race of vampires, basically,' Kestrel said. 'Look, there are two different kinds of vampires, OK? The kind who start out as humans and are changed when a vampire bites them, and the kind that are *born* vampires. That's the kind we are. Our line goes back – well, let's say a long way.'

'The longest,' Jade broke in again. 'We're Redferns; we go back to prehistoric times.'

Mary-Lynnette blinked. 'But *you three* don't go back

that far, do you?' she said nervously.

Rowan stifled a laugh. 'I'm nineteen; Kestrel's seventeen; Jade is sixteen. We haven't stopped aging yet.'

Kestrel was looking at Mary-Lynnette. 'How old did our aunt look to you?'

'Um, around seventy, seventy-five, I guess.'

'When we last saw her she looked maybe forty,' Kestrel said. 'That was ten years ago, when she left our island.'

'But she'd actually been alive for seventy-four years at that point,' Rowan said. 'That's what happens to us – if we stop holding off the aging process, it all catches up at once.'

'Which if you've been alive for five or six hundred years can be quite interesting,' Kestrel said dryly.

Mary-Lynnette said, 'So this island where you come from – is that the Night World?'

Rowan looked startled. 'Oh, no, it's just a safe town. You know, a place where our people all live without any humans. Hunter Redfern founded it back in the sixteenth century so we'd have somewhere safe to live.'

'The only problem,' Kestrel said, golden eyes glinting, 'is that people there are still *doing* things the way they did in the sixteenth century. And they made a rule that nobody could *leave* – except for some of the men and boys that they trusted completely.'

Like Ash, I guess, Mary-Lynnette thought. She was about to say this, but Rowan was speaking again.

'So that's why we ran away. We didn't want to have to get married when our father told us to. We wanted to see the human world. We wanted—'

'To eat *junk* food,' Jade carolled. 'And read magazines and wear pants and watch TV.'

'When Aunt Opal left the island, she didn't tell anybody where she was going – except me,' Rowan said.

'She told me she was going to this little town called Briar Creek where her husband's family had built a house a hundred and fifty years ago.'

Mary-Lynnette ran her fingers through the silky tassels of a forest-green pillow. 'OK, but – where *is* the Night World, then?'

'Oh . . . it's not a place . . .' Rowan looked uncertain. 'This is – it's kind of hard to tell you, actually,' she said. 'You're not even supposed to know it *exists*. The two very first laws of the Night World are that you never let a human find out about it . . . and that you never fall in love with a human.'

'And Jade's breaking both this minute,' Kestrel murmured.

Jade just looked pleased.

'And the penalty for both is death – for everybody involved,' Rowan said. 'But . . . you're family. Here goes.' She took a steadying breath. 'The Night World is a sort of secret society. Not just of vampires. Of witches and werewolves and shape-shifters, too. All the different kinds of Night People. We're everywhere.'

Everywhere? Mary-Lynnette thought. It was an unnerving idea – but an interesting one. So there was a whole world out there she'd never known about – a place to explore, as alien as the Andromeda galaxy.

Mark didn't seem too disturbed by the thought of vampires everywhere. He was grinning at Jade, leaning with one elbow on the arm of the dark green couch. 'So, can you read *minds*? Can you read my mind *right now*?'

'Soulmates can read each other's minds without even trying,' Jade told Mark firmly.

Soulmates . . . Mary-Lynnette wanted to get on to a different subject. She felt uncomfortable, tingly.

'I wish you'd stop saying that. What you have is much

better than being soulmates,' Rowan was telling Jade. 'With love you get to find out about a person first. Being soulmates is involuntary – you don't even have to *like* the person when you meet them. They may be completely wrong for you in every way – wrong species, wrong temperament, wrong age. But you know you'll never be completely happy again without them.'

More and more tingly. Mary-Lynnette had to say something. 'And what if that happened to you – if you found somebody and you were soulmates with them and you didn't want to be?' she asked Rowan. She realized that her voice was strange – thick. 'Isn't there any way you could – get rid of it?'

There was a pause. Mary-Lynnette saw everyone turn to look at her.

'I've never heard of one,' Rowan said slowly. Her brown eyes were searching Mary-Lynnette's. 'But I guess you could ask a witch . . . if you had that problem.'

Mary-Lynnette swallowed. Rowan's eyes were gentle and friendly – and Mary-Lynnette felt a very strong need to talk to *someone*, someone who would understand.

'Rowan—'

She didn't get any further. Rowan, Kestrel, and Jade all looked suddenly toward the front door – like cats who have heard something their humans can't. An instant later, though, Mary-Lynnette heard it, too. The sound of feet on the front porch – *tap, tap, tap* – as quick as that. And then a thud.

'Hey, somebody's *out* there,' Jade said, and before Mark could stop her, she was up and heading for the door.

CHAPTER

11

'Jade – wait a minute!' Mark said.

Jade, of course, didn't wait even a second. But she lost time undoing the bolts on the front door, and Mary-Lynnette could hear the quick *tap, tap, tap* of somebody running away.

Jade threw the door open, darted out onto the porch – and screamed. Mary-Lynnette crowded forward and saw that Jade had put her foot into one of the holes where the porch was missing a board. Everybody who didn't know the place did that. But that wasn't what had made her scream.

It was the goat.

'Oh, God,' Mark said. 'Oh, God – who would do that?'

Mary-Lynnette took one look and felt a burning in her chest and arms – a painful, bad feeling. Her lungs seemed to contract and her breath was forced out. Her vision blurred.

'Let's get it inside,' Rowan said. 'Jade, are you all right?'

Jade was taking in ragged, whooping breaths. She sounded the way Mary-Lynnette felt. Mark leaned over to help pull her out of the hole.

Rowan and Kestrel were lifting the goat by its legs. Mary-Lynnette was backing into the house, teeth clamped on her already-bitten lip. The taste of copper was like a blood clot in her mouth.

They put the goat on an old-fashioned patterned rug in the entrance to the living room. Jade's whooping breaths turned into gasping sobs.

'That's Ethyl,' Mary-Lynnette said. She felt like sobbing too.

She knelt beside Ethyl. The goat was pure white, with a sweet face and a broad forehead. Mary-Lynnette reached out to touch one hoof gently. She'd helped Mrs B trim that hoof with pruning shears.

'She's dead,' Kestrel said. 'You can't hurt her.' Mary-Lynnette looked up quickly. Kestrel's face was composed and distant. Shock rippled under Mary-Lynnette's skin.

'Let's take them out,' Rowan said.

'The hide's ruined already,' Kestrel said.

'Kestrel, please—'

Mary-Lynnette stood. 'Kestrel, *shut up*!'

There was a pause. To Mary-Lynnette's astonishment, the pause went on. Kestrel stayed shut up.

Mary-Lynnette and Rowan began to pull the little wooden stakes out of the goat's body.

Some were as small as toothpicks. Others were longer than Mary-Lynnette's finger and thicker than a shish kebab skewer, with a dull point at one end. Somebody *strong* did this, Mary-Lynnette thought. Strong enough to punch splinters of wood through goat hide.

Over and over again. Ethyl was pierced everywhere. Hundreds of times. She looked like a porcupine.

'There wasn't much bleeding,' Rowan said softly. 'That means she was dead when it was done. And look here.' She gently touched Ethyl's neck. The white coat was crimson there – just like the deer, Mary-Lynnette thought.

'Somebody either cut her throat or bit it,' Rowan said. 'So it was probably quick for her and she bled out. Not like . . .'

'What?' Mary-Lynnette said.

Rowan hesitated. She looked up at Jade. Jade sniffled and wiped her nose on Mark's shoulder.

Rowan looked back at Mary-Lynnette. 'Not like Uncle Hodge.' She looked back down and carefully loosened another stake, adding it to the pile they were accumulating. 'You see, they killed Uncle Hodge this way, the Elders did. Only he was alive when they did it.'

For a moment Mary-Lynnette couldn't speak. Then she said, '*Why?*'

Rowan pulled out two more stakes, her face controlled and intent. 'For telling a human about the Night World.'

Mary-Lynnette sat back on her heels and looked at Mark.

Mark sat down on the floor, bringing Jade with him.

'That's why Aunt Opal left the island,' Rowan said.

'And now somebody's staked Aunt Opal,' Kestrel said. 'And somebody's killed a goat in the same way Uncle Hodge was killed.'

'But *who*?' Mary-Lynnette said.

Rowan shook her head. 'Somebody who knows about vampires.'

Mark's blue eyes looked darker than usual and a little glazed. 'You were talking before about a vampire hunter.'

'That gets my vote,' Kestrel said.

'OK, so who around here is a vampire hunter? *What's* a vampire hunter?'

'That's the problem,' Rowan said. 'I don't know how you could tell who is one. I'm not even sure I *believe* in vampire hunters.'

'They're supposed to be humans who've found out about the Night World,' Jade said, pushing tears out of her eyes with her palms. 'And they can't get other people to believe them – or maybe they don't want other people to know. So they hunt us. You know, trying to kill us one by one. They're supposed to know as much about the Night World as Night People do.'

'You mean, like knowing how your uncle was executed,' Mary-Lynnette said.

'Yes, but that's not much of a secret,' Rowan said. 'I mean, you wouldn't have to actually know about Uncle Hodge to think of it – it's the traditional method of execution among the lamia. There aren't many things besides staking and burning that will kill a vampire.'

Mary-Lynnette thought about this. It didn't get them very far. Who would want to kill an old lady and a goat?

'Rowan? Why did your aunt have goats? I mean, I always thought it was for the milk, but . . .'

'It was for the blood, I'm sure,' Rowan said calmly. 'If she looked as old as you said, she probably couldn't get out into the woods to hunt.'

Mary-Lynnette looked at the goat again, trying to find other clues, trying to be a good observer: detached, methodical. When her eyes got to Ethyl's muzzle, she blinked and leaned forward.

'I – there's something in her mouth.'

'Please tell me you're joking,' Mark said.

Mary-Lynnette just waved a hand at him. 'I can't – I need something to . . . hang on a sec.' She ran into the kitchen and opened a drawer. She snagged a richly decorated sterling silver knife and ran back to the living room.

'OK,' she grunted as she pried Ethyl's teeth farther open. There *was* something in there – something like a flower, but black. She worked it out with her fingers.

'Silence of the Goats,' Mark muttered.

Mary-Lynnette ignored him, turning the disintegrating thing over in her hands. 'It looks like an iris – but it's spray-painted black.'

Jade and Rowan exchanged grim glances. 'Well – this has *something* to do with the Night World,' Rowan said. 'If we weren't sure of that before, we are now. Black flowers are the symbols of the Night World.'

Mary-Lynnette put the sodden iris down. 'Symbols, like . . . ?'

'We wear them to identify ourselves to each other. You know, on rings or pins or clothes or things like that. Each species has its own kind of flower, and then there are other flowers that mean you belong to a certain club or family. Witches use black dahlias, werewolves use black foxglove; made vampires use black roses . . .'

'And there's a chain of clubs called the Black Iris,' Kestrel said, coming to stand by the others. 'I know because Ash belongs to one.'

'*Ash* . . .' Jade said, staring at Kestrel with wide green eyes.

Mary-Lynnette sat frozen. Something was tugging insistently at the corner of her consciousness. Something about a black design . . .

'Oh, God,' she said. 'Oh, God – I know somebody who wears a ring with a black flower on it.'

Everyone looked at her.

'Who?' Mark said, at the same time as Rowan said it. Mary-Lynnette didn't know which of them looked more surprised.

Mary-Lynnette struggled with herself for a minute.

'It's Jeremy Lovett,' she said finally. Not too steadily.

Mark made a face. 'That oddball. He lives by himself in

a trailer in the woods, and last summer . . .' Mark's voice died out. His jaw dropped, and when he spoke again, it was more slowly. 'And last summer they found a body right out near there.'

'Can you tell?' Mary-Lynnette asked Rowan quietly. 'If somebody's a Night Person?'

'Well . . .' Rowan looked dismayed. 'Well – not for sure. If somebody was experienced at shielding their mind . . . Well, we *might* be able to startle them into revealing something. But otherwise, no. Not for *certain*.'

Mark leaned back. 'Oh, terrific. Well, I think Jeremy would make a great Night Person. Actually, so would Vic Kimble and Todd Akers.'

'Todd,' Jade said. 'Now, wait a minute.' She picked up one of the toothpicks that had been embedded in the goat and stared at it.

Rowan was looking at Mary-Lynnette. 'No matter what, we should go and see your friend Jeremy. He'll probably turn out to be completely innocent – sometimes a human gets hold of one of our rings or pins, and then things get *really* confusing. Especially if they wander into one of our clubs . . .'

Mary-Lynnette wasn't so sure. She had a terrible, terrible sick feeling. The way Jeremy kept to himself, the way he always seemed to be an outsider at school – even his untamed good looks and his easy way of moving . . . No, it all seemed to lead to one conclusion. She had solved the mystery of Jeremy Lovett at last, and it was *not* a happy ending.

Kestrel said, 'OK, fine; we can go check this Jeremy guy out. But what about Ash?'

'What about Ash?' Rowan said. The last stake was out. She gently turned one side of the rug over the body of the goat, like a shroud.

'Well, don't you see? It's his club flower. So maybe somebody from his club did it.'

'Um, I know I'm starting to sound like a broken record,' Mark said. 'But I don't know what you're talking about. Who's Ash?'

The three sisters looked at him. Mary-Lynnette looked away. After so many missed opportunities, it was going to sound extremely peculiar when she casually mentioned that, oh, yes, she'd met Ash. Twice. But she didn't have a choice anymore. She had to tell.

'He's our brother,' Kestrel was saying.

'He's crazy,' Jade said.

'He's the only one from our family who might know that we're here in Briar Creek,' Rowan said. 'He found me giving a letter to Crane Linden to smuggle off the island. But I don't *think* he noticed Aunt Opal's address on it. He's not much good at noticing things that aren't about him.'

'You can say that again,' Jade said. 'All Ash thinks about is Ash. He's completely self-centred.'

'All he does is chase girls and party,' Kestrel said, with one of those smiles that made Mary-Lynnette wonder if she really disapproved. 'And hunt.'

'He doesn't like humans,' Jade said. 'If he didn't like chasing human girls and playing with them, he'd probably be planning to *wipe out* all the humans and take over the world.'

'Sounds like a great guy,' Mark said.

'Well, he's sort of conservative,' Rowan said. 'Politically, I mean. Personally, he's—'

'Loose,' Kestrel suggested, eyebrows up.

'To put it mildly,' Jade agreed. 'There's only one thing he wants when he goes after human girls – besides their cars, I mean.'

Mary-Lynnette's heart was pounding. With every

second that passed it was getting harder to speak up. And every time she took a breath, somebody else started talking.

'So, wait – you think *he* did all this stuff?' Mark asked.

'I wouldn't put it past him,' Kestrel said.

Jade nodded vigorously.

'But his own *aunt*,' Mark said.

'He'd do it if he thought the honour of the family was involved,' Kestrel said.

'Yes, well, there's one problem with all that,' Rowan said tightly. 'Ash isn't *here*. He's in California.'

'No, he's not,' Ash said casually, from the back of the living room.

CHAPTER

12

What happened then was interesting. Mary-Lynnette got to see the sisters do all the things she'd missed earlier in the clearing. All the hissing and the clawed fingers. Just like the movies.

Except that when a vampire hissed, it sounded *real*. Like a cat, not like a person imitating a cat. All three girls jumped up and stood ready to fight.

There wasn't any weird grimacing. But Jade and Kestrel were showing teeth that were long and beautifully curved, coming to delicate feline points that indented the lower lip.

And something else. Their eyes changed. Jade's silvery-green eyes went even more silvery. Kestrel's golden eyes looked jewel-yellow, like a hawk's. Even Rowan's eyes had a dark light in them.

'Oh, boy,' Mark whispered. He was standing beside Jade, staring from her to Ash.

Ash said, 'Hi.'

Don't look at him, Mary-Lynnette told herself. Her heart was pounding wildly and her knees were trembling. The attraction of particle to anti–particle, she thought, remembering a line from last year's physics class. But there was another, shorter name for it, and no matter what she said to herself, she couldn't keep it out of her mind.

Soulmates.

Oh, God, I really don't want this. Please, *please*, I didn't ask for this. I want to discover a supernova and study mini-quasars at the Gamma Ray Observatory. I want to be the one who solves the mystery of where all the dark matter in the universe is.

I don't want this.

It should have happened to someone like Bunny Marten, someone who spent time *longing* for romance. The only thing Mary-Lynnette longed for was somebody to understand . . .

. . . *to understand the night with you*, a distant part of her mind whispered.

And instead here she was, stuck with a guy whose own sisters were terrified of him.

It was true. That was why they were standing poised to fight, making threatening noises. Even *Kestrel* was afraid of him.

The moment Mary-Lynnette realized that, anger washed out the trembling dismay inside her. Whatever she felt about Ash, she wasn't afraid of him.

'Don't you ever *knock*?' she said and walked toward him. *Strode* toward him.

She had to hand it to her new family. Both Jade and Kestrel tried to grab her and keep her from getting close to their brother. Protecting her. Mary-Lynnette shook them off.

Ash eyed her warily.

'Oh. You,' he said. Unenthusiastically.

'What are you doing here?'

'It's my uncle's house.'

'It's your aunt's house and you weren't invited.'

Ash looked at his sisters. Mary-Lynnette could just see little wheels turning in his head. Had they already told about the Night World or not? Of course, if they hadn't, their behaviour should be giving somebody a clue. Most human girls didn't hiss.

Ash held one finger up. 'OK. Now, listen—'

Mary-Lynnette kicked him in the shins. She knew it was inappropriate, she knew it was uncalled-for, but she couldn't stop herself. She just *had* to.

'Oh, for God's sake,' Ash said, hopping backward. 'Are you *crazy?*'

'Yes, she is,' Mark said, abandoning Jade and hurrying forward to take Mary-Lynnette's arm. 'Everybody knows she's crazy. She can't help it.' He backed up, pulling. He was looking at Mary-Lynnette as if she'd taken all her clothes off and started to dance the mambo.

So were Kestrel and Jade. Their eyes had gone ordinary, their teeth retracted. They'd never seen anyone treat their brother quite this way. And to have a *human* doing it . . .

If the girls had superhuman strength, Ash was undoubtedly even stronger. He could probably flatten Mary-Lynnette with one blow.

She *still* couldn't help it. She wasn't afraid of him, only of herself and the stupid floating feeling in her stomach. The way her legs wanted to fold under her.

'Will somebody just tell her not to do that anymore?' Ash was saying.

Kestrel and Jade looked sideways at Mary-Lynnette. Mary-Lynnette shrugged at them, her breath coming quickly.

She saw that Rowan was looking at her, too, but not in the same dumbfounded way. Rowan looked worried and surprised and sorry.

'You've met,' she said.

'I should have told you,' Mary-Lynnette said. 'He came to our house. He was asking my stepmother about you and your friends – saying that he needed to approve them because he was head of the family.'

All three girls looked at Ash with narrowed eyes.

'So you *have* been around,' Kestrel said. 'For how long?'

Rowan said quietly, 'What are you really doing here?'

Ash let go of his shin. 'Can we all sit down and talk about this like reasonable people?'

Everyone looked at Mary-Lynnette. She took a deep, calming breath. She still felt as if her entire skin was electrified, but her heart was slowing down. 'Yes,' she said and worked at looking normal so they'd know her temporary insanity was over.

As he helped her to the couch, Mark whispered, 'I have to tell you, I've never seen you act so immature before. I'm proud of you.'

Even big sisters have to have some off time, Mary-Lynnette thought. She patted him vaguely and sat, feeling tired.

Ash settled in a plush-covered chair. Rowan and Kestrel sat beside Mary-Lynnette. Mark and Jade shared an ottoman.

'All right,' Ash said. 'Now can we first introduce ourselves? I presume that's your brother.'

'Mark,' Mary-Lynnette said. 'Mark, that's Ash.'

Mark nodded. He and Jade were holding hands. Mary-Lynnette saw Ash's eyes drop to their intertwined fingers. She couldn't tell anything from his expression.

'OK. Now.' Ash looked at Rowan. 'I'm here to take you back home, where everyone misses you violently.'

Jade breathed, 'Give me a break.'

Kestrel said, 'What if we don't want to be taken?' and showed her teeth briefly. Mary-Lynnette didn't find that strange. What she found strange was that Ash didn't return the smile. He didn't look lazy or sardonic or smug right then. He looked like somebody who wants to get a job over with.

Rowan said, 'We can't go home, Ash.' Her breathing was slightly irregular, but her chin was high.

'Well, you have to come home. Because otherwise there are going to be some fairly drastic consequences.'

'We knew that when we left,' Jade said, with as little emotion as Rowan. Her chin was high, too.

'Well, I don't think you've really thought it *through*.' Ash's voice had an edge.

'We'd rather die than go back,' Jade said.

Kestrel glanced at her quickly, one eyebrow raised.

'Oh, well, fine, I'll just make a note of that,' Ash said tightly. Then his expression darkened. He looked more determined than Mary-Lynnette would have thought he *could* look. Not in the least like a big blond cat. Like a lanky, elegant pale tiger.

'Now, listen,' he said. 'There are a few small things that you don't understand, and I don't have any time to play games. So how about we send your little friends home and then we can all have a family talk.'

Mary-Lynnette's hands clenched into fists.

Mark clutched at Jade, who pushed him away slightly with her elbow. She was frowning. 'I think maybe you'd better,' she said.

'I'm not going to leave you.'

Rowan bit her lip. 'Mark . . .'

'I'm not *going*. Don't try to protect me. He's not stupid; sooner or later he's going to find out that we know about the Night World.'

Rowan drew in her breath involuntarily. Kestrel's expression never changed, but her muscles tensed as if for a fight. Jade's eyes went silver. Mary-Lynnette sat very still.

They all looked at Ash. Ash looked heavenward.

'I know you know,' he said with deadly patience. 'I'm trying to get you out, you poor sap, before I find out how *much* you know.'

The sisters stared. Mary-Lynnette opened her mouth and then shut it again.

'I thought you didn't like humans,' Mark said.

'I don't; I hate them,' Ash said with brittle cheer.

'Then why would you want to cut me a break?'

'Because if I kill you, I have to kill your sister,' Ash informed him, with a smile that would have fit in perfectly at the Mad Hatter's tea party.

'So what; she kicked you.'

Ash stopped tossing answers back like footballs. 'Yeah, well, I may change my mind any minute.'

'No, *wait*,' Jade said. She was sitting with legs folded under her, staring at her brother fiercely. 'This is just too weird. Why would you care what happens to a human?'

Ash didn't say anything. He looked at the fireplace bitterly.

It was Rowan who said softly, 'Because they're soulmates.'

An instant of silence, then everybody started talking explosively.

'They're what? You mean, like what Jade and I are?'

'Oh, Ash, this is rich. I just wish our father were here to see this.'

'It is *not my fault*,' Mary-Lynnette said. She found everyone turning toward her, and realized that her eyes were full.

Rowan leaned across Kestrel to put her hand on Mary-Lynnette's arm.

'You mean it's really true?' Mark said, looking from Mary-Lynnette to Ash.

'It's true. I guess. I don't know what it's supposed to be like,' Mary-Lynnette said, concentrating on making the tears go away.

'It's true,' Ash said moodily. 'It doesn't mean we're going to *do* anything about it.'

'Oh, you've got *that* right,' Mary-Lynnette said. She was glad to be angry again.

'So let's all just pick up our toys and go home,' Ash said in the general direction of his sisters. 'We'll forget all about this; we'll just agree that it never happened.'

Rowan was watching him, shaking her head slightly. There were tears in her eyes, but she was smiling.

'I never thought I'd hear you say something like that,' she said. 'You've changed so much – I can't believe it.'

'I can't believe it, either,' Ash said bleakly. 'Maybe it's a dream.'

'But you have to admit now that humans aren't vermin. You couldn't be soulmates with vermin.'

'Yes. Fine. Humans are terrific. We all agree; now let's go home.'

'When we were kids, you were like this,' Rowan said. 'Before you started acting like you were better than everyone. I always knew a lot of that was just show. To hide how scared you were. And I always knew you didn't really believe a lot of the horrible stuff you said. Somewhere inside, you're still that nice little kid, Ash.'

Ash produced his first really *flashing* smile of the evening. 'Don't bet on it.'

Mary-Lynnette had listened to all this feeling shakier and shakier. To conceal it, she said to Rowan,

'I don't think your aunt thought so.'

Ash sat up. 'Hey, where is the old hag, anyway? I need to have a talk with her before we leave.'

This silence seemed endless.

'Ash . . . don't you know?' Rowan said.

'Of course he knows. Ten to one, he *did* it,' Kestrel said.

'What is it that I'm supposed to know?' Ash said, with every sign of being about to lose his patience.

'Your aunt's dead,' Mark told him.

'Somebody staked her,' Jade added.

Ash looked around the room. His expression said he suspected it was a practical joke. Oh, God, Mary-Lynnette thought numbly, when he's startled and bewildered like that he looks so young. Vulnerable. Almost human.

'Somebody . . . murdered . . . Aunt Opal. That's what you're telling me?'

'Are you telling *us* that you don't know?' Kestrel asked. 'What have you been *doing* all night, Ash?'

'Banging my head against a rock,' Ash said. 'Then looking for you. When I walked in you were talking about me.'

'And you didn't run across any livestock tonight? Any – let's say – goats?'

Ash gave her a long, incredulous look. 'I fed, if that's what you're asking. Not on a goat. *What* does this have to do with Aunt Opal?'

'I think we'd better show him,' Rowan said.

She was the one who got up and lifted the fold of rug away from the goat. Ash walked around the couch to see what she was doing. Mary-Lynnette turned to watch his face.

He winced. But he controlled it quickly.

Rowan said quietly, 'Look at what was in the goat's mouth.'

Ash picked up the black flower gingerly. 'An iris. So?'

'Been to your club recently?' Kestrel asked.

Ash gave her a weary look. 'If *I* had done this, why would I sign it with an iris?'

'Maybe to tell us who did it.'

'I don't have to kill goats to say things, you know. I *can* talk.'

Kestrel looked unimpressed. 'Maybe this way the message has a little more impact.'

'Do I *look* like the kind of person who wastes time turning goats into pin cushions?'

'No. No, I don't think you did this,' Rowan said in her quiet way. 'But *somebody* did – probably whoever killed Aunt Opal. We've been trying to figure out who.'

'Well, who have we got for suspects?'

Everyone looked at Mary-Lynnette. She looked away.

'There's one who's pretty prime,' Mark said. 'His name's Jeremy Lovett. He's a real—'

'Quiet guy,' Mary-Lynnette interrupted. If anyone was going to describe Jeremy, it was going to be her. 'I've known him since elementary school, and I would never, *ever* have believed he could hurt anybody – especially an old lady and an animal.'

'But his uncle was crazy,' Mark said. 'And I've heard things about his family—'

'Nobody *knows* anything about his family,' Mary-Lynnette said. She felt as if she were struggling to keep her head above water, with barbells tied to her wrists and ankles. What was dragging her down wasn't Mark's suspicion – it was her own. The little voice in her head that was saying, 'But he *seemed* like such a nice guy' – and which meant, of course, that he wasn't.

Ash was watching her with a brooding, intent expression. 'What does this Jeremy look like?'

Something about the way he said it irritated Mary-Lynnette beyond belief. 'What do you care?'

Ash blinked and shifted his gaze. He shrugged minimally and said with forced blandness, 'Just curious.'

'He's *very* handsome,' Mary-Lynnette said. Good – a way to let out her anger and frustration. 'And the thing is that he looks very intelligent and sensitive – it's not empty good looks. He's got hair that's sort of the colour of Ponderosa pinecones and the most wonderful brown eyes . . . He's thin and tan and a little bit taller than me, because I'm normally looking at his mouth . . .'

Ash didn't look pleased. 'I saw somebody vaguely like that at the gas station in town.' He turned to Rowan. 'You think he's some kind of outlaw vampire?'

'Obviously not a made vampire because Mary-Lynnette has watched him grow up,' Rowan said. 'I was thinking more that he might be renegade lamia. But there's not much use in trying to figure it out from here. Tomorrow we can go and *see* him, and then we'll know more. Right?'

Mark nodded. Jade nodded. Mary-Lynnette took a deep breath and nodded.

Ash nodded and said, 'All right, I see why you can't go home until this is solved. So, we'll figure out who killed Aunt Opal, and then we'll take the appropriate action, and *then* we'll go home. Got it?'

His sisters exchanged glances. They didn't answer.

As she and Mark walked back to their house, Mary-Lynnette noticed that Sirius had lifted above the eastern horizon. It hung like a jewel, brighter than she had ever seen it before – much brighter. It seemed almost like a miniature sun, flashing with blue and gold and violet rays.

She thought the effect must be psychological, until she remembered that she'd exchanged blood with three vampires.

CHAPTER

13

Jade sat in the wing chair, holding Tiggy upside down on her lap, petting his stomach. He was purring but mad. She stared down into indignant, glowing green eyes.

'The other *goat*,' Kestrel announced from the doorway, saying the word as if it were something not mentioned in polite society, 'is just fine. So you can let the cat out.'

Jade didn't think so. There was somebody crazy in Briar Creek, and she planned to keep Tiggy safe where she could see him.

'*We're* not going to have to feed on the goat, are we?' Kestrel asked Rowan dangerously.

'Of course not. Aunt Opal did because she was too old to hunt.' Rowan looked preoccupied as she answered.

'I like hunting,' Jade said. 'It's even better than I thought it would be.' But Rowan wasn't listening – she was biting her lip and staring into the distance. 'Rowan, *what*?'

'I was thinking about the situation we're in. You and Mark, for one thing. I think we need to talk about that.'

Jade felt reflexive alarm. Rowan was in one of her organizing moods – which meant you could blink and find that she'd rearranged all your bedroom furniture or that you were moving to Oregon. 'Talk about what?' she said warily.

'About what you two are going to *do*. Is he going to stay human?'

'It's illegal to change him,' Kestrel put in pointedly.

'Everything we've done this week is illegal,' Rowan said. 'And if they exchange blood again – well, it's only going to take a couple of times. Do you *want* him a vampire?' she asked Jade.

Jade hadn't thought about it. She thought Mark was nice the way he was. But maybe *he* would want to be one. 'What are you going to do with yours?' she asked Ash, who was coming slowly downstairs.

'My what?' He looked sleepy and irritable.

'Your soulmate. Is Mary-Lynnette going to stay human?'

'That's the other thing I've been worrying about,' Rowan said. 'Have you thought at all, Ash?'

'I can't think at this hour in the morning. I don't have a brain yet.'

'It's almost noon,' Kestrel said scornfully.

'I don't care when it is. I'm still asleep.' He wandered toward the kitchen. 'And you don't need to worry,' he added, looking back and sounding more awake. 'Because I'm not doing *anything* with the girl and Jade's not doing anything with the brother. Because we're going *home*.' He disappeared.

Jade's heart was beating hard. Ash might act frivolous, but she saw the ruthlessness underneath. She looked at Rowan.

'Is Mary-Lynnette *really* his soulmate?'

Rowan leaned back, her brown hair spreading like a waterfall on the green brocade of the couch. 'I'm afraid so.'

'But then how can he want to leave?'

'Well . . .' Rowan hesitated. 'Soulmates don't always stay together. Sometimes it's too much – the fire and lightning and all that. Some people just can't stand it.'

Maybe Mark and I aren't really soulmates, Jade thought. And maybe that's *good*. It sounds painful.

'Poor Mary-Lynnette,' she said.

A clear voice sounded in her mind: *Why doesn't anybody say 'Poor Ash'?*

'Poor Mary-Lynnette,' Jade said again.

Ash reappeared. 'Look,' he said and sat down on one of the carved mahogany chairs. 'We need to get things straight. It's not just a matter of *me* wanting you to come home. I'm not the only one who knows you're here.'

Jade stiffened.

Kestrel said, almost pleasantly, 'You *told* somebody?'

'I was staying with somebody when the family called to say you were missing. And he was there when I realized where you must have gone. He also happens to be an extremely powerful telepath. So just consider yourself lucky I convinced him to let me try to get you back.'

Jade stared at him. She did consider herself lucky. She also considered it strange that Ash would go to such trouble for her and Rowan and Kestrel – for *anybody* besides Ash. Maybe she didn't know her brother as well as she thought.

Rowan said, very soberly, 'Who was it?'

'Oh, nobody.' Ash leaned back and looked moodily at the ceiling. 'Just Quinn.'

Jade flinched. Quinn . . . that *snake*. He had a heart like a glacier and he despised humans. He was the sort to take Night World law into his own hands if he didn't think it was being enforced properly.

'He's coming back on Monday to see if I've taken care of the situation,' Ash said. 'And if I haven't, we're all dead

– you, me, *and* your little human buddies.'

Rowan said, 'So we've got until Monday to figure something out.'

Kestrel said, 'If he tries anything on *us*, he's in for a fight.'

Jade squeezed Tiggy to make him growl.

Mary-Lynnette had been sleeping like a stone – but a stone with unusually vivid dreams. She dreamed about stars brighter than she'd ever seen and star clouds shimmering in colours like the northern lights. She dreamed about sending an astronomical telegram to Cambridge, Massachusetts, to register her claim for discovering a new supernova. About being the first to see it with her wonderful new eyes, eyes that – she saw in a mirror – were all pupil, like an owl's or a cat's . . .

Then the dream changed and she *was* an owl, swooping down in a dizzying rush from a hollow Douglas fir. She seized a squirrel in her talons and felt a surge of simple joy. Killing felt so natural. All she had to do was be the best owl she could be, and grab food with her feet.

But then a shadow fell over her from somewhere above. And in the dream she felt a terrible sick realization – that even hunters could be hunted. And that something was after *her* . . .

She woke up disoriented – not as to *where* she was, but as to *who* she was. Mary-Lynnette or a hunter being chased by something with white teeth in the moonlight? And even when she went downstairs, she couldn't shake off the sick feeling from her dream.

'Hi,' Mark said. 'Is that breakfast or lunch?'

'Both,' Mary-Lynnette said, sitting down on the family room couch with her two granola bars.

Mark was watching her. 'So,' he said, 'have you

been thinking about it, too?'

Mary-Lynnette tore the wrapper off a granola bar with her teeth. 'About what?'

'*You* know.'

Mary-Lynnette did know. She glanced around to make sure Claudine wasn't in earshot. '*Don't* think about it.'

'Why not?' When she didn't answer, he said, 'Don't tell me you haven't been wondering what it would be like. To see better, hear better, be telepathic . . . and live *forever*. I mean, we could see the year three thousand. You know, the robot wars, colonizing other planets . . . Come on, don't tell me you're not even a *little* curious.'

All Mary-Lynnette could think of was a line from a Robert Service poem: *And the skies of night were alive with light, with a throbbing, thrilling flame . . .*

'I'm curious,' she said. 'But there's no point in wondering. They do things we couldn't do – they *kill*.'

She put down her glass of milk as if she'd lost her appetite. She hadn't, though – and wasn't that the problem? She ought to be sick to her stomach at just the thought of killing, of drinking blood from a warm body.

Instead, she was scared. Of what was out there in the world – and of herself.

'It's *dangerous*,' she said aloud to Mark. 'Don't you see? We've gotten mixed up in this Night World – and it's a place where bad things can happen. Not just bad like flunking a class. Bad like . . .'

. . . white teeth in the moonlight . . .

'Like getting killed *dead*,' Mary-Lynnette said. 'And that's serious, Mark. It's not like the movies.'

Mark was staring at her. 'Yeah, but we knew that already.' His tone said 'What's the big deal?'

And Mary-Lynnette couldn't explain. She stood up abruptly. 'If we're going over there, we'd better get moving,' she said. 'It's almost one o'clock.'

The sisters and Ash were waiting at Burdock Farm. 'You and Mark can sit in the front with me,' Mary-Lynnette told Jade, not looking at Ash. 'But I don't think you'd better bring the cat.'

'The cat goes,' Jade said firmly, getting in. 'Or I don't.'

Mary-Lynnette put the car in gear and pulled out.

As they came in sight of the small cluster of buildings on Main Street, Mark said, 'And there it is, downtown Briar Creek in all its glory. A typical Friday afternoon, with absolutely nobody on the streets.'

He didn't say it with his usual bitterness. Mary-Lynnette glanced at him and saw that it was Jade he was talking to. And Jade was looking around with genuine interest, despite the cat's claws embedded in her neck.

'*Somebody's* on the streets,' she said cheerfully. 'It's that boy Vic. And that other one, Todd. And grown-ups.'

Mary-Lynnette slowed as she passed the sheriff's office but didn't stop until she reached the gas station at the opposite corner. Then she got out and looked casually across the street.

Todd Akers was there with his father, the sheriff – and Vic Kimble was there with *his* father. Mr Kimble had a farm east of town. They were all getting into the sheriff's car, and they all seemed very excited. Bunny Marten was standing on the sidewalk watching as they left.

Mary-Lynnette felt a twinge of fear. This is what it's like when you have a terrible secret, she thought. You worry about everything that happens, and wonder if it's got something to do with you, if it's going to get you caught.

'Hey, Bunny!' she called. 'What's going on?'

Bunny looked back. 'Oh, hi, Mare.' She walked unhurriedly – Bunny never hurried – across the street.

'How're you doing? They're just going to check out that horse thing.'

'What horse thing?'

'Oh . . . didn't you hear?' Bunny was looking behind Mary-Lynnette now, at Mark and the four strangers who were getting out of the station wagon. Suddenly her blue eyes got rounder and she reached up to fluff her soft blond hair.

Now, I wonder who she's just seen, Mary-Lynnette thought ironically. Who *could* it be?

'Hi,' Ash said.

'We didn't hear about the horse thing,' Mary-Lynnette said, gently prompting.

'Oh . . . um, one of Mr Kimble's horses cut his throat on barbed wire last night. That's what everybody was saying this morning. But just now Mr Kimble came into town and said that he didn't think it was barbed wire after all. He thinks . . . somebody did it on purpose. Slashed its throat and left it to die.' She hunched her shoulders in a tiny shiver. Theatrically, Mary-Lynnette thought.

'You see?' Jade said. 'That's why I'm keeping my eye on Tiggy.'

Mary-Lynnette noticed Bunny eyeing Jade. 'Thanks, Bun.'

'I've got to get back to the store,' Bunny said, but she didn't move. Now she was looking at Kestrel and Rowan.

'I'll walk you there,' Ash said gallantly. With what, Mary-Lynnette thought, must be his usual putting-the-moves-on manner. 'After all, we don't know what could be lurking around here.'

'It's broad daylight,' Kestrel said disgustedly, but Ash was already walking Bunny away. Mary-Lynnette decided she was glad to get rid of him.

'Who was that girl?' Rowan asked, and something in her voice was odd.

Mary-Lynnette glanced at her in surprise. 'Bunny Marten. I know her from school. What's wrong?'

'She was staring at us,' Rowan said softly.

'She was staring at Ash. Oh, and probably you three, too. You're new and you're pretty, so she's probably wondering which boys you'll take from her.'

'I see.' But Rowan still looked preoccupied.

'Rowan, what is it?'

'It's nothing. I'm sure it's nothing. It's just that she's got a lamia name.'

'*Bunny?*'

'Well.' Rowan smiled. 'Lamia are traditionally named after natural things – gems and animals and flowers and trees. So "Bunny" would be a lamia name – and isn't a marten a kind of weasel?'

Something was tugging at the edges of Mary-Lynnette's consciousness again. Something about Bunny . . . about Bunny and . . . wood . . .

It was gone. She couldn't remember. To Rowan she said, 'But – can you sense something suspicious about her or anything? I mean, does she *seem* like one of you? Because otherwise I just can't see Bunny as a vampire. I'm sorry; I just *can't.*'

Rowan smiled. 'No, I don't sense anything. And I'm sure you're right – humans can have names like ours, too. Sometimes it gets confusing.'

For some bizarre reason Mary-Lynnette's mind was still on wood. 'You know, I don't see why you name yourselves after trees. I thought wood was dangerous for you.'

'It is – and that makes it powerful. Tree names are supposed to be some of the most powerful names we have.'

Ash was coming out of the general store. Immediately Mary-Lynnette turned around and looked for Jeremy.

She didn't see him in the empty gas station, but she heard something – something she realized she'd been hearing for several minutes. Hammering.

'Come on, let's go around back,' she said, already walking, not waiting for Ash to reach them. Kestrel and Rowan went with her.

Jeremy was around back. He was hammering a long board across a broken window. There were shards of thick, greenish-tinted glass all over the ground. Light brown hair was falling in his eyes as he struggled to hold the board steady.

'*What happened?*' Mary-Lynnette said. She moved automatically to hold the right end of the board in place for him.

He glanced up at her, making a grimace of relief as he let go of the board. 'Mary-Lynnette – thanks. Hang on a sec.'

He reached into his pocket for nails and began driving them in with quick, sure blows of the hammer. Then he said, 'I don't know what happened. Somebody broke it last night. Made a real mess.'

'Last night seems to have been a busy night,' Kestrel said dryly.

Jeremy glanced back at the voice. And then . . . his hands went still, poised with the hammer and nail. He was looking at Kestrel, and at Rowan beside her, looking a long time. At last he turned to Mary-Lynnette and said slowly, 'You need more gas already?'

'Oh – no. No.' I should have siphoned some out, Mary-Lynnette thought. Nancy Drew would definitely have thought of that. 'I just – it's been knocking a lot – the engine – and I thought you could look at it – under the hood – since you didn't last time.'

Incoherent and pathetic, she decided in the silence that followed. And Jeremy's clear brown eyes were still searching her face.

'Sure, Mary-Lynnette,' he said – not sarcastically, but gently. 'As soon as I get finished.'

Oh, he *can't* be a vampire. And so what am I doing here, lying to him, suspecting him, when he's only ever been nice to me? He's the type to *help* old ladies, not kill them.

Sssssss.

She started as the feral hiss tore through the silence. It came from behind her, and for one horrible instant she thought it was Kestrel. Then she saw that Jade and Mark had rounded the corner, and that Tiggy was fighting like a baby leopard in Jade's arms. The kitten was spitting and clawing, black fur standing on end. Before Jade could get a better grip, he climbed up her shoulder and leaped, hitting the ground running.

'*Tiggy!*' Jade shrieked. She took off after him, silvery-blond hair flying, agile as a kitten herself. Mark followed, ricocheting off Ash who was just coming around the corner himself. Ash was knocked into the gas station wall.

'Well, that was fun,' Kestrel said.

But Mary-Lynnette wasn't really listening. Jeremy was staring at Ash – and his expression gave Mary-Lynnette cold chills.

And Ash was staring back with eyes as green as glacier ice. Their gazes were locked in something like instantaneous, instinctive hatred. Mary-Lynnette felt a quiver of fear for Jeremy – but Jeremy didn't seem afraid for himself. His muscles were tight and he looked ready to defend himself.

Then, deliberately, he turned away. Turned his back on Ash. He readjusted the board – and Mary-Lynnette did what she should have done in the beginning. She looked at his hand. The ring on his index finger glinted gold, and she could just make out the black design on the seal.

A tall cluster of bell-shaped flowers. Not an iris, not a dahlia, not a rose. No – there was only one flower Rowan had mentioned that this could possibly be. It grew wild around here and it was deadly poison.

Foxglove.

So now she knew.

Mary-Lynnette felt hot and sick. Her hand began to tremble on the board she was holding. She didn't want to move, but she couldn't stay here.

'I'm sorry – I have to get something—' The words came out in a painful gasp. She knew everyone was staring at her. She didn't care. She let go of the board and almost ran away.

She kept going until she was behind the boarded-up windows of the Gold Creek Hotel. Then she leaned against the wall and stared at the place where town ended and the wilderness began. Motes of dust danced in the sunlight, bright against a dark background of Douglas fir.

I'm so *stupid*. All the signs were there, right in front of my face. Why didn't I see before? I guess because I didn't *want* to . . .

'Mary-Lynnette.'

Mary-Lynnette turned toward the soft voice. She resisted the impulse to throw herself into Rowan's arms and bawl.

'I'll be OK in just a few minutes. Really. It's just a shock.'

'Mary-Lynnette . . .'

'It's just – it's just that I've known him so long. It's not easy to picture him – you know. But I guess it just goes to show you. People are never what they seem.'

'Mary-Lynnette—' Rowan stopped and shook her head. 'Just what are you talking about?'

'*Him.* Jeremy. Of course.' Mary-Lynnette took a breath. The air felt hot and chokingly dusty. 'He did it. He really did it.'

'Why do you think so?'

'*Why?* Because he's a *werewolf.*'

There was a pause and Mary-Lynnette suddenly felt embarrassed. She looked around to make sure nobody was in earshot, and then said more quietly, 'Isn't he?'

Rowan was looking at her curiously. 'How did you know?'

'Well – you said black foxglove is for werewolves. And that's foxglove on his ring. How did *you* know?'

'I just sensed it. Vampire powers are weaker in sunlight, but Jeremy isn't trying to hide anything. He's right out there.'

'He sure is,' Mary-Lynnette said bitterly. '*I* should have sensed it. I mean . . . he's the only person in town who was interested in the lunar eclipse. And the way he moves, and his eyes . . . and he lives at Mad Dog Creek, for God's sake. I mean, that land's been in his family for generations. *And*' – Mary-Lynnette gave a sudden convulsive sniffle – 'people say they've seen the Sasquatch around there. A big hairy monster, half person and half beast. Now, what does *that* sound like?'

Rowan was standing quietly, her expression grave – but her lips were twitching. Mary-Lynnette's vision blurred and wetness spilled onto her cheeks.

'I'm sorry.' Rowan put a hand on her arm. 'I'm not laughing.'

'I thought he was a nice guy,' Mary-Lynnette said, turning away.

'I still think he is,' Rowan said. 'And actually, really,

you know, it means he *didn't* do it.'

'The fact that he's a nice guy?'

'The fact that he's a werewolf.'

Mary-Lynnette turned back. *'What?'*

'You see,' Rowan said, 'werewolves are different. They're not like vampires. They can't drink a little blood from people and then stop without doing any real harm. They kill every time they hunt – because they have to *eat.*' Mary-Lynnette gulped, but Rowan went on serenely. 'Sometimes they eat the whole animal, but they *always* eat the internal organs, the heart and liver. They have to do it, the same way that vampires need to drink blood.'

'And that means . . .'

'He didn't kill Aunt Opal. Or the goat. They were both intact.' Rowan sighed. 'Look. Werewolves and vampires traditionally hate each other. They've been rivals forever, and lamia think of werewolves as sort of – lower class. But actually a lot of them are gentle. They only hunt to eat.'

'Oh,' Mary-Lynnette said hollowly. Shouldn't she be happier about this? 'So the guy I thought was nice just has to eat the odd liver occasionally.'

'Mary-Lynnette, you can't blame him. How can I explain? It's like this: Werewolves aren't people who sometimes turn into wolves. They're wolves who sometimes look like people.'

'But they still kill,' Mary-Lynnette said flatly.

'Yes, but only animals. The law is *very* strict about that. Otherwise humans catch on in no time. Vampires can disguise their work by making it look like a cut throat, but werewolf kills are unmistakable.'

'OK. Great.' I should be more enthusiastic, Mary-Lynnette thought. But how could you ever really trust someone who was a wolf behind their eyes? You might admire them the way you admire a sleek and handsome predator, but trust them . . . no.

'Before we go back – we may have a problem,' Rowan said. 'If he realizes that you recognized his ring, he may know we've told you about – you know.' She glanced around and lowered her voice. 'The Night World.'

Mary-Lynnette understood. 'Oh, God.'

'Yes. That means it's his duty to turn us all in. Or kill us himself.'

'Oh, God.'

'The thing is, I don't think he will. He likes you, Mary-Lynnette. A lot. I don't think he could bring himself to turn you in.'

Mary-Lynnette felt herself flushing. 'But then, that would get *him* in trouble, too, wouldn't it?'

'It could, if anybody ever finds out. We'd better go back and see what's going on. Maybe he *doesn't* realize you know. Maybe Kestrel and Ash have managed to bluff him.'

CHAPTER
14

They walked back to the gas station quickly, their shoulders almost touching. Mary-Lynnette found comfort in Rowan's nearness, in her level-headedness. She'd never had a friend before who was completely her equal, who found it as easy to take care of people as to be taken care of.

As they reached the gas station, they could see that the little group was now clustered around Mary-Lynnette's car. Jeremy was peering under the hood. Mark and Jade were back, hand in hand, but there was no sign of Tiggy. Kestrel was leaning against a gas pump, and Ash was talking to Jeremy.

'So the werewolf walks into the second doctor's office and he says, "Doc, I think I have rabies." And the doctor says . . .'

So much for bluffing him, Mary-Lynnette thought.

Rowan, eyes shut and shoulders tensed, said, 'Ash, that isn't funny.' She opened her eyes. 'I'm sorry,' she said to Jeremy. 'He doesn't mean it.'

'He does, but it doesn't matter. I've heard worse.' Jeremy bent over the engine again. He replaced a cap with careful, even twists. Then he looked up at Mary-Lynnette.

Mary-Lynnette didn't know what to say. What's the etiquette when you've just discovered that somebody's a werewolf? And that it may be their duty to eat you?

Her eyes filled. She was completely out of control today.

Jeremy looked away. He shook his head slightly. His mouth was bitter. 'That's what I figured. I thought you'd react this way. Or I'd have told you myself a long time ago.'

'You would?' Mary-Lynnette's vision cleared. 'But – then *you* would have gotten in trouble. Right?'

Jeremy smiled faintly. 'Well, we're not really sticklers for Night World law around here.'

He said it in a normal tone of voice. Ash and the sisters looked around reflexively.

Mary-Lynnette said, ' "We"?'

'My family. They first settled here because it was so far out of the way. A place where they wouldn't bother anybody, and nobody would bother them. Of course, they're all gone now. There's only me left.'

He said it without self-pity, but Mary-Lynnette moved closer. 'I'm sorry.'

Jade moved in on the other side, silvery-green eyes wide. 'But that's why we came here, too! So nobody would bother us. We don't like the Night World, either.'

Jeremy gave another faint smile – that smile that showed mostly in his eyes. 'I know,' he said to Jade. 'You're related to Mrs Burdock, aren't you?'

'She was our aunt,' Kestrel said, her golden gaze fixed unwaveringly on him.

Jeremy's expression changed slightly. He turned around to look at Kestrel directly. ' "Was"?'

'Yes, she met with a slight accident involving a stake,' Ash said. 'Funny how that happens sometimes . . .'

Jeremy's expression changed again. He looked as if he were leaning against the car for support. 'Who did it?' Then he glanced back at Ash, and Mary-Lynnette saw a gleam of teeth. 'Wait – you think *I* did. Don't you?'

'It did cross our minds at one point,' Ash said. 'Actually, it seemed to keep crossing them. Back and forth. Maybe we should put in a crosswalk.'

Mary-Lynnette said, 'Ash, stop it.'

'So you're saying you *didn't* do it,' Mark said to Jeremy, at the same time as Rowan said, 'Actually, Kestrel thinks it was a vampire hunter.'

Her voice was soft, but once again, everybody looked around. The street was still deserted.

'There's no vampire hunter around here,' Jeremy said flatly.

'Then there's a vampire,' Jade said in an excited whisper. 'There *has* to be, because of the way Aunt Opal was killed. And the goat.'

'The goat . . . ? No, don't even tell me. I don't want to know.' Jeremy swung Mary-Lynnette's hood shut. He looked at her and said quickly, 'Everything's fine in there. You should get the oil changed sometime.' Then he turned to Rowan. 'I'm sorry about your aunt. But if there *is* a vampire around here, it's somebody staying hidden. *Really* hidden. Same if it's a vampire hunter.'

'We already figured that out,' Kestrel said. Mary-Lynnette expected Ash to chime in, but Ash was staring across the street broodingly, his hands in his pockets, apparently having given up on the conversation for the moment.

'You haven't seen anything that could give you a clue?' Mary-Lynnette said. 'We were going to look around town.'

He met her eyes directly. 'If I knew, I'd tell you.' There

was just the slightest emphasis on the last word. 'If I could help you, I would.'

'Well, come along for the ride. You can put your head out of the window,' Ash said, returning to life.

That did it. Mary-Lynnette marched over, grabbed him by the arm, and said to the others, 'Excuse us.' She hauled him in a series of tugs to the back of the gas station. 'You jerk!'

'Oh, look . . .'

'*Shut up!*' She jabbed a finger at his throat. It didn't matter that touching him set off electrical explosions. It just gave her another reason to want to kill him. She found that the pink haze was a lot like anger when you kept shouting through it.

'You have to be the centre of every drama, don't you? You have to be the centre of attention, and act smart, and mouth off!'

'Ow,' Ash said.

'Even if it means hurting other people. Even if it means hurting somebody who's only had rotten breaks all his life. Well, *not this time.*'

'Ow . . .'

'Rowan said you guys think all werewolves are low class. And you know what that is? Where I come from, they call that prejudice. And humans have it, too, and *it is not a pretty picture*. It's about the most hateful thing in the world. I'm *ashamed* to even stand there while you spout it off.' Mary-Lynnette realized she was crying. She also realized that Mark and Jade were peering around the edge of the gas station.

Ash was flat against the boarded-up window, arms up in a gesture of surrender. He looked at a loss for words – and ashamed. Good, Mary-Lynnette thought.

'Should you keep poking him that way?' Mark said

tentatively. Mary-Lynnette could see Rowan and Kestrel behind him and Jade. They all looked alarmed.

'I can't be friends with anybody who's a bigot,' she said to all of them. She gave Ash a jab for emphasis.

'*We're* not,' Jade said virtuously. '*We* don't believe that stupid stuff.'

'We really don't,' Rowan said. 'And Mary-Lynnette – our father is always yelling at Ash for visiting the wrong kind of people on the Outside. Belonging to a club that admits werewolves, having werewolves for friends. The Elders all say he's *too* liberal about that.'

Oh. 'Well, he's got a funny way of showing it,' Mary-Lynnette said, deflating slightly.

'I just thought I'd mention that,' Rowan said. 'Now we'll leave you alone.' She herded the others back toward the front of the station.

When they were gone, Ash said, 'Can I move now, please?' He looked as if he was in a very bad mood.

Mary-Lynnette gave up. She felt tired, suddenly – tired and emotionally drained. Too much had happened in the last few days. And it *kept* happening, it never let up, and . . . well, she was tired, that's all.

'If you'd go away soon, it would be easier,' she said, moving away from Ash. She could feel her head sag slightly.

'Mary-Lynnette . . .' There was something in Ash's voice that she'd never heard before. 'Look – it's not exactly a matter of me *wanting* to go away. There's somebody else from the Night World coming on Monday. His name is Quinn. And if my sisters and I don't go back with him, the whole *town* is in trouble. If he thinks anything irregular is going on here . . . You don't know what the Night People can do.'

Mary-Lynnette could hear her heart beating distinctly.

She didn't turn back to look at Ash.

'They could wipe Briar Creek out. I mean it. They've *done* things like that, to preserve the secret. It's the only protection they have from your kind.'

Mary-Lynnette said – not defiantly, but with simple conviction, 'Your sisters aren't going to leave.'

'Then the whole town's in trouble. There's a rogue werewolf, three renegade lamia, and a secret vampire killer wandering around somewhere – not to mention two humans who know about the Night World. This is a paranormal disaster area.'

A long silence. Mary-Lynnette was trying very hard not to see things from Ash's point of view. At last she said, 'So what do you want me to do?'

'Oh, I don't know, why don't we all have a pizza party and watch TV?' Ash sounded savage. 'I have no idea what to do,' he added in more normal tones. 'And you'd better believe I've been thinking about it. The only thing I can come up with is that the girls have to go back with me, and we all have to lie through our teeth to Quinn.'

Mary-Lynnette tried to think, but her head was throbbing.

'There is one other possibility,' Ash said. He said it under his breath, as if he wouldn't mind if she pretended not to hear him.

Mary-Lynnette eased a crick in her neck, watching blue-and-yellow images of the sun on her shut eyelids. 'What?'

'I know you and the girls did a blood-tie ceremony. It was illegal, but that's beside the point. *You're* part of the reason they don't want to leave here.'

Mary-Lynnette opened her mouth to point out that they didn't want to leave because life had been unbearable for them in the Night World, but Ash hurried on. 'But maybe if you were – like us, we could work something out. I could take the girls back to the island, and then in a few months I could get them out again. We'd go someplace where nobody would know us. Nobody would suspect there was anything irregular about you. The girls would be free, and you'd be there, so there's no reason they shouldn't be happy. Your brother could come, too.'

Mary-Lynnette turned around slowly. She examined Ash. The sun brought out hidden warm tones in his hair, making it a shimmering blond somewhere between Jade's and Kestrel's. His eyes were shadowed, some dark colour. He stood lanky and elegant as ever, but with one hand in his pocket and a pained expression on his face.

'Don't frown; you'll spoil your looks,' she said.

'For God's sake, don't patronize me!' he yelled.

Mary-Lynnette was startled. Well. OK.

'I *think*,' she said, more cautiously but with emphasis to let him know that she was the one with a right to be upset, 'that you are suggesting changing me into a vampire.'

The corner of Ash's mouth jerked. He put his other hand in his pocket and looked away. 'That was the general idea, yes.'

'So that your sisters can be happy.'

'So that you don't get killed by some vigilante like Quinn.'

'But aren't the Night People going to kill me just the same if you change me?'

'Only if they *find* you,' Ash said savagely. 'And if we can get away from here clean, they wouldn't. Anyway, as a vampire you'd have a better chance of fighting them.'

'So I'm supposed to become a vampire and leave everything I love here so your sisters can be happy.'

Ash just stared angrily at the roof of the building across the street. 'Forget it.'

'Believe me, I wasn't even thinking about it in the first place.'

'Fine.' He continued to stare. All at once Mary-Lynnette had the horrible feeling that his eyes were wet.

And I've cried I don't know how many times in the last two days – and I only used to cry when the stars were so beautiful it hurt. There's something *wrong* with me now. I don't even know who I am anymore.

There seemed to be something wrong with Ash, too.

'Ash . . .'

He didn't look at her. His jaw was tight.

The problem is that there isn't any tidy answer, Mary-Lynnette thought. 'I'm sorry,' she said huskily, trying to shake off the strange feelings that had suddenly descended on her. 'It's just that everything's turned out so . . . *weird*. I never asked for any of this.' She swallowed. 'I guess you never asked for it, either. First your sisters running away . . . and then me. Some joke, yeah?'

'Yeah.' He wasn't staring off into the distance anymore. 'Look . . . I might as well tell you. I *didn't* ask for this, and if somebody had said last week that I'd be in . . . involved . . . with a human, I'd have knocked his head off. I mean, after howls of derisive laughter. But.'

He stopped. That seemed to be the end of his confession: *but*. Of course, he didn't really need to say more. Mary-Lynnette, arms folded over her chest, stared at a curved piece of glass on the ground and tried to think of other phrases that started with *in*. Besides the obvious. She couldn't come up with any.

She resisted the impulse to nudge the glass with her foot. 'I'm a bad influence on your sisters.'

'I said that to protect you. To try and protect you.'

'I can protect myself.'

'So I've noticed,' he said dryly. 'Does that help?'

'You noticing? No, because you don't really believe it. You'll always think I'm weaker than you, softer . . . even if you didn't *say* it, I'd know you were thinking it.'

Ash suddenly looked crafty. His eyes were as green as hellebore flowers. 'If you were a vampire, you wouldn't *be* weaker,' he said. 'Also, you'd know what I was really thinking.' He held out his hand. 'Want a sample?'

Mary-Lynnette said abruptly, 'We'd better get back. They're going to think we've killed each other.'

'Let them,' Ash said, his hand still held out, but Mary-Lynnette just shook her head and walked away.

She was scared. Wherever she'd been going with Ash, she'd been getting in too deep. And she wondered how much of their conversation had been audible around front.

When she rounded the corner, her eyes immediately went to Jeremy. He was standing with Kestrel by the gas pump. They were close together, and for just an instant Mary-Lynnette felt something like startled dismay.

Then her inner voice asked, Are you *insane*? You can't be jealous over him while you're worrying whether he's jealous over *you*, and meanwhile worrying about what to do with your soulmate . . . It's *good* if he and Kestrel like each other.

'I don't care; I can't wait anymore,' Jade was saying to Rowan on the sidewalk. 'I've got to find him.'

'She thinks Tiggy's gone home,' Rowan said, seeing Mary-Lynnette. Ash went toward Rowan. Kestrel did, too. Somehow Mary-Lynnette was left beside Jeremy.

Once again, she didn't know the etiquette. She glanced at him – and stopped feeling awkward. He was watching her in his quiet, level way.

But then he startled her. He threw a look at the sidewalk and said, 'Mary-Lynnette, be careful.'

'What?'

'Be *careful*.' It was the same tone he'd used when warning her about Todd and Vic. Mary-Lynnette followed his gaze . . . to Ash.

'It's all right,' Mary-Lynnette said. She didn't know how to explain. Even his own sisters hadn't believed Ash wouldn't hurt her.

Jeremy looked bleak. 'I know guys like that. Sometimes they bring human girls to their clubs – and you don't want to know why. So just – just watch yourself, all right?'

It was a nasty shock. Rowan and the girls had said similar things, but coming from Jeremy it sank in, somehow. Ash had undoubtedly done things in his life that . . . well, that would make her want to kill him if she knew. Things you couldn't just forget about.

'I'll be careful,' she said. She realized her fists were clenched, and she said with a glimmer of humour, 'I can handle him.'

Jeremy still looked bleak. His brown eyes were dark and his jaw was tight as he looked at Ash. Under his quietness, Mary-Lynnette could sense leashed power. Cold anger. Protectiveness. And the fact that he didn't like Ash *at all*.

The others were coming back. 'I'll be all right,' Mary-Lynnette whispered quickly.

Aloud, Jeremy said, 'I'll keep thinking about the people around town. I'll tell you if I come up with something.'

Mary-Lynnette nodded. 'Thanks, Jeremy.' She tried to give him a reassuring look as everybody got into the car.

He stood watching as she pulled out of the gas station. He didn't wave.

'OK, so we go home,' Mark said. 'And then what?'

Nobody answered. Mary-Lynnette realized that she had no idea what.

'I guess we'd better figure out if we still have any suspects,' she said at last.

'There's something else we've got to do, first,' Rowan said softly. 'We vampires, I mean.'

Mary-Lynnette could tell just by the way she said it. But Mark asked, 'What?'

'We need to feed,' Kestrel said with her most radiant smile.

They got back to Burdock Farm. There was no sign of the cat. The four vampires headed for the woods, Jade calling for Tiggy, and Mary-Lynnette headed for Mrs B's rolltop desk. She got engraved stationery – only slightly mildewed at the edges – and a silver pen with a fussy Victorian pattern on it. 'Now,' she said to Mark as she sat at the kitchen table. 'We're going to play List the Suspects.'

'There's nothing in this house to eat, you know,' Mark said. He had all the cupboards open. 'Just things like instant coffee and green Jujyfruits. The ones everybody leaves.'

'What can I say, your girlfriend is undead. Come on. Sit down and concentrate.' Mark sat down and sighed. 'Who have we got?'

'We should have gone to find out what the deal was with that horse,' Mark said.

Mary-Lynnette stopped with her pen poised over the stationery. 'You're right, that must be connected. I forgot about it.' Which just goes to show you, detective work doesn't mix with l— with idle dawdling.

'All right,' she said grimly. 'So let's assume that whoever killed the horse was the same person who killed

Aunt Opal and the goat. And maybe the same person who broke the gas station window – that happened last night, too. Where does that get us?'

'I think it was Todd and Vic,' Mark said.

'You're not being helpful.'

'I'm serious. You know how Todd is always chewing on that toothpick. And there were toothpicks stuck in the goat.'

Toothpicks . . . now, what did *that* remind her of? No, not toothpicks, the bigger stakes. Why couldn't she *remember*?

She rubbed her forehead, giving up. 'OK . . . I'll put Todd and Vic, vampire hunters, with a question mark. Unless you think they're vampires themselves.'

'Nope,' Mark said, undeterred by her sarcasm. 'I think Jade would've noticed *that* when she drank their blood.' He eyed her thoughtfully. 'You're the smart one. Who do *you* think did it?'

'I have no idea.' Mark made a face at her, and she doodled a stake on the stationery. The doodle changed into a very small stake, more like a pencil, held by a feminine hand. She never could draw hands . . .

'Oh, my God. *Bunny*.'

'Bunny did it?' Mark asked ingenuously, prepared to be straight man for a joke.

But Mary-Lynnette said, '*Yes*. I mean – no, I don't know. But those stakes in the goat – the big ones – I've seen her *using* them. She uses them on her nails. They're cuticle sticks.'

'Well . . .' Mark looked dismayed. 'But I mean . . . *Bunny*. C'mon. She can't kill a mosquito.'

Mary-Lynnette shook her head, agitated. 'Rowan said she had a lamia name. And she said something strange to me – Bunny – the day I was looking for Todd and Vic.' It

was all coming back now, a flood of memories that she
didn't particularly want. 'She said, "Good hunting." '

'Mare, it's from *The Jungle Book*.'

'I know. It was still weird for her to say. And she's
almost *too* sweet and scared – what if it's all an act?' When
Mark didn't answer, she said, 'Is it any more unlikely than
Todd and Vic being vampire hunters?'

'So put her down, too.'

Mary-Lynnette did. Then she said, 'You know there's
something I keep meaning to ask Rowan – about how
they wrote to Mrs B from that island—' She broke off and
tensed as the back door banged.

'Am I the first one back?'

It was Rowan, windblown and glowing, slightly
breathless. Her hair was a tumbling chestnut cloud
around her.

'Where's everybody else?' Mary-Lynnette asked.

'We separated early on. It's the only way, you know,
with four of us in this small of an area.'

'Small!' Mark looked offended. 'If Briar Creek has one
good thing – and I'm not saying it does – it's space.'

Rowan smiled. 'For a hunting range, it *is* small,' she
said. 'No offence. It's fine for us – we never got to hunt at
all on the island. They brought our meals to us,
tranquilized and completely passive.'

Mary-Lynnette pushed away the image this evoked.
'Um, you want to register a guess on Whodunit?'

Rowan sat down in a kitchen chair, smoothing a wisp
of brown hair off her forehead. 'I don't know. I wonder if
it's somebody we haven't even thought of yet.'

Mary-Lynnette remembered what she'd been talking
about when the door banged. 'Rowan, I always meant to
ask you – you said that only Ash could have figured out
where you were going when you ran away. But what

about the guy who helped you smuggle letters off the island? *He* would know where your aunt lived, right? He could see the address on the letters.'

'Crane Linden.' Rowan smiled, a sad little smile. 'No, he wouldn't know. He's . . .' She touched her temple lightly. 'I don't know what you call it. His mind never developed completely. He can't read. But he's very kind.'

There were illiterate vampires? Well, why not? Aloud Mary-Lynnette said, 'Oh. Well, I guess it's one more person we can eliminate.'

'Look, can we just brainstorm a minute?' Mark said. 'This is probably crazy, but what if Jeremy's uncle isn't really dead? And what if—'

At that moment, there was a crash from the *front* porch.

No, a *tap-tap-crash*, Mary-Lynnette thought. Then she thought, Oh, God . . . *Tiggy*.

CHAPTER

15

*T*iggy.

She was running. Throwing the door open. Visions of kittens impaled by tiny stakes in her mind.

It wasn't Tiggy on the front porch. It was Ash. He was lying flat in the purple twilight, little moths fluttering around him.

Mary-Lynnette felt a violent wrench in her chest. For a moment everything seemed suspended – and changed.

If Ash were dead – if Ash had been killed . . .

Things would never be all right. *She* would never be all right. It would be like the night with the moon and stars gone. Nothing that anybody could do would make up for it. Mary-Lynnette didn't know why – it didn't make any sense – but she suddenly knew it was true.

She couldn't breathe and her arms and legs felt strange. Floaty. Out of her control.

Then Ash moved. He lifted his head and pushed up with his arms and looked around.

Mary-Lynnette could breathe again, but she still felt dizzy. 'Are you hurt?' she asked stupidly. She didn't dare touch him. In her present state one blast of electricity could fry her circuits forever. She'd melt like the Wicked Witch of the West.

'I fell in this *hole*,' he said. 'What do you think?'

That's right, Mary-Lynnette thought; the footsteps *had* ended with more of a crash than a thud. Not like the footsteps of last night.

And that meant something . . . if only she could follow the thought to the end . . .

'Having problems, Ash?' Kestrel's voice said sweetly, and then Kestrel herself appeared out of the shadows, looking like an angel with her golden hair and her lovely clean features. Jade was behind her, holding Tiggy in her arms.

'He was up in a tree,' Jade said, kissing the kitten's head. 'I had to talk him down.' Her eyes were emerald in the porch light, and she seemed to float rather than walk.

Ash was getting up, shaking himself. Like his sisters, he looked uncannily beautiful after a feeding, with a sort of weird moonlight glow in his eyes. Mary-Lynnette's thought was long gone.

'Come on in,' she said resignedly. 'And help figure out who killed your aunt.'

Now that Ash was indisputably all right, she wanted to forget what she'd been feeling a minute ago. Or at least not to think about what it meant.

What it means, the little voice inside her head said sweetly, is that you're in *big* trouble, girl. Ha ha.

'So what's the story?' Kestrel said briskly as they all sat around the kitchen table.

'The story is that there is no story,' Mary-Lynnette said. She stared at her paper in frustration. 'Look – what if we start at the beginning? We don't know who did it, but we do know some things about them. Right?'

Rowan nodded encouragingly. 'Right.'

'First: the goat. Whoever killed the goat had to be strong, because poking those toothpicks through hide wouldn't have been easy. And whoever killed the goat had to know how your uncle Hodge was killed, because the goat was killed in the same way. And they had to have some reason for putting a black iris in the goat's mouth – either because they knew Ash belonged to the Black Iris Club, or because they belonged to the Black Iris Club themself.'

'Or because they thought a black iris would represent all lamia, or all Night People,' Ash said. His voice was muffled – he was bent over, rubbing his ankle. 'That's a common mistake Outsiders make.'

Very good, Mary-Lynnette thought in spite of herself. She said, 'OK. And they had access to two different kinds of small stakes – which isn't saying much, because you can buy both kinds in town.'

'And they must have had some reason to hate Mrs B, or to hate vampires,' Mark said. 'Otherwise, why kill her?'

Mary-Lynnette gave him a patient look. 'I hadn't gotten to Mrs B yet. But we can do her now. First, whoever killed Mrs B obviously knew she was a vampire, because they staked her. And, second . . . um . . . second . . .' Her voice trailed off. She couldn't think of anything to go second.

'Second, they probably killed her on impulse,' Ash said, in a surprisingly calm and analytical voice. 'You said she was stabbed with a picket from the fence, and if they'd been planning on doing it, they'd probably have brought their own stake.'

'*Very* good.' This time Mary-Lynnette said it out loud. She couldn't help it. She met Ash's eyes and saw something that startled her. He looked as if it mattered to him that she thought he was smart.

Well, she thought. Well, well. Here we are, probably for the first time, just talking to each other. Not arguing, not being sarcastic, just talking. It's nice.

It was *surprisingly* nice. And the strange thing was, she knew Ash thought so, too. They understood each other. Over the table, Ash gave her a barely perceptible nod.

They kept talking. Mary-Lynnette lost track of time as they sat and argued and brainstormed. Finally she looked up at the clock and realized with a shock that it was near midnight.

'Do we *have* to keep thinking?' Mark said pathetically. 'I'm tired.' He was almost lying on the table. So was Jade.

I know how you feel, Mary-Lynnette thought. My brain is stalled. I feel . . . extremely stupid.

'Somehow, I don't think we're going to solve the murder tonight,' Kestrel said. Her eyes were closed.

She was right. The problem was that Mary-Lynnette didn't feel like going to bed, either. She didn't want to lie down and relax – there was a restlessness inside her.

I want . . . what do I want? she thought. I want . . .

'If there weren't a psychopathic goat killer lurking around here, I'd go out and look at the stars,' she said.

Ash said, as if it were the most natural thing in the world, 'I'll go with you.'

Kestrel and Jade looked at their brother in disbelief. Rowan bent her head, not quite hiding a smile.

Mary-Lynnette said, 'Um . . .'

'Look,' Ash said. 'I don't think the goat killer is lurking out there every *minute* looking for people to skewer. And if anything does happen, I can handle it.' He stopped, looked guilty, then bland. 'I mean – *we* can handle it, because there'll be two of us.'

Close but no cigar, buddy, Mary-Lynnette thought. Still, there was a certain basic truth to what he was saying.

He was strong and fast, and she had the feeling he knew how to fight dirty.

Even if she'd never seen him do it, she thought suddenly. All those times she'd gone after him, shining light in his eyes, kicking him in the shins – and he'd never once tried to retaliate. She didn't think it had even occurred to him.

She looked at him and said, 'OK.'

'Now,' Mark said. 'Look . . .'

'We'll be fine,' Mary-Lynnette told him. 'We won't go far.'

Mary-Lynnette drove. She didn't know exactly where she was going, only that she didn't want to go to her hill. Too many weird memories. Despite what she'd told Mark, she found herself taking the car farther and farther. Out to where Hazel Green Creek and Beavercreek almost came together and the land between them was a good imitation of a rain forest.

'Is this the best place to look at stars?' Ash said doubtfully when they got out of the station wagon.

'Well – if you're looking straight up,' Mary-Lynnette said. She faced eastward and tilted her head far back.

'See the brightest star up there? That's Vega, the queen star of summer.'

'Yeah. She's been higher in the sky every night this summer,' Ash said without emphasis.

Mary-Lynnette glanced at him.

He shrugged. 'When you're out so much at night, you get to recognize the stars,' he said. 'Even if you don't know their names.'

Mary-Lynnette looked back up at Vega. She swallowed. 'Can you – can you see something small and bright below her – something ring-shaped?'

'The thing that looks like a ghost doughnut?'

Mary-Lynnette smiled, but only with her lips. 'That's the Ring Nebula. I can see that – with my telescope.'

She could feel him looking at her, and she heard him take a breath as if he were going to say something. But then he let the breath out again and looked back up at the stars.

It was the perfect moment for him to mention something about how Vampires See It Better. And if he had, Mary-Lynnette would have turned on him and rejected him with righteous anger.

But since he *didn't*, she felt a different kind of anger welling up. A spring of contrariness, as if she were the Mary in the nursery rhyme. What, so you've decided I'm not good enough to be a vampire or something?

And what did I really bring you out here for, to the most isolated place I could find? Only for star-watching? I don't *think* so.

I don't even know who I am anymore, she remembered with a sort of fatalistic gloom. I have the feeling I'm about to surprise myself.

'Aren't you getting a crick in your neck?' Ash said.

Mary-Lynnette rolled her head from side to side slightly to limber the muscles. 'Maybe.'

'I could rub it for you?' He made the offer from several feet away.

Mary-Lynnette snorted and gave him a look.

The moon, a waning crescent, was rising above the cedars to the east. Mary-Lynnette said, 'You want to take a walk?'

'Huh? Sure.'

They walked and Mary-Lynnette thought. About how it would be to see the Ring Nebula with her own eyes, or the Veil Nebula without a filter. She could feel a longing for them so strong it was like a cable attached to her chest, pulling her upward.

Of course, *that* was nothing new. She'd felt it lots of times before, and usually she'd ended up buying another book on astronomy, another lens for her telescope. Anything to bring her closer to what she wanted.

But now I have a whole new temptation. Something bigger and scarier than I ever imagined.

What if I could be – more than I am now? The same person, but with sharper senses? A Mary-Lynnette who could *really* belong to the night?

She'd already discovered she wasn't exactly who she'd always thought. She was more violent – she'd kicked Ash, hadn't she? Repeatedly. And she'd admired the purity of Kestrel's fierceness. She'd seen the logic in the kill-or-be-killed philosophy. She'd dreamed about the joy of hunting.

What else did it take to be a Night Person?

'There's something I've been wanting to say to you,' Ash said.

'Hm.' Do I want to encourage him or not?

But what Ash said was 'Can we stop fighting now?'

Mary-Lynnette thought and then said seriously, 'I don't know.'

They kept walking. The cedars towered around them like pillars in a giant ruined temple. A dark temple. And underneath, the stillness was so enormous that Mary-Lynnette felt as if she were walking on the moon.

She bent and picked a ghostly wildflower that was growing out of the moss. Death camas. Ash bent and picked up a broken-off yew branch lying at the foot of a twisted tree. They didn't look at each other. They walked, with a few feet of space between them.

'You know, somebody told me this would happen,' Ash said, as if carrying on some entirely different conversation they'd been having.

'That you'd come to a hick town and chase a goat killer?'

'That someday I'd care for someone – and it would hurt.'

Mary-Lynnette kept on walking. She didn't slow or speed up. It was only her heart that was suddenly beating hard – in a mixture of dismay and exhilaration.

Oh, God – whatever was going to happen was happening.

'You're not like anybody I've ever met,' Ash said.

'Well, *that* feeling is mutual.'

Ash stripped some of the papery purple bark off his yew stick. 'And, you see, it's difficult because what I've always thought about humans – what I was always raised to think . . .'

'I know what you've always thought,' Mary-Lynnette said sharply. Thinking, *vermin*.

'But,' Ash continued doggedly, 'the thing is – and I know this is going to sound strange – that I seem to love you sort of desperately.' He pulled more bark off his stick.

Mary-Lynnette didn't look at him. She couldn't speak.

'I've done everything I could to get rid of the feeling, but it just won't *go*. At first I thought if I left Briar Creek, I'd forget it. But now I know that was insane. Wherever I go, it's going *with* me. I can't kill it off. So I have to think of something else.'

Mary-Lynnette suddenly felt *extremely* contrary. 'Sorry,' she said coldly. 'But I'm afraid it's not very flattering to have somebody tell you that they love you against their will, against their reason, and even—'

'Against their character,' Ash finished for her, bleakly. 'Yeah, I know.'

Mary-Lynnette stopped walking. She stared at him. 'You have *not* read *Pride and Prejudice*,' she said flatly.

'Why not?'

'Because Jane Austen was a human.'

He looked at her inscrutably and said, 'How do you know?'

Good point. *Scary* point. How could she really know *who* in human history had been human? What about Galileo? Newton? Tycho Brahe?

'Well, Jane Austen was a *woman*,' she said, retreating to safer ground. 'And you're a chauvinist pig.'

'Yes, well, that I can't argue.'

Mary-Lynnette started walking again. He followed.

'So now can I tell you how, um, ardently I love and admire you?'

Another quote. 'I thought your sisters said you *partied* all the time.'

Ash understood. 'I do,' he said defensively. 'But the morning after partying you have to stay in bed. And if you're in bed you might as well read something.'

They walked.

'After all, we *are* soulmates,' Ash said. 'I can't be *completely* stupid or I'd be completely wrong for you.'

Mary-Lynnette thought about that. And about the fact that Ash sounded almost – humble. Which he had certainly never sounded before.

She said, 'Ash . . . I don't know. I mean – we *are* wrong for each other. We're just basically incompatible. Even if I were a *vampire*, we'd be basically incompatible.'

'Well.' Ash whacked at something with his yew branch. He spoke as if he half expected to be ignored. 'Well, about that . . . I think I could *possibly* change your mind.'

'About what?'

'Being incompatible. I think we could be sort of fairly compatible if . . .'

'If?' Mary-Lynnette said as the silence dragged on.

'Well, if you could bring yourself to kiss me.'

'*Kiss* you?'

'Yeah, I know it's a radical concept. I was pretty sure you wouldn't go for it.' He whacked at another tree. 'Of course humans *have* been doing it for thousands of years.'

Watching him sideways, Mary-Lynnette said, 'Would you kiss a three-hundred-pound gorilla?'

He blinked twice. 'Oh, thank you.'

'I didn't mean you looked like one.'

'Don't tell me, let me guess. I smell like one?'

Mary-Lynnette bit her lip on a grim smile. 'I mean you're that much stronger than I am. Would you kiss a female gorilla that could crush you with one squeeze? When you couldn't do anything about it?'

He glanced at *her* sideways. 'Well, you're not *exactly* in that position, are you?'

Mary-Lynnette said, 'Aren't I? It looks to me as if I'd have to become a vampire just to deal with you on an equal level.'

Ash said, 'Here.'

He was offering her the yew branch. Mary-Lynnette stared at him.

'You want to give me your stick.'

'It's not a stick, it's the way to deal with me on an equal level.' He put one end of the branch against the base of his throat, and Mary-Lynnette saw that it was *sharp*. She reached out to take the other end and found the stick was surprisingly hard and heavy.

Ash was looking straight at her. It was too dark to see what colour his eyes were, but his expression was unexpectedly sober.

'One good push would do it,' he said. 'First here and then in the heart. You could eliminate the problem of me from your life.'

Mary-Lynnette pushed, but gently. He took a step back. And another. She backed him up against a tree, holding the stick to his neck like a sword.

'I actually meant only if you were really serious,' Ash said as he came up short against the cedar's bare trunk. But he didn't make a move to defend himself. 'And the truth is that you don't even need a spear like that. A pencil in the right place would do it.'

Mary-Lynnette narrowed her eyes at him, swirling the yew stick over his body like a fencer getting the range.

Then she removed it. She dropped it to the ground.

'You really have changed,' she said.

Ash said simply, 'I've changed so much in the last few days that I don't even recognize myself in the mirror.'

'And you didn't kill your aunt.'

'You're just now figuring that out?'

'No. But I always wondered just a bit. All right, I'll kiss you.'

It was a little awkward, lining up to get the position right. Mary-Lynnette had never kissed a boy before. But once she started she found it was simple.

And . . . *now* she saw what the electric feeling of being soulmates was for. All the sensations she'd felt when touching his hand, only intensified. And not unpleasant. It was only unpleasant if you were afraid of it.

Afterward, Ash pulled away. 'There. You see,' he said shakily.

Mary-Lynnette took a few deep breaths. 'I suppose that's what it feels like to fall into a black hole.'

'Oh. Sorry.'

'No, I mean – it was interesting.' Singular, she thought. Different from anything she'd ever felt before. And she had the feeling that *she* would be different from now on, that she could never go back and be the same person she had been.

So who am I now? Somebody fierce, I think.

Somebody who'd enjoy running through the darkness, underneath stars bright as miniature suns, and maybe even hunt deer. Somebody who can laugh at death the way the sisters do.

I'll discover a supernova and I'll hiss when somebody threatens me. I'll be beautiful and scary and dangerous and of course I'll kiss Ash a lot.

She was giddy, almost soaring with exhilaration.

I've always loved the night, she thought. And I'll finally belong to it completely.

'Mary-Lynnette?' Ash said hesitantly. 'Did you *like* it?'

She blinked and looked at him. Focused.

'I want you to turn me into a vampire,' she said.

It didn't feel like a jellyfish sting this time. It was quick and almost pleasant – like pressure being released. And then Ash's lips were on her neck, and that was *definitely* pleasant. Warmth radiated from his mouth. Mary-Lynnette found herself stroking the back of his neck and realized that his hair was soft, as nice to touch as cat's fur.

And his mind . . . was every colour of the spectrum. Crimson and gold, jade and emerald and deep violet-blue. A tangled thorn-forest of iridescent colours that changed from second to second. Mary-Lynnette was dazzled.

And half frightened. There was darkness in among those gemlike colours. Things Ash had done in the past . . . things she could sense he was ashamed of now. But shame didn't change the acts themselves.

I know it doesn't – but I'll make up for them, somehow. You'll see; I'll find a way . . .

So that's telepathy, Mary-Lynnette thought. She could *feel* Ash as he said the words, feel that he meant them with desperate earnestness – and feel that there was a lot to make up for.

I don't care. I'm going to be a creature of darkness, too. I'll do what's in my nature, with no regrets.

When Ash started to lift his head, she tightened her grip, trying to keep him there.

'Please don't tempt me,' Ash said out loud, his voice husky, his breath warm on her neck. 'If I take too much, it will make you seriously weak. I *mean* it, sweetheart.'

She let him go. He picked up the yew stick and made a small cut at the base of his throat, tilting his head back like a guy shaving his chin.

'Ow.'

Mary-Lynnette realized he'd never done this before. With a feeling that was almost awe, she put her lips to his neck.

I'm drinking blood. I'm a hunter already – sort of Anyway, I'm drinking blood and liking it – maybe because it doesn't *taste* like blood. Not like copper and fear. It tastes weird and magic and old as the stars.

When Ash gently detached her, she swayed on her feet.

'We'd better go home,' he said.

'Why? I'm OK.'

'You're going to get dizzier – and weaker. And if we're going to finish changing you into a vampire—'

'*If?*'

'All right, *when*. But before we do, we need to talk. I need to explain it all to you; we have to figure out the details. And *you* need to rest.'

Mary-Lynnette knew he was right. She wanted to stay here, alone with Ash in the dark cathedral of the forest – but she *did* feel weak. Languid. Apparently it was hard work becoming a creature of darkness.

They headed back the way they had come. Mary-Lynnette could feel the change inside herself – it was stronger than when she'd exchanged blood with the three girls. She felt simultaneously weak and hypersensitive. As if every pore were open.

The moonlight seemed much brighter. She could see colours clearly – the pale green of drooping cedar boughs, the eerie purple of parrot-beak wildflowers growing out of the moss.

And the forest wasn't silent anymore. She could hear faint uncanny sounds like the soft seething of needles in the wind, and her own footsteps on moist and fungus-ridden twigs.

I can even smell better, she thought. This place smells like incense cedar, and decomposing plants, and something really wild – feral, like something from the zoo. And something hot . . . burny . . .

Mechanical. It stung her nostrils. She stopped and looked at Ash in alarm.

'What *is* that?'

He'd stopped, too. 'Smells like rubber and oil . . .'

'Oh, God, the *car*,' Mary-Lynnette said. They looked at each other for a moment, then simultaneously turned, breaking into a run.

It was the car. White smoke billowed from under the closed hood. Mary-Lynnette started to go closer, but Ash pulled her back to the side of the road.

'I just want to open the hood—'

'No. Look. There.'

Mary-Lynnette looked – and gasped. Tiny tongues of flame were darting underneath the smoke. Licking out of the engine.

'Claudine always said this would happen,' she said grimly as Ash pulled her back farther. 'Only I think she meant it would happen with me in it.'

'We're going to have to walk home,' Ash said. 'Unless maybe somebody sees the fire . . .'

'Not a chance,' Mary-Lynnette said. And *that's* what you get for taking a boy out to the most isolated place in Oregon, her inner voice said triumphantly.

'I don't suppose you could turn into a bat or something and fly back,' she suggested.

'Sorry, I flunked shapeshifting. And I wouldn't leave you here alone anyway.'

Mary-Lynnette still felt reckless and dangerous – and it made her impatient.

'I can take care of myself,' she said.

And *that* was when the club came down and Ash pitched forward unconscious.

CHAPTER

16

After that, things happened very fast, and at the same time with a dreamy slowness. Mary-Lynnette felt her arms grabbed from behind. Something was pulling her hands together – something *strong*. Then she felt the bite of cord on her wrists, and she realized what was happening.

Tied up – I'm going to be helpless – I've got to *do* something fast . . .

She fought, trying to wrench herself away, trying to kick. But it was already too late. Her hands were secure behind her back – and some part of her mind noted distantly that no wonder people on cop shows yell when they're handcuffed. It *hurt*. Her shoulders gave a shriek of agony as she was dragged backward up against a tree.

'Stop fighting,' a voice snarled. A thick, distorted voice she didn't recognize. She tried to see who it was, but the tree was in the way. 'If you relax it won't hurt.'

Mary-Lynnette kept fighting, but it didn't make any difference. She could feel the deeply furrowed bark of the tree against her hands and back – and now she couldn't move.

Oh, God, oh, God – I can't get *away*. I was already weak

from what Ash and I did – and now I can't move at all.

Then stop panicking and *think*, her inner voice said fiercely. Use your *brain* instead of getting hysterical.

Mary-Lynnette stopped struggling. She stood panting and tried to get control of her terror.

'I told you. It only hurts when you fight. A lot of things are like that,' the voice said.

Mary-Lynnette twisted her head and saw who it was.

Her heart gave a sick lurch. She shouldn't have been surprised, but she was – surprised and infinitely disappointed.

'Oh, Jeremy,' she whispered.

Except that it was a different Jeremy than the one she knew. His face was the same, his hair, his clothes – but there was something weird about him, something powerful and scary and . . . *unknowable*. His eyes were as inhuman and flat as a shark's.

'I don't want to hurt you,' he said in that distorted stranger's voice. 'I only tied you up because I didn't want you to interfere.'

Mary-Lynnette's mind was registering different things in different layers. One part said, *My God, he's trying to be friendly*, and another part said, *To interfere with what?*, and a third part just kept saying *Ash*.

She looked at Ash. He was lying very still, and Mary-Lynnette's wonderful new eyes that could see colours in moonlight saw that his blond hair was slowly soaking with blood. On the ground beside him was a club made of yew – made of the hard yellow sapwood. No wonder he was unconscious.

But if he's bleeding he's not dead – oh, God, please, he *can't* be dead – Rowan said that only staking and burning kill vampires . . .

'I have to take care of him,' Jeremy said. 'And then

I'll let you go, I promise. Once I explain everything, you'll understand.'

Mary-Lynnette looked up from Ash to the stranger with Jeremy's face. With a shock, she realized what he meant by 'take care of'. Three words that were just part of life to a hunter – to a werewolf.

So now I know about werewolves. They're killers – and I was right all along. I was right and Rowan was wrong.

'It'll only take a minute,' Jeremy said – and his lips drew back.

Mary-Lynnette's heart seemed to slam violently inside her chest. Because his lips went farther up than any human's lips could. She could see his gums, whitish-pink. And she could see why his voice didn't sound like Jeremy's – it was his *teeth*.

White teeth in the moonlight. The teeth from her dream. Vampire teeth were nothing compared to this. The incisors at the front were made for cutting flesh from prey, the canines were two inches long, the teeth behind them looked designed for slicing and shearing.

Mary-Lynnette suddenly remembered something Vic Kimble's father had said three years ago. He'd said that a wolf could snap off the tail of a full-grown cow clean as pruning shears. He'd been complaining that somebody had let a wolf-dog crossbreed loose and it was going after his cattle . . .

Except that of course it wasn't a crossbreed, Mary-Lynnette thought. It was Jeremy. I saw him every day at school – and then he must have gone home to look like *this*. To hunt.

Just now, as he stood over Ash with his teeth all exposed and his chest heaving, Jeremy looked completely, quietly insane.

'But *why*?' Mary-Lynnette burst out. '*Why* do you want to hurt him?'

Jeremy looked up – and she got another shock. His eyes were different. Before she'd seen them flash white in the darkness. Now they had no whites at all. They were brown with large liquid pupils. The eyes of an animal.

So it doesn't need to be a full moon, she thought. He can change anytime.

'Don't you know?' he said. 'Doesn't anybody *understand*? This is *my* territory.'

Oh. *Oh* . . .

So it was as simple as that. After all their brainstorming and arguing and detective work. In the end it was something as basic as an animal protecting its range.

'*For a hunting range, it is small,*' Rowan had said.

'They were taking *my* game,' Jeremy said. 'My deer, my squirrels. They didn't have any right to do that. I tried to make them leave – but they wouldn't. They stayed and they kept killing . . .'

He stopped talking – but a new sound came from him. It started out almost below the range of Mary-Lynnette's hearing – but the deep rumbling of it struck some primal chord of terror in her. It was as uncanny and inhuman as the danger-hum of an attacking swarm of bees.

Growling. He was growling. And it was *real*. The snarling growl a dog makes that tells you to turn and run. The sound it makes before it springs at your throat . . .

'Jeremy!' Mary-Lynnette screamed. She threw herself forward, ignoring the white blaze of pain in her shoulders. But the cord held. She was jerked back. And Jeremy fell on Ash, lunging down, head darting forward like a striking snake, like a biting dog, like every animal that kills with its teeth.

Mary-Lynnette heard someone screaming '*No!*' and

only later realized that it was her. She was fighting with the cord, and she could feel stinging and wetness at her wrists. But she couldn't get free and she couldn't stop seeing what was happening in front of her. And all the time that eerie, vicious growling that reverberated in Mary-Lynnette's own head and chest.

That was when things went cold and clear. Some part of Mary-Lynnette that was stronger than the panic took over. It stepped back and looked at the entire scene by the roadside: the car, which was still burning, sending clouds of choking white smoke whenever the wind blew the right way; the limp figure of Ash on the pine needles; the blur of snarling motion that was Jeremy.

'Jeremy!' she said, and her throat hurt, but her voice was calm – and commanding. 'Jeremy – before you do that – don't you want me to *understand?* You said that was what you wanted. Jeremy, *help me understand.*'

For a long second she thought in dismay that it wasn't going to work. That he couldn't even hear her. But then his head lifted. She saw his face; she saw the blood on his chin.

Don't scream, don't scream, Mary-Lynnette told herself frantically. Don't show any shock. You have to keep him talking, keep him away from Ash.

Behind her back her hands were working automatically, as if trying to get out of ropes was something they'd always known how to do. The slick wetness actually helped. She could feel the cords slide a little.

'Please help me understand,' she said again, breathless, but trying to hold Jeremy's eyes. 'I'm your friend – you know that. We go back a long way.'

Jeremy's whitish gums were streaked with red. He still had human features, but there was nothing at all human about that face.

Now, though – slowly – his lips came down to cover his gums. He looked more like a person and less like an animal. And when he spoke, his voice was distorted, but she could recognize it as Jeremy's voice.

'We do go back,' he said. 'I've watched you since we were kids – and I've seen you watching me.'

Mary-Lynnette nodded. She couldn't get any words out.

'I always figured that someday, when we were older – maybe we'd be together. I thought maybe I could make you understand. About me. About everything. I thought you were the one person who might not be afraid . . .'

'I'm not,' Mary-Lynnette said, and hoped her voice wasn't shaking too badly. She was saying it to a figure in a blood-spattered shirt crouching over a torn body like a beast still ready to attack. Mary-Lynnette didn't dare look at Ash to see how badly he was hurt. She kept her eyes locked on Jeremy's. 'And I think I can understand. You killed Mrs Burdock, didn't you? Because she was on your territory.'

'Not *her*,' Jeremy said, and his voice was sharp with impatience. 'She was just an old lady – she didn't hunt. I didn't mind having her in my range. I even did things for her, like fixing her fence and porch for free . . . And that's when she told me *they* were coming. Those girls.'

Just the way she told me, Mary-Lynnette thought, with dazed revelation. And he was there fixing the fence – of course. The way he does odd jobs for everybody.

'I *told* her it wouldn't work.' Mary-Lynnette could hear it again – the beginnings of a snarling growl. Jeremy was tense and trembling, and she could feel herself start to tremble, too. 'Three more hunters in this little place . . . I *told* her, but she wouldn't listen. She couldn't see. So then I lost my temper.'

Don't look at Ash, don't call attention to him, Mary-Lynnette thought desperately. Jeremy's lips were drawing back again as if he needed something to attack. At the same time the distant part of her mind said, *So that's why he used a picket – Ash was right; it was an impulse of the moment.*

'Well, anybody can lose their temper,' she said, and even though her voice cracked and there were tears in her eyes, Jeremy seemed to calm a little.

'Afterward, I thought maybe it was for the best,' he said, sounding tired. 'I thought when the girls found her, they'd know they had to leave. I waited for them to do it. I'm good at waiting.'

He was staring past her, into the woods. Heart pounding, Mary-Lynnette grabbed the opportunity to dart a look at Ash.

Oh, God, he's not moving at all. And there's so much *blood* . . . I've never seen so much blood . . .

She twisted her wrists back and forth, trying to find some give in the cords.

'I watched, but they didn't go away,' Jeremy said. Mary-Lynnette's eyes jerked back to him. 'Instead *you* came. I heard Mark talking to Jade in the garden. She said she'd decided she was going to like it here. And then . . . I got mad. I made a noise and they heard me.'

His face was changing. The flesh was actually moving in front of Mary-Lynnette's eyes. His cheekbones were broadening, his nose and mouth jutting. Hair was creeping between his eyebrows, turning them into a straight bar. She could *see* individual coarse hairs sprouting, dark against pale skin.

I'm going to be sick . . .

'What's wrong, Mary-Lynnette?' He got up and she saw that his body was changing, too. It was still a human body, but it was too thin – stretched out. As if it were just long bones and sinews.

'Nothing's wrong,' Mary-Lynnette got out in a whisper. She twisted violently at her cords – and felt one hand slide.

That's it. Now keep him distracted, keep him moving away from Ash . . .

'Go on,' she said breathlessly. 'What happened then?'

'I knew I had to send them a message. I came back the next night for the goat – but you were there again. You ran away from me into the shed.' He moved closer again and the moonlight caught his eyes – and *reflected*. The pupils shone greenish-orange. Mary-Lynnette could only stare.

That shadow in the clearing – those eyes I saw. Not a coyote. Him. He was following us everywhere.

The very thought made her skin creep. But there was another thought that was worse – the picture of him killing the goat. Doing it carefully, methodically – as a message.

That was why he didn't eat the heart and liver, Mary-Lynnette realized. *He didn't kill it for food – it wasn't a normal werewolf killing. And he's not a normal werewolf.*

He wasn't at all like what Rowan had described – a noble animal that hunted to eat. Instead he was . . . a mad dog.

Of all people, Ash had it right. Him and his jokes about rabies . . .

'You're so beautiful, you know,' Jeremy said suddenly. 'I've always thought that. I love your hair.'

He was right in her face. She could see the individual pores in his skin with coarse hairs growing out of them. And she could *smell* him – the feral smell of a zoo.

He reached out to touch her hair, and his hand had

dark, thick fingernails. Mary-Lynnette could feel her eyes getting wider. Say something . . . say something . . . don't show you're afraid.

'You knew how Mrs Burdock's husband was killed,' she got out.

'She told me a long time ago,' Jeremy said almost absently, still moving his fingers in her hair. He'd changed so much that his voice was getting hard to understand. 'I used little sticks from my models . . . you know I make models. And a black iris for *him*. Ash.' Jeremy said the name with pure hatred. 'I saw him that day with his stupid T-shirt. The Black Iris Club . . . my uncle belonged to that once. They treated him like he was second-class.'

His eyes were inches from Mary-Lynnette's; she felt the brush of a fingernail on her ear. Suddenly she had the strength to give a violent wrench behind her back – and one hand came free. She froze, afraid that Jeremy would notice.

'I threw the goat on the porch and ran,' Jeremy said, almost crooning the words as he petted Mary-Lynnette. 'I knew you were all in there. I was so mad – I killed that horse and I kept running. I smashed the gas station window. I was going to burn it down – but then I decided to wait.'

Yes, and yes, and yes, Mary-Lynnette thought, even as she carefully worked her other wrist free, even as she stared into Jeremy's crazy eyes and smelled his animal breath. Yes, of course it was you we heard running away – and you didn't fall into the hole in the porch because you knew it was there, because you were fixing it. And yes, you were the one who smashed the window – who else would hate the gas station but somebody who worked there?

Her fingers eased the cord off her other wrist. She felt

a surge of fierce triumph – but she controlled her expression and clenched her hands, trying to think of what to do. He was so strong and so quick . . . if she just threw herself at him, she wouldn't have a chance.

'And today you all came to town together,' Jeremy said, finishing the story quietly, through a mouth so inhuman it was hard to believe it could speak English. 'I heard the way *he* was talking to you. I knew he wanted you – and he wanted to change you into one of *them*. I had to protect you from that.'

Mary-Lynnette said almost steadily, 'I knew you wanted to protect me. I could tell, Jeremy.' She was feeling over the furrowed hemlock bark behind her. How could she attack him when she didn't even have a stick for a weapon? And even if she *had*, wood was no good. He wasn't a vampire.

Jeremy stepped back. Relief washed over Mary-Lynnette – for one second. Then she saw with horror that he was plucking at his shirt, pulling it off. And underneath . . . there was no skin. Instead there was hair. A pelt that twitched and shivered in the night air. 'I followed you here and I fixed your car so you couldn't leave,' Jeremy said. 'I heard you say you wanted to be a vampire.'

'Jeremy – that was just talk . . .'

He went on as if she hadn't spoken. 'But that was a mistake. Werewolves are much better. You'll understand when I show you. The moon looks so beautiful when you're a wolf.'

Oh, *God* – and so that was what he meant by protecting her, by making her understand. He meant changing her into something like him.

I need a weapon.

Rowan had said silver was harmful to werewolves, so

the old silver-bullet legend must be true. But she didn't *have* a silver bullet. Or even a silver dagger . . .

A silver dagger . . . a silver *knife* . . .

Behind Jeremy the station wagon was almost invisible in the clouds of smoke. And by now the smoke had the red glow of uncontrolled fire.

It's too dangerous, Mary-Lynnette thought. It's about to go. I'd never make it in and out . . .

Jeremy was still talking, his voice savage now. 'You won't miss the Night World. All their stupid restrictions – no killing humans, no hunting too often. *Nobody* tells me how to hunt. My uncle tried, but I took care of him –'

Suddenly the creature – it wasn't really a person anymore – broke off and turned sharply. Mary-Lynnette saw its lips go back again, saw its teeth parted and ready to bite. In the same instant she saw why – Ash was moving.

Sitting up, even though his throat was cut. Looking around dazedly. He saw Mary-Lynnette, and his eyes seemed to focus. Then he looked at the thing Jeremy had become.

'You – get away from her!' he shouted in a voice Mary-Lynnette had never heard before. A voice filled with deadly fury. Mary-Lynnette could see him change position in a swift, graceful motion, gathering his muscles under him to jump—

But the werewolf jumped first. Springing like an animal – except that Jeremy still had arms, and one hand went for the yew club. The club smashed sideways into Ash's head and knocked him flat. And then it fell, bouncing away on the carpet of needles.

The werewolf didn't need it – it was baring its teeth. It was going to tear Ash's throat out, like the horse, like the hiker . . .

Mary-Lynnette was running.

Not toward Ash. She couldn't help him barehanded. She ran toward the car, into the clouds of choking smoke.

Oh, God, it's hot. Please let me just get there . . .

She could feel the heat on her cheeks, on her arms. She remembered something from an elementary school safety class and dropped to her knees, scrambling and crawling where the air was cooler.

And then she heard the sound behind her. The most eerie sound there is – a wolf howling.

It knows what I'm doing. It's seen that knife every time I pry off my gas cap. It's going to stop me . . .

She threw herself blindly into the smoke and heat, and reached the car. Orange flames were shooting crazily from the engine, and the door handle burned her hand when she touched it. She fumbled, wrenching at it.

Open, open . . .

The door swung out. Hot air blasted around her. If she'd been completely human she wouldn't have been able to stand it. But she'd exchanged blood with four vampires in two days, and she wasn't completely human anymore. She wasn't Mary-Lynnette anymore . . . but was she capable of killing?

Flames were licking up beneath the dashboard. She groped over smoking vinyl and shoved a hand under the driver's seat.

Find it! Find it!

Her fingers touched metal – the knife. The silver fruit knife with the Victorian scrolling that she'd borrowed from Mrs Burdock. It was very hot. Her hand closed on it, and she pulled it from under the seat and turned . . . just as something came flying at her from behind.

The turning was instinctive – she had to face what was attacking her. But what she would always know afterward was that she could have turned without pointing the *knife* at what was attacking her. There was a moment in which she could have slanted it backward or toward the ground or toward herself. And if she'd been the Mary-Lynnette of the old days, she might have done that.

She didn't. The knife faced outward. Toward the shape jumping at her. And when the thing landed on top of her she felt impact in her wrist and all the way up her arm.

The distant part of her mind said, It went in cleanly between the ribs . . .

And then everything was very confused. Mary-Lynnette felt teeth in her hair, snapping for her neck. She felt claws scratching at her, leaving welts on her arms. The thing attacking her was hairy and heavy and it wasn't a person or even a half-person. It was a large, snarling wolf.

She was still holding the knife, but it was hard to keep her grip on it. It jerked around, twisting her wrist in an impossible direction. It was buried in the wolf's chest.

For just an instant, as the thing pulled away, she got a good look at it.

A beautiful animal. Sleek and handsome, but with crazy eyes. It was trying to kill her with its last panting breath.

Oh, God, you hate me, don't you? I've chosen Ash over you; I've hurt you with silver. And now you're dying. You must feel so betrayed . . .

Mary-Lynnette began to shake violently. She couldn't do this anymore. She let go of the knife and pushed and kicked at the wolf with her arms and legs. Half scrambling and half scooting on her back, she managed to get a few feet away. The wolf stood silhouetted against a background of fire. She could see it gather itself for one last spring at her—

There was a very soft, contained *poof*. The entire car

lurched like something in agony – and then the fireball was everywhere.

Mary-Lynnette cringed against the ground, half-blinded, but she had to watch.

So that's what it looks like. A car going up in flames. Not the kind of big explosion you hear in the movies. Just a *poof*. And then just the fire, going up and up.

The heat drove her away, still crawling, but she couldn't stop looking. Orange flames. That was all her station wagon was now. Orange flames shooting every which way out of a metal skeleton on tyres.

The wolf didn't come out of the flames.

Mary-Lynnette sat up. Smoke was in her throat, and when she tried to yell 'Jeremy!' it came out as a hoarse croak.

The wolf still didn't come out. And no wonder, with a silver knife in its chest and fire all around it.

Mary-Lynnette sat, arms wrapped around herself, and watched the car burn.

He would have killed me. Like any good hunter. I had to defend myself, I had to save Ash. And the girls . . . he would have killed all of them. And then he'd have killed more people like that hiker . . . He was crazy and completely *evil*, because he'd do anything to get what he wanted.

And she'd seen it from the beginning. Something under that 'nice guy' exterior – she'd seen it over and over, but she'd kept letting herself get convinced it wasn't there. She should have trusted her feelings in the first place. When she'd realized that she'd solved the mystery of Jeremy Lovett and that it wasn't a happy ending.

She was shaking but she couldn't cry.

The fire roared on. Tiny sparks showered upward.

I don't care if it was justified. It wasn't like killing in my dream. It wasn't easy and it wasn't natural and I'll never forget the way he looked at me . . .

Then she thought, *Ash*.

She'd been so paralyzed she'd almost forgotten him. Now she turned around, almost too frightened to look. She made herself crawl over to where he was still lying.

So much blood . . . how can he be all right? But if he's dead . . . if it's all been for nothing . . .

But Ash was breathing. And when she touched his face, trying to find a clean place in the blood, he moved. He stirred, then he tried to sit up.

'Stay there.' Jeremy's shirt and jeans were on the ground. Mary-Lynnette picked up the shirt and dabbed at Ash's neck. 'Ash, keep still . . .'

He tried to sit up again. 'Don't worry. I'll protect you.'

'Lie down,' Mary-Lynnette said. When he didn't, she pushed at him. 'There's nothing to do. He's dead.'

He sank back, eyes shutting. 'Did I kill him?'

Mary-Lynnette made a choked sound that wasn't exactly a laugh. She was trembling with relief – Ash could breathe and talk, and he even sounded like his normal fatuous self. She'd had no idea how good that could sound. And underneath the swabbing shirt she could see that his neck was already healing. What had been gashes were becoming flat pink scars.

Vampire flesh was incredible.

Ash swallowed. 'You didn't answer my question.'

'No. You didn't kill him. I did.'

His eyes opened. They just looked at each other for a moment. And in that moment Mary-Lynnette knew they were both realizing a lot of things.

Then Ash said, 'I'm sorry,' and his voice had never been less fatuous. He pushed the shirt away and sat up. 'I'm so sorry.'

She didn't know who reached first, but they were holding each other. And Mary-Lynnette was thinking about hunters and danger and laughing at death. About all the things it meant to *really* belong to the night. And about how she would never look in the mirror and see the same person she used to see.

'At least it's over now,' Ash said. She could feel his arms around her, his warmth and solidity, his support. 'There won't be any more killings. It's over.'

It was, and so were a lot of other things.

The first sob was hard to get out. So hard that she'd have thought there would be a pause before the next – but, no. There was no pause between that one and the next, or the next or the next. She cried for a long time. And the fire burned itself out and the sparks flew upward and Ash held her all the while.

CHAPTER

17

'**W**ell, she wasn't telling humans anything – but she did defy the authority of the Night World,' Ash said in his most lazy, careless voice.

Quinn said succinctly, 'How?'

It was late Monday afternoon and the sun was streaming through the western windows of the Burdock farmhouse. Ash was wearing a brand-new shirt bought at the Briar Creek general store, a turtleneck with long sleeves that covered the almost-healed scars on his throat and arms. His jeans were bleached white, his hair was combed over the scab on the back of his head, and he was playing the scene of his life.

'She knew about a rogue werewolf and didn't tell anybody about him.'

'So she was a traitor. And what did you do?'

Ash shrugged. 'Staked her.'

Quinn laughed out loud.

'No, really,' Ash said earnestly, looking into Quinn's face with what he knew were wide, guileless eyes – probably blue. 'See?'

Without taking his eyes from Quinn's he whipped a pink-and-green country quilt off the bundle on the couch.

Quinn's eyebrows flew upward.

He stared for a moment at Aunt Opal, who had been cleaned so that you'd never know she'd ever been buried, and who had the picket stake carefully replaced in her chest.

Quinn actually swallowed. It was the first time Ash had ever seen him falter.

'You really did it,' he said. There was reluctant respect in his voice – and definite shock.

You know, Quinn, I don't think you're quite as tough as you pretend. After all, no matter how you try to act like an Elder, you're only eighteen. And you'll *always* be eighteen, and next year maybe I'll be older.

'Well,' Quinn said, blinking rapidly. 'Well. Well – I have to hand it to you.'

'Yeah, I just decided the best thing to do was clean up the whole situation. She was getting on, you know.'

Quinn's dark eyes widened fractionally. 'I have to admit – I didn't think you were *that* ruthless.'

'You've gotta do what you've gotta do. For the family honour, of course.'

Quinn cleared his throat. 'So – what about the werewolf?'

'Oh, I took care of that, too.' Ash meandered over and whipped a brown-and-white quilt off Exhibit B. The wolf was a charred and contorted corpse. It had given Mary-Lynnette hysterics when Ash insisted on pulling it out of the car, and Quinn's nostrils quivered when he looked at it.

'Sorry, it does smell like burnt hair, doesn't it? I got a little sooty myself, keeping him in the fire . . .'

'You burned him *alive*?'

'Well, it is one of the traditional methods . . .'

'Just put the blanket back, all right?'

Ash put the blanket back.

'So, you see, everything's taken care of. No humans involved, no extermination necessary.'

'Yes, all right . . .' Quinn's eyes were still on the quilt. Ash decided the moment was right.

'And by the way, it turns out the girls had a perfectly legitimate reason for coming. They just wanted to learn to hunt. Nothing illegal about that, is there?'

'What? Oh. No.' Quinn glanced at Aunt Opal, then finally looked back at Ash. 'So they're coming back now that they've learned it.'

'Well, eventually. They haven't quite learned it yet . . . so they're staying.'

'They're *staying*?'

'Right. Look, I'm the head of the family on the West Coast, aren't I? And I say they're staying.'

'Ash . . .'

'It's about time there was a Night World outpost in this area, don't you think? You see what's happened without one. You get families of outlaw werewolves wandering around. Somebody's got to stay here and hold down the fort.'

'Ash . . . you couldn't *pay* Night People to strand themselves out here. Nothing but animals to feed on, nobody but humans to associate with . . .'

'Yeah, it's a dirty job, but someone's got to do it. Besides, wasn't it you who said it's not good living your whole life isolated on an island?'

Quinn stared at him, then said, 'Well, I don't think this is much better.'

'Then it serves my sisters right. Maybe in a few years they'll appreciate the island more. Then they can hand the job over to someone else.'

'Ash . . . no one else is going to *come* here.'

'Well.' With the battle won, and Quinn simply looking dazed and as if he wanted to get back to Los Angeles as fast as possible, Ash allowed himself a small measure of truth.

'I might come visit them someday,' he said.

'He did a beautiful job,' Rowan said that evening. 'We heard it all from the kitchen. You would have loved it.'

Mary-Lynnette smiled.

'Quinn can't wait to get away,' Jade said, intertwining her fingers with Mark's.

Kestrel said to Ash, 'I'd just like to be around when you explain all this to Dad.'

'That's funny,' Ash said. 'I feel just the opposite.'

Everyone laughed – except Mary-Lynnette. The big farm kitchen was warm and bright, but the windows were darkening. She couldn't see anything in the gathering darkness – in the last two days the effects of her blood exchange had faded. Her senses were ordinary human senses again.

'You're sure you won't get in trouble?' she asked Ash.

'No. I'll tell our dad the truth – mostly. That an outlaw werewolf killed Aunt Opal and that I killed the werewolf. And that the girls are better off here, hunting quietly and watching out for other rogues. There's sure to be some record of the Lovett family . . . Dad can check out the history all he wants.'

'A whole family of outlaw werewolves,' Kestrel said musingly.

'Of *crazy* werewolves,' Ash said. 'They were as dangerous to the Night World as any vampire hunters could be. God knows how long they've been here – long enough for their land to get named Mad Dog Creek.'

'And for people to mistake them for Sasquatch,' Mark said.

Rowan's brown eyes were troubled. 'And it was my fault that you didn't know,' she said to Mary-Lynnette. '*I* told you he couldn't be the killer. I'm sorry.'

Mary-Lynnette captured her gaze and held it. 'Rowan, you are *not* going to feel guilty for this. You couldn't have realized. He wasn't killing for food like a normal werewolf. He was killing to protect his territory – and to scare us.'

'And it might have worked,' Mark said. 'Except that you guys didn't have anywhere else to go.'

Ash looked at Mark, then at his sisters. 'I have a question. Is the territory around here going to be enough for *you*?'

'Of course,' Rowan said, with gentle surprise.

'We don't always need to *kill* the animals,' Jade said. 'We're getting it down pat now. We can take a little here and a little there. Heck, we can even try the *goat*.'

'I'd rather try Tiggy,' Kestrel said, and for a moment her golden eyes glimmered. Mary-Lynnette didn't say it, but she wondered sometimes about Kestrel. If maybe, someday, Kestrel might need a bigger territory of her own. She was a lot like Jeremy in some ways.

Beautiful, ruthless, single-minded. A true Night Person.

'And what about you?' Ash said, looking at Mark.

'Me? Uh . . . Well, when you get down to it, I'm kind of a hamburger guy . . .'

'I tried to take him hunting last night,' Jade interpreted. 'You know, just to show him. But he threw up.'

'I didn't actually—'

'Yes, you did,' Jade said calmly and cheerfully. Mark looked away. Mary-Lynnette noticed they didn't stop holding hands.

'So I take it you're not going to become a vampire,' Ash said to Mark.

'Uh, let's just say not any time soon.'

Ash turned to Mary-Lynnette. 'And what about the human end of things? Do we have that taken care of?'

'Well, I know everything that's going on in town – by which I mean that I talked with Bunny Marten this morning. I'm so glad she's not a vampire, incidentally . . .'

Mark said, 'I always knew it.'

'Anyway, here's the quick version.' Mary-Lynnette held up a finger. 'One, everybody knows that Jeremy is gone – his boss at the gas station missed him yesterday and went up to check the trailer. They found a lot of weird stuff there. But all they know is that he's disappeared.'

'Good,' Rowan said.

Mary-Lynnette held up another finger. 'Two, Dad is sorry but not surprised that the station wagon blew up. Claudine has been predicting it would for a year.'

Another finger. 'Three, Mr Kimble doesn't have any idea *what* killed his horse – but now he thinks it was an animal instead of a person. Vic Kimble thinks it was maybe Sasquatch. He and Todd are very spooked and want to get out of Briar Creek for good.'

'And let's have a moment of silence to show how we'll miss them,' Mark said solemnly, and blew a raspberry.

'Four,' Mary-Lynnette said, holding up a fourth finger, 'you girls are eventually going to have to mention that your aunt hasn't come back from her "vacation". But I think you can wait awhile. Nobody comes out here so nobody will notice she's gone. And I think we can bury her and Jeremy safely. Even if somebody finds them, what have they got? A mummy that looks about a thousand years old and a wolf. They won't be able to connect them to the missing people.'

'Poor old Aunt Opal,' Jade said, still cheerful. 'But she helped us in the end, didn't she?'

Mary-Lynnette looked at her. Yes, there it is, she thought. The silver in the eyes when you laugh about death. Jade is a true Night Person, too.

'She did help. And I'm going to miss her,' she said out loud.

Kestrel said, 'So everything is taken care of.'

'Seems like it.' Ash hesitated. 'And Quinn is waiting down the road. I told him it would only take a couple hours to finish making arrangements and say goodbye.'

There was a silence.

'I'll see you off,' Mary-Lynnette said at last.

They went together to the front door. When they were outside in the twilight Ash shut the door behind them.

'You still can come with me, you know.'

'With you and Quinn?'

'I'll send him away. Or I'll go and come back tomorrow and get you. Or I'll come back and stay . . .'

'You need to go tell your father about this. Make everything right with him, so it's safe for your sisters. You *know* that.'

'Well, I'll come back after *that*,' Ash said, with an edge of desperation to his voice.

Mary-Lynnette looked away. The sun was gone. Looking east, the sky was already the darkest purple imaginable. Almost black. Even as she watched, a star came out. Or – not a star. Jupiter.

'I'm not ready yet. I wish I were.'

'No, you don't,' Ash said, and he was right, of course. She'd known ever since she sat there by the road, crying while her car burned. And although she'd thought and thought about it since then, sitting in her darkened room, there was nothing she could do to change her own mind.

She would never be a vampire. She just wasn't cut out for it. She couldn't do the things vampires had to do – and stay sane. She wasn't like Jade or Kestrel or even Rowan with her pale sinewy feet and her instinctive love of the hunt. She'd looked into the heart of the Night World . . . and she couldn't join it.

'I don't *want* you to be like that,' Ash said. 'I want you to be like *you*.'

Without looking at him, Mary-Lynnette said, 'But we're not kids. We can't be like Jade and Mark, and just hold hands and giggle and never think about the future.'

'No, we're only soulmates, that's all. We're only destined to be together forever . . .'

'If we've got forever, then you can give me time,' Mary-Lynnette said. 'Go back and wander a little. Take a look at the Night World and make sure you want to give it up—'

'I know that already.'

'Take a look at humans and make sure you want to be tied to one of them.'

'And think about the things I've done to humans, maybe?'

Mary-Lynnette looked at him directly. 'Yes.'

He looked away. 'All right. I admit it. I've got a lot to make up for . . .'

Mary-Lynnette knew it. He'd thought of humans as vermin – and food. The things she'd seen in his mind made her not want to picture more.

'Then make up for what you can,' she said, although she didn't dare really hope that he would. 'Take time to do that. And give *me* time to finish growing up. I'm still in high school, Ash.'

'You'll be out in a year. I'll come back then.'

'It may be too soon.'

'I know. I'll come back anyway.' He smiled ironically. 'And in the meantime I'll fight dragons, just like any knight for his lady. I'll prove myself. You'll be proud of me.'

Mary-Lynnette's throat hurt. Ash's smile disappeared. They just stood looking at each other.

It was the obvious time for a kiss. Instead, they just stood staring like hurt kids, and then one of them moved and they were holding on to each other. Mary-Lynnette held on tighter and tighter, her face buried in Ash's shoulder. Ash, who seemed to have lost it altogether, was raining kisses on the back of her neck, saying, 'I wish I were a human. I wish I were.'

'No, you don't,' Mary-Lynnette said, seriously unsteady because of the kisses.

'I do. I do.'

But it wouldn't help, and Mary-Lynnette knew he knew it. The problem wasn't simply what he was, it was what he'd done – and what he was going to do. He'd seen too much of the dark side of life to be a normal person. His nature was already formed, and she wasn't sure he could fight it.

'Believe in me,' he said, as if he could hear her.

Mary-Lynnette couldn't say yes or no. So she did the only thing she could do – she lifted her head. His lips were in the right place to meet hers. The electric sparks weren't painful anymore, she discovered, and the pink haze could be quite wonderful. For a time everything was warm and sweet and strangely peaceful.

And then, behind them, somebody knocked on the door. Mary-Lynnette and Ash jumped and separated. They looked at each other, startled, emotions still too raw, and then Mary-Lynnette realized where she was. She laughed and so did Ash.

'Come out,' they said simultaneously.

Mark and Jade came out. Rowan and Kestrel were behind them. They all stood on the porch – avoiding the hole. They all smiled at Ash and Mary-Lynnette in a way that made Mary-Lynnette blush.

'Goodbye,' she said firmly to Ash.

He looked at her for a long moment, then looked at the road behind him. Then he turned to go.

Mary-Lynnette watched him, blinking away tears. She still couldn't let herself believe in him. But there was no harm in hoping, was there? In wishing. Even if wishes almost never came true . . .

Jade gasped. 'Look!'

They all saw it, and Mary-Lynnette felt her heart jump violently. A bolt of light was streaking across the darkness in the northeast. Not a little wimpy shooting star – a brilliant green meteor that crossed half the sky, showering sparks. It was right above Ash's path, as if lighting his way.

A late Perseid. The last of the summer meteors. But it seemed like a blessing.

'Quick, quick, wish,' Mark was telling Jade eagerly. 'A wish on that star you gotta get.'

Mary-Lynnette glanced at his excited face, at the way his eyes shone with excitement. Beside him, Jade was clapping, her own eyes wide with delight.

I'm so glad you're happy, Mary-Lynnette thought. My wish for you came true. So now maybe I can wish for myself.

I wish . . . I wish . . .

Ash turned around and smiled at her. 'See you next year,' he said. 'With slain dragon!'

He started down the weed-strewn path to the road. For a moment, in the deep violet twilight, he did look to Mary-Lynnette like a knight walking off on a quest. A knight-errant with shining blond hair and no weapons, going off into a very dark and dangerous wilderness. Then he turned around and walked backward, waving, which ruined the effect.

Everyone shouted goodbyes.

Mary-Lynnette could feel them around her, her brother and her three blood-sisters, all radiating warmth and support. Playful Jade. Fierce Kestrel. Wise and gentle Rowan. And Mark, who wasn't sullen and solitary anymore. Tiggy wound himself around her ankles, purring amiably.

'Even when we're apart, we'll be looking at the same sky!' Ash yelled.

'What a line,' Mary-Lynnette called back. But he was right. The sky would be there for both of them. She'd always know he was out there somewhere, looking up at it in wonder. Just knowing that was important.

And she was clear on who she was at last. She was Mary-Lynnette, and someday she'd discover a supernova or a comet or a black hole, but she'd do it as a human. And Ash would come back next year.

And she would always love the night.

ENCHANTRESS

For Maurice Ogden, with thanks

CHAPTER

1

Expelled.

It was one of the scariest words a high school senior could think of, and it kept ringing in Thea Harman's mind as her grandmother's car approached the school building.

'This,' Grandma Harman said from the front passenger seat, 'is your last chance. You do realize that, don't you?'

As the driver pulled the car to the curb, she went on. 'I don't know why you got thrown out of the last school, and I don't want to know. But if there's one *whiff* of trouble at this school, I'm going to give up and send both of you to your Aunt Ursula's. And you don't want *that*, now, do you?'

Thea shook her head vigorously.

Aunt Ursula's house was nicknamed the Convent, a grey fortress on a deserted mountain top. Stone walls everywhere, an atmosphere of gloom – and Aunt Ursula watching every move with thin lips. Thea would rather die than go there.

In the backseat next to her, Thea's cousin Blaise was shaking her head, too – but Thea knew better than to hope she was listening.

Thea herself could hardly concentrate. She felt dizzy

and very untogether, as if half of her were still back in New Hampshire, in the last principal's office. She kept seeing the look on his face that meant she and Blaise were about to be expelled – again.

But this time had been the worst. She'd never forget the way the police car outside kept flashing red and blue through the windows, or the way the smoke kept rising from the charred remains of the music wing, or the way Randy Marik cried as the police led him off to jail.

Or the way Blaise kept smiling. Triumphantly, as if it had all been a game.

Thea glanced sideways at her cousin.

Blaise looked beautiful and deadly, which wasn't her fault. She always looked that way; it was part of having smouldering grey eyes and hair like stopped smoke. She was as different from Thea's soft blondness as night from day and it was her beauty which kept getting them in trouble, but Thea couldn't help loving her.

After all, they'd been raised as sisters. And the sister bond was the strongest bond there was . . . to a witch.

But we can't get expelled again. We can't. *And I know you're thinking right now that you can do it all over again and good old Thea will stick with you – but this time you're wrong. This time I've got to stop you.*

'That's all,' Gran said abruptly, finishing with her instructions. 'Keep your noses clean until the end of October or you'll be sorry. Now, get out.' She whacked the headrest of the driver's seat with her stick. 'Home, Tobias.'

The driver, a college-age boy with curly hair who had the dazed and beaten expression all Grandma's apprentices got after a few days; muttered, 'Yes, High Lady,' and reached for the gearshift. Thea grabbed for the door handle and slid out of the car fast. Blaise was right behind her.

The ancient Lincoln Continental sped off. Thea was left standing with Blaise under the warm Nevada sun, in front of the two-storey adobe building complex. Lake Mead High School.

Thea blinked once or twice, trying to kick-start her brain. Then she turned to her cousin.

'Tell me,' she said grimly, 'that you're not going to do the same thing here.'

Blaise laughed. 'I never do the same thing twice.'

'You know what I *mean*.'

Blaise pursed her lips and reached down to adjust the top of her boot. 'I think Gran overdid it a little with the lecture, don't you? I think there's something she's not telling us about. I mean, what was that bit about the end of the month?' She straightened, tossed back her mane of dark hair and smiled sweetly. 'And shouldn't we be going to the office to get our schedules?'

'Are you going to answer my *question*?'

'Did you ask a question?'

Thea shut her eyes. 'Blaise, we are running out of relatives. If it happens again – well, do *you* want to go to the Convent?'

For the first time, Blaise's expression darkened. Then she shrugged, sending liquid ripples down her loose ruby-coloured shirt. 'Better hurry. We don't want to be tardy.'

'You go ahead,' Thea said tiredly. She watched as her cousin walked away, hips swaying in the trademark Blaise lilt.

Thea took another breath, examining the buildings with their arched doorways and pink plaster walls. She knew the drill. Another year of living with *them*, of walking quietly through halls knowing that she was different from everybody around her, even while she was carefully, expertly pretending to be the same.

It wasn't hard. Humans weren't very smart. But it took a certain amount of concentration.

She had just started toward the office herself when she heard raised voices. A little knot of students had gathered at the edge of the parking lot.

'Stay away from it.'

'Kill it!'

Thea joined the periphery of the group, being inconspicuous. But then she saw what was on the ground beyond the curb and she took three startled steps until she was looking right down at it.

Oh . . . how *beautiful*. Long, strong body . . . broad head . . . and a string of rapidly vibrating horny rings on the tail. They were making a noise like steam escaping, or melon seeds being shaken.

The snake was olive green, with wide diamonds down its back. The scales on the face looked shiny, almost wet. And its black tongue flickered so fast . . .

A rock whizzed past her and hit the ground beside the snake. Dust puffed.

Thea glanced up. A kid in cutoffs was backing away, looking scared and triumphant.

'Don't do that,' somebody said.

'Get a stick,' somebody else said.

'Keep away from it.'

'*Kill* it.'

Another rock flew.

The faces around Thea weren't vicious. Some were curious, some were alarmed, some were filled with a sort of fascinated disgust. But it was all going to end up the same for the snake.

A boy with red hair came running up with a forked branch. People were reaching for rocks.

I can't let them, Thea thought. Rattlers were actually

pretty fragile – their backbones were vulnerable. These kids might kill the snake without even meaning to.

Not to mention that a couple of the kids might get bitten in the process.

But she didn't have anything . . . no jasper against venom, no St John root to soothe the mind.

It didn't matter. She had to do *something*. The red-headed boy was circling with the stick like a fighter looking for an opening. The kids around him were alternately warning him and cheering him on. The snake was swelling its body, tongue-tips flickering up and down faster than Thea's eye could follow. It was *mad*.

Dropping her backpack, she slipped in front of the red-haired boy. She could see his shock and she heard several people yell, but she tried to block it all out. She needed to focus.

I hope I can do this . . .

She knelt a foot away from the rattler.

The snake fell into a striking coil. Front body raised in an S-shaped spiral, head and neck held like a poised javelin. *Nothing* looked so ready to lunge as a snake in this position.

Easy . . . easy, Thea thought, staring into the narrow cat-like pupils of the yellow eyes. She slowly lifted her hands, palms facing the snake.

Worried noises from the crowd behind her.

The snake was inhaling and exhaling with a violent hiss. Thea breathed carefully, trying to radiate peace.

Now, who could help her? Of course, her own personal protector, the goddess closest to her heart. Eileithyia of ancient Crete, the mother of the animals.

Eileithyia, Mistress of the Beasts, please tell this critter to calm *down*. Help me see into its little snaky heart so I'll know what to do.

And then it happened, the wonderful transformation that even Thea didn't understand. Part of her *became* the snake. There was a strange blurring of Thea's boundaries – she was herself, but she was also coiled on the warm ground, angry and excitable and desperate to get back to the safety of a creosote bush. She'd had eleven babies some time ago and had never quite recovered from the experience. Now she was surrounded by large, hot, fast-moving creatures.

Big-living-things . . . way too close. Not responding to my threat noises. Better bite them.

The snake had only two rules for dealing with animals that weren't food. 1) Shake your tail until they go away without stepping on you. 2) If they don't go away, strike.

Thea the person kept her hands steady and tried to pound a new thought into the small reptile brain. *Smell me. Taste me. I don't smell like a human. I'm a daughter of Hellewise.*

The snake's tongue brushed her palm. Its tips were so thin and delicate that Thea could hardly feel them flicker against her skin.

But she could feel the snake drop down from maximum alert. It was relaxing, ready to retreat. In another minute it would listen when she told it to slither away.

Behind her, she heard a new disturbance in the crowd.

'There's Eric!'

'Hey, Eric – rattlesnake!'

Block it out, Thea thought.

A new voice, distant but coming closer. 'Leave it alone, guys. It's probably just a bull snake.'

There was a swell of excited denial. Thea could feel her connection slipping. Stay focused . . .

But nobody could have stayed focused during what

happened next. She heard a quick footstep. A shadow fell from the east. Then she heard a gasp.

'Mojave rattler!'

And *then* something hit her, sending her flying sideways. It happened so fast that she didn't have time to twist. She landed painfully on her arm. She lost control of the snake.

All she could see as she looked east was a scaly olive-green head driving forward so fast it was a blur. Its jaws were wide open – amazingly wide – and its fangs sank into the blue-jeaned leg of the boy who had knocked Thea out of the way.

CHAPTER

2

The crowd erupted in panic.

Everything was happening at once; Thea couldn't sort out the different impressions. Half the people in front of her were running. The other half were yelling.

'Call nine-one-one—'

'It got Eric—'

'I *told* you to kill it!'

The red-headed boy was darting forward with his stick. Other kids were rushing around, looking for rocks. The group had become a mob.

The snake was rattling wildly, a terrifying sizzling sound. It was in a frenzy, ready to strike again at any moment – and there was nothing Thea could do.

'Hey!' The voice startled her. It came from Eric, the boy who'd been bitten. 'Calm down, you guys. Josh, give me that.' He was talking to the redhead with the forked branch. 'It didn't bite me. It just struck.'

Thea stared at him. Was this guy *crazy*?

But people were listening to him. A girl in baggy shorts and a midriff top stopped hefting her rock.

'Just let me get hold of it . . . then I can take it out into the brush where it won't hurt anybody.'

Definitely crazy. He was talking in such a matter-of-fact, reasonable way – and he was going to try to pin the snake down with that stick. *Somebody* had to act fast.

A flash of ruby-colour caught Thea's eye. Blaise was in the crowd, watching with pursed lips. Thea made her decision.

She dove for the snake.

It was watching the stick. Thea grabbed for its mind before grabbing its body – which kept it immobilized for the instant she needed to seize it just below the head. She hung on while its jaws gaped and its body lashed.

'Grab the tail and we'll get it out of here,' she said breathlessly to Eric the crazy guy.

Eric was staring at her grip on the snake, dumbfounded. 'For God's sake, don't let go. It can twist in a second . . .'

'I know. *Grab* it!'

He grabbed it. Most of the crowd scattered as Thea wheeled around with the snake's head held tightly at arm's length. Blaise didn't run, she just looked at the snake as if it smelled bad.

'I need this,' Thea whispered hastily as she passed her cousin. She snatched at Blaise's necklace with her free hand. The fragile gold chain broke and Thea's fingers closed around a stone.

Then she was heading out into the scrub brush, the weight of the snake dragging on her arm. She walked fast, because Eric didn't have much time. The grounds behind the school sloped up and then downward, getting wilder and more grey-brown. When the buildings were out of sight, Thea stopped.

'This is a good place,' Eric said. His voice was strained.

Thea glanced back and saw that he looked pale. Brave and very, very crazy, she thought. 'OK, we let go on three.' She jerked her head. 'Throw it that way and back up fast.'

He nodded and counted with her. 'One . . . two . . . *three.*'

Giving it a slight swing, they both let go. The snake flew in a graceful arc and landed near a clump of purple sage. It wriggled immediately into the brush without showing the slightest hint of gratitude. Thea felt its cool, scaly mind recede as it thought, *That smell . . . that shade . . . safety.*

She let out the breath she hadn't realized she'd been holding.

Behind her, she heard Eric sit down abruptly. 'Well, that's that.' His own breathing was fast and irregular. 'Now could I ask you a favour?'

He was sitting with his long legs straight out, his skin even paler than before. Perspiration beaded on his upper lip.

'You know, I'm not really sure it didn't bite me,' he said.

Thea knew – and knew Eric knew – that it *had*. Rattlers did sometimes strike without biting, and did sometimes bite without injecting venom. But not this time. What she couldn't believe was that any human would care enough about a snake to let a bite go untreated.

'Let me see your leg,' she said.

'Actually, I think maybe you'd better just call the paramedics.'

'Please let me see.' She kept her voice gentle, kneeling in front of him, reaching slowly. The way she'd approach a scared animal. He held still, letting her roll up his jeans leg.

There it was, the little double wound in the tanned skin. Not much blood. But surrounded by swelling already. Even if she ran back to the school, even if the paramedics broke every speed law, it wouldn't be fast enough. Sure, they'd save his life, but his leg would swell up like a sausage and turn purple and he'd have days of unbelievable pain.

Except that Thea had in her hand an Isis blood-stone. A deep red carnelian engraved with a scarab, symbol of the Egyptian Queen goddess, Isis. The ancient Egyptians had put the stones at the feet of mummies; Blaise used it to heighten passion. But it was also the most powerful purifier of the blood in existence.

Eric groaned suddenly. His arm was over his eyes, and Thea knew what he must be feeling. Weakness, nausea, disorientation. She felt sorry for him, but his confusion would actually work to her advantage.

She pressed her hand to the wounds, the carnelian hidden between her tightly closed fingers. Then she started to hum under her breath, visualizing what she wanted to happen. The thing about gems was that they didn't work on their own. They were just a means of raising psychic power, focusing it, and directing it to a certain purpose.

Find the poison, surround it, dispel it. Purify and eliminate. Then encourage the body's natural defenses. Finally, soothe away the swelling and redness, sending the blood back where it belonged.

As she knelt there, feeling the sun on the back of her head, she suddenly realized that she'd never done this before. She'd healed animals – puppies with toad poisoning and cats with spider bites – but never a person. Funny how she'd known instinctively that she could do it. She'd almost felt that she *had* to do it.

She sat back on her heels, pocketing the blood-stone. 'How are you feeling?'

'Huh?' He took his arm away from his eyes. 'Sorry – I think I sort of blanked out there for a minute.'

Good, Thea thought. 'But how do you feel now?'

He looked at her as if he were struggling under pressure to be gentle. He was going to explain to her that people who got bitten by rattlesnakes felt sick. But then his expression changed. 'I feel . . . it's weird . . . I think maybe it's gone numb.' He peered doubtfully at his calf.

'No, you were just lucky. You didn't get bitten.'

'*What?*' He scrambled to roll his jeans leg up higher. Then he just stared. The flesh was smooth and unmarked, with just the slightest trace of redness left. 'I was sure . . .'

He lifted his eyes to hers.

It was the first time Thea had really gotten a chance to look at him. He was a nice-looking guy, lean and sandy-haired and sweet-faced. Long legs. And those eyes . . . deep green with grey flecks. Just now they were both intense and bewildered, like those of a startled kid.

'How'd you do that?' he said.

Thea was shocked speechless.

He wasn't supposed to respond like this. What was wrong with him? When she could talk again, she said, 'I didn't do anything.'

'Yes, you did,' he said, and now his eyes were clear and direct, full of an odd conviction. Suddenly his expression changed to something like wonder. 'You . . . there's something so different about you.'

He leaned forward slowly, as if entranced. And then . . . Thea experienced an odd duality. She was used to seeing herself through the eyes of animals: a big, hairless creature in false skins. But now she saw herself as Eric saw her. A kneeling girl with yellow hair falling loose over her shoulders and soft brown eyes. A face that was too gentle, with a very worried expression.

'You're . . . beautiful,' Eric said, still wondering. 'I've never seen anybody . . . but it's like there's a mist all around you. You're so mysterious . . .'

A huge quivering stillness seemed to hang over the desert. Thea's heart was beating so hard that it shook her body. *What was happening?*

'It's like you're part of everything out here,' he said in that wise, childlike voice. 'You belong to it. And there's so much peace . . .'

'*No*,' Thea said. There was no peace at all in her. She was terrified. She didn't know what was going on, but she knew she had to get away.

'Don't go,' he said, when she shifted. He had the stricken expression of a heartbroken puppy.

And then . . . he reached for her. Not roughly. His fingers didn't close on her wrist. They just brushed the back of her hand, sliding away when she jerked.

But it didn't matter. That light touch had raised all the hairs on Thea's forearm. And when she looked back into the grey-flecked green eyes, she knew he'd felt it, too.

A sort of piercing sweetness, a dizzying exhilaration. And – a connection. As if something deeper than words was being communicated.

I know you. I see what you see . . .

Almost without knowing what she was doing, Thea raised her hand. Fingertips slightly outspread, as if she were going to touch a mirror or a ghost. He brought his hand up, too. They were staring at each other.

And then, just before their fingers made contact, Thea felt a jolt of panic like ice water.

What was she *doing*? Had she lost her mind?

Suddenly everything was clear – too clear. Her future stretched out before her, every detail sharp. Death for breaking Night World law. Herself centred in the Inner

Circle, trying to explain that she hadn't meant to betray their secrets, that she hadn't meant to . . . to get close to a human. That it was all a mistake, just a moment of stupidity because she'd wanted to heal him. And them bringing the Cup of Death anyway.

The vision was so clear it seemed like a prophecy. Thea jumped up as if the ground had lurched underneath her, and she did the only thing she could think of to do.

She said scathingly, 'Are you *nuts*? Or is your brain just overheated or something?'

He got the stricken look again.

He's a human. One of *them*, Thea reminded herself. She put even more scorn in her voice. 'I'm part of everything; I did something to your leg . . . yeah, sure. I bet you believe in Santa Claus, too.'

Now he looked shocked – and uncertain. Thea went for the coup de grâce. 'Or were you just trying to put the moves on me?'

'Huh? *No*,' he said. He blinked and looked around. The desert was the ordinary desert, grey-green and parched and flat. Then he looked at his leg. He blinked again, as if getting a fresh grip on reality. 'I . . . look, I'm sorry if I upset you. I don't know what's wrong with me.'

Suddenly he gave a sheepish smile. 'Maybe I'm kind of weird from being scared. I guess I'm not as brave as I thought.'

Relief trickled through Thea. He was buying it. Thank Isis that humans were stupider than chickens.

'And I wasn't trying to move in on you. I just—' He broke off. 'You know, I don't even know your *name*.'

'Thea Harman.'

'I'm Eric Ross. You're new here, aren't you?'

'Yes.' Stop talking and *go*, she ordered herself.

'If I can show you around or anything . . . I mean,

I *would* like to see you again . . .'

'No,' Thea said flatly. She would have liked to have kept it to that monosyllable, but she wanted to crush this new idea of his completely. 'I don't want to see *you*,' she said, too rattled to think of any more subtle way to put it.

And then she turned and walked away. What else was there to do? She certainly couldn't talk to him anymore. Even if she would always wonder why he'd been crazy enough to care about the snake, she couldn't ask. From now on she had to stay as far away from him as possible.

She hurried back to the school – and realized immediately that she was late. The parking lot was quiet. Nobody was walking outside the adobe buildings.

On my first day, too, Thea thought. Her backpack was on the ground where she'd dropped it, a notebook lying beside it on the asphalt. She grabbed them both and all but ran to the office.

It was only in physics class, after she'd handed her admission slip to the teacher and walked past rows of curious eyes to an empty seat in the back, that she realized the notebook wasn't hers.

It fell open to a page that had *Introduction to Flatworms* scribbled in sloping, spiky blue ink. Below were some pictures labelled *Class Turbellaria* and *Class Trematoda*. The worms were beautifully drawn, with their nervous systems and reproductive organs shaded in different colours of highlighter, but the artist had also given them big goofy smiling faces. Grotesque but lovable in a cross-eyed way. Thea turned the page and saw another drawing, the *Life Cycle of the Pork Tapeworm*.

Yum.

She leafed back to the beginning of the notebook. *Eric Ross, Honours Zoology I.*

She shut the book.

Now how was she going to get it back to him?

Part of her mind worried about this through physics and her next class, computer applications. Part of it did what it always did at a new school, or any new gathering of humans: it watched and catalogued, keeping alert for danger, figuring out how to fit in. And part of it simply said, I didn't know they had a zoology class here.

The one question she *didn't* want to ask herself was what had happened out there in the desert? Whenever the thought came up, she pushed it away brusquely. It must have had something to do with her senses being too open after merging with the snake.

Anyway, it hadn't meant anything. It had been a weird one-time fluke.

In the main hallway at break, Blaise came rushing up, quick as a lioness despite the high heels.

'How's it going?' Thea said, as Blaise drew her into a temporarily deserted classroom.

Blaise just held out her hand. Thea fished in her pocket for the carnelian.

'You ruined the chain, you know,' Blaise said as she shook back midnight hair and examined the stone for damage. 'And it was one I designed.'

'Sorry. I was in a hurry.'

'Yes, and *why*? What did you want with it?' Blaise didn't wait for a response. 'You healed that boy, didn't you? I knew he got bitten. But he was *human*.'

'Reverence for life, remember?' Thea said. ' "An ye harm none, do as you will." ' She didn't say it with much conviction.

'That doesn't mean humans. And what did he *think*?'

'Nothing. He didn't know I was healing him; he didn't even realize he got bitten.' It wasn't *exactly* a lie.

Blaise looked at her with smoky, suspicious grey eyes.

Then she glanced heaven ward and shook her head. 'Now if you'd been using it to *heat* his blood, I'd understand. But maybe you were doing a little of that, too . . .'

'No, I was *not*,' Thea said. And despite the warmth that rose in her cheeks her voice was cold and sharp. The horror of that death vision was still with her. 'In fact, I don't ever want to see him again,' she went on jaggedly, 'and I told him so, but I've got his stupid *notebook*, and I don't know what to do with it.' She waved the notebook in Blaise's face.

'Oh.' Blaise considered, head on one side. 'Well . . . *I'll* take it to him for you. I'll track him down somehow.'

'Would you?' Thea was startled. 'That's really nice.'

'Yes, it is,' Blaise said. She took the notebook, handling it carefully, as if her nails were wet. 'OK, well, I'd better get to my next class. Algebra.' She made a face. ' 'Bye now.'

Suspicion struck as Thea watched her go.

Blaise wasn't usually so accommodating. And that 'bye now' . . . too sweet. She was up to something.

Thea followed the ruby of Blaise's shirt as Blaise went back into the main hallway, then turned without hesitation into a locker-lined corridor. There, searching through one of the lockers, was a lean figure with long legs and sandy hair.

Fastest tracking I've ever seen, Thea thought sourly. She peered around the Mediterranean-blue door of a broken locker.

Blaise walked up behind Eric very slowly, hips swaying. She put a hand on his back.

Eric jumped slightly, then turned around.

Blaise just stood there.

It was all she needed to do. Blaise reeled guys in just by *being*. It was the glorious dark hair, the smouldering grey eyes . . . plus a figure that could stop traffic on the freeway. Curves galore, and clothes that emphasized every one. On another girl it might have been too much, but on Blaise it was just breathtaking. Guys who thought they liked the waif look dropped everything to follow her just as fast as guys who thought they liked blonds.

Eric blinked at her, looking hazy already. He didn't seem to know what to say.

That wasn't unusual. Guys always got tongue-tied around Blaise.

'I'm Blaise Harman.' The voice was low and liquid. 'And you're . . . Eric?'

Eric nodded, still blinking.

Yes, he's dazed all right, Thea thought. The *jerk*. She was surprised at her own vehemence.

'Good, because I wouldn't want to give this to the wrong person.' Blaise produced the notebook from behind her back like a magician.

'Oh – where'd you get that?' Eric looked relieved and grateful. 'I've been looking everywhere.'

'My cousin gave it to me,' Blaise said carelessly. She held onto the notebook as he tried to take it, and their fingers touched. 'Wait. You owe me something for bringing it back, don't you?'

Her voice was a purr. And now Thea knew, without a doubt, what was going to happen.

Eric was doomed.

CHAPTER

3

Done for, lost, a goner. Blaise had chosen him, and it was only a matter of how she was going to play him.

A parade of names marched through Thea's mind. Randy Marik. Jake Batista. Kristoffer Milton. Troy Sullivan. Daniel Xiong.

And now: Eric Ross.

But Eric was talking, sounding animated. 'Your cousin? Is she that other new girl? Thea?'

'Yes. Now—'

'Look, do you know where she is? I really want to talk to her.' The hazy look descended again, and Eric stared into the distance. 'She's just . . . I've never met anybody like her . . .'

Blaise let go of the notebook and stared.

From her hiding place, Thea stared, too.

It had never happened before. This guy didn't even seem to *see* Blaise.

That was strange enough. But by the Blue Monkey-headed Goddess of Inquisitiveness, what Thea really wanted to know was why she herself felt so relieved by it.

A bell rang. Blaise was still standing there flabbergasted. Eric stuffed the notebook in his backpack.

'Could you just let her know I asked about her?'

'She doesn't *care* if you asked about her!' Blaise snapped, voice no longer honeyed. 'She said very explicitly that she never wanted to see you again. And I'd watch out if I were you. Because she has a *temper*.' The last word was uttered in rising tones.

Eric looked slightly alarmed – and crestfallen. Thea saw his throat move as he swallowed. Then, without saying good bye to Blaise, he turned and walked out the far side of the corridor.

Well, by the Red Crow-headed Thunderbolt Goddess.

Blaise turned around and stalked up the corridor in Thea's direction. Thea didn't even try to hide.

'So you saw all that. Well, I hope you're happy,' Blaise said waspishly.

Thea wasn't. She was confused. Strangely agitated – and *scared*, because the Cup of Death was still floating before her eyes.

'I guess we should both just leave him alone,' she said.

'Are you kidding? I'm going to *have* him,' Blaise said. 'He's *mine*. Unless,' she added, eyes glittering, 'you've already staked a claim.'

Thea floundered, shocked. 'I . . . well, no . . .'

'Then he's mine. I like a challenge.' Blaise ran a hand through her hair, disordering the black waves. 'Isn't it nice that Gran has so many love charms in the shop,' she mused.

'Blaise . . .' Thea had a hard time collecting her thoughts. 'Don't you *remember* what Gran said? If there's any more trouble . . .'

'There isn't going to be any trouble for *us*,' Blaise said, her voice flat and positive. 'Only for *him*.'

Thea walked to her next class feeling oddly empty.

Ignore it, she thought. There's nothing you can do.

She didn't see many Night People along the way to class. A young kid, probably a freshman, who looked like a shapeshifter; a teacher who had the hunting light of the lamia – the born vampires – in his eyes. No made vampires, no werewolves. No other witches.

Of course, she couldn't be certain. All the people of the Night World were masters of secrecy, of blending in, of passing unseen. They had to be. It was what allowed them to survive in a world where there were so many more humans . . . and where humans loved to kill anything different.

But when she was sitting in the world literature classroom, Thea noticed a girl in the next row.

The girl was small-boned and pretty, with thick eyelashes and hair as black and soft as soot. She had a heart-shaped face – and dimples. But what caught Thea's eye was the girl's hand, which was playing with a pin on the girl's blue-and-white-striped vest. A pin in the shape of a black flower.

A dahlia.

Thea immediately turned to a blank page in her notebook. While the teacher read a passage from the story *Rashomon*, Thea began drawing a black dahlia, tracing it over and over until it was large enough for the girl to see distinctly. When she raised her head, she saw the girl was looking at her.

The girl's lashes swept down as she looked at the drawing, then up again. She smiled at Thea and nodded slightly.

Thea smiled and nodded back.

After class, without any need to discuss it, Thea followed the girl to the front of the school. The girl looked around to make sure no one was in earshot, then turned to Thea with something like resigned wistfulness.

'Circle Midnight?' she said.

Thea shook her head. 'Circle Twilight. Aren't you?'

The girl's face lit up with shy delight. Her eyes were dark and velvety. 'Yes!' she said and rushed on, 'But there are only two more of us – two seniors, I mean – and they're both Circle Midnight, and I was afraid to hope!' She thrust out her hand, dimpling. 'I'm Dani Abforth.'

Thea felt her heart lighten. The girl's laughter was infectious. 'Thea Harman. Unity.' It was the age-old greeting of the witches, the symbol of their harmony, their oneness.

'Unity,' Dani murmured. Then her eyes widened. 'Harman? You're a Hearth-Woman? A daughter of Hellewise? Really?'

Thea laughed. 'We're all daughters of Hellewise.'

'Yes, but – you know what I mean. You're a direct descendent. I'm honoured.'

'Well, I'm honoured, too. Abforth is "All-bringing-forth", isn't it? That's a pretty impressive line itself.' Dani was still looking awed, so Thea said quickly, 'My cousin's here, too – Blaise Harman. We're both new – but you must be, too. I've never seen you around Vegas before.'

'We moved in last month, just in time to start school,' Dani said. Her brow puckered. 'But if *you're* new, what do you mean you haven't seen me around?'

Thea sighed. 'Well, it's kind of complicated . . .'

A bell rang. Both she and Dani looked at the school building in frustration, then at each other.

'Meet me here at lunch?' Dani asked.

Thea nodded, asked which way her French class was, and then flew off toward the other side of the building.

She sat through her next two classes trying to actually listen to the teachers. She didn't know what else to do. She had to concentrate to keep the image of grey-flecked green eyes out of her mind.

At lunch, she found Dani sitting on the steps out front. Thea settled beside her and opened a bottle of Evian water and a chocolate yogurt she'd bought at the snack bar.

'You were going to explain how you know Vegas,' Dani said. She spoke softly because there were kids everywhere in the front courtyard, sprawled in the sun with paper bags.

Thea eyed a row of sago palms and felt herself sighing again. 'Blaise and I – our mothers died when we were born. They were twin sisters. And then both our *dads* died. So we grew up sort of moving around from relative to relative. We usually spend the summers with Grandma Harman, and we live with somebody else during the school year. But these last couple of years . . . well, we've been in five high schools since we were sophomores.'

'*Five?*'

'Five. I think five. Isis knows, it could be six.'

'But *why*?'

'We keep getting expelled,' Thea said succinctly.

'But—'

'It's Blaise's fault,' Thea said. She was mad at Blaise. 'She does – *things* – to boys. Human boys. And somehow it always ends up getting us kicked out of school. Both of us, because I'm always too stupid to tell them she's the one responsible.'

'Not stupid, I bet. Loyal,' Dani said warmly, and put her hand on Thea's. Thea squeezed it, taking some comfort in the sympathy.

'Anyway, this year we were in New Hampshire living with our Uncle Galen – and Blaise did it again. To the captain of the football team. His name was Randy Marik . . .'

When Thea stopped, Dani said, 'What happened to him?'

'He burned the school down for her.'

Dani made a sound halfway between a snort and a giggle. Then she straightened out her face quickly. 'Sorry, not funny. *For* her?'

Thea leaned against the wrought-iron stair railing.

'That's what Blaise likes,' she said bleakly. 'Having power over guys, messing with their minds. Getting them to do things they would never ordinarily do. To prove their love, you know. But the thing is, she's never satisfied until they're completely destroyed . . .' She shook her head. 'You should have seen Randy at the end. He'd lost his mind. I don't think he'll ever get it back.'

Dani wasn't smiling anymore. 'Power like that . . . she sounds like Aphrodite,' she said softly.

And that's right, Thea thought. Aphrodite, the Greek goddess of love who could turn passion into a weapon that brought the whole world to its knees.

'Remind me sometime to tell you what she's done to the other guys she's played. In a way, Randy was lucky . . .'

Thea took a breath. 'So, anyway, we got shipped back here to Grandma Harman because there weren't any other relatives willing to take us. They figured if Gran couldn't straighten us up, nobody could.'

'But that must be *wonderful*,' Dani said. 'I mean, living with *the* Crone. Part of the reason my mom moved us here was that she wanted to study with your grandmother.'

Thea nodded. 'Yeah, people come from all over to take her classes, or to buy her amulets and things. She's not always easy to live with, though,' Thea added wryly. 'She goes through a couple of apprentices a year.'

'So is she going to straighten Blaise up?'

'I don't think *anybody* can. What Blaise does – it's just her nature, the way it's a cat's nature to play with mice.

And if we get in trouble again, Gran says she's going to send us to our aunt Ursula at the Connecticut enclave.'

'The Convent?'

'Yeah.'

'Then you'd better stay out of trouble.'

'I *know*. Dani, what's this school like? I mean, is it the kind of place where Blaise *can* keep out of trouble?'

'Well . . .' Dani looked dismayed. 'Well – I told you before, there's only two other witches in our class, and they're both Circle Midnight. Maybe you know them . . . Vivienne Morrigan and Selene Lucna?'

Thea's heart sank. Vivienne and Selene – she'd seen them going to summer Circles, wearing the darkest robes of any of the Circle Midnight girls. The two of them plus Blaise would make . . . well, a lethal combination.

'Maybe if you explain to them how important it is, they might help you keep Blaise under control,' Dani said. 'You want to go talk to them now? They'll be on the patio by the cafeteria – I usually eat with them there.'

'Um . . .' Thea hesitated. Talking to those two – well, she doubted it would help. But on the other hand, she didn't have a better idea. 'Why not?'

On the way to the cafeteria, she saw something that made her stop dead. Taped to the stucco wall was a giant piece of butcher paper, painted orange and black at the margins. In the centre was a grotesque figure: an old woman with a black dress, dishevelled white hair, and a wart-covered, haglike face. She was straddling a broom and wearing a pointy hat. Lettering under the picture said COMING OCTOBER 31ST . . . THE ULTIMATE HALLOWEEN PARTY.

Hands on hips, Thea said, '*When* will they learn that witches never wore pointy hats?'

Dani snorted, her heart-shaped face surprisingly

dangerous. 'You know, maybe your cousin has the right idea after all.'

Thea looked at her, startled.

'Well, they *are* an inferior species. You have to admit that. And maybe it sounds prejudiced, but then they're so prejudiced themselves.' She leaned closer to Thea. 'You know, they even have prejudices against *skin*.'

She held out her arm. Thea looked at the flawless skin, which was a deep, clear brown. 'They'd think *we* were two different races,' Dani said, pressing her arm against Thea's tan one. 'And that maybe one was better than the other one.'

Thea couldn't deny it. All she could say, feebly, was, 'Well, two wrongs don't make a right . . .'

'But three lefts do!' Dani burst out, finishing the old witch carol. Then she dissolved into laughter and led Thea to the patio.

'Let's see, they should be over there . . . Oh. Oops.'

Oops, Thea thought.

Vivienne and Selene were at a secluded table on the far side. Blaise was with them.

'I should have known she'd find them first thing,' Thea muttered. From the way the three girls had their heads together, it looked as if trouble were brewing already.

As Thea and Dani approached the table, Blaise looked up. 'Where've you been?' she said, waving a finger reproachfully. 'I've been waiting to introduce you.'

Everybody said hello. Then Thea sat down and studied the other two girls.

Vivienne had fox-red hair and looked tall even sitting down. Her face was animated; she seemed sparkling with energy. Selene was a platinum blond with sleepy blue eyes. She was smaller, and moved with languid grace.

Now, how do I politely say, 'Please help me suppress

my cousin?' Thea wondered. She could already tell it wouldn't be much use. Viv and Selene seemed to be under Blaise's spell already – they turned to her every other second as if checking for approval. Even Dani was watching Blaise with something like fascinated awe.

Blaise had that effect on people.

'So we were just talking about guys,' Selene said, twirling a straw languorously in her bottle of Snapple iced tea. Thea's heart plummeted.

'Toyboys,' Vivienne clarified in a lovely melodious voice. Thea felt the beginnings of a bad headache.

No wonder Blaise is smirking, she thought. These girls are *just like her*. She'd seen it at other schools: young witches who seemed to flirt with breaking Night World law by flaunting inhuman power over boys.

'Aren't there any of *our* kind of guys here?' Thea asked, as a last hope.

Vivienne rolled her eyes. 'One sophomore. Alaric Breedlove, Circle Twilight. That's *it*. This place is a desert – no pun intended.'

Thea wasn't really surprised. There were always more witch girls than guys – and nobody seemed to know why. More girls got born, more survived to grow up. And in some places the ratio was particularly unbalanced.

'So we just have to make do,' Selene drawled. 'But that can be fun sometimes. Homecoming dance is this Saturday, and I've got my boy all picked out.'

'So,' Blaise said, 'have I.' She glanced at Thea significantly.

And there it was. Thea felt her throat close.

'Eric Ross,' Blaise said, savouring the words. 'And Viv and Sel have told me *allll* about him.'

'Eric?' Dani said. 'He's the basketball star, isn't he?'

'And the baseball star,' Vivienne said in her beautiful

voice. 'And the tennis star. And he's smart – he takes honours courses and works at the animal hospital, too. He's studying to get into UC Davis. To be a vet, you know.'

So that's why he cared about the snake, Thea thought. And why he's got flatworms in his notebook.

'And he's so cute,' Selene murmured. 'He's so shy with girls – he can hardly talk around them. None of us have gotten anywhere with him.'

'That's because you used the wrong methods,' Blaise said, and her eyes were very smoky.

Thea's insides seemed hollow and there was a circlet of pain around her head. She did the only thing she could think of.

'Blaise,' she said. She looked her cousin directly in the face, making an open appeal. 'Blaise, listen. I hardly ever ask anything of you, right? But now I'm asking something. I want you to leave Eric alone. Can you do that – for me? For the sake of Unity?'

Blaise blinked slowly. She took a long drink of iced tea. 'Why, Thea, you're getting all worked up.'

'I am *not*.'

'I didn't know you cared.'

'I *don't*. I mean – of course I don't care about *him*. But I'm worried about you, about all of us. I think . . .' Thea hadn't meant to say this, but she found the words spilling out anyway. 'I think he might have some suspicions about us. This morning he told me that I seemed so different from other girls . . .' She managed to stop herself before she mentioned that he'd guessed she had healed him. *That* would be incredibly dangerous, especially since she didn't know who Vivienne or Selene might blab to.

Blaise's pupils were large. 'You mean – you think he's a psychic?'

'No, no.' She knew he *wasn't* a psychic. She'd been inside his mind, and he wasn't from any lost witch family. He didn't have any powers. He was as much a human as that snake had been a snake.

'Well, then,' Blaise said. She chuckled, a rich, rippling sound. 'He just thinks you're different – and *that's* hardly something to worry about. We *want* them to think we're different.'

She didn't understand. And Thea couldn't explain. Not without getting herself into very hot water.

'So, if you don't mind, we'll just consider my claim staked,' Blaise said courteously. 'Now, let's see, what to do with the boys at the dance. First, I think we need to spill their blood.'

'Spill *what*?' Dani said, sitting up.

'Just a little blood,' Blaise told her absently. 'It's going to be absolutely vital for some of the spells we'll want to do later.'

'Well, good luck,' Dani said. 'Humans don't like blood – they're going to run like bunnies from you after that.'

Blaise regarded her with a half-smile. 'I don't think so,' she said. 'You don't understand this business yet. If it's done right, they don't run. They're scared; they're shocked; and they just keep coming back for more.'

Dani looked shocked herself – and still fascinated. 'But why do you want to hurt them?'

'We're just doing what comes naturally,' Blaise purred.

I don't care Thea thought, it's none of my business.

She heard herself say, 'No.'

She was staring at a pile of squashed napkins in her hand. Out of the corner of her eye she could see Blaise's exasperated expression. The others might not know what Thea was saying no *to*, but Blaise always understood her cousin.

'I asked you before if you wanted him,' Blaise said. 'And you said you didn't. So now you're changing your mind? You're going to play him?'

Thea stared at her wad of napkins. What could she say? I can't because I'm scared? I can't because something happened between him and me this morning and I don't know what it was? I can't because if I keep seeing him I have this feeling I might break the law, and I don't mean the one about never telling humans that we exist; I mean the other one, the one about never falling in love . . .

Don't be *ridiculous*.

That sort of thing is out of the question, she told herself. All you want is to keep him from ending up like Randy Marik. And you can do *that* without getting involved.

'I'm saying I want him,' she said out loud.

'You're going to play him?'

'I'm going to play him.'

'Well.' Instead of snarling, Blaise laughed. 'Well, congratulations. My little cousin is growing up at last.'

'Oh, please.' Thea gave her a look. She and Blaise had been born on two different days – just barely. Blaise had been born one minute before midnight, and Thea one minute after. It was another reason they were so connected – but Thea hated it when Blaise acted older.

Blaise just smiled, her grey eyes glinting. 'And, look – there's lover boy right now,' she said, feigning elaborate surprise. Thea followed her nod and saw a figure with sandy hair and long legs at the other side of the patio.

'What luck,' Blaise said. 'Why don't you just walk over and ask him to the dance?'

CHAPTER
4

At that moment Thea almost hated her cousin.

But there was no choice. Four pairs of eyes were watching her: Blaise's grey eyes, Vivienne's emerald green, Selene's clear blue, and Dani's velvety dark ones. They were waiting.

Thea got up and began the long walk across the patio.

She felt as if *everyone* was watching her. She tried to keep her steps measured and confident, her face serene. It wasn't easy. The closer she got to that sandy hair, the more she wanted to turn and run. She had tunnel vision now: everything on the sides was a blur; the only clear thing was Eric's profile.

Just as she got within earshot, he glanced up and saw her coming.

He looked startled. For a moment his eyes met hers: a deeper green than Vivienne's, more intense and more innocent.

Then, without a word, he turned away and walked quickly down a path between two buildings. He was gone before Thea knew what was happening.

She stood rooted to the ground. There was a huge amount of empty space inside her, with only her uncomfortably pounding heart trying to fill it.

OK; he hates me. I don't blame him. Maybe it's good; maybe Blaise will say we can all forget him now.

But when she went back to the shady table, Blaise was frowning thoughtfully.

'You just don't have the technique yet,' she said. 'Never mind. I can coach you.'

'Viv and I can help, too,' Selene murmured. 'You'll learn fast.'

'*No* – thank you,' Thea said. Her pride was hurt and her cheeks were on fire. 'I can do it myself. Tomorrow. I have a plan already.'

Dani squeezed her hand under the table. 'You'll do fine.'

Blaise said, 'Just make sure it's tomorrow. Or I might think you don't really want him.'

And then, to Thea's immense relief, the bell rang.

'Hawthorne, yarrow, angelica . . .' Thea peered through the thick blue glass of an unlabelled jar. 'Some kind of nasty powder . . .'

She was in the front room of her grandmother's shop, deserted now because it was closed for the evening. Just being with all these herbs and gems and amulets gave her a feeling of comfort. Of control.

I love this place, she thought, looking around at the floor-to-ceiling shelves of bottles and boxes and dusty vials. One whole wall was devoted to trays of stones – unpolished and polished, rare and semi-precious, some with symbols or words of power engraved on them, some dirty and fresh from the earth. Thea liked putting her hands in them and murmuring their names: tourmaline, amethyst, honey topaz, white jade.

And then there were the good-smelling herbs: everything you needed to cure indigestion or to call a lover; to soothe arthritis or to curse your landlord. Some of these – the simples – worked whether you were a witch or not. They were just natural remedies, and Gran even sold them to humans. But the *real* spells required both arcane knowledge and psychic power, and no human could make them active.

Thea was whipping up a real spell.

First, heartsease. That was good for any love charm. Thea opened a canister and fingered the dried purple and yellow flowers gently. Then she dropped a handful of them into a fine mesh bag.

What else? Rose petals were a given. She unstopped a large ceramic jar and got a whiff of sweetness as she sprinkled them in.

Chamomile, yes. Rosemary, yes. Lavender . . . she twisted the cork out of a small vial of lavender essence. She could use some of *that* right this minute. She mixed it in her palm with a teaspoon of jojoba oil, then dabbed the fragrant liquid on her temples and at the back of her neck.

Blood, flow! Headache, go!

The tension in her neck started to ease almost instantly. She took a long breath and looked around.

Some bones of the earth would help. Rose quartz carved in the shape of a heart for attraction. A lump of raw amber for charm. Oh, and throw in a lodestone for magnetism and a couple of small garnets for fire.

It was done. Tomorrow morning she'd take a bath, letting this giant tea bag infuse the water while she burned a circle of red candles. She'd soak in the potent mixture, letting the smell of it, the essence of it, seep into her skin. And when she got out, she'd be irresistible.

She was about to walk away when a leather pouch caught her eye.

No. Not *that*, she told herself. You've got a mixture here

to promote interest and affection. It's plenty strong enough just to get him to listen to you.

You don't *want* anything stronger.

But she found herself picking up the soft pouch anyway. Opening it, just to look inside.

It was full of reddish-brown chips, each about the size of a thumbnail with a woody, aromatic smell.

Yemonja root. Guaranteed to draw an unwilling heart. But usually forbidden to maidens.

Recklessly, not letting herself think about it, Thea transferred half a dozen chips to her mesh bag. Then she put the worn leather pouch back on its shelf.

'Figured it out yet?' a voice behind her said.

Thea whirled. Gran was standing at the foot of the narrow stairway that led to the apartment above the store.

'Uh – what?' She held the mesh bag behind her back.

'Your specialty. Herbs, stones, amulets . . . I hope you're not going to be one of those chanting girls. I hate that whiny music.'

Thea loved the music. In fact, she loved all the things Gran had mentioned – but she loved animals even better. And there wasn't much of a place for animals in witch life, not since familiars had been outlawed during the Burning Times.

You could use *bits* of animals, sure. Lizard foot and nightingale tongue. Blaise was always trying to get hold of Thea's animals for just that purpose, and Thea was always fighting her off.

'I don't know, Gran,' she said. 'I'm still thinking.'

'Well, you've got time – but not too *much*,' her grandmother said, walking slowly toward her. Edgith Harman's face was a mass of creases, she hunched, and she used two canes, but that wasn't bad for a woman over a hundred who ran her own business and tyrannized every witch in the country.

'Remember, you've got some decisions to make when you hit eighteen. You and Blaise are the last of our line. The last two direct descendants of Hellewise. That means you have a responsibility – you have to set an example.'

'I know.' At eighteen, she would have to decide not just her specialty, but which Circle she would join for life: Twilight or Midnight. 'I'll think about it, Gran,' she promised, putting her free arm around the old woman. 'I've still got six months.'

Gran stroked Thea's hair with a veined, gentle hand. It chased the last of Thea's headache away. Still holding the mesh bag behind her back, she said, 'Gran? Are you really mad about having us here for the school year?'

'Well, you eat too much and you leave hair in the shower . . . but I guess I can stand it.' Gran smiled, then frowned. 'Just as long as you stay in line until the end of the month.'

There it was again. 'But what's happening at the end of the month?'

Gran gave her a look. 'Samhain, of course! All Hallow's Eve.'

'I know *that*,' Thea said. Even the humans celebrated Halloween. She wondered if Gran was having one of her vague spells.

'Samhain – and the Inner Circle,' Gran said abruptly. 'They've picked the desert for their ceremony this year.'

'The desert – you mean *here*? The Inner Circle is coming *here*? Mother Cybele and Aradia and all of them?'

'All of them,' Gran said. Suddenly her wrinkles looked grim. 'And by Air and Fire, I'm not having them come here just to see you girls screw up. I have a reputation, you know.'

Thea nodded a little dazedly. 'I – well, no wonder you were worried. We won't embarrass you. I promise.'

'Good.'

As Thea discreetly tucked the mesh bag under her arm and started for the stairs, the old woman added, 'You'd better toss some plantain into that mix to bind it all together.'

Thea felt herself blushing furiously. 'Uh . . . thanks, Gran,' she said, and went to look for plantain.

Above the shop were two tiny bedrooms and a kitchenette. Grandma had one bedroom and Thea and Blaise shared the other. Tobias, Gran's apprentice, had been bumped to the workshop downstairs.

Blaise was lying on her bed, reading a thick book with a red cover. Poetry. Despite her frivolous act, she wasn't stupid.

'Guess what,' Thea said, and without waiting for Blaise to guess, told her about the Inner Circle coming.

She watched to see if the news would scare Blaise – or at least alarm her into good intentions. But Blaise just yawned and stretched like a well-fed cat.

'Good. Maybe we can watch how they summon the ancestors again.' She raised her eyebrows at Thea meaningfully. Two years ago in Vermont, while the human world was trick-or-treating, they'd hidden behind maple trees and spied on the Samhain summoning. They'd seen the elders use the magic of Hecate, the most ancient witch of all, the goddess of moon and night and sorcery, to bring spirits across the veil. For Thea it had been scary but exciting, for Blaise just exciting.

Thea gave up on trying to alarm Blaise.

Thea looked at the three star-shaped blue flowers lying on her palm. Then, one by one, she ate them.

'Now say "*Ego borago guadia semper ago*",' Selene instructed. 'It means, "I, borage, always bring courage." Old Roman spell.'

Thea muttered the words. For the second day in a row, she was on the patio looking at a sandy head across the room.

'Go get 'im, tiger,' Blaise said. Vivienne and Dani nodded encouragingly. Thea squared her shoulders and started across the room.

As soon as Eric saw her coming he went down the side path.

You *idiot*, Thea thought. You don't know what's good for you. Maybe I should just let Blaise have you.

But she followed him. He was standing just beyond the buildings, staring into the distance. She could only see his profile, which was nice – clean and somehow lonely.

Thea swallowed, tasting a lingering sweetness from the borage flowers. What to say? She wasn't used to talking to humans – especially human boys.

I'll just say 'What's up?' and be casual, she thought. But when she opened her mouth, what came out was, 'I'm sorry.'

He turned immediately. He looked startled. 'You're sorry?'

'Yes. I'm sorry I was so mean. What do you think I was following you for?'

Eric blinked – and Thea thought his cheeks coloured under his tan. 'I thought you were mad because I kept staring at you. I was trying not to get you madder.'

'You were staring at me?' Thea felt a little flushed herself. As if the herbs from her bath were steaming fragrantly out of her skin.

'Well – I kept trying not to. I think I've got it down to one look every thirty seconds now.' He said it seriously.

Thea wanted to laugh. 'It's OK. I don't mind,' she said. Yes, she could definitely smell the love potion now. The heady floral scent of rose and heartsease, plus the spice of yemonja root.

Eric seemed to take her at her word. He was definitely staring. '*I'm* sorry I acted like such a jerk before. With the snake, I mean. I really wasn't trying to feed you a line.'

Alarm whispered through Thea. She didn't want to think about what had happened in the desert.

'Yes, OK, I know,' she said. He was watching her so intently, his eyes such a deep green. 'Well – you see, the reason I wanted to talk to you was . . . you know, there's the Homecoming dance this Saturday. So I thought we could maybe go together.'

She remembered at the last instant that in human society boys frequently asked girls to dances. Maybe she'd been too direct.

But he looked – well, extremely pleased. 'You're kidding! You're serious? You'd go with me?'

Thea just nodded.

'But that's terrific. I mean – *thanks*.' He was as excited as a kid at Beltane. Then his face clouded over.

'I forgot, though. I promised Dr Salinger – that's my boss at the pet hospital – that I'd spend the night there Saturday. Midnight to eight A.M. Somebody needs to watch the animals that stay overnight, and Dr Salinger's going to a conference out of town.'

'It doesn't matter,' Thea said. 'We'll just go to the dance before midnight.' She was relieved. It meant less time play-acting in front of Blaise.

'It's a date, then.' He still looked so happy. 'And, Thea?' He said the name shyly, as if almost afraid to use it. 'Maybe – maybe we could do something else sometime. I mean, we could go out, or you could come over to my house . . .'

'Uh . . .' The yemonja smell was *really* making her dizzy. 'Uh . . . well, this week – I'm trying to get adjusted to the new school and all. But maybe later.'

'OK. Later.' His smile was unexpected, astonishing. It transformed his face, turning the sweet, serious shyness into charismatic radiance. 'If there's any way I can help, just ask.'

Why, he's handsome, Thea thought. She felt a sort of tug at her insides, like a bird being charmed out of a tree. She hadn't realized how attractive he was, or how the grey flecks in his eyes seemed to catch sunlight . . .

Stop that! she told herself abruptly. This is *business*, and he's *vermin*. She felt a flush of shame at using the word, even in thought. But she had to do something. Without meaning to, she'd moved closer to him, so she was looking up into his face. Now they were only inches apart and she was feeling distinctly giddy.

'I have to go – *now*. I'll see you later,' she murmured, and made herself back up.

'Later,' he said. He was still glowing.

Thea fled.

Wednesday, Thursday, and Friday, she tried to ignore him. Avoided him in the halls, acting as busy as possible. He seemed to understand, and didn't chase her down. She just wished he wouldn't look so dreamy and *happy* all the time.

And then there was Blaise. Blaise already had a couple of husky football players who followed her everywhere, Buck and Duane – but neither of them was invited to the dance. Blaise had a unique method of choosing a partner. She told them all to go away.

'You don't want me,' she said to a gorgeous Asian-American guy with one earring.

It was lunch break on Thursday, and the witches had a whole table to themselves: Vivienne and Selene with Blaise on one side; Dani with Thea on the other. The gorgeous guy had one knee on a chair and was looking very nervous.

'You can't afford me, Kevin. I'll ruin you. Better get out of here,' Blaise said, all the while looking up with sleeping fire in her grey eyes.

Kevin shifted. 'But I'm rich.' He said it simply, without affectation.

'I'm not talking about money,' Blaise said. She gave a deprecating smile. 'And anyway, I don't think you're really interested.'

'Are you kidding? I'm crazy about you. Every time I see you . . . I don't know; it just makes me crazy.' He glanced at the other girls and Thea knew he was uncomfortable at having an audience. But not uncomfortable enough to stop talking. 'I'd do anything for you.'

'No, I don't think so.' Blaise was toying with a ring on her left index finger.

'What's that?' Vivienne interjected nonchalantly.

'Hm? Oh, just a little diamond,' Blaise said. She held out her hand and light scintillated. 'Stuart Mac-Ready gave it to me this morning.'

Kevin shifted again. 'I can buy you dozens of rings.'

Thea felt sorry for him. He seemed like an OK guy, and she'd heard him talk about wanting to be a musician. But she knew from long experience that it wouldn't do any good to tell him to get out of here. It would only make him more stubborn.

'But I wouldn't want a ring from you,' Blaise was saying in a soft, chiding voice. 'Stuart gave this to me because it was the only memento he had of his mom. It meant everything to him – so he wanted me to have it.'

'I'd do the same thing,' Kevin said.

Blaise just shook her head. 'I don't think so.'

'Yes, I would.'

'No. The thing that means the most to you is your car, and you'd never give that up.'

Thea had seen the car. It was a silver-grey Porsche. Kevin lovingly touched it up with a chamois in the school parking lot every morning.

Now Kevin looked confused. 'But – that car's not really mine. It belongs to my parents. They just let me use it.'

Blaise nodded understandingly. 'You see? I told you you wouldn't. Now, why don't you go away like a good boy?'

Kevin seemed to collapse internally. He stared at Blaise pleadingly, not making a move to go away. At last, Blaise tilted her head at the football flunkies.

'C'mon, man,' one flunky – Thea thought it was Duane – said. They took Kevin by the shoulders and propelled him away. Kevin kept looking back.

Blaise dusted her fingers off briskly.

Selene pushed back pale hair and drawled, 'Think he'll cough up the car?'

'Well . . .' Blaise smiled. 'Let's just say I think I'll have transportation to the dance. Of course, I'm still not sure who I'm taking . . .'

Thea got up. Dani had sat silently through lunch, and now she was watching Blaise, her velvety dark eyes half horrified and half admiring.

'I'm getting out of here,' Thea said significantly, and was relieved when Dani stopped staring at Blaise and stood up.

'Oh, by the way,' Blaise said, picking up her backpack, 'I forgot to give you this.' She handed Thea a small vial, the size that perfume samples came in.

'What's it for?'

'For the dance. You know, to put the boys' blood in.'

CHAPTER
5

What? Thea said. This was something she *could* speak out about. 'Blaise, are you out of your mind?'

'I hope you're not saying you don't want to do spells,' Blaise said dangerously. 'That's part of it, you know.'

'I'm saying there's no way we can get enough blood to fill *this* without them noticing. What are we going to tell them? "I just want a little to remember you by?" '

'Use your ingenuity,' Vivienne said musically, twining a red-gold strand of hair around her fingers.

'In a pinch we could always use the Cup of Lethe,' Blaise added calmly. 'Then no matter what we do, they won't remember.'

Thea nearly fell over. What Blaise was suggesting was like using a nuclear bomb to swat a fly. 'You *are* crazy,' she said quietly. 'You know that maidens aren't allowed to use that kind of spell, and we probably won't even be able to use it when we're mothers, and probably not even when we're *crones*. That's stuff for the *Elders*.' She stared at Blaise until the grey eyes dropped.

'I don't believe in classifying some spells as forbidden,' Blaise said loftily, but she didn't look back at Thea and she didn't pursue the subject.

As she and Dani left the patio, Thea noticed that Dani had taken one of the small vials.

'Are you going to the dance?'

'I guess so.' Dani shrugged lithe shoulders. 'John Finkelstein from our world lit class asked me a couple weeks ago. I've never been to one of *their* dances before – but maybe this is the time to start.'

Now what did *that* mean? Thea felt uneasy. 'And you're planning to put a spell on him?'

'You mean this?' She twisted the vial in her fingers. 'I don't know. I figured I'd take it just in case . . .' She looked up at Thea defensively. 'You took one for Eric.'

Thea hesitated. She hadn't talked to Dani about Eric yet. Part of her wanted to and part of her was scared. What did Dani really think of Outsiders, anyway?

'After all,' Dani said, her sweet face tranquil, 'they're only humans.'

Saturday night Thea took a dress out of the closet. It was pale green – so pale that it almost looked white – and designed along Grecian lines. Witch clothes had to feel good as well as look good, and this dress was soft and light-weight, swirling beautifully when she turned.

Blaise wasn't wearing a dress. She was wearing a tuxedo. It had a red silk bow tie and cummerbund and it looked fantastic on her.

This is probably going to be the only dance in history where the most popular girl has on cufflinks, Thea thought.

Eric arrived right on time. He knocked at the front door of the shop, the door that only Outsiders used. Night People came around back, to a door that was unmarked except for what looked like a bit of graffiti – a spray-painted black dahlia.

OK, Thea thought. She took a deep breath before she

unlocked the door and let him in.

This is business, business, business . . .

But the first moment wasn't as awkward as she'd feared. He smiled and held out a corsage of white orchids. She smiled and took it. Then she said, 'You look nice.'

His suit was pale fatigue brown, loose and comfortable looking. 'Me? *You* look nice. I mean – you look wonderful. That colour makes your hair look just like gold.' Then he glanced down at himself apologetically. 'I don't go to many dances, I'm afraid.'

'Don't you?' She'd heard girls talking about him at school. It seemed as if everyone liked him, wanted to get close to him.

'No, I'm usually pretty busy. You know, working, playing sports.' He added more softly, 'And I have a hard time thinking of things to say around girls.'

Funny, you never seem to have a problem around *me*, Thea thought. She saw him looking the shop over.

'It's my grandmother's store. She sells all kinds of things here, from all around the world.' She watched him closely. This was an important test. If he – a human – believed in this stuff, he was either a New Age geek or dangerously close to the truth.

'It's cool,' he said, and she was happy to see that he was lying. 'I mean,' he said, obviously struggling to find a polite way to praise the voodoo dolls and wand crystals, 'I think people can really affect their bodies by changing their state of mind.'

You don't know how right you are, Thea thought.

There was a clack of high heels on wood, and Blaise came down the stairs. Her shoes appeared first, then her fitted trouser legs, then all the curves, emphasized here and there with brilliant red silk. Finally came her shoulders and head, her midnight hair half up and half down, framing her face in stormy dark curls.

Thea glanced sideways at Eric.

He was smiling at Blaise, but not in the goofy, dying-sheep way other guys smiled. His was just a genuine grin.

'Hi, Blaise,' he said. 'Going to the dance? We can take you if you need a lift.'

Blaise stopped dead. Then she gave him a blistering glare. 'Thank you, I have my own date. I'm just going to pick him up now.'

On the way to the door, she looked hard at Thea. 'You do have everything you need for tonight – don't you?'

The vial was in Thea's pale green clutch purse. Thea still didn't know how she could possibly get it filled, but she nodded tightly.

'Good.' Blaise swept out and got into a silver-grey Porsche that was parked at the curb. Kevin's car. But, as Thea knew, she wasn't going to pick up Kevin.

'I think I made her mad,' Eric said.

'Don't worry. Blaise likes being mad. Should we go now?'

Business, business, business, Thea chanted to herself as they walked into the school cafeteria. It had been completely transformed from its daytime identity. The lights and music were oddly thrilling and the whirl of colour out on the dance floor was strangely inviting.

I'm not here to have fun, Thea told herself again. But her blood seemed to be sparkling. She saw Eric glance at her conspiratorially and she could almost feel what he was feeling – as if they were two kids standing hand in hand at the edge of some incredible carnival.

'Uh, I should tell you,' Eric said. 'I can't really dance, except for slow ones.'

Oh, great. But of course this was what she was here to do. To put on a show of romancing Eric for Blaise.

A slow song was starting that minute. Thea shut her eyes briefly and resigned herself to fate – which didn't seem all *that* awful as she and Eric stepped out onto the floor.

Terpsichore, Muse of the Dance, help me not make a fool of myself. She'd never been so close to a human boy, and she'd never tried to dance to human music. But Eric didn't seem to notice her lack of experience.

'You know, I can't believe this,' he said. His arms were around her lightly, almost reverently. As if he were afraid she'd break if he held her too hard.

'What can't you believe?'

'Well . . .' He shook his head. 'Everything, I guess. That I'm here with you. And that it all feels so easy. And that you always *smell* so good.'

Thea laughed in spite of herself. 'I didn't use any yemonja this time—' she began, and then she almost bit her tongue. Adrenalin washed over her in a wave of painful tingles.

Was she crazy? She was blurting out *spell ingredients*, for Earth's sake. He was too easy to talk to, that was the problem. Every so often she'd forget he wasn't a witch.

'You OK?' he said as her silence stretched on. His voice was concerned.

No, I am not OK. I've got Blaise on one side and the laws of the Night World on the other, and they're both out to get me. And I don't even know if you're worth it . . .

'Can I ask you something?' she said abruptly. 'Why did you knock me out of the way of that snake?'

'Huh? It was in a striking coil. You could have got bit.'

'But so could you.' So *did* you.

He frowned as if stricken by one of those unsolvable

mysteries of life. 'Yeah . . . but that didn't seem so bad somehow. I suppose that sounds stupid.'

Thea didn't know how to answer. And she was suddenly in terrible conflict about what to do. Her body seemed to want her to lean her head against Eric's shoulder, but her mind was yelling in alarm at the very thought.

At that moment she heard loud voices at the edge of the dance floor.

'Get out of the way,' a guy in a blue jacket was saying. 'She smiled at me, and I'm going over there.'

'It was *me* she was smiling at, you jerk,' a guy in a grey jacket snapped back. 'So just back off and let me go.'

Expletives. 'It was *me*, and you'd better get out of the way.'

More expletives. 'It was *me*, and you'd better let go.'

A fistfight started. Chaperones came running.

Guess who's here? Thea asked herself. She had no trouble at all locating Blaise. The red-trimmed tuxedo was surrounded by a ring of guys, which was surrounded by a ring of abandoned and angry girls.

'Maybe we should go over and say hi,' Thea said. She wanted to warn Blaise about starting a riot.

'OK. She sure is popular, isn't she?'

They managed to worm their way through the encircling crowd. Blaise was in her element, glorying in the adulation and confusion.

'I waited for an hour and a half, but you never showed up,' a very pale Kevin was saying to her. He was wearing an immaculate white silk shirt and exquisitely tailored black pants. His eyes were hollow.

'Maybe you gave me the wrong address,' Blaise said thoughtfully. 'I couldn't find your house.' She had her hand tucked into the arm of a very tall guy with shoulder-length blond hair, who looked as if he worked out four or five hours a day. 'Anyway, you want to dance?'

Kevin looked at the blond guy, who looked back impassively, his cleft chin rock hard.

'Don't mind Sergio,' Blaise said. 'He was just keeping me company. Do you *not* want to dance?'

Kevin's eyes fell. 'Well, yeah, of course I want to . . .'

As Blaise detached herself from Sergio, Thea leaned forward. 'You'd better not do anything too public,' she hissed in her cousin's ear. 'There's already been one fight.'

Blaise just gave her an amused glance and took Kevin's arm. Most of the boys followed her, and with the crowd gone, Thea saw Dani at a small table. She was wearing a sparkling gold dress and she was alone.

'Let's go sit,' Eric said, before Thea could even get a word out. She threw him a grateful look.

'Where's John?' Thea asked as they pulled chairs to the table.

Dani nodded toward the pack following Blaise.

'I don't mind, though,' she said, sipping a cup of punch philosophically. 'He was kind of boring. I don't know about all this dance stuff.'

Thea knew she meant it was different from Circle dances, where everyone was in harmony and there was no pairing off. You danced with the elements and with everybody else, all one big inter-connected whole.

Eric volunteered to get more punch.

'How's it going with him?' Dani asked in a low voice when he was gone. Her velvety dark eyes searched Thea's curiously.

'Everything's OK so far,' Thea said evasively. Then she looked out toward the dance floor. 'I see Viv and Selene are here.'

'Yeah. I think Vivienne already got her blood. She

stabbed Tyrone with her corsage pin.'

'How clever,' Thea said. Vivienne was wearing a black dress that made her hair look like flame, and Selene was in deep violet that showed off her blondness. They both seemed to be having a wonderful time.

Dani yawned. 'I think I'll probably go home early—' she began, and then she broke off.

Some kind of a disturbance had begun on the other side of the room, in front of the main entrance. People were scuffling. At first, Thea thought it was just another minor fracas over Blaise – but then a figure came staggering out under the lights of the dance floor.

'I want to *know*,' the voice said in dissonant tones that rose over the music. 'I want to *knoooow*.'

The band stopped. People turned. Something about the voice made them do that. It was so obviously abnormal, the cadence wrong even for somebody who was drunk. This was someone who was *disturbed*.

Thea stood up.

'I want to *knoooow*,' the figure said again, sounding lost and petulant. Then it turned and Thea felt ice down her spine.

The person was wearing a Halloween mask.

A kid's plastic mask of a football player, the kind held on with an elastic string. Perfectly appropriate for a Halloween dance. But at Homecoming, it was grotesque.

Oh, Eileithyia, Thea thought.

'Can you *tell* me?' the figure asked a short girl in black ruffles. She backed away, reaching for her dance partner.

Mr Adkins, Thea's physics teacher, came jogging up, his tie fluttering. None of the other chaperones seemed to be around – probably because they were out somewhere trying to control fights over Blaise, Thea thought.

'OK, let's settle; settle,' Mr Adkins said, making

motions as if the figure were an unruly class. 'Let's just take it easy . . .'

The guy in the Halloween mask pulled something out of his jacket. It glinted like a rainbow under the coloured dance floor lights, reflective as a mirror.

'A straight razor,' Dani said in a hushed voice. 'Queen Isis, where'd he get that?'

Something about the weapon – maybe the fact that it was so weird, so old-fashioned – made it scarier than a knife. Thea pictured the way even a safety razor could slice flesh.

Mr Adkins was backing away, arms held out as if to protect the students behind him. His eyes were frightened.

I have to stop this, Thea thought. The problem was that she had no idea how. If it had been an animal, she could have stepped out and tried mind control. But she couldn't control a person.

She started walking anyway, slowly, so as not to attract attention. She skirted the edge of the crowd around the dance floor until she drew parallel with the masked guy.

Who by now had switched to a new question. 'Have you *seen* her?' he said. He kept asking it as he walked, and people kept backing away. Vivienne and Selene drew to either side with their dates. The razor glittered.

Thea looked toward the opposite end of the dance floor, where Blaise was standing with Kevin Imamura.

With no Buck, no Duane to protect her. But Blaise didn't look frightened. That was one thing about Blaise – she had magnificent physical courage. She was standing with one hand on her hip and Thea could tell that she knew exactly who was coming her way.

In between moving couples, Thea glimpsed something else. Eric was on the other side of the dance floor, holding two cups of punch in one hand and one in the other. He was keeping pace with the masked guy, just as she was.

She tried to catch his eye, but the crowd was too thick.

'Have you *seen* her?' the masked guy asked a couple right in front of Blaise. 'I want to *knoooow* . . .'

The couple split like bowling pins. Blaise stood exposed, tall and elegant in her black suit, lights shimmering off her midnight hair.

'Here I am, Randy,' she said. 'What is it you want to know?'

Randy Marik stopped, panting. His breath made a muffled noise against the plastic. The rest of the huge room was eerily silent.

Thea moved closer, walking silently. Eric was pulling in from the other side, and he saw her for the first time. He shook his head at her and mouthed, 'Stay away.'

Yeah. And you're going to tackle him armed with three party cups of punch. She gave him a look and mouthed, '*You* stay away.'

Randy's hand was trembling, making the razor flash. His chest was heaving.

'What *is* it, Randy?' Blaise said. The toe of one high heeled shoe tapped the floor impatiently.

'I feel bad,' Randy said. It was almost a moan. Suddenly his head didn't seem well connected to his neck. 'I miss you.'

His voice made Thea's flesh creep. He sounded like a person with the body of an eighteen-year-old and the mind of a four-year-old.

'I cry all the time,' he said.

With his left hand, he pulled off the Halloween mask. Kevin recoiled. Thea herself felt a wave of horror.

He was crying *blood*. Bloody streams ran down from each of his eyes, mingling with regular tears.

A spell? Thea wondered. Then she thought, no; he's cut himself.

That was it. He'd made two crescent-shaped incisions under his eyes and the blood was coming from them.

The rest of his face was ghastly, too. He was white as a corpse and there was fuzzy stubble on his chin. His eyes stared wildly. And his hair, which had always been strawberry blond and silky, stood up all over his head like bleached hay.

'You came all the way from New Hampshire to tell me *that*?' Blaise said. She rolled her eyes.

Randy let out a sobbing breath.

This seemed to make Kevin braver. 'Look, man, I don't know who you are, but you'd better keep away from her,' he said. 'Why don't you go home and sober up?'

It was a mistake. The wild eyes above the bloodstained cheeks focused on him.

'Who are *you*?' Randy said thickly, advancing a step. 'Who . . . are . . . *you*?'

'Kevin, move!' Thea said urgently.

It was too late. The hand with the razor flashed out, lightning quick. Blood spurted from Kevin's face.

CHAPTER
6

Kevin howled, clapping a hand to his cheek. 'He cut me! This guy cut me!' Blood ran between his fingers.

Randy lifted the razor again.

Thea reached out with her mind. Not reached. She *leaped*. It was completely instinctive; she was scared to death, and all she could think of was that he was going to kill Kevin, and maybe Blaise, too.

She caught – something. Pain and grief and fury that seemed to be bouncing around like a baboon in a cage. She could hold it for only an instant, but in that instant Eric threw two cups of punch in Randy's face. Randy yelled and turned away from Kevin, toward Eric.

Thea felt a surge of pure terror. Randy slashed with the razor, but Eric was fast; he jumped back out of the way, circling to get behind Randy. Randy wheeled and slashed again. They were doing a macabre dance, going round and round.

Thea felt as if the fear was winding tighter inside her with each turn. But Eric kept out of the way of the flashing razor until a rush of movement on the dance floor caught her eye. It was Mr Adkins and two other teachers. They converged on Randy and there was a lot of confusion. When it was over, Randy was on the ground.

Sirens wailed outside, coming closer. Eric stepped away from the pile on the floor.

Breathing hard, he looked at Thea. She nodded that she was all right, then shut her eyes.

She felt limp and wrung out and awful. They were going to take Randy away now, and she didn't think there was much help for him. He definitely seemed too far gone.

At that moment she was ashamed of being a witch.

'All right, people,' Mr Adkins was saying. 'Let's move out of here. Let's get this place cleared.' He looked at Blaise, who was bending over a seated Kevin, holding a napkin to his cheek. 'You two can stay.' Then he put a hand on Blaise's shoulder. 'Are you OK here?'

Blaise looked up with wide, tragic grey eyes. 'I think so,' she said bravely.

Mr Adkins swallowed. His hand on Blaise's shoulder squeezed. Thea heard him mutter something like, 'Poor kid.'

Oh, give me a break, Thea thought. But a small, selfish part of her was relieved. Blaise wasn't going to get in trouble over this one; neither of them was going to get expelled. Grandma wasn't going to be disgraced in front of the Inner Circle.

And Blaise *did* seem worried about Kevin. She was bending over him again solicitously. As if she really cared.

Thea slipped past a teacher's outstretched arm. '*Are* you OK?' she whispered to Blaise.

Blaise looked up enigmatically. That was when Thea saw that she had a tiny vial concealed in the napkin. It was full of blood.

'You . . .' Thea couldn't find the words.

Blaise made a slight grimace that meant: *I know. But it was just too good a chance to miss.*

Thea backed up and ran into Eric. He put a steadying arm around her.

'Is she all right?'

'*She's* fine. *I* have to get out of here.'

Eric looked into her face. He was rumpled: his hair mussed, his eyes dark. All he said was, 'Let's go.'

They passed Vivienne and Selene on the way out. Thea had to give them credit; they both looked shocked and unhappy. The question was, would it last?

Dani was in the parking lot with John Finkelstein. 'I'm going home,' she said significantly to Thea, and tossed something into a clump of bitterbrush.

It was an empty vial.

Thea felt a tiny uncoiling of relief. She touched Dani's arm lightly. 'Thanks.'

Dani looked back at the cafeteria. 'I wonder what it was he wanted to know?' she murmured.

And just then a howl came from the lighted doorway, as if answering her question. It didn't sound like a person; it sounded like an animal in anguish.

'*Whyyyyyy?*'

Thea turned blindly and almost ran for Eric's jeep.

When they were driving on darkened streets, Eric said quietly, 'I'm presuming he was an old boyfriend?'

'Last month's.'

Eric glanced at her. 'He was pretty messed up, poor guy.'

And *that*, Thea thought, summed it up nicely. He was pretty messed up forever. Poor guy.

'It's Blaise,' she said. She hadn't meant to talk to him about this, but the words were so crowded in her throat that she thought she'd burst if she didn't let them out. 'She does this and *does* this, and I can't stop her. She picks guys up everywhere, and they fall in love with her, and then she dumps them.'

'Love? Hm,' Eric said.

Thea looked at him, astonished. He was looking straight ahead, his long, supple fingers steady on the wheel.

Well. And I thought you were so naive. Maybe you see more than I realized.

'It's a kind of love,' she said. 'It's like – do you know, in ancient Greece they worshiped the goddess Aphrodite. She was the goddess of love – and the thing about her was that she was absolutely merciless.' Thea shook her head. 'I saw this play once about a queen named Phaedra. And Aphrodite made her fall in love with her own stepson, and by the end of the play just about everybody was dead on the stage. But Aphrodite just kept smiling. Because she was just doing what a goddess does – the same way that a tornado rips houses apart or a fire burns down a forest.'

She stopped. Her chest was aching and she didn't have any breath left. But in a way she felt better, as if some pressure had been relieved.

'And you think Blaise is like that.'

'Yes. Sort of a natural force that can't help itself. Does that sound completely crazy?'

'Actually, no.' Eric gave a wry smile. 'Nature's rough. Hawks grab rabbits. Male lions kill cubs. It's a jungle out there.'

'But that doesn't make it right. Maybe for goddesses and animals, but not when it gets to the level of humans.' It was a moment before she realized what she'd said. She was using 'humans' to mean 'people'.

'Well, humans aren't very far from animals, after all,' Eric said softly.

Thea sagged back against the seat. She was still confused and unhappy, but what scared her most was that she felt a strong urge to keep talking to Eric about it. He seemed to *understand* so well . . . better than anybody else ever had. And not only to understand, but to care.

'I know what you need,' Eric said suddenly, brightening. 'I was going to suggest we go to the late buffet at Harrah's, but I know something better.'

Thea glanced at the clock, saw that it was almost eleven. 'What?'

'Puppy therapy.'

'*What?*'

He just grinned and turned the jeep south. They pulled up at a modest grey building with a sign that read SUN CITY ANIMAL HOSPITAL.

'This is where you work.'

'Yup. We can let Pilar off early,' Eric said, getting out and unlocking the front door of the building. 'Come on.'

A pretty girl with shoulder-length brown hair looked up from behind the office counter. Thea recognized her as Pilar Osorio from school. A quiet girl who looked like a good student.

'How was the dance?' she said. Thea thought her eyes lingered on Eric wistfully as she said it.

Eric shrugged. 'Pretty awful, to tell the truth. There was a fight and we left.' Thea noticed he didn't mention his part in stopping the fight.

'How awful,' Pilar said sympathetically – but Thea thought she wasn't entirely sorry that the dance hadn't gone well.

'Yeah. So how's our boy?'

'OK – a little hyper. You might want to take him for a walk later.' Pilar picked up her jacket. She nodded politely to Thea as she headed for the door. 'See you Monday.'

She likes him.

When the door was shut, Thea looked around the office. 'So the clinic's not open.'

'No, but somebody has to stay overnight when we've got animals boarding here.' He gave her the grin again. 'Follow me.'

He led her through an exam room into a corridor and then to a kennel room at the back. Thea looked around with interest. She'd never been in the inner sanctum of an animal hospital before.

There were several dog runs. Eager whining was coming from the last.

Eric looked at her mischievously. 'Three, two, one . . .'

He opened the cage. A big Labrador puppy tumbled out, tail wagging frantically. He was a beautiful colour that ranged from deep gold on his back to almost white on his legs and paws.

'Hey, Bud,' Eric said. 'Hey, pal; who's a good boy?' He looked at Thea solemnly. 'This is the ultimate cuddle dog.'

Thea collapsed on the sheet vinyl floor and made a lap, holding both arms out.

'Uh – your dress—' Eric began mildly, but the puppy was already in mid-air. Thea caught him and he crawled up her, legs on her shoulders, hot breath blowing in her ear.

'I think I'm in love,' Thea gasped, her arms full of warm, heavy puppy sweetness.

Happiness surrounded her. She didn't have to try to merge with the puppy's mind; he practically took over by force. All his thoughts were good ones, and they were all about *now*. About how terrific everything smelled this minute, and how great that scratch behind the ear felt on a fleabite.

Good feelings, happy feelings . . . I really like this big bald dog . . . Wonder which of us is dominant?

The puppy bit her and Thea play-bit him back. 'Wrong; I'm the pack leader,' she informed him, holding his jowls.

There was only one odd thing. She could see the way the world looked to the pup – and there was nothing on the right. Just a void.

'Is there something wrong with his eyes?'

'You noticed the cataract. Lots of people don't see that right away. Yeah, he's blind in the right eye. When he gets older he may come back for surgery.' Eric sat back against the wall, grinning madly. 'You've really got a way with animals,' he said. 'But you don't own any pets?'

The question was gentle, not intrusive. Thea said absently, 'Well, usually just temporary ones. I pick them up and when they're cured I put them back – or find homes for them if they *want* to be pets.'

'You cure them.'

Once again, the question was gentle, but Thea felt a little shock. Why couldn't she guard her tongue around this guy? She looked up and found he was looking at her steadily and searchingly, his green eyes alert.

She took a breath. 'I feed them, take them to the vet if they need it. Then I wait until they heal up.'

He nodded, but the searching look didn't go away. 'Did you ever think of being a vet yourself?'

Thea had to look down. She bluffed by kissing the puppy.

'Uh, not really,' she muttered into blond fur.

'But you've got a *gift*. Look, I've got some material on UC Davis. They have a great undergraduate program – and their graduate school is one of the best in the country. It's not easy to get in, but you could do it. I know you could.'

'I wouldn't bet on it,' Thea muttered. She had several dramatic blotches on her academic record – like four expulsions.

But that wasn't the real problem. The real problem was

that witches weren't veterinarians. They just *weren't*.

She could choose to specialize in gems or herbs or ritual clothing; in chants or runes or research or amulets . . . in hundreds of things, but nothing taught at UC Davis.

'It's hard to explain,' Thea said. She didn't have much room left to be surprised, or she'd have been surprised to find she *wanted* to explain to a human. 'It's just – my family wouldn't really approve. They want me to be something else.'

Eric opened his mouth, then shut it again.

The puppy sneezed.

'Well, maybe you could help me with *my* application sometime,' Eric said at last. 'I'm trying to do the essay question and dying.'

You sneak, Thea thought.

'Maybe,' she said.

At that moment a buzzer sounded – far away but insistent. Bud barked.

'What the . . . that's the outside buzzer,' Eric said. 'But nobody should be here at this time of night.' He got up and headed for the front of the building. Thea followed, her fingertips just brushing Bud's head to control him.

Eric opened the door, then stepped back in surprise.

'Rosamund . . . what are you *doing* here? Does Mom know you're out?'

Something like a miniature whirlwind entered the waiting room. It was a kid, a little girl with a mop of sandy hair sticking out from under a baseball cap. She was carrying a rolled-up blue blanket, and what could be seen of her expression under the hair was ferocious.

'Mom said Madame Curie wasn't really sick, but she is. Call Dr Joan.' With that, the kid marched into the office and dumped the blue blanket on the counter, pushing aside a clipboard and some vaccination reminder cards.

'Hey. Don't.' When she ignored him, Eric looked at Thea. 'Uh, this is my sister Rosamund. And I don't know how she got here—'

'I rode my bike and I want Madame Curie fixed *now*.'

Bud was rearing up and trying to sniff the blue blanket. Thea pushed him down gently. 'Who's Madame Curie?'

'Madame Curie is a guinea pig,' Eric said. He touched the blanket. 'Roz – Dr Joan is gone. She's out of town at a conference.'

Rosamund's ferocious expression never wavered, but her chin began to quiver.

'OK, listen. I'll take a look at Madame Curie now, see if I can see anything. But first we have to call Mom and let her know you're alive.' He reached for the phone.

'I'll take Bud back,' Thea said. 'I think he thinks Madame Curie is lunch.' She led the puppy into the back room and coaxed him into the run with a promise of extra petting later.

When she came back to the office, Eric was bent over a small brown-and-white guinea pig. He looked frustrated.

'Well, there's *something* wrong with her – I guess. She seems weaker than usual and sort of lethargic . . .' Suddenly he jerked his hand back with a yelp.

'Not *too* lethargic,' he said, eyeing the blood welling up from his thumb. He wiped it on a tissue and bent over the guinea pig again.

'She's in a bad mood,' Rosamund said. 'And she's not eating right. I told you yesterday she was sick.'

'No, you didn't,' Eric said calmly. 'You told me she was tired of living under patriarchy.'

'Well, she *is* tired. *And* she's sick. *Do* something.'

'Kid, I don't know what to do yet. Hang on.' He bent closer to the little animal, muttering to himself. 'She's not coughing . . . so it's not strep. Her lymph nodes are OK . . .

but her joints seem swollen. Now, that's weird.'

Rosamund was watching him, her green eyes full of fierce trust. Eyes like Eric's, Thea realized.

She reached out gently and just touched the guinea pig's soft fur with her fingers. Her mind reached gently, too.

Frightened-little-animal thoughts. The guinea pig didn't like being here, wanted the sawdust of her cage, wanted safety. She didn't like the clinical smells, didn't like huge, strange fingers descending from the sky.

Home-place, nest-place, she was thinking. And then, something odd. A concept – more smell and taste than picture. Madame Curie was imagining eating something . . . something crunchy and slightly sharp. Eating and eating and eating.

'Is there some treat she really likes?' Thea asked doubtfully. 'Something like cabbage?'

Eric blinked, then straightened up as if he'd gotten an electric shock. His green eyes stared straight into hers. 'That's it! You're brilliant!'

'What's it?'

'What you said. She's got *scurvy*!' He dashed out of the office and came back with a thick book full of small print. 'Yeah, here it is. Anorexia, lethargy, enlarged limb joints . . . she's got all the symptoms.' He turned pages feverishly and then said triumphantly, 'All we have to do is give her some of those veggies, or maybe some ascorbic acid in her water.'

Scurvy – wasn't that a disease sailors used to get? When they were on long trips with no fresh fruits or vegetables? And ascorbic acid was . . . 'Vitamin C!'

'Yeah! It's been hot and we've got hard water at our house – all that could deplete the vitamin C in her diet. But it's easy to fix.' Then Eric looked at Thea and shook his head wonderingly. 'I've been studying for years, besides working here, and you just *look* at the animal and you know. How do you *do* that?'

'She asked Madame Curie,' Rosamund said flatly.

Thea gave her a wary glance. How come this whole family was so observant? 'Ha ha,' she said, her voice light.

'I like you,' Rosamund said, just as flatly as before. 'Now where can I get some cabbage?'

'Go look in the vaccine fridge in back,' Eric said. 'If there isn't any, we can always use vitamin drops.'

Rosamund trotted off. Eric watched her, openly fond.

'She's an interesting kid,' Thea said.

'She's sort of a genius. Also the world's smallest militant feminist. She's suing the local Boy Trekkers, you know. They won't let her in, and the Girl Trekkers don't trek. They do macramé.'

Thea looked at him. 'And what do you think of that?'

'Me? I drive her to the lawyer's office whenever Mom can't make it. I figure it stops her griping. Besides, she's right.'

Simple as that, Thea thought. She watched Eric as he folded the blue blanket, and heard a voice in her mind like the voice of an announcer describing a game-show prize.

Now. Look at this guy. He's tender but intense. Brave. Profoundly insightful. Shy but with a wicked sense of humour. He's smart, he's honest, he's an animal lover . . .

He's human.

I don't care.

She was feeling – well, strange. As if she'd been breathing too much yemonja root. The air seemed sweet and heavy and *tingly* somehow, as if laced with tropical electricity.

'Eric . . .'

And she found herself touching the back of his hand.

He let go of the blanket instantly and turned his hand to close on hers. He wasn't looking at her, though. He was still staring at the office desk. His chest heaved.

'Eric?'

'Sometimes I think if I blink, you'll disappear.'

Oh, Eileithyia, Thea thought. Oh, Aphrodite. I'm in terrible trouble.

The thing was, it was terrible and wonderful. She felt awkward and tremendously safe at once, scared to death and not scared of anything. And what she wanted was so simple. If he only felt the same, everything would be all right.

'I just can't even imagine life without you anymore, but I'm so afraid you'll go away,' Eric said, still looking fatalistically at the computer on the desk. Then he turned to her. 'Are you mad?'

Thea shook her head. Her heart was threatening to leave her body. When she met his eyes it was as if some circuit had closed. They were connected, now, and being pulled together as if Aphrodite herself was gathering them into her arms.

And then everything was warm and wonderful. Better than holding the puppy, because Eric could hold her, too. And the thrills of fear that had been shooting through her seemed somehow to burst like fireworks and turn into exhilaration.

Her cheek was against Eric's. And she'd never felt anything so blissful before. Eric's cheek was smooth and firm – and she was safe here, loved here. She could rest like this forever. Peace filled her like cool water. They were two birds enfolding each other with their wings.

Swans mate for life . . . and when they see their mate, they *know*, she thought. That's what happened in the desert. We knew each other; it was as if we each could see the other one's soul. Once you see into someone's soul, you're attached forever.

Yeah, and there's a word for it in the Night World, part of her mind said, trying to shatter her peace. The soulmate principle. You're trying to say that your one and only is a human?

But Thea couldn't be frightened, not now. She felt insulated from the Night World and the human world both. She and Eric formed their own reality; and it was enough just to stand here and *breathe* and to feel his breathing, without worrying about the future . . .

A door creaked and a blast of cool air blew in.

Thea's eyes were startled open. And then her heart gave a terrible lurch and started thudding painfully.

It wasn't the door that Rosamund had gone through. It was the front door, which Eric must have left unlocked. And Blaise was standing there in the waiting room.

CHAPTER
7

'I've been looking *everywhere* for you,' Blaise said. 'I had to call Mrs Ross to find out you were here.'

Her black hair was wild and windblown, tumbling over her shoulders. She had taken off her red bow tie and unbuttoned the top button of her dress shirt. There was colour in her cheeks and dark light in her grey eyes. She looked extremely beautiful and very, very witchy.

Thea and Eric had moved apart and Thea had the feeling they were both blushing.

'We were just . . .' Eric said. 'Um. Heh.' While Blaise scrutinized him, he picked up the blue blanket and started refolding it. 'Uh, can I show you around?'

'I don't care much for animals unless they've been shish-kebabed.' Blaise surveyed the room with one hand on her hip.

Oh, she's in a *terrific* mood.

Thea's palms were getting damp. She wasn't sure what Blaise thought of the embrace she'd walked in on . . . but Thea was *supposed* to be leading Eric on, wasn't she?

Her eye fell on the Kleenex daubed with Eric's blood. Unobtrusively, she reached for it and crumpled it in her hand.

'So you left the dance,' she said to Blaise. 'Where's . . .' Who'd actually been Blaise's date tonight? Sergio? Kevin? Someone else?

'There is no dance,' Blaise said. 'They shut it down. Leave it to Randy, he was always a royal pain.' Then her face changed; she blinked and put on a sweet smile. 'And who are you, darling?'

In the doorway to the corridor, Rosamund backed up, Madame Curie clutched to her chest. She didn't say a word, but her hostile green eyes never left Blaise.

'Uh, sorry,' Eric said. 'That's my sister. She's shy.'

'So this is a family affair,' Blaise said. 'How nice.'

Thea said, 'I think it's time to be going home.' She needed to talk to Eric, but alone, not with a disgruntled munchkin and a suspicious witch looking on.

She glanced at Eric, feeling a little shy herself. He looked the same.

'Well – see you at school.'

'Yeah.' Suddenly he smiled. 'You know, that's something else I was going to mention. If you're even thinking about going to Davis, you might want to get into honours zoology. It's a good class.'

'Um – we'll see.' She was aware of Blaise watching her.

But outside, all Blaise said was, 'Sorry if I was rude. But I've been looking all over for you, so I could tell you what a great time I wasn't having. And' – she shook her midnight hair out with a charming smile – 'it's so much *fun* to be a bitch when you want to be.'

Thea sighed, then stopped in her tracks. 'Blaise, the car!'

Kevin's silver-grey Porsche looked as if it had been through a war. The front bumper was caved in, the passenger door was mangled, and the windshield was cracked.

'I had a little trouble,' Blaise said coolly. 'It's all right, though; I met a guy tonight named Luke Price, who's got a Maserati.' She looked at Thea, then added, 'You don't *disapprove*, do you? Of treating humans that way?'

'No – of course not. I just don't want to get expelled again.'

'It's not illegal to have an accident. Here, you have to get in through the driver's side now.'

She drove, not seeming to choose any particular direction. Thea sat quietly, acutely aware of the probing glances cast her way every so often.

'So,' Blaise said at last in her silkiest voice, 'did you get *it*?'

'What?'

'Don't be funny.'

Thea held out her hand with the crumpled Kleenex on her palm. 'I didn't fill the vial; that was ridiculous. But I used my ingenuity and got enough.'

'Hmm.' Blaise's tapering fingers, tipped with blood-red nails, closed delicately on the tissue. Startled, Thea snatched it back and the Kleenex tore. She ended up with only a corner.

'Hey—'

'What's the problem? I just want it for safekeeping,' Blaise said smoothly. 'And so how did everything else go?'

'Fine,' Thea said. Her palms were getting damp, but she managed to keep her voice airy. 'I think he's hooked,' she added, trying to imitate Blaise's most languid and arrogant tones.

'Oh, really?' They had ended up on the strip, which meant the car was now crawling through traffic. Neon highlighted the curious half-smile on Blaise's lips. 'And what was that about Davis?'

'Nothing. It's where he's going to college, so of course

he'd like me to be with him.'

'He's already thinking about the future. Well, that was fast work. Congratulations.'

Thea didn't like the way she said it. More than ever, she wanted to protect Eric from Blaise, but she wasn't sure how. It depended on how much Blaise suspected.

'You know, I think it's the pop that's the most fun,' Blaise went on reminiscently. 'Human boys are all different, but in the end, they're all the same. And when they give in completely, you can almost hear it. There's a "pop". Like a balloon breaking.'

Thea swallowed, staring at the huge golden lion in front of the MGM Grand Hotel. Its green eyes reminded her of Eric. 'Really? Sounds interesting.'

'Oh, it is. And after the pop, they just kind of collapse, and everything they are, their whole *self*, just sort of pours out in this internal haemorrhage. And after that, of course, they're useless. Like a stag that's too old to mate. They're just – over.'

'How nice.'

'You know, I think Eric's ready for that pop. He's already in love with you; I could see that. I think it's time.'

Thea just sat. A vampire girl, wearing a dress with a black rose design, threaded her way through stopped traffic. Finally, Thea said, 'Blaise . . .'

'What, is that a problem with you? Are you having difficulty with that? Are you a little soft on him, maybe? Are you a little *too* fond of him?'

'Blaise—'

'Are you in love with him?'

Shock waves went through Thea, and the last question seemed to vibrate in the air.

At last she whispered, 'Don't be ridiculous.'

'And don't *you* try to fool me. Remember who you're

talking to. I know that dopey look you get when you're mooning over some animal. I saw the way you were holding him.'

Thea felt desperate. It wasn't just Blaise she was afraid of here. Night World law couldn't be clearer about the penalty for loving a human.

Death. Not only for her, but for Eric, too.

There was only one thing Thea could do. She turned and looked at her cousin directly.

'All right, Blaise, you do know me. We've always been like sisters, and I know that however you act sometimes, you still love me—'

'Of course I do,' Blaise said impatiently, and Thea realized that was part of the problem. In the changing light of the Bally hotel's neon pillars, she could see that Blaise's eyes were wet. She was *frightened* for Thea – and angry at being frightened.

Thea grabbed her cousin's hand. 'Then you have to listen to me.' It was a naked plea. 'Blaise – when I first met Eric, something *happened*. I can't explain it – I can't even really describe it. But there was a connection. And I know this is going to sound insane, and I know you're not going to like it, but . . .' She had to stop to breathe. 'Blaise, what if you found your soulmate, and they were something that everybody said you shouldn't love . . .'

She stopped again, this time because Blaise had frozen. For a moment they both just sat, and then, very slowly, Blaise withdrew her hand from Thea's.

'Found . . . your . . . soulmate?' she said.

Warmth pooled in Thea's eyes. She had never felt so alone. 'I think so,' she whispered.

Blaise turned to face the windshield. Purple light shone on her black hair. 'This is more serious than I thought.'

The tears overflowed. 'But will you help me?'

Blaise tapped her slender fingers on the steering wheel a few times. Finally she said, 'Of course I'll help you. I *have* to. We're like sisters – I would never abandon you when you're in trouble.'

Thea was so relieved she felt dizzy. Paradoxically, it made her cry more. 'I've just been so scared . . . Ever since it happened, I've been trying to figure things out.' She hiccupped. Blaise was looking at her again, smiling, grey eyes glittering oddly. 'Blaise?'

'I'm going to help you,' Blaise said, still smiling, 'by getting him myself. And then I'm going to kill him for putting my sister in danger.'

There was a moment when everything inside Thea seemed absolutely still – and the next instant it all exploded into chaos.

'*Never*,' she said. 'Do you hear me, *sister*? *Never.*'

Blaise stayed calm, driving. 'I know you don't think it's best – now. But one day you'll thank me.'

'Blaise, *listen to me*. If you do anything to him – if you hurt him – it's me you're hurting.'

'You'll get over it.' In the rainbow light of the Riviera, Blaise looked like some ancient goddess of fate. 'It's better to hurt a little now than to be executed later.'

Thea was so angry she was shaking. So angry that she made a mistake. If she'd kept on arguing the same points, she thought later, Blaise might eventually have started to listen. But she was furious and terrified and she blurted out, 'Well, I don't think you *can* do it. I don't think you could take him from me if you tried.'

Blaise stared, as if caught for once at a loss for words. Then she threw back her head and laughed.

'Thea,' she said. 'I can take *any* boy from *anybody*. Any time, any place, any way I want to. That's what I *do*.'

'Not this time. Eric loves me, and you can't change that. You can't take him.'

Blaise was wearing a secret smile. But she said only two words as she turned off the strip and onto darkened streets again.

'Watch me.'

Thea didn't sleep well. She kept seeing Randy Marik's face, and when she dreamed, it turned into Eric's face, blood-streaked and vacant-eyed.

She woke up to see sunshine streaming in the room.

It was a bedroom with a split personality. One side was fairly neat and decorated in pale blues and spring greens. The other side was messy and was decorated in *the* colour, the primal colour, the one that roused emotions, that meant passion and hatred both. Red.

And usually Blaise was lying on that side underneath her red velvet Ralph Lauren bedspread, but this morning she was gone already. A bad omen. Blaise only got up early for a reason.

Thea got dressed and went downstairs warily.

The shop was empty except for Tobias sitting gloomily in his usual place beside the cash register. He grunted when Thea said hello and went on staring at the wall, one hand clutching his curly brown hair. Wishing, undoubtedly, to be outside on the weekend like other nineteen-year-old guys.

Thea went into the workshop.

Blaise was sitting at the long table, wearing earphones and humming to herself. A project was spread in front of her.

Thea stalked up close.

She could see right away that it was beautiful. Blaise was a genius at creating jewellery, most of it based on ancient designs. She made necklaces of bees and butterflies, spiraling flowers, serpents, leaping dolphins. It was all alive, all joyous . . . all magical.

That was where the real genius came in. Blaise put each element of the piece together with a purpose in mind. The gems were chosen to enhance each other: ruby for desire, black opal for obsession, topaz for yearning, garnet for heat. And asteria, the smoke-grey form of sapphire with a six-pointed star. Blaise's stone, just the colour of her eyes.

Blaise had them all laid out loose. But her magic wasn't just in the gems. Interwoven into every piece were herb caches, tiny compartments that could be filled with potions or powders. She could literally *drench* the jewellery in sorcery.

Even the design itself could be a spell. Every line, every curve, every flower stem could have a meaning, could make the eye follow a pattern that was as powerful as any symbol traced on the floor in chalk. Just looking at the piece could be enough to charm you.

Right now Blaise was working on a necklace to knock you dead.

Thea could see it taking shape. Blaise used the lost wax method of jewellery-making, which meant that she carved out her pieces in stiff blue wax before casting them in silver or copper or gold. What she was carving now was breathtaking. Heart-stopping. An intricate masterpiece that was going to have roughly the same effect as Aphrodite's magic girdle – which meant no male was going to be able to look at it without falling under the spell.

And she had some of Eric's blood. The vital ingredient that meant she'd be able to personalize this spell for him.

The one good thing was that it would take Blaise a few days to finish this piece. But once it was done . . .

Eric didn't have a chance in Hades.

Thea backed up, not knowing – and not caring – whether Blaise had noticed her. She headed blindly for her bedroom.

She and Eric were soulmates. But Blaise was, in some ways, Aphrodite herself. And who could resist that?

What am I going to *do*?

She had a little of Eric's blood herself on the corner of the tissue. But she could never outmatch Blaise in creating love spells. Blaise had years of experience and a natural talent that left everyone else in the dust.

So I have to think of something else. Something to keep her from getting to him in the first place. To protect him . . .

Thea straightened up.

I can't. It's too dangerous. The summoning spells aren't for maidens. Even the Inner Circle has to be careful with those.

But Grandma has the materials. I know she does. I've seen the box.

It may kill me even to try.

An odd serenity came over her. If she concentrated on that – on the risk – she felt better than if she thought about what Gran would say if she found out. She wasn't afraid to face danger for Eric. And as long as she kept thinking about *that*, she could block out the thought that her idea was not only dangerous, but *wrong*.

This time she went down the stairs almost as if she were sleepwalking. Calm and detached.

'Toby, where's Gran?'

He lifted his head a bare inch. 'She went to see Thierry Descouedres, something about his land. Told me to come and pick her up tonight.'

Thierry was a vampire and a Night Lord. He owned a

lot of the land northeast of Las Vegas – but what did Gran have to do with that?

It didn't matter. The important thing was that Gran wouldn't be back all day.

'Well, then, why don't you go out and have some fun? I can watch the shop.'

Tobias looked at her with dazed blue eyes – and then his round face lit up. 'Seriously? You'd do that? I could kiss you. Let's see, I'll go visit Kishi . . . no, maybe Zoe . . . no, maybe Sheena . . .'

Like all boy witches, he was in tremendous demand with the girl witches in town.

Still muttering, he checked his wallet, grabbed the car keys, and headed for the door as if Thea might change her mind any second. 'I'll be back in time to pick her up, I promise,' he said hastily and was out the door.

The instant he was gone, Thea turned the sign on the door to CLOSED, locked up, and tiptoed to the counter.

It was in the locked lower shelf, an iron chest that looked five hundred years old. Thea picked it up with an effort – it was *heavy*. With her teeth gritted and her eyes on the bead curtain that separated the store from Grandma's workshop, she staggered up the stairs.

She made two other trips downstairs to gather materials. The bead curtain never stirred.

Last, she went to Gran's bedroom. On a nail near the headboard was a heavy ring with dozens of keys. Thea took it. Back in her own bedroom she shut the door and stuffed a towel underneath so Blaise wouldn't smell the smoke.

OK, now let's get this thing open.

She sat crosslegged on the floor in front of the chest. It wasn't hard to find the key that would fit the lock – she just looked for the oldest and crudest iron key on the ring.

It fit perfectly and the chest opened.

Inside was a bronze box, and inside *that* a silver box.

And inside the silver box was an ancient book with yellowing, brittle pages, and a small green bottle with wax and ribbons securing its cork. There were also thirty or forty amulets. Thea picked one up and examined it.

A lock of blond hair had been twisted and woven into a knot, and then sealed in that shape with a round piece of clay. The clay was dark earthy red, and Thea touched it reverently. It had been made with mud – and the blood of a witch. An entire Circle had probably worked on this for weeks: charging the blood, chanting, mixing it with secret ingredients, baking it in a ritual fire.

I'm touching a witch, Thea thought. The very essence of somebody who's been dead hundreds of years.

The cabalistic sign stamped on the front of the amulet was supposed to show *who* the witch was. But lots of the pieces of clay were so worn that Thea couldn't make out any trace of a symbol.

Don't worry. Find a description of somebody in the book, and then match the amulet to them.

She turned the fragile pages of the book carefully, trying to read the spidery, faded writing.

Ix U Sihnal, Annie Butter, Markus Klingelsmith . . . no, they all sound too dangerous. *Lucio Cagliostro* – maybe. But I don't really want an alchemist. *Dewi Ratih, Omiya Inoshishi* . . . wait a minute. *Phoebe Garner*.

She scanned the page on Phoebe eagerly. A gentle girl from England who had lived before the Burning Times and had kept familiars. She'd died young of tuberculosis, but had been considered a blessing by everyone who'd known her – even humans, who appreciated her ability to deflect spells from her village. Human villagers had mourned at her grave.

Perfect, Thea thought.

Then, she began scrabbling through the amulets, looking for one with the same symbol impressed on the clay as the book showed by Phoebe's name.

There it was! She cradled the amulet in her palm. Phoebe's hair had been auburn and very fine.

OK. Now get the balefire ready.

It had to be made from oak and ash, the two kinds of wood that had been burned to bake the clay. Thea put the dry sticks in her grandmother's largest bronze bowl and lit them.

Now add quassia chips, blessed thistle, mandrake root. Those were just for general power raising. The real magic was in the tiny bottle that had been carved out of a single piece of malachite. It was the summoning potion, and Thea had no idea at all what was in it.

She dug at the wax with her fingernails until the cork twisted freely. Then she paused, her hands shaking with every beat of her pulse.

Up until now, she'd only examined things she shouldn't: bad but forgivable. *Now* she was going to kindle a forbidden fire . . . and that *wasn't* forgivable. If the Elders discovered what she'd done . . .

She pulled the cork out.

CHAPTER

8

A sharp, acrid odour assaulted her nostrils. She had to blink away tears as she held the bottle over the fire and very carefully tipped it.

One drop, two drops, *three*.

The fire flared, burning blue.

It was ready. The balefire that was the only way to get a spirit from the other side – apart from crossing the veil and fetching it back yourself.

Thea took Phoebe's amulet in both hands and snapped it, cracking the clay and breaking the seal. Then, holding the broken amulet over the fire, she said the words of power she'd heard the elders speaking last Samhain.

'*May I be given the Power of the Words of Hecate.*'

Instantly, she found words coming to her, rolling off her tongue. She heard them as if it were somebody else talking.

From beyond the veil . . . I call you back!
Through the mist of years . . . I call you back!
From the airy void . . . I call you back!
Through the narrow path . . . I call you back!
To the heart of the flame . . . I call you back!
Come speedily, conveniently, and without delay!

She felt a rumbling vibration like an earthquake rock the floor. Above the ordinary fire different flames seemed to burn; cold, ghostly flames that were pale blue and violet and rose to lick at her knuckles.

She started to open her hands, to let the amulet fall into the magical flame. But just as she was about to do it, there was a bang.

The door to her bedroom swung open, and for the second time in twelve hours she found herself horrified to see Blaise.

'The whole place is shaking – what are you *doing*?'

'Blaise – just stay back!'

Blaise stared. Her jaw dropped and she lunged forward. *'What are you doing?'*

'It's almost finished—'

'You're crazy!' Blaise grabbed at the amulet in Thea's hands, and then, when Thea snatched her hands back, at the silver box.

'Leave it alone!' Thea grabbed the other side of the box. They were struggling with it, each trying to pull it from the other. Fire scorched Thea's hands.

'Let *go*!' Blaise shouted, trying to twist the box away. 'I'm warning you—'

Thea's fingers were damp with sweat. The box slipped.

That was when it happened.

The silver box flipped in Blaise's hands, sending a spray of amulets everywhere. Locks of grey hair, black hair, red hair, all flying. Most of them hit the floor – but one landed directly in the balefire.

Thea heard a crack as the clay seal broke.

For one second she was frozen, then she plunged her hand into the fire. But the clay was already burning – not red hot, but white hot. She couldn't close her fingers around it. For just an instant she seemed to see a symbol etched in blue flames, and then a flash like sheet lightning exploded from the fire. It knocked her into Blaise's bed and Blaise into the wall.

The lightning formed a column and *something* shot out.

Thea didn't so much see it as sense it. A wraith shape that tore around the room like a blast of arctic wind. It sent books and articles of clothing flying. When it reached the window, it seemed to pause for an instant, as if gathering itself, and then it shot through as if the glass didn't exist.

It was gone.

'Great Mother of Life,' Blaise whispered from against the wall. She was staring at the window with huge luminous eyes – and she was scared. Blaise was scared.

That was when Thea realized how bad things were.

'What have we done?' she whispered.

'What have *we* done – what have *you* done, that's the question,' Blaise snapped, sitting up and looking more like her ordinary self. 'What *was* that thing?'

Defensively, Thea gestured at the scattered amulets. 'What do you think? A witch.'

'But *who*?'

'How should I know?' Thea almost yelled, fear giving way to anger. '*This* is the one I was going to call back.' She snatched up the auburn hair and cracked amulet of Phoebe Garner. '*That* one was just whichever one fell out when you grabbed the box.'

'Don't try to make this my fault. *You're* the one doing forbidden spells. *You're* the one summoning ancestors. And whatever happens with that one' – Blaise pointed at the window – '*you're* the one responsible.'

She got up and shook out her hair, standing tall. 'And *that's* what you get for trying to sic the spirits on me!' She turned and stalked out the door.

'I wasn't trying to sic the spirits on you!' Thea shouted – but the door had already slammed shut.

Thea's anger collapsed. Feeling numb, she looked at the overturned silver box, where she had temporarily stored the tissue with Eric's blood.

I was just trying to find a protector for him. Somebody who'd help him fend off your spells, who'd understand that he's a person even though he's a human.

She looked forlornly around the room. Then, feeling older than Gran, she struggled to her feet and started mechanically cleaning up the mess.

When she dumped the ashes out of the bowl she found some sort of residue sticking to the bottom. She couldn't wash it off and she couldn't pry it off with a steak knife. She stashed the entire bowl under her bed.

All the while she cleaned, her mind kept churning.

Who got out? No way to know. Process of elimination wouldn't help, not with all those unmarked amulets.

What to do now? She didn't know that either.

If I tell anyone – even Gran – they'll want to know why I was trying to summon the dead. But if they find out the truth, it means death for me and Eric.

Around sunset, a limousine pulled up in the back alley. Thea saw it from her window and rushed downstairs in alarm.

Grandma was being helped out of the car by two politely expressionless vampires. Servants of Thierry's.

'Gran, what happened?'

'Nothing happened. I had a little weak spell, that's all!' She whacked at one of the vampires with her cane. 'I can help myself, son!'

'Ma'am,' said the vampire – who might have been three or four times Grandma's age. To Thea, he said, 'Your grandmother fainted – she was pretty sick there for a while.'

'And that good-for-nothing apprentice of mine never showed up,' Gran said, making her way to the back door.

Thea nodded goodbye to the vampires. 'Gran, it was my fault about Tobias. I let him have the day off.' Her stomach, which had been clenched like a fist all day, seemed to draw even tighter now. 'Are you really sick?'

'I'm good for a few years yet.' She began labouriously working her way up the stairs. 'Vampires just don't understand old age.'

'What did you go there for?'

Gran stopped to cough. 'None of your business, but I had to settle some arrangements with Thierry. He's agreed to let the Inner Circle use his land on Samhain.'

Upstairs, Thea made some herb tea in the tiny kitchenette. And then, when Gran was in bed with the tea, she gathered her courage.

'Gran, when the Elders call up the spirits on Samhain – how do they send them *back*?'

'Why should you want to know?' Gran said crossly. But when Thea just looked at her, she went on. 'There are certain spells that are used for summoning – and don't you ask me what they are – and you say those backwards to send them back. The witch who calls a spirit has to be the one to dismiss it.'

So only I can do it. 'And that's all?' Thea asked.

'Oh, of course not. It's a long process of kindling the fire and strewing the herbs – but if you do it all right, you can draw the spirit down from between the standing stones and send it back where it came from.' Grandma went on muttering, but Thea had snagged on a earlier phrase.

'From between – the standing stones . . . ?' she got out.

'The standing stones that encircle the spirits. Well, think, Thea! If you didn't have a circle of some kind to hold them in, they'd just – *voom*.' Gran made a gesture. 'They'd zip out and how would you ever find them again? That's why I went to Thierry today,' she added, taking a noisy sip of tea. 'We need a place where the sandstone forms a natural circle . . . and naturally it's up to me to arrange everything . . .' She went on grumbling softly.

Thea felt faint.

'You *have* to be – physically close to them – to send them back?'

'Of course. You have to be within spitting distance. And don't think I don't know why you're asking.'

Thea stopped breathing.

'You're planning something for Samhain – and it's probably all Blaise's idea. You two are like Maya and Hellewise. But you can forget about it right now – those spells are for the Elders, not for girls.' She stopped to cough. 'I don't understand why you want to be crones before you're done being maidens. You ought to enjoy your youth while you have it . . .'

Thea left her still grumbling.

She hadn't cast any kind of a circle before calling the spirit. She hadn't realized she was supposed to.

And now . . . how could she ever get close enough to the spirit to send it back?

Well, it'll just have to *stay* out in the world, she told herself bravely. Too bad . . . but it's not as if there aren't other spirits floating around out there. Maybe if it doesn't like roaming around, it'll come back.

But she was sick with guilt and disheartened. Not to mention worried – if only a little – about Gran's fainting spell.

Blaise didn't come to bed. She stayed downstairs and worked on her necklace long into the night.

* * *

On Monday, everyone at school was talking about Randy Marik and the ruined dance. The girls were annoyed about it and furious with Blaise; the boys were annoyed and furious with Randy.

'Are you OK?' Dani asked Thea after world lit class. 'You look kind of pale.'

Thea smiled wanly. 'It was a busy weekend.'

'Really? Did you do something with Eric?' The way she said 'do something' alerted Thea. Dani's heart-shaped face looked as sweet and concerned as ever . . . but Thea couldn't trust even her. She was a Night Person, a witch, a human-hater.

It didn't matter. Thea was so edgy that the words just seemed to burst out. 'Do something like what? Smash his car? Turn him into a toad?'

Dani looked shocked, her velvet-dark eyes wide.

Thea turned and walked quickly away.

Stupid, *stupid*, she told herself. That was so *dumb* of you. You may not have to pretend to be playing with Eric in front of Blaise anymore – but in front of the other witches you've *got* to keep acting.

She headed almost blindly for Eric's locker, ignoring the people she passed.

I've only been here a week. How can everything in my life have become so awful? I'm at war with Blaise; I've worked a forbidden spell; I don't dare talk to Gran – and I've broken Night World law.

'Thea! I was looking for you.'

It was Eric's voice. Warm, eager – everything that Thea wasn't. She turned to see green eyes flecked with dancing grey and an astonishing smile. A smile that drew her in, changing the world.

Maybe everything was going to be all right, after all.

'I called you yesterday, but I just kept getting

the machine.'

Thea hadn't even looked at the answering machine. 'I'm sorry – there was a lot going on.' Eric looked so kind that she groped for something that had been going on that she could *tell* him about. 'My grandmother's been sick.'

He sobered at once. 'That's terrible.'

'Yes.' Thea fished in her backpack for the small herb pillow she'd put there this morning. Then she hesitated. 'Eric . . . is there somewhere we could go to talk alone? Just for a few minutes? I want to give you something.'

He blinked, then waggled his eyebrows. 'Nothing I'd like better. And I know just the place. Come on.'

He led her across campus to a large building that stood apart from the rest of the complex. It had a shabby look and the paint on the double doors was blistered. A banner announced in orange and black letters: DON'T MISS THE ULTIMATE HALLOWEEN PARTY.

'What is this?'

Eric, who was opening the door, put a finger to his lips. He glanced inside, then beckoned to her.

'It's the old gym. They're supposed to be renovating it as a student centre, but there isn't enough money.' He snorted. 'Probably because they're spending too much on renovating downtown. Now – what was it you wanted to give me?'

'It . . .' Thea stopped dead as she took in her surroundings. All thoughts of the herb pillow vanished. 'Eric . . .' She stared around her, feeling a slow wave of sickness roil through her stomach. 'Is this . . . for the Halloween party?'

'Yeah. They do a couple of fund-raisers a semester here. This is kind of a weird one – but they did it last year and it brought in a lot.'

Not weird, Thea thought numbly. Weird doesn't begin to describe it.

Half the room was empty, just scuffed hardwood floor, a broken basketball backboard, and exposed pipes in the ceiling. But the other half looked like a cross between a medieval dungeon and a casino. She walked slowly toward it, her footsteps echoing.

Wooden booths of various sizes were decorated with orange and black crepe paper and fake spider webs. Thea read one banner after another.

'Fortune telling . . . Drench a Wench . . . *Bobbing for Shrunken Heads?'*

'It's bobbing for apples really,' Eric said, seeming embarrassed. 'And the gambling isn't real. You do it all with goblin money and exchange it for prizes.'

Thea couldn't stop looking at the booths. Wheel of Torture: a money wheel with a dummy dressed like a witch spreadeagled in the middle. Bloody Blackjack. Devil's Darts . . . a dart game with a cork witch as a target.

And there were witch figures everywhere. Cloth witches on nooses hanging from the overhead pipes. Cardboard witches leering from the tops of booths. Paper witches dancing on the wall. They were fat, skinny, white-haired, grey-haired, cross-eyed, squint-eyed, warty, funny, scary . . . and *ugly*. That was the one thing they all had in common.

That's what they think of us. Humans. All humans . . .

'Thea? Are you OK?'

Thea whirled. 'No, I am not *OK*.' She gestured around the room. 'Will you *look* at this stuff? Do you really think it's funny? Something to party about?' Hardly aware of what she was doing, she spun him around to face The Iron Maiden – a wooden replica with rubber spikes.

'What are people going to do? Pay to step into that?

Don't they realize that it used to be *real*? That *real* people were put in it, and that when the door closed, those spikes went into them, into their arms and their stomachs and their eyes . . .' She couldn't go on.

Eric looked as stricken as Dani had earlier. He'd never seen her like this. 'Thea – look, I'm sorry . . . I never thought . . .'

'Or *that*.' Thea gestured toward the Wheel of Torture, the words tumbling out. 'Do you know how they *really* put a witch on the wheel? They broke every bone in her body so they could just thread her arms and legs through the spokes like spaghetti. Then they put the wheel on a pole and left her up there to die . . .'

Eric's face contracted with horror. 'God, Thea . . .'

'And these pictures – the witches who got tortured didn't have green skin and evil eyes. They weren't monsters, and they didn't have anything to do with devils. They were *people*.'

Eric reached out for her, but she spun away, staring at a particularly ugly hag on the wall. 'Do *you* think this place is all right for a party? That this is good fun? That witches look like *that*?' She flung out an arm, close to being hysterical. 'Well, *do you*?'

In her mind's eye she could see the world: Dani and Blaise and all other witches on the left; Eric and the students here and all other humans on the right, both races hating and despising each other, and herself somewhere in the middle.

Eric caught her shoulders. '*No, I don't think it's all right.* Thea, will you just *listen* to me for a second?'

He was almost shaking her – but she could see that there were tears forming at the corners of his eyes.

'I feel *awful*,' he said. 'I never thought about taking this stuff seriously – and that's my own stupid fault, and I know it's not an excuse. But now that you say it, I do see how terrible it is, and I'm sorry. And I never should have brought *you* here, of all people . . .'

Thea, who had been starting to relax, stiffened again. 'Why me "of all people"?' she demanded.

He hesitated a moment, then met her eyes and spoke quietly. 'Because of your grandma's store. I mean, I know it's just herbs and positive thinking – but I also know that in the old days, there would have been somebody out there pointing a finger and calling her a witch.'

Thea relaxed again. It was OK for people to think Gran was a witch – if by 'witch' they meant someone who talked to plants and mixed up homemade hair tonic. And she couldn't disbelieve Eric, not under the intensity of those steady green eyes.

But she saw an opportunity and seized it.

'Yeah, and they'd probably have burned *me* for giving you this present,' she said, opening her hand. 'And you'd probably have been scared or superstitious if I asked you to keep it with you all the time: you'd think I was putting some kind of a spell on you—'

'I wouldn't think anything,' he said firmly, taking the little green pillow from her. It smelled like fresh New Hampshire pine needles, which was what was in it – mainly. She'd also added a few protective herbs and an Ishtar crystal, a golden beryl in a star cut with thirty-three facets, carved with the name of the Babylonian mother goddess. The charm was the best she could do to help him fend off Blaise's spells.

'I would just kiss it and put it in my pocket and never let it out of my sight,' Eric went on. And he did, stopping after the kiss to say, 'Mm, smells good.'

Thea couldn't help smiling at him. She chanced saying, 'Actually, it's just to remind you of me.'

'It will never leave my pocket,' he said solemnly.

Well, that worked out nicely.

'Look, there's probably something we can do about this place,' Eric said, glancing around again. 'The school board doesn't want any bad publicity. Why don't I run and borrow a camera from the journalism class, and we can take some pictures so people will see what we mean when we complain?'

Thea glanced at her watch. 'Why not? I think I've already missed French.'

He grinned. 'Back in a minute.'

When he was gone, Thea wandered slowly among the silent booths, lost in her own thoughts.

For a few minutes there, when I was ranting, I almost told him the truth. And then later I thought maybe he'd figured it all out for himself.

And would that be so terrible? He's already under sentence of death just because I love him; it doesn't matter if he knows or not.

But if he did know . . . what would he say? Witches may be OK in the abstract, but does he really want one for a girlfriend?

The only way to find out was to tell him.

She leaned against a ladder and gazed sightlessly at an oilcloth lying beneath a hanging noose. Of course, it was probably all academic anyway. What kind of future could they possibly have . . . ?

Suddenly Thea realized what she was looking at.

Underneath that oilcloth was a shoe – and the shoe was connected to something. Subconsciously, she'd been assuming it was another witch dummy . . . but now she focused. And she felt the hairs on her arms lift and tingle.

Why would they dress a witch in black Nike hightops?

CHAPTER

9

The shoe was so incongruous that for an instant Thea thought her eyes must be playing tricks on her. It was the atmosphere here – the dim, echoing room with all its macabre booths. If she looked away and then looked back . . .

It was still there.

I should wait, I should call somebody. This could be something terrible. There are human authorities; I should at least wait for Eric . . .

Thea found herself moving in dreamlike, slow speed.

She took the edge of the oilcloth between finger and thumb and lifted it just an inch or so.

There was a leg attached to the shoe.

A blue-jeaned leg. Not part of a dummy. And another shoe.

Horror and adrenalin washed over Thea. And, strangely, that helped. Her first thought was, *It's a person and she may be hurt*. She went into emergency mode, slamming a wall between herself and her fear.

Hang on, are you OK, just let me see . . .

She pulled the rest of the oilcloth off, tugging to get it free. She saw legs, a body, curled fingers clutching the sleeve of a black-dressed witch dummy . . .

Then she saw the head and she reeled backward, both hands pressed over her mouth. She'd only gotten a glimpse, but the picture was burned into her mind.

Blue-grey face, hideously swollen. Grotesquely bulging eyes. Tongue like a sausage protruding from between black lips . . .

Thea's knees gave out.

She'd seen the dead before. She'd been to leave-taking ceremonies where the mortal remains of witches were returned to the earth. But those had been natural deaths, and the corpses had been peaceful. While this . . .

I think it was a boy. It had short hair and a flat chest. But there was no way to recognize the face. It was so distorted – didn't even look human . . .

He died violently. May his spirit be released; not held here by the need for revenge. Oh, Sekhmet, Lionheaded goddess of Egypt; Mistress of Death, Opener of Ways, Sekhmet Who Reduceth to Silence . . .

Her disjointed thoughts were interrupted as sunlight fanned into the room. At the door, Eric shouted, 'I'm back!'

Thea stood up. Her legs wanted to cave again. She opened her mouth, but what came out was a whisper. 'Eric—'

He was hurrying toward her. 'What's wrong? Thea?'

'It's somebody dead.'

She saw his eyes widen in absolute disbelief – and then he looked past her. He took a step toward the thing on the floor, stopped, crouched, and stared for a second. Then he whirled back and grabbed her as if he could somehow protect her from what he'd seen.

'Don't look at it; don't look over there,' he gasped. 'Oh, God, it's bad.'

'I know. I saw it.'

'It's bad; it's so bad . . .'

They were both holding on to each other. It was the only safety in this nightmare.

'He's dead. That guy is dead,' Eric said. It was obvious, but Thea understood the need to babble. 'There's nothing we can do for him. Oh, God, Thea, I think it's Kevin Imamura.'

'*Kevin?*' Black dots danced in front of Thea's eyes. 'No, it can't be—'

'I've seen him wearing that shirt before. And the hair . . . And he's on the committee to decorate this place. He must have been setting up that dummy.'

Thea's mind showed her a terrible picture. A crusted dark line on that bloated face – like the wound made by a slashing razor. And the soft black hair . . . Yes, it could have been Kevin. And that meant—

Blaise.

'Come on,' Eric was saying, his voice dazed and quenched. 'We've got to tell the office.'

Numbly, Thea let him guide her. Her mind was in another place.

Blaise. Did Blaise know . . . could Blaise have . . .

She didn't want to form the thought even to herself, but she couldn't help it.

. . . finally gone all the way? Not just spilled blood, but taken a life?

It was forbidden to witches. But the Harmans were part lamia, and vampires sometimes killed for power. Could Blaise have gone that far into the darkness?

After they got to the office, things happened fast, but Thea couldn't really take it in. Activity whirled around her. The secretaries. The principal. The police. She was grateful for Eric, who kept telling the story over and over so she didn't have to.

I need to find Blaise.

They were back at the gym. The police were cordoning off the whole building with yellow tape. A throng of students and teachers was watching. Thea's eyes skimmed the crowd, but she didn't see Blaise anywhere.

Voices rose around her.

'I heard it was Kevin Imamura.'

'Somebody said that guy from the dance came back and got him.'

'Eric! Eric, did you really *see* him?'

Then one voice outshouted the others. 'Hey, Mrs Cheng, what about the Halloween party? Is the gym gonna be open by then?'

The principal, who had been huddled with a couple of police officers, turned around. Black hair riffling over her forehead in the breeze, she addressed the entire crowd.

'I don't know what is going to happen with the gym. There's been a tragedy, and now there's going to be an investigation. We'll just have to wait and see what comes of that. Now, I want everybody to go back to their classes. Teachers, please take your students back to your classrooms.'

'I can't go back,' Thea whispered. She and Eric were standing at a little distance from the thinning crowd. Everyone seemed to have forgotten about them.

'I'll take you home,' Eric said immediately.

'No, I need to find Blaise. I have some things to ask her.' She tried to make her stupefied brain work. 'Eric, I should have told you this before. You've got to be careful.'

'Of what?'

'Of Blaise.'

He looked incredulous. 'Thea . . .' He glanced at the old

gym. 'You can't think *she* had anything to do with – what happened to Kevin.'

'I don't know. She could have had somebody do it, or made him do it himself.' Thea kept her voice low. She looked straight into Eric's face, willing him to believe her. 'Eric, I know you don't understand, but it's like I told you before. She's like Aphrodite. Or Medea. She laughs when she destroys things. Especially when she gets mad . . . and she's mad at *you*.'

'Why?'

'Because you picked me instead of her – because I like you – lots of things. *That* doesn't matter. The point is that she may come after you. She may try to . . . seduce you. And' – Thea glanced at the bobbing yellow tape surrounding the old gym – 'she may try to hurt you. So will you just be *careful* if you see her? Will you promise me that?'

Eric looked windblown and bewildered, but he nodded slowly. 'I promise.'

'Then I'll see you later. We still have things to talk about – but I have to find Blaise first.'

She walked toward the crowd, leaving Eric standing there in the wind. She knew he was watching her.

A waving hand caught Thea's eye. It was Dani, her face full of sympathy and concern.

'Thea, are you all right?'

'Sort of.' Thea gave a laugh she didn't recognize. 'Have you seen Blaise around?'

Dani's soft little hand crept into hers. 'She and Vivienne went home – I mean, to your place. I'll go back with you, if you want. You shouldn't be alone.'

Thea squeezed her hand. 'Thanks. I'd appreciate it.' She was grateful, and relieved that Dani didn't hate her. 'Dani, about the way I acted earlier . . .'

'Forget it. I don't know what I said, but I didn't mean to make you mad.' She added gently, 'Thea, are you really OK? Really? Because I don't want to upset you more . . .'

'Why?' And then: '*What*, Dani?'

'Your grandma's sick. That's why Blaise and Vivienne went home – Vivienne's mom paged her. She's a healer – Vivienne's mom, I mean – and I think she's taking your grandma to her house.'

Thea was disturbed. Gran hadn't moved to Las Vegas for the same reason other Night People did. Lamia and made vampires came because so many of the humans here were transients – the kind that wouldn't be missed if they disappeared. Other witches came because of the power vortexes in the desert. But Gran had come because of the warm, dry climate. Her lungs had been bad since she was a kid.

Please don't let it be serious, Thea kept thinking as Dani drove her home. She felt as if her skin had been rubbed too thin all over her body.

When they got to the shop, Gran was already gone. Tobias and Vivienne were downstairs.

'Is she OK?' Thea asked. 'Is it something bad?'

'Not too bad,' Tobias said. 'She just kept getting dizzy today, and then she had a coughing fit and couldn't stop. She finally decided maybe she'd better get somebody to sing it out. So she called Ms Morrigan.'

Oh, great – chanting. Just what Gran loved. But she must have been really sick to *ask* to have it done.

'Can I call her?'

'I wouldn't,' Vivienne put in. Her green eyes were kind, her voice reassuring. 'I'm sure Mom's working on her by now, and when she does a singing, it takes all night. You shouldn't disturb them. But don't worry, Thea, my mom's really good.'

'Yes, it's not that I'm worried about.' Thea looked around distractedly, finally coming back to Vivienne's face. 'Did you hear about what happened at school?'

'No.' Vivienne looked mildly curious. '*What* happened?'

Instead of answering. Thea said, 'Where's Blaise?'

'Upstairs packing. She's going to stay overnight at my house. You can come, too – Thea?'

Thea was already racing up the stairs.

She burst into the bedroom she and Blaise shared. Blaise had a small suitcase open on her bed.

Thea didn't waste words. 'Did you kill Kevin Imamura?'

Blaise dropped a black silk teddy. 'Did I *what*? What are you talking about?'

'He's dead.'

'And you thought *I* did it? Thanks a lot, but it's not him I want to kill.' Blaise narrowed her eyes and Thea felt cold. Then she tilted her head. 'So how did he die?'

'He was strangled. Somebody *murdered* him.'

Blaise just raised her eyebrows and murmured, 'Hm. I wonder where Randy is?' She held a shirt up, considered it, and added, 'Do you want to come stay at Viv's with me? It's better than staying here by yourself.'

'I don't know. Do I have to watch you to make sure *Eric* doesn't end up like Kevin?'

Blaise gave her a scorching look. 'When I go after a boy, I *get* him first. I don't strangle him before the fun begins.'

She slammed her suitcase closed and stalked out.

Thea sat on the bed.

In spite of her sharp words, Thea now knew Blaise hadn't done it. Her cousin had been genuinely surprised.

And Randy? I suppose it could have been, if he somehow got out of wherever they've taken him. He had a reason to hate Kevin. But . . .

The alternate explanation slid into place so quickly that Thea realized it must have been in her mind all along.

The spirit.

She sat there for an endless time, trying to think. It was like trying to find her way through a thick fog.

Gran's gone . . . and if she's sick I can't bother her anyway . . . of course, Blaise won't help . . . but I need to trust *somebody* . . .

Dani gently pushed the door open. 'Can I come in?' When Thea nodded, she walked in and sat down on Blaise's bed.

'They left. I told Tobias to go too – he had a girlfriend he wanted to see. I'll stay here tonight, if you want.'

Thea took a shaky breath. 'Thanks, Dani.'

'Look, Thea, I don't want to pry, but . . . *are* you OK? I mean, you're as pale as a corpse—' Dani bit her lip. 'Sorry, bad choice of words. But I *am* your friend, and if there's anything I can do, I'd like to help.'

Another breath. Then Thea made her decision.

'I worked a forbidden spell.'

Dani looked shocked, but not appalled. 'Which one?'

'Calling back the spirits.'

When Dani didn't scream or faint, Thea told the whole story. All about her summoning – everything except why she'd been doing it. 'And now I'm scared,' she finished. 'I let *something* out yesterday, and today Kevin gets murdered. Blaise didn't kill him. She thinks Randy may be involved, but . . .' Thea shook her head.

'But, Thea, be logical. Why should it have anything to do with your spell?' Dani's rational voice was soothing. 'You let some*one* out, not some*thing*. The Elders summon the ancestors all the time without anything bad happening. You just feel guilty because you know you weren't *supposed* to be doing it.'

'No. Dani, I can't explain it, but the thing I let out – it wasn't friendly. It knocked Blaise and me down. None of the spirits I saw the elders summon ever did that.'

'Well . . .' Dani looked doubtful. 'But why would one of the ancestors want to murder a human?'

'I don't know.' Somehow talking about it had cleared Thea's mind. She said slowly, 'But . . . maybe the book would tell us.'

Ten minutes later, they were sitting side by side on Thea's bed, with the iron chest on the floor and the book between them.

'First, could you tell *anything* about the amulet that fell in the fire?' Dani asked in scientific tones. 'Like, if the hair was grey, it could mean—'

'The witch was old.' Thea caught on immediately. 'No, it wasn't grey or white. It was dark, sort of like mahogany.' She closed her eyes, trying to remember. 'It all happened so fast, but I think it was *long*. It was doubled up lots of times in the clay.'

'So maybe a woman.'

'Yes.' Thea read for several minutes. 'Wait a minute. Look at this.'

' "Suzanne Blanchet," ' Dani read with difficulty. ' "Born sixteen thirty-four in Esgavans on the day that they made bonfires for the peace between France and Spain. Tried sixteen fifty-three at Ron-chain, prisoner at the court of Rieux." '

'And listen to the charges,' Thea said grimly. ' "Bewitching men's corn, killing cattle, bringing hunger into the country, *and strangling babies at night with her long hair*." '

'Strangling,' Dani breathed.

'She denied it, so they tortured her. Listen: "Being a little stretched on the rack, she screamed ceaselessly that she was not a witch, but being more tightly stretched, said that it was true." '

'And then they tortured her *family*,' Dani said, her finger skimming the lines. 'Oh, Isis, look at this. She had a ten-year-old brother named Clément and a six-year-old sister named Lucienne. They tortured them both.'

'And burned them.' Thea had begun to tremble involuntarily. The room wasn't cold, but she had a feeling like ice deep inside her. 'Look. "The children having been promised the mercy of being strangled before burning, but the executioner not having been paid, they were committed alive to the flames . . ." ' She couldn't finish.

' " . . . before the eyes of their sister," ' Dani whispered. She was shaking, too, and huddling close to Thea. 'How could they *do* that?'

'I don't know,' Thea said flatly.

'I mean, no wonder Night World laws are so strict. No wonder we have to keep ourselves a secret – look at what they *do* to us when they find out.'

Then swallowed, she didn't want to think about Night World rules. 'And then they burned Suzanne,' she said quietly, keeping her eyes on the book. ' "Being consigned to the fire, she uttered several exclamations, crying out upon revenge." '

'I would too,' Dani said, her soft voice threaded with steel. 'I'd come back and *kill* them.'

She stopped and she and Thea looked at each other.

'And maybe that's just what she did,' Thea said slowly. 'Only she couldn't get to her torturers. But she found something that looked similar – a reproduction torture chamber. And there was Kevin, doing something to a witch dummy – hanging it, maybe. Maybe treating it in some way that reminded her of . . .' Thea nodded toward the book. 'Anyway, doing *something* that made her lose it.'

'And kill him. By strangling him – what she'd been accused of doing. Thea?' Dani grimaced, then went on. 'When you saw Kevin's body – was there anything around his neck?'

Thea stared at the window curtains, trying to remember. That awful bloated face . . . the protruding tongue . . . and dark bruises on the throat.

'No,' she said softly. 'There were marks, but whatever strangled him was gone.'

'She took it with her.' Dani shivered, then put both hands on the book. 'Or maybe not. Look, Thea, this may make a great bonfire story, but, really, it's all speculation.'

Thea was staring at the yellowed page beneath Dani's fingers. 'I don't think so,' she said quietly. 'See this symbol by Suzanne Blanchet's name? I recognize it. I saw it for just a second – on the amulet in the fire.'

'You're sure?'

Thea looked away. 'Yeah. It's her, Dani. And it's my fault. I let her out . . . and now she's killing people. Because of me, somebody's *dead*.'

It was only when she said it that the full realization hit, as if forming the words had somehow made it true. Kevin was *dead*. He wasn't going to school anymore, he wasn't going to get a chance to repair his Porsche. He wouldn't ever smile at a girl again. He'd lost everything a person had to lose.

'And I just – I just feel so *bad*,' Thea said. The ache in her throat rose up in a sort of spasm, as if she were going to be sick. But what came out was tears.

Dani held her while she sobbed. And at last, when Thea was crying more quietly, she said, 'You didn't know. You didn't mean to do anything bad. You were just playing around and it went wrong. *You didn't know.*'

'It doesn't matter.' Thea wiped her face on her sleeve,

sitting up. The ache in her chest was duller now, and she was slowly realizing that something else was there, something that felt hot and bright. A need to *act*.

'It doesn't matter,' she said again. 'I still made it happen. But I'll tell you one thing, I'm not going to let it *keep* happening. I've got to stop her. Which means I've got to send her back.'

'I'm with you there,' Dani said, her small jaw set in determination. 'But *how*?'

Thea stared at the wall a moment, then said, 'I have an idea.'

CHAPTER

10

'Gran told me that the only person who can send a spirit back is the one who called it up,' Thea said. 'But the problem is that you have to be able to *see* the spirit, you have to be close to it. Then you can do the sending-back spell.'

'OK,' Dani said, nodding. 'But—'

'Wait, I'm getting to it.' Thea got up and began to pace the few steps between her bed and Blaise's. She spoke slowly at first, then more rapidly. 'What I'm thinking is that this can't be the first time this has happened. Sometime, somewhere, somehow, some witch must have called up a spirit and let it get away. And then had to go out and get hold of it again.'

'I'm sure that's true. But so what?'

'So if we could find a record of how she did it – how she tracked the spirit down – we might be in business.'

Dani was getting excited. 'Yeah, and it wouldn't even have to be a case of a *summoned* spirit. I mean, some spirits just won't go to the other side at all after they've died, right? Maybe there's a record about how one of *them* got sent across the veil.'

'Or a story. Or a poem. *Anything* that would give us

a clue about how to get them to stay in the same room with you while you do the spell.' Thea stopped and grinned at Dani. 'And if there's one thing Gran has lots of, it's records and stories and poems. There are hundreds of books in the workshop.'

Dani jumped up, dark eyes snapping. 'I'll call my mom and tell her I'm staying over tonight. Then – we find it.'

After Dani called her mother, Thea called Eric to make sure he was OK. Now that she knew there was a demented spirit on the loose she was worried about him.

'You're sure *you're* all right?' he said. 'I mean, I still feel awful about taking you to that place. I wanted, well, I'd like it if we could see each other *without* something terrible happening.'

Thea felt as if someone had squeezed her heart. 'Me, too.'

'Maybe we could do something tomorrow. If you're up to it.'

'That would be good.' She didn't dare to keep talking to him with Dani around. It would be too easy for anyone listening to guess her feelings.

The first thing Thea noticed in the workshop was that Blaise had taken her new project with her.

She must be close to finishing it.

'I'll start here,' Dani said, standing in front of a large bookcase. 'Some of these look really old.'

Thea picked another case. There were books of every kind: leather-bound, paper-bound, cloth-bound, suede-bound, unbound. Some were printed, some were handwritten, some were illuminated. Some were in languages Thea didn't know.

The first shelf yielded nothing except an interesting spell titled 'HOW TO MAKE AN ELIXIR OF ABHORRENCE, which works quite as well, or perhaps a little worse than the traditional Elixirs of Loathing or Detestation, and is less delicate and expensive than the Elixir of Odium used by royals and members of the nobility, and will also keep extremely well for a very long time'.

Hmm . . .

Thea put that book aside. She'd looked through another half a shelf when Dani said, 'Hey, I found your family tree.'

Thea scooted over. 'Yeah, that's the one Gran keeps. It doesn't go anywhere near back to Hellewise.' She laughed.

'Who's this guy?' Dani put her finger on a name. ' "Hunter Redfern." I thought the Redferns were that hotshot vampire family.'

'Lamia family. I mean, there's a difference, you know. Someone who's *made* into a vampire can't have kids.'

'But what's the lamia guy doing in your family tree?'

'He's the one who did a kinship ceremony with Maeve Harman, back in the sixteen hundreds. She was the leader of the Harmans then. See? And we're all descended from their daughter Roseclear.'

'She did it with a *vampire*? Creepy.'

Thea smiled. 'She did it to stop their families from fighting – they had a feud going on. And so now all of us modern Harmans have a little vampire blood.'

'I'll remember to watch out if you start looking at my throat.' Dani traced a finger down the tree. 'It looks like you and Blaise are the last of the female Harmans.'

'Yeah, we're it. The last Hearth-Women.'

'That's a big responsibility.'

It was almost exactly what Gran had said. Thea suddenly felt uncomfortable with family trees. 'Yeah. Um, I guess we'd better keep reading.'

It was several hours later when Dani said quietly, 'I've got it.'

'What?' Thea went to sit by her. The book on Dani's knees was bound in green with a crescent moon and three stars on the front – a Night World symbol for witches.

'It's a book of humourous stories, but they're supposed to be true. This one is about a guy named Walstan Harman back in seventeen-seventy. He died, but he didn't cross over. He just hung around town playing jokes on everybody – appearing at night with his head under his arm and stuff like that. He never stayed in one place long enough for them to catch him, though.'

'So how did they track him down?'

Dani flashed a triumphant smile. 'They didn't. They *lured* him *in*.'

Light dawned for Thea. 'Of course, I'm so stupid. But *how*?'

Dani's slender finger swept down the page. 'Well, first they waited till Samhain, so the veil between the worlds would be thinnest. Then Nicholas Harman had this big feast prepared, this huge table piled up with Walstan's favourite food.' Dani made a face. 'Which happened to be mince pie made with bear meat and pumpkin, with a cornmeal crust. They have a recipe for it here, too. Gah.'

'Never mind that. Did it work?'

'Apparently. They set up the table with the pies in an empty room, then they cast a circle around it. Old Walstan was attracted to the food – I guess he just couldn't resist taking a look, even if he couldn't eat it. And when he came down to check it out, they opened the door and nabbed him.'

' "Sent him speedily and conveniently through the narrow path to the airy void," ' Thea read over Dani's shoulder. The story sounded genuine, only someone who'd actually seen a summoning or a sending-back would know those words.

'So now we know how to do it,' Dani said. 'We wait until Halloween and then we *lure* her. We just have to find something she likes—'

'Or . . . something she *hates*,' Thea broke in as an idea struck her.

They stared at each other.

'Like what she saw at the old gym,' Dani breathed. 'Something that reminded her of what they did to her.'

'Yes, except . . .' Thea stopped. Her mind was racing on, but she didn't want to share her thoughts with Dani. Except that the humans might already be doing something on Halloween, something that would attract Suzanne. If the police opened the old gym, the Halloween party would be an incredibly strong lure. All those horror booths . . .

So if I wanted to draw her somewhere else, I'd need to be doing something even *worse*, something that would remind her even more of what happened to her. And I'd need bait, somebody she'd want to kill. A human. Somebody who'd work with me, who'd be willing . . .

Not Eric.

Her thoughts came up short as she realized where they were leading. She found that her hands were icy cold and her heart was pounding slowly.

No. Not Eric, no matter what. Not even to save lives.

She pushed the thought from her mind. Of course there was some other way, and she'd find it. There was time . . .

'Thea? You still with me?' Dani was watching her.

'I was just trying to figure it all out.' Thea forced herself to speak calmly, to focus on Dani. 'Um, listen, there's one good thing I just thought of, we may have a little time. If

Suzanne is *still* watching the old gym, it could work for us. As long as the gym is closed up, people won't go in there, and she won't be able to get anybody.'

'I hope so,' Dani said. 'I mean, I understand why she's upset, but nobody deserves to die the way Kevin did. Not even a human.'

Late that night, while Dani was breathing peacefully in Blaise's bed, Thea lay and stared at the faint glow above the window curtains.

It wasn't just visions of Kevin. Her mind kept returning to what Dani and Gran had said about her responsibility.

Even if I send Suzanne back, even if Gran gets well, even if I manage to keep Blaise from killing Eric . . . where am I?

I'm a renegade witch. And there's no future for Eric and me . . . unless we run away. But that would mean him leaving his family forever, and us being hunted wherever we went. And me betraying the Hearth-Women and the Night World.

One last thought glimmered before she could force her mind into blankness.

There's no way everybody is going to come out of this happy.

The next morning Thea was late for school. And she had a hard time tracking down Blaise, it wasn't until lunchtime that she and Dani found the Circle Midnight witches in the front courtyard.

'Please let us see it,' Selene was saying as Thea and Dani walked up. 'Just one peek. Please?'

'I want to do a trial run first,' Blaise said, looking very pleased with herself. She took a drink of iced tea, ignoring Thea and Dani.

'How's Gran?' Thea broke in without preamble.

Blaise turned. 'Better, no thanks to you. Why didn't

you call this morning?'

'I overslept.' After terrible nightmares about strangled people.

'We were up late last night,' Dani said. 'It's not Thea's fault.'

'Your grandma's really doing well,' Vivienne said kindly. 'She just needs to rest for a while, Mom'll probably keep her at our place for a couple of days. Sleep heals, you know.'

Thea felt a tiny breath of relief, like a spring breeze. If Gran was getting better she had one less thing to worry about. 'Thanks, Viv. Please thank your mom, too.'

Blaise raised her eyebrows and made a tiny sound like 'Hmf.' Then she tapped her chin with one long nail. 'A trial run . . .' she said again, gazing far away.

She was dressed unusually, in a bronze silk jacket with a high collar that was zipped up to her chin. Thea had a sudden sinking feeling.

'What are you trying out?' Dani asked.

Blaise gave them a slow smile. 'Hang around and you'll see.' She scanned the courtyard and said sweetly, 'And *there* is the perfect mark. Selene, will you go ask him to come here?'

Selene got up and languidly drifted to the boy Blaise had pointed at.

Thea recognized him. He was Luke Price, a guy who drove a sleek red Maserati and looked like a bad-boy Hollywood star. He was fashionably unshaven and unkempt, had electric blue eyes, and right now looked vaguely surprised to find himself following Selene back to Blaise.

'Luke, how's it going?' Blaise said pleasantly.

Luke shrugged. 'OK. What do you want?' His electric blue eyes lingered on Blaise, but he was obviously used to playing the tough guy with girls.

Blaise laughed shortly, as if taken off guard by the question. 'Nothing I can have,' she murmured – and then looked slightly startled at herself. 'I want to talk to you,' she said smoothly, recovering. 'And . . . ' She tilted her head thoughtfully. 'Maybe the keys to your car.'

Luke laughed out loud. He leaned one hip against the concrete wall by the stairs, two fingers fishing in his T-shirt pocket for a cigarette.

'You're crazy,' he said indistinctly.

Dani coughed as smoke drifted toward her. Thea swirled her plastic bottle of Evian water in one hand.

Blaise made a face. 'Put that out; it's disgusting,' she said.

Luke blew smoke toward her. 'If you've got something to say, say it.' He was eyeing Blaise's zipped-to-the-neck jacket with disfavour. 'Otherwise stop wasting my time.'

Blaise smiled.

She touched the zipper at her throat. 'You want to guess what's under here?'

Luke's eyes went up and down the silk of the jacket, particularly where Blaise made it curve. 'Maybe you'd better show me.'

'You want me to show you? You're *sure*, now?'

Thea looked heaven-ward, thumb playing with the opening to her Evian bottle.

Luke was scowling, blowing smoke between tight lips. His electric blue eyes were narrow. 'I think you're some kind of tease . . .'

Blaise took the zipper between two fingers and slid it down.

The necklace fit like a collar, lying against the pale skin of her throat and the matte black of her simple blouse. And it was everything Thea had known it would be.

It was delicate, exquisite, magical. Swirls of stars and moons in enchanted patterns. Gems of all kinds tucked into the mysterious curves. Green garnet, imperial topaz, sunstone, cinnabar. Violet sapphire, African emerald, smokestone.

It seemed to move as you looked at it, the lines changing and flowing. Pulling you into the centre of its mystery, winding around you like strands of softly burnished hair. Holding you fast . . .

Thea pulled herself away with a physical jerk. She had to shut her eyes and put up a hand to do it.

And if it does that to *me* . . .

Luke was staring. Thea could actually *see* the change in his face as the necklace worked its spell. Like some Oscar-winning actor transforming from bad boy to vulnerable kid right there on screen. His jaw softened, his tight lips relaxed. The muscles around his eyes shifted and he lost his tense squint. He looked surprised, then defenseless. Open. Those electric blue eyes seemed dazzled, pupils widening. He sucked in a breath as if he couldn't get enough air. Now he looked awed; now hypnotized; now yearning . . .

Spellbound.

Luke had been transformed. His whole body seemed smaller. His lips were parted. His eyes were huge and full of light. He looked as if at any second he might fall down and start worshiping Blaise.

Blaise sat like a queen, with her midnight hair tumbling around the necklace, her chest moving slightly as she breathed, her eyes as brilliant as jewels.

'Put the disgusting cigarette down,' she said.

Luke dropped the cigarette and stamped on it as if it were a spider.

Then he looked back at Blaise. 'You . . . you're

beautiful.' He reached a hand toward her.

'Wait,' Blaise said. Her face assumed a tragic, wistful expression. 'First, I'm going to tell you a sad story. I used to have a little dog that I loved, a cocker spaniel, and we would take long walks together around dusk.'

Thea gave her cousin a narrow sideways look. She'd never heard such a lie. And what was Blaise talking about *dogs* for?

'But he was run over by an eighteen-wheel Piggly Wiggly truck,' Blaise murmured. 'And ever since, I've been so lonely . . . I miss him so much.' She fixed her eyes on the boy in front of her. 'Luke . . . will you be my little dog?'

Luke looked confused.

'You see,' Blaise went on, slipping a hand in her pocket, 'if I could just have somebody to remind me of him, I'd feel so much better. So if you'd wear this for me . . .'

She was holding a blue dog collar.

Luke looked even more confused. Redness was creeping up his neck and jaw. His eyes filled.

'For me?' Blaise coaxed, jingling the collar – which was way too big for a spaniel, Thea noticed. 'I'd be *so* grateful.'

Luke looked as if he were having a tremendous internal struggle. His breathing was uneven. He swallowed. A muscle in his jaw twitched.

Then, very slowly, he reached for the collar. Blaise held it down low.

Luke's eyes followed the collar. Jerkily, as if his muscles were fighting each other, he knelt down at Blaise's side. He stayed there, stone-faced, as Blaise fastened the dog collar around his neck.

When it was secure, Blaise laughed. She glanced at the other girls, then jingled the metal loop for the dog tag. 'Good boy,' she said, and patted his head.

Luke's face lit up with an excitement that bordered on ecstasy. He stared into Blaise's eyes.

'I love you,' he said huskily, still squatting.

Blaise wrinkled her nose and laughed again. Then she zipped up the bronze jacket.

The change on Luke's face was much quicker this time than his first transformation. For an instant he looked completely blank, then he glanced around as if he'd suddenly woken up in a classroom.

His fingers went to the dog collar. His face contracted in anger and horror and he jumped up.

'What's going on? What am I doing?'

Blaise just gazed at him serenely.

Luke tore the collar off and kicked it. Although he was glaring at Blaise, he didn't seem to remember the last few minutes. 'You gonna tell me what you want or not?' he snapped, his upper lip trembling. 'Because I'm not going to wait all day.'

Then, when nobody said anything, he walked huffily off. His buddies across the courtyard were roaring with laughter.

'Oops,' Blaise said. 'I forgot about the car keys.' She turned to the other girls. 'But I'd say it works.'

'I'd say it's *scary*,' Dani whispered.

'I'd say it's incredible,' Selene murmured.

'I'd say it's unbelievable,' Vivienne added.

And *I'd* say it's the Armageddon of accessories, Thea thought. And, incidentally, so much for Selene and Vivienne changing their ways. They may have been shocked at what happened to Randy and Kevin, but it sure didn't last.

'Blaise,' she said tightly, 'if you walk around school showing that, you are going to cause a riot.'

'But I'm not *going* to walk around school showing it,'

Blaise said. 'There's only one guy I'm interested in right now. And this' – she touched her throat – 'has *his* blood in it. If it works like that on other people, I wonder what it will do to him?'

Thea took a few deep breaths to relax her stomach. She had never gone one-on-one with Blaise in a matter of witchcraft. And no one had ever challenged Blaise for a boy.

But she didn't have a choice, and putting this off wouldn't help.

'I suppose you're planning to find some time to ambush him,' she said. 'Some time when I'm not around.'

It worked. Blaise stood, tall and regal in her bronze silk jacket, hands in her pockets, hair like a waterfall behind her. She gave Thea a slow smile.

'I don't need to ambush anybody,' she said with dreadful confidence. 'In fact . . . why don't we set up a meeting after school? Just the three of us. You, me, and Eric, a showdown. And may the best witch win.'

CHAPTER
11

'I don't understand,' Eric said pitifully as Thea towed him toward the bleachers.

'Well, that's reasonable.'

'Blaise wants to talk to me alone and you want me to *do* it.'

'That's right.' Thea hadn't realized it was possible to sound bright and bleak at the same time. 'I told you she'd probably go after you—'

'And you told me to be careful of her. You made the point very strongly.'

'I know. It's just . . .' Thea searched for an explanation that wouldn't be too much of a lie and clutched her bottle of Evian water. She didn't need to ask him if he had the protective charm with him – she could smell New Hampshire pine needles.

'It's just that I think it's better to get things settled,' she said finally. 'One way or the other. So maybe if you talk to her face-to-face . . . well, you can decide what you want, and we can get this over with.'

'Thea . . .' Eric stopped, forcing Thea to stop, too. He looked completely bewildered. 'Thea, I don't know what you're thinking, but I don't *need* to talk to Blaise to know what I want.' He put his hands gently on her upper arms. 'Nothing she can say could make any difference.'

Thea looked at him, at his clean, good features and his expressive eyes. He thought things were so simple.

'Then you can just tell her that,' she said, trying to sound optimistic. 'And the whole thing will be resolved.'

Eric shook his head, but allowed her to guide him onward.

Blaise was leaning against a concrete dugout by the baseball diamond. When they were about ten feet away, Thea stopped and nodded at Eric to keep going.

He walked to Blaise, who slowly straightened with the leisurely grace of a snake uncoiling.

Thea put her thumb into the Evian bottle and jiggled it gently.

'Thea said you wanted to talk to me.' Eric's voice was polite, but not encouraging. He looked back at Thea after he said it.

'I did,' Blaise said in her liquid, persuasive voice. But to Thea's surprise, she addressed the ground, as if she felt awkward. 'But now . . . well, I feel so embarrassed. I know what you probably think of me – trying to say something like this while your girlfriend is standing there.'

'Well . . .' Eric glanced back at Thea again. 'It's OK,' he added, his voice softer. 'I mean, it's better to say whatever it is in front of her than behind her back.'

'Yes. Yes, that's true.' Blaise took a deep breath as if steeling herself and then lifted her head to meet Eric's eyes.

What on *earth* is she doing? Thea stared at her cousin. Where did this scene come from?

'Eric . . . I don't know how to say this, but . . . I care about you. I know how that sounds. You're thinking that I have dozens of guys, and the way I treat them I can't possibly care about any of them. And I don't blame you if you just want to walk away right now, without even listening to any more.' Blaise fiddled with the zipper at her throat.

'Oh, look, I'm not going to walk away. I wouldn't do that to you,' Eric said, and his voice was even more gentle.

'Thank you. You're being so nice, much nicer than I deserve.'

Absently, as if it were the most casual of gestures, Blaise reached for the zipper at her throat and pulled it down.

The necklace was revealed.

Don't look directly at it, Thea told herself. She stared instead at the back of Eric's sandy head, which suddenly went very still.

'And you know, this is going to sound strange, but most of those boys don't really like me.' Blaise's voice was soft now, seductive but vulnerable. 'They just – want me. They look at the surface, and never even try to see any deeper. And that makes me feel . . . so lonely sometimes.'

In Thea's peripheral vision, gold stars and moons were shifting and flowing. Yemonja root and other delicious scents wafted toward her. She hadn't even noticed that the first time; she'd been too deep in the necklace's spell to analyze it. And a faint, high resonance hung in the air – two or three notes that seemed to shimmer almost above the threshold of hearing.

Singing crystals. Of course. Blaise was assaulting every sense, weaving an inescapable golden web . . . and the whole thing was tuned to Eric's blood.

'All I've ever wanted is a guy who cares enough about me to look deeper than the surface.' Blaise's voice had a slight catch now. 'And – well, before I knew Thea liked you, I guess I thought you might be that guy. Eric, please tell me – is that completely impossible?

Should I just totally give up hope? Because if you say so, I will.'

Eric was standing oddly now, as if he were crippled. Thea could see his breath coming faster. She didn't want to see his face, she knew what it would be like. Like Luke's. Blank wonder changing into slow adulation for Blaise.

'Just tell me,' Blaise said, raising one hand in a gesture full of pathos. 'And if you say no, I'll go away forever. But if . . . if you think you could care about me . . . even just a little . . .' She gazed at him with luminous, yearning eyes.

'I . . .' Eric's voice was thick and hesitant. 'I . . . Blaise . . .' He couldn't seem to get started on a sentence.

And no wonder. He's lost already.

Certainty hit Thea, and she stopped shaking her plastic bottle. Her little Elixir of Abhorrence didn't stand a chance against Blaise's magic. Eric was hooked and Blaise was reeling him in.

And it wasn't his fault. Nobody could be expected to hold out against the kind of enchantment Blaise was using. Enchantment and psychology so beautifully mixed that even Thea found herself half believing Blaise's story.

But she had to try anyway. She couldn't let Eric go without a fight.

With one final, violent shake, Thea took her thumb out of the bottle neck. Colourless liquid skyrocketed, spraying up and then raining down on Eric. A geyser of loathing.

Only one thing went wrong. As soon as the mysterious downpour hit Eric, he turned to see where it was coming from. Instead of looking at Blaise when the elixir soaked into his skin, he was looking at Thea.

She stared back into his grey-flecked eyes with a kind of horror.

Twice. He'd been twice enchanted now, once to love Blaise and once to hate *her*.

Oh, Eileithyia, it's over . . .

It was a crisis, and Thea responded instinctively. She reached for Eric, to save him, to be saved herself. She flung out a thought the way she'd fling out a hand to someone going over a cliff.

Eric.

A connection . . .

Like closing a circuit – and that was all it took. Thea felt a wave of . . . *something*, something hot and sweet, more magical than Blaise's magic. Distilled lightning, maybe. The air between her and Eric was so charged that she felt as though her skin was being brushed with velvet. It was like being at the intersection of cosmic force lines.

And it was all OK. Eric's face was his ordinary face. Alive, alert, full of warmth – for her. Not zombie worship for Blaise.

Thea.

It can't be this simple.

But it was. She and Eric were staring at each other in the quivering air and the universe was just one big singing crystal.

We're right together.

A yell shattered the silent communion. Thea looked toward the dugout and saw that Blaise the vulnerable had disappeared.

'I'm *wet*,' Blaise shrieked. 'Are you crazy? Do you have any *idea* what water drops do to silk?'

Thea opened her mouth, then shut it again. She felt giddy with the sweetness of relief. She had no idea if Blaise really thought the elixir was only water, but one thing was clear. However strong Blaise's spell had been, it was broken now. And Blaise knew it.

Blaise jerked the zipper up and stalked off.

'She's mad,' Eric said.

'Well . . .' Thea was still dizzy. 'I told you she likes getting mad.' She took Eric's arm, very gently, and partly to steady herself. 'Let's go.'

They'd only gone a few steps when Eric said, 'Thank God you hit me with that water.'

'Yes.' Even if the elixir hadn't worked it had somehow broken Eric's concentration or distracted Blaise or something. She'd have to see if she could figure out what had happened to disrupt a spell as potent as the one Blaise had created . . .

'Yeah, because, you know, it was getting really awkward,' Eric went on. 'I kept trying to think of a polite way to tell her there wasn't a chance, but I couldn't. And just when I realized I was going to have to *say* it and hurt her feelings – well, you soaked us.'

Thea stopped dead. She stared at him.

He was serious.

'I mean, I know I hurt her feelings anyway. Or she wouldn't have gone away mad. Uh, are *you* mad now? Thea?'

She started walking again. 'Are you saying you didn't even *want* to be with her? Not even just a little?'

He stopped. 'How could I want to be with her when I want to be with you? I told you that before this whole thing started.'

Maybe it's because we're soulmates. Maybe it's because he's so *stubborn*. But, whatever, I'd better never tell Blaise. She'll have a whole new reason for killing him if she finds out her spell bounced off like water off a duck.

'Well, anyway, it's resolved now,' she murmured – and at that moment she really believed it. She was too happy to think about anything dreadful.

'Is it? Does that mean that we can finally go out? Like on a date?'

He sounded so wistful that Thea laughed. She felt light and free and full of energy. 'Yeah. We could go right now. Or . . . we could go *in*. Your house, I mean. I'd like to see your sister and Madame Curie again.'

Eric made an 'ouch' face. 'Well, Madame Curie would probably like that. But Roz lost her case – the court ruled that the Boy Trekkers are a private organization. And she is not – pardon the pun – a happy camper.'

'All the more reason we should go see her. Poor kid.'

Eric looked at her quizzically. 'You're serious? You have a choice of anywhere in Las Vegas and you'd like to go to *my house*?'

'Why not?' Thea didn't mention that a human house was more exotic to her than anywhere else in Vegas.

She was happy.

It turned out to be a modest frame house, shaded by a couple of honest-to-goodness trees, not palms. Thea felt a twings of shyness as they went inside.

'Mom's still at work. And' – Eric checked his watch – 'Roz is supposed to be in her room until five. Home detention. This morning she microwaved her Barbie dolls.'

'That doesn't sound good for the microwave.'

Rosamund's door was plastered with homemade signs. DO NOT ENTER. KEEP OUT AND THIS MEANS ERIC. FEMINISM IS THE RADICAL NOTION THAT WOMEN ARE PEOPLE.

When Eric opened the door a piggy bank shaped like a skunk came flying toward him. He ducked. It hit the wall and, amazingly, didn't break.

'Roz—'

'I hate everybody! And everybody hates me!' A hardback book came soaring.

Eric shut the door fast. *Bang.*

'Everybody doesn't hate you!' he yelled.

'Well, I hate them! *Go away!*'

Bang. Bang. *Crash.*

'I think maybe we'd better leave her alone,' Eric said. 'She gets a little moody sometimes. Want to see *my* room?'

His room was nice, Thea decided. Lots of books, some smelling of mildew – 'I get them at the used book stores.' *Comparative Vertebrate Anatomy. Development and Structure of the Fetal Pig. The Red Pony*. Most of them were about animals in some form or other.

And lots of trophies. Baseball trophies, basketball trophies, a few tennis trophies. 'I have to switch between baseball and tennis different years.' Sports equipment was scattered carelessly around, mixed with the books and some dirty socks.

Not so different from a teenager's room in the Night World. Just a *person's* room.

There was a picture of a man on the desk, a man with sandy hair and a glorious, lightning-bolt smile like Eric's.

'Who is it?'

'My dad. He died when Roz was little – a plane crash. He was a pilot.' Eric said it simply, but his eyes went dark.

Thea said softly, 'My parents died when I was little, too. What's sad is that I don't really remember them.'

Eric looked at the picture again. 'You know, I never thought about it, but I'm glad I *do* remember. At least we had him that long.'

They smiled at each other.

By the bed was a tank that gave off a pleasant percolating sound. Thea sat next to it and watched iridescent blue fish dart around. She turned off the bedside lamp to see the lighted tank better.

'You like it?'

'I like everything,' Thea said. She looked at him. 'Everything.'

Eric blinked. He eyed the bed Thea was sitting on, then slowly sat at the desk. He stuck out a casual elbow to lean on and papers showered to the floor.

'Oops.'

Thea stifled a laugh. 'Is that the UC Davis application?'

He looked up hopefully from gathering them. 'It sure is. Want to see it?'

Thea almost said yes. She was in such a cheerful mood, ready to agree to anything, be open to anything. But a moment of thought changed her mind. Some things were just going too far.

'Not right now, thanks.'

'Well . . .' He put the papers back. 'You know, you still might think about transferring to the zoology class at school. Ms Gasparro is a great teacher. And you'd really like what we're studying.'

Maybe I could, Thea thought. What would it hurt?

'And if you were ever interested, Dr Salinger is always looking for extra help. It doesn't pay much, but it's good experience.'

And . . . what would *that* hurt? It's not as if I would be breaking any laws. I wouldn't have to use any powers, either, I could just be close to the animals.

'I'll think about it,' she said. She could hear the suppressed excitement in her own voice. She looked at Eric, who was sitting with his elbows on his knees, leaning forward, watching her earnestly. 'And – thanks,' she said softly.

'For what?'

'For . . . wanting the best for me. For caring.'

The light from the fish tank threw wavering blue patterns on the walls and ceiling. It made the bedroom seem like its own little underwater world. It danced over Thea's skin.

Eric stared at her. Then he swallowed and shut his eyes. With his eyes still shut, he said in a muted voice, 'I don't think you know how *much* I care.'

Then he looked at her.

That connection again. It seemed to be drawing them together – an almost physical feeling of attraction. It was exciting, but scary.

Eric got up very slowly and crossed the room. He sat by Thea. Neither of them looked away.

And *then* things just seemed to happen by themselves. Their fingers were intertwined. Thea was looking up and he was looking down. They were so close that their breath mingled. Thea shivered with the electricity.

Everything seemed wrapped in a golden haze.

Crash.

Something hit the other side of the wall.

'Ignore it; it's poltergeists,' Eric murmured. His lips were an inch from hers.

'It's Rosamund,' Thea murmured back. 'She feels bad – and it's not really fair. We should try and make her feel better.' She was so happy that she wanted everyone else to be happy, too.

Eric groaned. 'Thea . . .'

'Let me just go see if I can cheer her up. I'll come back.'

Eric shut his eyes, opened them, and turned on the lamp. He gave her a pained smile. 'OK. I have to water Mom's outside plants and feed the rabbits and stuff, anyway. Let me know when she's cheered up enough. I'll be waiting.'

Thea knocked and ducked as she entered Rosamund's room. 'Roz? Can I just talk to you for a minute?'

'Don't call me that. I want you to call me Fred.'

'Uh, how come Fred?' Thea sat cautiously on the edge of the bed – or not the bed, actually, the box springs. The mattress was across the room, standing on its side in a corner. The entire room looked as if it had been hit simultaneously by a hurricane and an earthquake, and it smelled strongly of guinea pig.

Slowly, part of a sandy head appeared above the mattress. One green eye regarded Thea directly.

'Because,' Rosamund said with terrible maturity, 'I'm not a girl anymore. Things have always been this way for girls and they will always be this way and they are never going to change. And don't give me any of that BS about how females hear better and do better in submarines and have better fine motor skills, because *I don't care*. I'm going to be a boy now.'

'You're a smart kid,' Thea said. She was surprised at how smart Roz was, and at how much she wanted to comfort her. 'But you need to study your history. Things *haven't* always been this way. There were times when women and men were equals.'

Rosamund just said, 'When?'

'Well, in ancient Crete, for one thing. They were all children of Eileithyia, the Great Goddess, and boys and girls both did dangerous stuff, like acrobatics on wild bulls. Of course . . .' Thea paused, struck by a thought. 'The Greeks did come and conquer them.'

'Uh-huh.'

'But, um' – Thea wracked her brain for human history – 'Well, the ancient Celts were OK – until the Romans came and conquered *them*. And . . . and . . .'

Human history was a problem.

'I told you,' Rosamund said bitterly. 'It always turns out the same. Now go away.'

'Well . . .' Thea hesitated.

It was the excitement that did it. The giddy feeling of everything being right with the world. It made her over-confident, made her feel as if Night World law were a little thing that could be dispensed with if necessary.

Don't, a part of her mind whispered. *Don't or you'll be sorry*.

But Rosamund was so miserable. And the golden glow was still around Thea, making her feel protected. Invulnerable.

'Look,' she said. 'This may not help much, but I'll tell you a story, a story that always made me feel better when I was a little girl. Only you have to keep it a secret.'

There was a flicker of interest in Rosamund's green eyes. 'A true story?'

'Well – I can't really say it's true.' And *that's* true – I *can't*. 'But it's a good story, and it's about a time when women were leaders. About a girl called Hellewise.'

CHAPTER

12

Thea settled on the box springs, not the most comfortable seat. 'Now, this all happened back in the days when there was still magic, OK? And Hellewise could do magic, and so could most of the people in her tribe. She was the daughter of Hecate Witch-Queen—'

'She was a witch?' Roz sounded intrigued.

'Well, they didn't call it that then. They called her a Hearth-Woman. And she didn't look like a Halloween witch. She was beautiful: tall, with long yellow hair—'

'Like you.'

'Huh? Oh.' Thea grinned. 'Thanks, but, no. Hellewise was *really* beautiful – and she was smart and strong, too. And when Hecate died, Hellewise became co-leader of the tribe. The other leader was her sister, Maya.'

Rosamund's whole head was above the mattress now. She was listening with fierce, if skeptical, interest.

'Now, Maya.' Thea chewed her lip. 'Well, Maya was beautiful, too: tall, but with long black hair.'

'Like that girl who came to the vet's after you.'

Thea was briefly startled. She'd forgotten Rosamund had seen Blaise. 'Well – uh, maybe a little. Anyway, Maya was smart and strong, too – but she didn't like having to share the leadership with Hellewise. She wanted to rule alone, and she wanted something else. To live forever.'

'Sounds like a good idea to *me*,' Rosamund growled.

'Well, yeah, there's nothing wrong with being immortal, I agree. Except, see, that it all depends on how much you're willing to *pay* to be it. OK? Following me?'

'Nope.'

'Well . . .' Thea floundered. Any Night Person would know immediately what she was talking about, even if by some outrageous chance they hadn't already heard the story. But of course humans were different. 'Well, you see, it was a matter of what she had to do. No ordinary spell would make her immortal. She tried all sorts of things, and Hellewise even helped her. And finally they figured out what kind of spell would do it, but then Hellewise refused.'

'Why?'

'Because it was too awful. No, don't *ask* me,' Thea added as Rosamund's interest level immediately shot up. 'I'm not going to tell you. It's not a subject for kids.'

'What, *what*? If you *don't* tell me, I'm just going to imagine even worse things.'

Thea sighed. 'It had to do with babies, OK? And blood. But that's not the point of this story—'

'They killed babies?'

'Not Hellewise. Maya did. And Hellewise tried to stop her, but—'

'I bet she drank the blood.'

Thea stopped and looked hard at Rosamund. Human kids were ignorant, but not dumb. 'OK, yes, she drank the blood. Satisfied?'

Roz grinned, nodded, and sat back, listening avidly.

'OK, so then Maya became immortal. But the thing was, she didn't know until afterward the price she'd have to pay. She would live forever – but only if she drank the blood of a mortal creature every day. Otherwise, she'd die.'

'Like a vampire,' Rosamund said with relish.

Thea was shocked for an instant, then she laughed at herself. Of course humans knew about vampires – the same way they knew about witches. Silly legends filled with misinformation.

But that meant Thea could tell her own story without fear of being believed.

'*Just* like a vampire, actually,' she said impressively, holding Rosamund's eyes. 'Maya was the first vampire of all. And all her children were cursed to be vampires, too.'

Roz snorted. 'Vampires can't have children.' She looked doubtful. 'Can they?'

'The ones descended from Maya can,' Thea said. She wasn't going to say the word 'lamia' to a human. 'It's only the kind who get made into vampires by being bitten that can't. Maya had a vampire son called Red Fern *and* she bit people. That's the story, you see – Maya wanted to make everybody like her. So she started biting people in the tribe. And eventually Hellewise decided she had to stop it.'

'How?'

'Well, that was the problem. Hellewise's tribe wanted to fight with Maya and the other vampires. But Hellewise knew if they did that, they'd probably *all* get killed. Both sides. So Hellewise challenged Maya alone to a duel. Single combat.'

Rosamund pushed the mattress over with a thump. 'I'd fight a duel with Mr Hendries – he's the boys' trekleader.' She jumped on the mattress and attacked a pillow with hands and feet – and teeth. 'I'd win, too. He's out of shape.'

'Well, Hellewise didn't want to fight, but she had to.

She was scared, because as a vampire Maya was a lot stronger now.'

For a moment, Thea thought about it, visualizing the old story the way she had as a child. Seeing Hellewise in her white leather shift, standing in the dark forest and waiting for Maya to come. And knowing that even if she won the fight, she'd probably die – and being brave enough to *keep* standing there. Being willing to give up everything for the people she loved, and for peace.

I don't think I could ever be that brave. I mean, I'd certainly *hope* I would be, but I have a terrible feeling that I wouldn't.

And then a strange thing happened. At that instant, she seemed to hear a voice, not her usual mind-voice, but one that was urgent and almost accusatory. Asking a question as if Thea hadn't just decided on the answer.

Would you give up everything?

Thea shifted. She didn't usually hear voices.

I suppose that's what Hellewise must have been thinking, she told herself uneasily.

'So what happened? Hey! Thea! What *happened*?' Rosamund was war-dancing on the mattress.

'Oh. Well, it was a terrible fight, but Hellewise won. She drove Maya away. And the tribe was left in peace, and they all lived happily ever after . . . um, except Hellewise. She died of her wounds.'

Rosamund stopped dancing and stared in disbelief. 'And you're telling me this to make me feel *better*? I never heard such a lousy story.' Her chin began to tremble.

Thea forgot she was dealing with a human child. She held out her arms the way she had to Bud the puppy, the way she would have to any creature in pain – and Rosamund threw herself into them.

'No, no,' Thea said, anxiously cuddling. 'You see, the

point is that Hellewise's people lived on, and they were free. And that may seem like a little thing, because they were just a little tribe, but that little tribe got bigger and bigger, and they *stayed free*. And all the witches in the world are descended from them, and they all remember Hellewise and honour her. It's a story every mother tells her daughters.'

Rosamund breathed irregularly for a moment. 'What about her sons?'

'Well, her sons, too. When I say "daughters" I mean "sons and daughters". It's just shorter.'

One green eye looked up from a mop of shaggy hair. 'Like "he" and "him" are supposed to mean "she" and "her," too?'

'Yeah.' Thea thought. 'I guess maybe neither is the best system.' She shrugged. 'The important thing is that one woman's courage kept us – them – all free.'

'Look.' Rosamund straightened up, staring through the hair. 'Are you just jerking my chain or is that a *true* story? Because frankly you seem like a witch to me.'

'That's what I was going to say,' an amused voice behind Thea said.

Thea's head snapped around. The door was open a few inches and a woman was standing there. She was tall and lanky, with little glasses and long silky brown hair. Her expression reminded Thea of a look Eric got sometimes, a look of very sweet puzzlement, as if he'd suddenly been struck by one of life's overwhelming mysteries.

But that didn't matter. What mattered was that she was a stranger. An Outsider.

A human.

Thea had been blurting out the secrets of the Night World, the history of the witches, and a human adult had been listening.

Suddenly her hands and feet went numb. The golden haze disappeared, leaving her in a cold, grey reality.

'I'm sorry,' the human was saying, but to Thea the voice seemed to come from a distance. 'I didn't mean to startle you. I was just kidding. I really was enjoying the story – sort of a modern legend for kids, right?'

Thea's eyes focused on another human behind the adult. Eric. He'd been listening, too.

'Mom's such a kidder,' he said nervously. His green eyes were apologetic – and intense. As if he were trying to make a connection with Thea.

But Thea didn't want to be connected. Couldn't be, to these people. She was surrounded by humans, trapped in one of their houses. She felt like the rattlesnake in a circle of big creatures with sticks.

Sheer, raw panic overtook her.

'You should be a writer, you know?' the human woman was saying. 'All that creativity . . .' She took a step inside the room.

Thea stood up, dumping Rosamund on the floor. They were coming at her – by now, the very walls seemed to be closing in. They were alien, cruel, sadistic, terrorizing, evil, *not-her-kind*. They were Cotton Mather and the Inquisition and they *knew* about her. They were going to point at her in the street and cry 'Witch!'

Thea ran.

She slipped between Eric and his mother like a frightened cat, not touching either of them. She ran down the hall, through the living room, out the door.

Outside, the sky was clouded over and it was getting dark. Thea only stopped long enough to get her bearings, then headed west, walking as fast as she could. Her heart was pounding and telling her to go faster.

Get away, get away. Go to earth. Find home.

She turned corners and zigzagged, like a fox being chased by the hounds.

She was ten minutes from the house when she heard an engine pacing her. She looked. It was Eric's jeep. Eric was driving and his mother and Rosamund were passengers.

'Thea, *stop. Please* wait.' Eric stopped the jeep and jumped out.

He was on the sidewalk in front of her. Thea froze.

'Listen to me,' he said in a low voice, turning away from the jeep. 'I'm sorry they came, too – I couldn't stop them. Mom feels awful. She's crying, Roz is crying . . . *please*, won't you come back?'

He looked close to crying himself. Thea just felt numb.

'It's OK. I'm fine,' she said at random. 'I didn't mean to upset anybody.' *Please let me go away.*

'Look, we shouldn't have eavesdropped. I know that. It was just . . . you're so good with Rosamund. I never saw anybody she liked so much. And . . . and . . . I *know* you're sensitive about your grandma. That's why you're upset, isn't it? That story is something she told you, isn't it?'

Dimly, somewhere in the pit of Thea's mind, a light shone. At least he thought it was a story.

'We have family stories too,' Eric was saying, an edge of desperation in his voice. 'My grandpa used to tell us he was a Martian – I swear to God this is true. And then he went to my kindergarten Back to School and I'd told all the kids he was a Martian, and they made these beep-beep noises at him and laughed, and I felt so bad. He was really embarrassed . . .'

He was babbling. Thea's numbness had receded enough that she felt sorry for him. But then a shape loomed up and she tensed again. It was his mother, silky hair flying.

'Look, Thea,' Eric's mother said. Her expression was

wretched and earnest. 'Everybody knows your grandma, knows how old she is, how she's a little . . . quirky. But if she's scaring you – if she's telling you any kind of weird stuff—'

'Mom!' Eric shouted through his teeth.

She waved a hand at him. Her little glasses were steamed up. 'You don't *need* to deal with that, OK? No kid needs to deal with that. If you want a place to stay; if you need anything – if we need to call social services—'

'Mom, please, I'm *begging* you. *Shut up.*'

Social services, Thea was thinking. Dear Isis, there'll be some sort of *investigation*. The Harmans in court. Gran accused of being senile – or being part of some cult. And then the Night World coming in to enforce the law . . .

Her terror peaked and left her deadly calm.

'It's OK,' she said, turning her gaze toward Eric. Not looking at him, but going through the motions exactly. 'Your mom's just trying to be helpful. But really' – she turned the same face toward his mother – 'everything's OK. Gran isn't strange or anything. She does tell stories, but she doesn't scare anybody.'

Is that good enough? Close enough to whatever you believe? Will it make you leave me alone?

Apparently so. 'I just don't want to be responsible for you and Eric – well . . .' Eric's mom exhaled nervously, almost a laugh.

'Breaking up?' Thea made a sound that was also almost a laugh. 'Don't worry. I'd never want that.' She turned a smile on Eric, looking down because she couldn't meet his eyes. 'I'm sorry if I got – touchy. I was just – embarrassed, I guess. Like you said about your grandpa.'

'Will you come back with us? Or let us take you home?' Eric's voice was soft. He wanted her to go back to his house.

'Just home, if you don't mind. I've got homework.' She lifted her eyes, making herself smile again.

Eric nodded. He didn't look happy, but he wasn't as upset as he had been.

In the backseat of the jeep, Rosamund pushed up against Thea and squeezed her hand.

'Don't be mad,' she hissed, fierce as ever. 'Are you mad? I'm sorry. Want me to kill somebody for you?'

'I'm not mad,' Thea whispered, looking over the top of Rosamund's shaggy head. 'Don't worry about it.'

She had reverted to the strategy of any trapped animal. Wait and watch for your chance. Don't fight until you see a real opportunity to get away.

'See you tomorrow,' Eric said as she got out of the jeep. His voice was almost a plea.

'See you tomorrow,' Thea said. It wasn't time to get away yet. She waved until the jeep was gone.

Then it was time. She dashed inside, up the stairs, and straight to Blaise.

'Wait a minute,' Blaise said. 'Go back. So you're saying they *didn't* believe any of it.'

'Right. At worst Eric's mom thinks Gran's bonkers. But it was a close call. For a while there I thought she might want to get Gran declared unfit or something.'

The two of them were sitting on the floor by Blaise's bed where Thea had collapsed. Blaise was eating candy corn with one hand and scribbling on a yellow legal pad with the other, all the while listening attentively.

Because that was the thing about Blaise. She might be vain and self-centred, quarrelsome, hot-tempered, lazy, unkind to humans, and generally hard to live with, but she came through for family. She was a witch.

I'm sorry I said you might be a little like Maya, Thea

thought.

'It's my fault,' she said out loud.

'Yes, it is,' Blaise said, scribbling.

'I should have just found some way to keep him at a distance in the beginning.'

But of course, it was because of Blaise that she hadn't. She'd thought Eric was safer with her than he would have been with Blaise. She'd thought that somehow ... somehow ...

Things would work out. That was it. There had always been some secret underlying hope that there could be a future with Eric. Some little hiding place where she'd kept the hope that things could be all right.

But now she had to face reality.

There was no future.

The only thing she could give Eric was death. And that was all he could give her. She'd realized that, all in one terrible explosion of insight when she'd seen Eric's mother in the room.

There was no way for them to be together without being discovered. Even if they ran away, someday, somewhere, the Night People would find them. They'd be brought before the joint Night World Council, the vampire and witch Elders. And then the law would be fulfilled ...

Thea had never seen an execution, but she'd heard of them. And if the Harmans tried to stop the Council from killing her, it would start a war. Witches against vampires. Maybe even witches against witches. It could mean the end of everything.

'So it doesn't look like we have to kill the mother,' Blaise said, frowning at her scribbles. 'On the other hand, if we kill the kids, the mother's bound to be unhappy, and might make a connection. So to be safe—'

'We can't kill any of them,' Thea said. Her voice was

muted but final.

'I don't mean *ourselves*. I'm going to call one of our friendly vampire cousins. Ash, he's supposed to be out on the West Coast somewhere, isn't he? Or Quinn, he likes that kind of thing. One quick bite, let the blood run out—'

'Blaise, I am not going to let vampires kill Eric. Or anybody,' she added as Blaise opened her mouth. 'It's not *necessary*. Nobody needs to die.'

'So you have a better idea?'

Thea looked at a statue of Isis, the Queen of Egyptian Goddesses, on the desk. 'I . . . don't know. I thought of the Cup of Lethe. Make them forget everything about me. But it might look suspicious – this entire family with a gap in their memory. And kids at school would wonder why Eric doesn't remember my name anymore.'

'True.'

Thea stared at the moon held between Isis's golden horns. Her brain, which had been working so coldly and logically, helping her to survive, was stalling now. There had to be a way to save Eric and his family – or what was the point of living herself?

Then she saw it.

'What I really think would be best,' she said slowly, because it hurt like a physical pain, 'would be for Eric to stop caring about me. To fall in love with someone else.'

Blaise sat back. She stirred the candy corn with long, elegant nails. She ate a piece.

'I admire you,' she said. 'Very sensible.'

'*Not* you,' Thea said through clenched teeth. 'You understand that, right? A human. If he falls in love with another girl he'll forget about me without any Lethe. Nobody will disappear or have amnesia; nobody will get suspicious.'

'OK. Although I would've liked to try him. He's got a strong will, I think he'd have held out for a while. Been a challenge.'

Thea ignored this. 'I still have some of his blood. The question is, do you have something you've been holding back, some love spell that will completely blow him out of the water?'

Blaise ate another piece of candy corn. 'Of course I do.' She narrowed her grey eyes. 'Also, of course, it's a forbidden spell.'

'I figured. Blaise, I'm now the princess of forbidden spells. One more doesn't matter. But I'll do the actual working, I don't want you to get in trouble.'

'You won't like it. It involves the bezoar stone from the stomach of an ibex – which I just happened to pick up while we were living with Aunt Gerdeth.'

Ibex were an endangered species. But this one was already dead. 'I'll do the working,' Thea said stubbornly.

'You really care about him, don't you?'

'Yes,' Thea whispered. 'I still think we're soulmates. But . . .'

Would you give up everything?

'I don't want to be the reason he dies. Or the reason a war starts between the Harmans and the rest of the Night World. And if I have to give him up, I'd rather do it myself, make sure he's safe with somebody else who loves him.'

'Have you got somebody picked out?'

'Her name is Pilar.' Thea looked at her cousin suddenly. 'Blaise? When Luke asked you what you wanted, and you said nothing you could have . . . what did you mean?'

Blaise tilted her head back and examined the ceiling. Then she looked down. 'Does anybody ever want anything they can have? Really?'

'I . . . don't know.'

Blaise clasped her knees and rested her chin on them. 'If we can have things, we don't really want them anymore. So there's always something out there that we're wanting and not able to get . . . and maybe that's *good*.'

It didn't sound good to Thea. It sounded like one of those terrible lessons in Life 101 that were supposed to make you more mature.

'Let's do the spell,' she said.

CHAPTER
13

'You know, he probably only loved you because of the yemonja,' Blaise said.

Thea looked up from her seat in the empty chemistry lab. It was morning break, and this was the most private place they could find at school. 'Thanks, Blaise. I needed that.'

But maybe it was true. She'd almost forgotten that she'd used a spell to get him in the first place.

That should make a difference, she told herself. If it was all artificial, I shouldn't even miss it.

She still felt as if she were encased in ice.

'Did you get it?'

'Sure.' Blaise tossed a ring on the high table. 'I asked her if I could look at it, then pretended I dropped it in the bushes. She's still out there searching.'

Thea pulled the binding spell out of her backpack.

Two anatomically correct dolls, both made with the blue wax Blaise used for her jewellery. Beautiful little creatures – Blaise was an artist. The male one contained the Kleenex with Eric's blood and a single sandy hair Thea had found clinging to her shoulder.

Thea put Pilar's turquoise ring around the feet of the

female doll and tied it with a red thread to keep it on. She held out a hand.

From her backpack, Blaise produced a corked hexagonal bottle. The liquid inside was made up of all sorts of disgusting things, including ground bezoar stone. Thea held her breath as she poured it over the two figures, which immediately began to smoke.

'Now bind them together,' Blaise said, coughing and waving a hand to clear a space to breathe.

'I know.' Thea took a thin scarlet ribbon seven feet long and patiently began winding it around the two figures. It wrapped them like mummies. She tucked the loose end into a loop.

'And there they are,' Blaise said. 'Bound till death. Congratulations. Let's see, it's ten-fifteen now, so he should have forgotten your existence by about . . . say, ten-sixteen.' She reached up and her hair ran like black water through her hands as she stretched.

Thea tried to smile.

The pain was bad. It was as if some part of Thea's physical body had been cut off. She felt raw and bleeding and not at all able to deal with things like French or trigonometry.

There must be more to life. I'll go somewhere and do something for other people; I'll work in third world countries or try to save an endangered species.

But thinking about future good works didn't help the raw ache. Or the feeling that if the ache stopped she would just be numb and never be happy again.

And all this for a human . . .

It didn't work anymore. She couldn't go back to her old way of thinking. Humans might be alien, but they were still people. They were as good as witches. Just different.

She managed to get through the school day without

running into Eric – which mainly meant scuttling around corridors after bells rang and being tardy for classes. She was scuttling after the last bell toward Dani's US government class when she almost collided with Pilar.

'Thea!'

The voice was surprised. Thea looked up.

Deep amber-brown eyes, framed by spiky black lashes. Pilar was looking at her very strangely.

Wondering at your good luck? Thea thought. Has Eric proposed to you yet? 'What?' she said.

Pilar hesitated, then just shook her head and walked off.

Thea ducked into the history classroom.

Dani said, 'Thea!'

Everybody sounds the same.

'Where've you *been*? Eric's looking all over for you.'

Of course, I should have realized. Blaise was wrong – he's not just going to forget about me and walk away. He's a gentleman; he's going to *tell* me he's walking away.

'Can I go home with you?' she asked Dani wretchedly. 'I need some space.'

'Thea . . .' Dani dragged her to a corner and looked her over with anxious eyes. 'Eric really wants to find you . . . but what's wrong?' she whispered. 'Is it something about Suzanne? The old gym's still closed, isn't it?'

'It's nothing to do with that.' She was about to suggest they get moving when a tall figure walked in the door.

Eric.

He walked straight to Thea.

The kids hanging around the teacher's desk were looking. The teacher was looking. Thea felt like a freak show.

'We have to talk,' Eric said flatly.

She'd never seen him look quite like this before. He

was pale, glassy-eyed, hollow-cheeked. He somehow managed to look as if he'd missed a week's worth of sleep since that morning.

And he was right. They had to talk to end it. She had to explain that it was OK, or he'd never be able to go.

I can do that.

'Somewhere private,' Thea said.

They left Dani and walked through the campus, past the old gym with its yellow ribbon of police tape hanging limp and still. Through the football field. Thea didn't know where they were going, and suspected Eric didn't either – they just kept moving until they were out of sight of *people*.

The green of the tended grass gave way to yellow-green, and then brown, and then desert. Thea wrapped her arms around herself, thinking about how cold it had gotten in just a week and a half. The last trace of summer was gone.

And now we're going to talk about it, she thought as Eric stopped. *OK. I don't have to think, just say the right words.* She forced herself to look at him.

He turned the haggard, haunted face on her and said, 'I want you to stop it.'

Funny choice of words. You mean end it, break it off, put it quietly out of its misery.

She couldn't get all that out, so she just said, 'What?'

'I don't know what you're doing,' he said, 'but I want it stopped. Now.'

His green eyes were level. Not apologetic, more like demanding. His voice was flat.

Thea had a sudden sense of shifting realities. All the hairs on her arms were standing up.

Caught without a working brain, she said, 'I – what are you talking about?'

'You know what I'm talking about.' He was still looking at her steadily.

Thea shook her head no.

He shrugged. It was a you-asked-for-it shrug. 'Whatever you're doing,' he said with terrible distinctness, 'to try and make me like Pilar, it has got to stop. Because it's not fair to her. She's upset right now because I'm acting crazy. But I don't want to be with her. It's you I love. And if you want to get rid of me, then *tell* me, but don't try and foist me off on somebody else.'

Thea listened to the whole speech feeling as if she were floating several feet above the ground. The sky and desert seemed too bright, not warm, just very shiny. While her brain ran around frantically like Madame Curie in a new cage, she managed to get out, 'What could I possibly have to do – with you liking Pilar?'

Eric looked around, found a rock, and sat on it. He stared down at his hands for a minute or so. Finally he looked up, his expression helpless.

'Give me a break, Thea,' he said. 'How stupid do you think I am?'

Oh.

'Oh.' Then she thought, don't just *stand* there. You bluffed him before. You talked him out of knowing he'd been bitten by a snake. For *Earth's* sake, you can talk him out of whatever he's thinking now.

'Eric, I guess we've all been under a lot of stress . . .'

'Oh, please don't give me that.' He seemed to be talking to a clump of silver cholla, eyeing the halos of awful spines as if he might jump into them. '*Please* don't give me that.'

He took a deep breath and spoke deliberately. 'You charm snakes and read guinea pigs' minds. You cure rattler bites with a touch. You tap into people's brains. You make up magical potpourri bags and your insane cousin is the goddess Aphrodite.' He looked at her. 'Did I miss anything?'

Thea found another rock and backed up to it blindly. She sat. Of everything in the universe, right then what she was most aware of was her own breathing.

'I have this feeling,' Eric said, watching her with his green eyes, 'that you guys are in fact the descendants of good old Hecate Witch-Queen. Am I close?'

'You think you win a prize?' Thea still couldn't think, couldn't put a meaningful remark together. Could only gabble.

He paused and grinned, a wry and painful grin, but the first one she'd seen today. Then the smile faded. 'It's true, isn't it?' he said simply.

Thea looked out over the desert, toward the huge, bare cliffs of rock in the distance. She let her eyes unfocus, soaking in the expanse of brown-green. Then she put her fingers to the bridge of her nose.

She was going to do something that all her ancestors would condemn her for, something that nobody she'd grown up with would understand.

'It's true,' she whispered.

He breathed out, a lonely human figure in that vastness of the desert.

'How long have you known?' she asked.

'I . . . don't know. I mean, I think I always sort of knew. But it wasn't possible – and you didn't want me to know. So I *didn't* know.' A kind of excitement was creeping into his haggardness. 'It's really true, then. You can do magic.'

Say it, Thea told herself. You've done everything else. Say the words to a human.

'I'm a witch.'

'A Hearth-Woman, I thought you called it. That's what Roz was telling me.'

At that, Thea was horrified out of her daze of horror. Stricken. 'Eric, you can't talk about this with *Roz*. You don't *understand*. They'll *kill* her.'

He didn't look as shocked as she might have expected. 'I knew you were scared of something. I thought it was just that people might hurt *you* – and your grandma.'

'They will; they'll kill me. But they'll kill you and Roz, too – and your mom and any other human they think may have learned about them—'

'*Who* will?'

She looked at him, floundered a moment, and then made the ultimate betrayal of her upbringing.

'It's called the Night World.'

'OK,' he said slowly, half an hour later. They were sitting side by side on his rock. Thea wasn't touching him, although her whole side was aware of his presence.

'OK, so basically, the descendants of Maya are lamia and the descendants of Hellewise are witches. And together they're all this big secret organization, the Night World.'

'Yes.' Thea had to fight the instinct to whisper. 'It's not just lamia and witches, though. It's shapeshifters and made vampires and werewolves and other things. All the races that the human race couldn't deal with.'

'Vampires,' Eric muttered to the cholla, his eyes going glassy again. 'That's what really gets me, real vampires. I don't know why, it follows logically . . .' He looked at Thea, his gaze sharpening. 'Look, if all you people have supernatural powers, why don't you just take over?'

'Not enough of us,' Thea said. 'And too many of *you*. It doesn't matter how supernatural we are.'

'But, look—'

'You breed much faster, have more children – and you

kill us whenever you find us. The witches were on the verge of extinction before they got together with the other races and formed the Night World. And that's why Night World law is so strict about keeping our secrets from humans.'

'And that's why you tried to hand me over to Pilar,' Eric said.

Thea could feel his eyes on her like a physical sensation. She stared at a patch of rock nettle between her feet. 'I didn't want you dead. I didn't want me dead, either.'

'And they'd really kill us for being in love.'

'In a *minute*.'

He touched her shoulder. Thea could feel warmth spread from his hand and she had to work to make sure she didn't tremble. 'Then we'll keep it a secret,' he said.

'Eric, it's not like that. You don't understand. There's nowhere we could go, no place we could hide. The Night People are everywhere.'

'And they all follow these same rules.'

'*Yes*. It's what allows them to survive.'

He breathed for a moment, then said in a voice that had gone husky, 'There's got to be a way.'

'That's what I let myself think – for a while.' Her own voice sounded shaky. 'But we have to face reality. The only *chance* we have of even living through this is for us to just go our separate ways. And for you to try as hard as you can to forget me and everything I've told you.'

She *was* trembling now, and her eyes had filled. But her hands were balled into fists and she wouldn't look at him.

'Thea—'

The tears spilled. '*I won't be your death!*'

'And I can't forget you! I can't stop loving you.'

'Well, and maybe that was just a spell, too,' she said,

sniffling. Tears were falling straight off her face and onto the rock. Eric looked around for something to give her, then tried to wipe her wet cheeks with his thumb.

She whacked his hand away. '*Listen* to me. You did miss something when you were adding up what I did. I also make love spells for *me*. I put one on you, and that's why you fell in love in the first place.'

Eric didn't look impressed. 'When?'

'When did I put the spell on you? The day I asked you to the dance.'

Eric laughed.

'You—'

'Thea.' He shook his head. 'Look,' he said gently, 'I fell in love with you *before* that. It was when we were out here with that snake. When we just looked at each other and . . . and . . . I saw you surrounded by mist and you were the most beautiful thing in the world.' He shook his head again. 'And maybe *that* was magic, but I don't think it was any spell you were putting on me.'

Thea wiped her eyes on her sleeve. OK, so the yemonja had nothing to do with it. Anyway, love spells just seemed to bounce off Eric – even the dolls hadn't worked . . .

She bent suddenly and picked up her backpack. 'And I don't know *why* this didn't work,' she muttered. She took out a quilted make-up bag, unzipped it, and reached inside.

The dolls came out as a bundle. At first glance they looked all right. Then Thea saw it.

The male doll had turned around. Instead of being face-to-face with the female doll, it had its back to her.

The scarlet ribbon was still wound tightly around them. There was no way that it could have slipped, that this could have happened by accident. But the dolls had been inside the case, and the case had been inside her backpack all day.

Eric was watching. 'That's Pilar's ring. Hey, is that the spell on me and Pilar? Can I see it?'

'Oh, why not?' Thea whispered. She felt dazed again.

So it couldn't have been an accident, and no human could have done it. And no witch could have done it either.

Maybe . . .

Maybe there was a magic stronger than spells. Maybe the soulmate principle was responsible, and if two people were meant to be together, nothing could keep them apart.

Eric was gingerly unwinding the scarlet ribbon. 'I'll give the ring back to Pilar,' he said. He reduced the binding spell to its constituent parts, put them gently back in the make-up bag.

Then he looked at her.

'I've always loved you,' he said. 'The only question is . . .' He broke off and looked like the shy Eric she knew again. 'Is, do you love me?' he finished at last. His voice was soft, but he was looking at her steadily.

Maybe there are some things you just can't fight . . .

She made herself look at him. The image wobbled and split.

'I love you,' she whispered. 'I don't know what's going to happen, but I do.'

They fell – slow as a dream, but still falling – into each other's arms.

'There's a problem,' Thea said some time later. 'Besides all the other problems. I'm going to be doing something next week, and I just need you to give me some time.'

'What kind of something?'

'I can't tell you.'

'You have to tell me,' he said calmly, his breath against

her hair. 'You have to tell me everything now.'

'It's magic stuff and it's dangerous—' A second too late she realized her mistake.

'What do you mean, dangerous?' He straightened up. His voice told her the peaceful interlude was over. 'If you think I'm going to let you do something dangerous by yourself . . .'

He wore her down. He was good at that – even better than his sister – and Thea was no good at refusing him. In the end she told him about Suzanne Blanchet.

'A dead witch,' he said.

'A spirit. And a very angry one.'

'And you think she's coming back,' he said.

'I think she's been here all along. Maybe hanging around the old gym, which hasn't done her any good since nobody's been there assaulting dummies. But if they open it to have the Halloween party . . .'

'It'll be full of humans, all visiting those booths, all reminding her of what she hates. She can pick them off like ticks off a dog.'

'Something like that. I think it could be bad. So what I've got to do is quietly lure her somewhere else and then send her back where she came from.'

'And how are you going to do that?'

'I don't know.' Thea rubbed her forehead. The sun was dipping toward the cliffs and long afternoon shadows had fallen across the desert.

'You've got a plan,' Eric said matter-of-factly.

Not you, Thea thought. I promised myself I wouldn't use you. Not even to save lives.

'You've got a plan you think is dangerous for humans. For me, since I'm going to be helping you.'

I will not use you . . .

'Let's make this easy on everybody. You *know* I'm not

going to let you do it alone. We might as well take that as given and go on from there.'

This is the crazy guy who ignores snakebites and attacks people with punch, she reminded herself. Do you *really* expect to talk him out of helping you?

But if something were to happen to him . . .

The voice came back again, and Thea didn't understand it and she didn't like it at all.

Would you give up everything?

CHAPTER
14

A week passed more or less quietly. Grandma Harman came home, her cough better. She didn't seem to notice anything different about Thea.

Night came earlier, and everyone at school talked about parties and costumes. The air got colder and there was an announcement that the old gym would be opened for Halloween.

Thea heard that Randy Marik had been moved to a psychiatric hospital and was in intensive therapy. He was making some progress.

Thea and Eric worked every day on their plan.

The only real excitement came the night when Thea walked in, sat on Blaise's bed, and said, 'Bullets won't stop him.'

'*What?*' Blaise looked up from creaming her elbows.

'I mean, spells won't stop him. Eric. They just bounce off. I'm telling you this because you're going to notice that he's not with Pilar.'

Blaise snapped the tube of cream shut. She stared at Thea for a full minute before she said tightly, 'What are you saying?'

Thea's humour drained away. She looked at the floor.

'I'm saying we're soulmates,' she said quietly. 'And that I can't help it. There is really, truly, nothing I can do about it.'

'I can't believe, after all that—'

'Right. After all that work. And after me trying and trying to stop, because I'm scared to death. But there's no way to *fight* it, Blaise. That's what I'm trying to tell you. I've got to find some way to try to live with it.' She looked at her cousin. 'OK?'

'You know it's not OK. You know it's completely not OK.'

'I guess what I mean is, OK, will you please not kill him or turn us in? Because I can't stand being in another fight with you. And I can't stop breaking the law.'

Blaise tossed the cream jar in the direction of the dresser. 'Thea, are you all right?' she said, seriously. 'Because you're acting very . . .'

'Fatalistic?'

'Fatalistic and generally scary.'

'I'm OK. I just . . . I don't know what's going to happen, but I am sort of . . . calm. I'm going to do my best. Eric's going to do his best. And beyond that, nothing's guaranteed.'

Blaise stared for another minute, her grey eyes searching Thea's face. Then she shook her head. 'I won't turn you in. You *know* I would never turn you in. We're sisters. And as for trying to kill him . . .' She shrugged, looking grim. 'It probably wouldn't work. That guy is impossible.'

'Thank you, Blaise.' Thea touched her cousin's arm lightly.

Blaise covered Thea's hand with her own red-nailed fingers, just for a moment. Then she sat back and straightened her pillows with a little jerk.

'Just don't *tell* me anything, all right? I wash my hands of you two and I don't want to know what's going on. Besides, I've got worries of my own. I have to decide between a Maserati and a Karmann Ghia.'

Halloween.

Thea looked out the window at the darkened world. There weren't any kids in the alley, but she knew they were flitting around the city. Goblins and ghosts and witches and vampires – all fakes. Real vampires were sitting inside at fireplaces, or maybe at exclusive parties, chuckling.

And real witches were getting dressed for their Samhain Circles.

Thea put on a white shift, sleeveless, made out of one piece of material. She pulled a soft white belt around her waist and made a loop pointing up with one side of the tie, then wrapped the other end around the base of the loop three times. A thet knot. Witches had used them for four thousand years.

She took a breath and looked outside again.

Enjoy the peace while you can, she told herself. It's going to be a busy night.

Eric's jeep pulled into the alley. The horn honked once.

Thea grabbed the backpack, which had been stuffed under her bed. It was full of materials. Oak, ash, quassia chips, blessed thistle, mandrake root. The hardened residue from the bronze bowl, which she had painstakingly scraped off with one of Blaise's art knives. A wooden seal, also carved with Blaise's tools. And an ounce vial with three precious drops of summoning potion stolen from the malachite bottle.

She started for the stairs.

'Hey, are you leaving already?' Blaise said, emerging

from the bathroom. 'You've got – what? – an hour and a half before Circle.'

Blaise looked gorgeous, and more herself than at any other time of year. Her shift was black, also sleeveless, also made in one piece. Her hair hung loose to her hips, woven with little bells. Her arms were pale and beautiful against the darkness of hair and shift, and she was barefoot, wearing one ankle bracelet.

'I'm going to run out and do something before Circle,' Thea said. 'Don't ask me what.'

Blaise of course didn't know what Thea and Eric were planning. Not even Dani knew. It was better that way.

'Thea . . .' Blaise stood at the top of the stairs and looked down as Thea dashed out. 'You be *careful*!'

Thea waved at her cousin.

The back of the jeep was full of wood.

'I thought I'd better bring some more, just in case we need it,' Eric said, throwing her backpack in. Then he added in a different voice, 'You look – amazing – like that.'

She smiled at him. 'Thanks. It's traditional. You look nice, too.'

He was wearing the costume of a seventeenth-century French soldier at Ronchain – or as close as they could get from looking at woodcuts in old books.

They drove into the desert, past the huge bare cliffs, off the main road and far out among the Joshua trees, until they found the place. It was tiny, just a dip in the ground almost enclosed in red sandstone pillars. The pillars didn't look like the monoliths at Stonehenge – they were knobby and squished sideways, like towers of Play-doh that some kid had smashed – but they served the same purpose.

They'd found this place all by themselves, and Thea was very proud of it.

'The fire's still going,' she said. 'That's good.'

It had been burning for the last three days inside the circle. Thea's hope had been that it would keep Suzanne interested – and away from the people setting up in the old gym. And it seemed to have worked.

Not just the fire, of course. The three dummies lying on the ground tied to stakes were supposed to be interesting, too.

'These guys all look OK,' Eric said. He picked up the smallest dummy and dusted it off. It looked something like a scarecrow when he thrust the stick into a hole in the ground, standing it up.

A scarecrow dressed in a black shift tied with a thet knot. With a sign hanging around the neck: LUCIENNE.

The other small dummy had a sign that said CLÉMENT. The big dummy's sign said SUZANNE.

'OK,' Thea said when they had unloaded the wood, leaving her backpack in the jeep. 'Now, remember, you don't do *anything* until I get back, right? Not anything. And if I'm a few minutes late, you just wait.'

He stopped nodding. 'The Halloween party starts at nine. If you're not here at nine exactly, I might—'

'*No*. Don't touch anything, don't do anything.'

'Thea, we might lose her. What if she decides that nothing's happening here, so she might as well go to the party—'

'I won't be late,' Thea said flatly. It seemed the only way to win the argument. 'But do *not* burn those witches before I'm here to cast the circle. OK?'

'Good luck,' he said.

He looked handsome and mysterious in his exotic clothes. Not like himself. They kissed under the half-full moon.

'Be safe,' Thea whispered, making herself let go of him.

'Come back safe,' he whispered. 'I love you.'

She drove the jeep back to the city, to the maidens' Circle Twilight meeting.

It was being held this year at a Night World club on the southern edge of town. There was no sign on the door, but the doormat, between two grinning jack-o'-lanterns, had been painted with a black dahlia.

Thea knocked and the door opened.

'Dani! You look great.'

'So do you,' Dani said. She was dressed in white, in a pleated sheer gown that hung to her ankles and looked Egyptian. Black braids clasped with silver cascaded from a sort of crown at her head, falling over her shoulders and back and arms. She made a beautiful Queen Isis. 'You didn't wear a costume,' she said, making it a question.

'Blaise and I are sort of going as Maya and Hellewise,' Thea said. The truth was that she was most comfortable in her ordinary Circle clothes, and that Blaise knew she looked best in *hers*.

'Well, come on down. You're the last one,' Dani said, taking Thea's hand.

They went down a flight of stairs to an underground room. It had a makeshift, thrown-together look, with crates to sit on, and white fairy lights strung between concrete pillars. Metal chairs had been pushed to the periphery.

'Thea! Hey, there! Merry meet!' people called. Thea turned around and around, smiling and getting hugs.

'Good Samhain,' she kept saying. 'Unity.'

For those few minutes, she forgot about what was going to happen tonight. It was so good to see them all again, all her friends from summer Circles.

Kishi Hirata, dressed as Amaterasu, the Japanese sun goddess, in gold and orange. Alaric Breedlove – the sophomore from Lake Mead High – as Tammuz the shepherd, son of the mother goddess Ishtar. Claire Blessingway as the Navajo goddess Changing Woman, in a dress decorated with red flower petals and turquoise. Nathaniel Long as Herne, Celtic god of the hunt, in forest green, with stag's antlers.

Humans put on costumes to disguise themselves tonight. Witches put on costumes to try to reflect their inner selves – what they were inside, what they wanted to be.

'Here, taste,' Claire said, handing Thea a paper cup. It was full of a thick red herb drink spiced with cinnamon and cloves. 'It's hibiscus – my dad's recipe.'

Someone else was passing around shortbread cakes in the shape of crescent moons. Thea took one. Everything here was so bright, so warm, and she would have been so happy if all she had to do tonight was enjoy it. Have a normal Samhain Circle. Celebrate . . .

But Eric was waiting out there in the dark and cold of the desert. And Thea was counting the minutes until she could leave.

'OK, people, it's time to get started.'

Lawai'a Ikua, a pretty, sturdy girl with hair like black nylon, was standing in the centre of the room. She was wearing a red shift and lei-Pele, the Hawaiian fire goddess, Thea guessed.

'Let's get our circle, here. That's good, come on. Chang Xi, you're the youngest now.'

A little girl with big almond-shaped eyes came shyly into the ring of people. Thea hadn't seen her before – she must have turned seven since the last summer Circle. She was dressed in jade green as Kuan Yin, the Chinese goddess of compassion.

Still shy, she took a sprig of broom – real broom, the plant – and swept the area inside the ring.

'Thea, you do the salt.'

Thea was surprised and pleased. She took the bowl of sea salt that Lawai'a offered, and walked slowly around the perimetre of the circle, sprinkling it.

'Alaric, you take the water—'

Lawai'a broke off, looking toward the stairway, seeming startled. Thea saw other people look. She turned around.

Two adults, mothers, were coming down the stairs. As the light shone on the first woman's face, Thea felt a jolt.

It was Aunt Ursula.

In a grey suit, her expression as bleak as Thea had ever seen it.

Nobody in the room made a noise. They all stood still as Joshua trees, watching until the women reached the bottom. Interrupting a Circle in the middle of casting was unheard of.

'Good Samhain,' Lawai'a said faintly.

'Good Samhain.' Aunt Ursula was polite, but she didn't smile. Like a displeased teacher. 'I'm very sorry to bother you, but this will only take a minute.'

Thea's heart had begun to pound, slow and hard.

It's just guilty conscience, she tried to tell herself. This doesn't *have* to be about you.

But it did. And something inside her knew even before Aunt Ursula looked the Circle over and said, 'Thea Sophia Harman.'

As if she doesn't know what I look like, Thea thought dazedly.

She clamped down hard on a wild impulse simply to brush past Aunt Ursula and head for the street. Now she knew why rabbits were so stupid as to leave a good hiding place and run blindly when a dog came near. Just panic, that's all.

She stepped away from a staring Kishi on her left and

a dismayed Nat on her right. She could feel every pair of eyes in the place on her.

'What is it?' she said, trying to look surprised.

Aunt Ursula's eyes met hers directly, as if to say, *You know*. But she didn't say anything, which was almost as bad.

'Dani Naete Mella Abforth.'

Oh, *Eileithyia*. Not Dani, too . . .

Dani was stepping out of the circle. Her small head was held proudly, but Thea could see the fear in her eyes. She walked, linen swaying around her ankles, to stand beside Thea.

Dani, I'm sorry . . .

'That's all,' Aunt Ursula said. 'The rest of you go on with your Circle. Good Samhain, everybody.' To Thea and Dani, she said, 'You need to come outside.'

They followed her silently. There was nothing else to do.

When they were out in the cool night air, Dani said, 'Is – something wrong?' She looked from Aunt Ursula to the other woman, who was short but had considerable presence.

And seemed familiar to Thea . . . and then she had it.

It's Nana Buruku. From the Inner Circle.

This isn't a Harman family matter. The Inner Circle itself is calling us.

'There are some things we need to talk about. Come on and let's get it all cleared up fast,' Nana Buruku said quietly, putting a cinnamon-coloured hand on Thea's arm. Gran's ancient Lincoln Continental was sitting at the curb. Nana Buruku took the wheel herself.

Dani and Thea held hands in the backseat. Dani's fingers were icy cold.

The car wound up and down streets lined with human

trick-or-treaters, to a big ranch-style house with high block walls screening the backyard. Selene's house, Thea realized, seeing the name Lucna on the mailbox.

It must be where they're having the maidens' Circle Midnight meeting.

Aunt Ursula got out. Thea and Dani sat in the car with Nana Buruku. In a few minutes, Aunt Ursula came back with Blaise.

Selene, dressed in silver, and Vivienne in black, followed as far as the driveway. They looked sober and scared, not like wicked witches at all.

Blaise did. Barefoot and apparently indifferent to the cold, little bells ringing, she looked flushed and angry and proud. She opened the door with a jerk and sat down hard beside Thea, who scooted over.

'What's going on?' she said, almost out loud. 'I'm missing the moon cakes, I'm missing *everything*. What kind of Samhain is this?'

Thea had never admired her more.

'We'll get back in time,' Dani said, and her voice was steady, even if her fingers were still cold.

They're both brave, Thea thought. And me? But however much she wanted to, she couldn't get a word out through the tightness in her throat.

She half expected Nana Buruku to get on the freeway and head out toward the desert, toward Thierry's land. But instead the Lincoln headed down familiar streets and pulled up in the alley behind Grandma Harman's store.

Thea could feel Dani's questioning eyes on her. But she had no idea what was going on, and she was afraid to look Dani in the face.

'Come on,' Aunt Ursula said, and shepherded them through the back door, into the shop, through the bead curtain that led to the workshop.

All the chairs for Gran's students had been pushed into a rough circle. People were sitting in them, or standing and talking quietly, but when Thea stepped through the curtain behind Nana Buruku, they all stopped and looked.

Thea's eyes moved from face to face, seeing each in a sort of disconnected, dreamlike flash. Grandma Harman, looking so grim and tired. Mother Cybele, who was *the* Mother of the Inner Circle, just as Gran was *the* Crone, looking anxious. Aradia, the Maiden, her lovely face serious and sad.

Others she recognized from two years ago, people who were so famous she knew them by their first names. Rhys, Belfana, Creon, Old Bob.

Aunt Ursula and Nana Buruku made up the last two of the nine.

They looked like ordinary people, working men and women and still-sharp-as-a-tack retired seniors, the kind you'd see any day on the street.

They weren't.

This was the biggest concentration of magical talent anywhere in the world. These people were the witch geniuses, the prodigies and the sages, the far-seers, the teachers, the policy-makers. They were the Inner Circle.

And they were all looking at Thea.

'The girls are here,' Mother Cybele said softly to Aradia. 'They're standing in the middle.'

Gran said, 'All right, let's get this thing started. Will everybody find themselves a seat.' It wasn't a question, it was an order. Gran was senior to all these celebrities.

But she wouldn't *look* at Thea. And that was the most terrible, nightmarish thing of all. She acted as if Thea and Blaise were strangers.

Everyone was sitting, nudging their chairs into a more evenly spaced circle. They were all wearing their ordinary clothes, Thea realized: business suits or uniforms or pants and tops. In Aradia's case, jeans. In Old Bob's case, dirty overalls.

Which means they never even started their own ceremony tonight. This is important enough to skip Samhain over.

This is a trial.

Red-haired Belfana pushed Creon's wheelchair to an empty spot. She was the last to sit down.

I'm centred, Thea thought numbly.

It was her worst fear, the very thing that had driven her away from Eric in the desert, the first time she'd felt the soulmate connection with him. And now it was *true*.

She could hear Dani breathing irregularly, and the faint tinkle of bells as Blaise shifted from foot to foot.

'All right,' Grandma Harman said, sounding tired but formal. 'By Earth, by Air, by Water, and by Fire, I call this Circle to unity.' She went on, reciting the age-old formula for a meeting of deliberation.

For Thea, the words blended into the pounding of blood in her ears. It was strange, how terrifying it could be to be surrounded in all directions by people. Everywhere she looked, another grave, unreadable face. She felt as trapped as if they had been humans.

'Thea Sophia Harman,' Gran said, and suddenly Thea was listening again. 'You stand accused . . .'

There seemed to be an endless, empty pause, although Thea knew it was probably no time at all.

'. . . of working forbidden spells in direct disobedience to the laws of Hellewise and of this Circle . . .'

All Thea heard for a while was *'working forbidden spells'*. It seemed to hang in the air, echoing. Part of her kept waiting to hear the other, more terrible charges of betraying the secrets of the Night World and falling in love with a human. But they didn't come.

'. . . summoning a spirit from the far places beyond the veil . . . binding two humans with a forbidden love charm . . .'

And then Gran was reading Blaise's name.

Blaise was charged with fashioning a necklace out of forbidden materials and binding humans with a forbidden charm. Dani was charged with aiding and abetting Thea in the summoning of a spirit from the far places – which was wrong, of course, Thea thought dizzily.

Her whole body was tingling, from the soles of her feet, to her palms, to her scalp. With fear . . . and with something like relief.

They don't know. They don't know the worst part of it, or they would have said so – wouldn't they? And if I just keep quiet, why should they ever know?

Then she focused on Gran, who had finished reading the charges and was now talking in an ordinary voice again. 'And I have to say that I'm disappointed in all three of you. Especially you, Thea. I'd expect this from *her*, of course' – she nodded at Blaise, speaking to the rest of the Circle – 'that descendant of mine there who's dressed up like Hecate's bad daughter. But I honestly thought Thea had more sense.'

She *looked* disappointed. And that hurt. Thea had always been the good girl, the golden girl, youngest and most promising of the Hearth-Woman line. Now, as she looked from face to face, she saw disappointment everywhere.

I've failed them; I've disgraced my heritage. I'm so ashamed . . .

She wanted to curl up and disappear.

Just then, there was a silvery ripple of bells. Blaise was tossing her dark head. She looked defiant and scornful and very proud and a little bored.

'What *I* want to know is who turned us in,' she said in an almost inaudible but definitely menacing whisper. 'Whoever it is, they're going to be *sorry*.'

And suddenly, somehow, Thea was less frightened. The disappointment didn't mean so much. It was possible to shock the Inner Circle and still be standing up. Blaise proved it.

It was then that irony struck Thea. She'd spent her life getting in trouble because of Blaise, and now here they were, in the worst trouble imaginable – because of her.

And Dani was in trouble, too. Her velvety eyes were filled with tears. When she saw *that*, Thea found the tightness in her throat easing. She could talk again.

'Look, excuse me, but there's something you need to know. Before this goes any further—'

'You'll have a chance to speak later,' Mother Cybele said, her voice soft and firm, like her little dumpling-shaped body.

'No, I have to say it now.' Thea turned to Gran, speaking, for just these few seconds, to her grandmother rather than to the Crone of the Inner Circle. 'Grandma, Dani shouldn't be here. Really. *Really*. She didn't know anything about the summoning; I did it all. I *promise*.'

Gran's expression gentled slightly, the creases on her face shifting. Then she was impassive again.

'All right, all right, we'll see about that later. The first thing is to find out just what *you've* been doing. Since you seem to be the instigator here.'

It was when she said 'later' that realization hit Thea like a tsunami. And everything changed.

Later . . . time . . . *what time is it?*

She looked frantically around for the clock. There – behind Old Bob's grey head . . .

Ten minutes to ten.

Eric.

Somehow, in the stress she'd felt since Aunt Ursula came to get her, she had completely forgotten that he was waiting in the desert.

But now she could *see* him, the vision in her mind's eye as clear as if she were standing there with him. Eric watching the clock, minutes going by, and Thea still not arriving. Eric looking at the bonfire and at the three black-clothed dummies tied to their stakes.

And the party. The Halloween party at school. Blistered metal doors being opened and people flooding in. Shoes walking across the scuffed wooden floor, costumed kids standing underneath the dangling witch figures. Kids shrieking with laughter, handing over goblin money, crowding into the torture booths.

While something lurked around the exposed pipes on the ceiling. Maybe invisible, maybe looking like a white figure and feeling like a blast of arctic wind. Maybe like a woman with long mahogany hair.

Lurking . . . then suddenly sweeping down . . .

She's going to *kill* them. They're completely defenceless . . .

Fear tore into Thea like jagged metal.

It was all happening right now, and she wasn't doing anything to stop it. It had been happening for almost an hour, and she hadn't even given it a thought.

CHAPTER

15

'Thea.' Dani was shaking her arm. 'They're *talking* to you.'

The visions were gone. Thea was standing in Gran's workshop, seeing everything as if through a distorting lens. People's faces seemed to stretch; their voices seemed to drag.

'I *asked*, how did you learn the invocation for summoning spirits?' Gran said slowly.

Eric. He won't wait; he'll start without me. Or will he? I told him not to. But he'll be worrying about the party . . .

The party. All those kids . . . even *little* kids. Humans, but *people*. Like baby chicks with a hawk up above. How many of them will end up like Kevin?

'The invocation for summoning spirits!' Gran was shouting, as if Thea were hard of hearing.

'I . . . we . . . *I* heard you at Samhain two years ago. In Vermont. I saw the summoning the Inner Circle did.' Even her own voice sounded weird and distorted.

'*We* saw you. Both of us. We were hiding behind the trees and you never even noticed,' Blaise said clearly, and the bells rang again.

Dimly, Thea felt appreciation. But most of her mind

was reeling from horrible thought to thought.

Eric . . . but if I try to get to him, if the Inner Circle finds out he's involved . . . *that* will get him killed. A human who knows about the Night World. Immediate death sentence.

But Suzanne. If he burns those dummies, Suzanne will kill him the way she killed Kevin.

No matter what happened, Eric was going to end up dead.

Unless . . .

'Which . . . of the spirits . . . did you call?' Gran was shouting, as if Thea was now not only hard of hearing but slow of understanding.

Unless . . .

'That's what I want to tell you,' Thea said.

She could see the way. It would mean the end for her, but she might possibly save Eric. If there was enough time, if they would let her alone, if Eric wasn't right now trying to be a hero . . .

'I *want* to tell you about it,' Thea said again. And then the words were tumbling out in a rush, faster and faster, as if some dam had broken inside her. 'And I'll tell you everything, but *please*, Grandma, *please*, you have to let me go out now. Just for a little while. There's something I have to do. You *have* to let me go, and then I'll come back here and you can do whatever you want to me.'

'Hold on a minute,' Mother Cybele said, but Thea couldn't stop.

'Please, *please*, Grandma. I've done a terrible thing – and I'm the only one who can take care of it. I'll come back—'

'Wait, wait, wait. Calm down,' Gran said. She looked agitated herself. 'What's this rush all of sudden? Try it slowly. What do you think you have to do?'

'I have to put her *back*.' Thea saw that she was going to have to give some explanation. She tried to speak clearly and slowly, to make them understand. 'The spirit I let out, Grandma. Her name is Suzanne Blanchet and she was burned in the sixteen hundreds. And she's out, out *there*, and she's already killed a human.'

Everyone was listening now, some leaning forward, some frowning. Thea looked around at the circle of faces, talking to all of them. She was still terrified, but what did that matter? Eric mattered.

'Last week she killed a boy at my high school. And tonight she's going to kill more people, at the high school Halloween party. I can't explain how I know – there isn't *time*. But I do know. And I'm the only one who can stop her. I called her; I'm the only one who can put her back.'

'Yes, but unfortunately it's not that easy,' a low voice said. Thea turned and identified Rhys, a wiry man in a white lab coat. 'If the spirit's at large—'

'I know about that, but I have a way to trap her. It's all set up, and I . . .' Thea hesitated. 'I've tricked somebody into helping me,' she said slowly. 'And he's in danger right now. Which is why you have to let me go, let me take care of this. *Please*.'

'You want to go to the high school, where the party is,' Aunt Ursula said. Although her lips were as thin as ever, she didn't sound angry. More – astute.

Thea opened her mouth to say no, and then stopped, confused again.

The party – or the desert? If Suzanne was really killing people at the party, she should go there. But only if Eric wasn't doing something to attract Suzanne to the desert. He was still more important to her than anyone else. But if he *wasn't* doing something – and if Suzanne was at the party – she might kill before Thea and Eric could lure her . . .

I'm going crazy.

She felt, literally, as if she might faint. Her head was swimming. There were too many possibilities. It all depended on where Suzanne was right now, and there was no way to know that.

Thea began to shake violently, black dots dancing in front of her eyes.

I don't know what to do.

'I'm sorry . . . could everybody listen for a moment? I'm seeing something.'

It was Aradia's voice, quiet and gently self-possessed. Mature, even though she was only a little older than Thea. Thea tried to see her through the black dots.

'I think it's something important, something about what we're talking about,' Aradia said. Her beautiful face, with its smooth skin the colour of coffee with cream, was turned toward Thea. Her wide brown eyes looked straight ahead without focus, the way they always did.

Aradia couldn't see with those eyes – but then she didn't need to. She saw with her mind – and saw things that were hidden to most people.

'I'm seeing a boy, he's dressed in some old-fashioned costume. He's beside a fire, inside a circle of stones.'

Eric . . .

'He's got a stick – an ember. He's looking around. Now he's going to . . . it looks like a scarecrow. I can't see it well. There's a pile of sticks underneath it. He's bending. He's lighting the sticks.'

No.

'I have to go,' Thea said. She wasn't asking permission anymore.

Aradia was still speaking. 'OK, the sticks are catching

fire. Now I can see better . . . and it's not a scarecrow; it looks sort of like a witch. A doll.' She stopped, her lovely blind eyes widening. 'It's – and it's moving – no, there's something moving it. I can see it now – a spirit. A spirit is moving the doll. It's coming out now – toward the boy—'

'I have to go,' Thea said. And then she was moving, pushing her way between Rhys and Old Bob, breaking out of the circle. The beads of the curtain struck her face, clattering as they fell back behind her.

'Thea, wait a minute!'

'Thea, come back here!'

'Ursula, you go get her—'

The jeep. My backpack's in the *jeep*. I have to get it first.

The keys to the Lincoln were hanging on a nail by the back door. Thea grabbed them.

She pushed the back door open just as three or four people came hurrying through the bead curtain. She slammed the door in their faces.

Get to the car. *Fast*. Now drive.

She backed out of the alley, tyres squealing. She could see light spill as the door to the shop opened, but by then she was turning onto Barren Street.

Eric . . .

She found herself driving at some new level, squeezing through the tail end of yellow lights, recognizing shortcuts in the dark. In just a few minutes she was at the Night World club with the jack-o'-lanterns on the porch.

There was no place to park the Lincoln. She left it in the middle of the street, with the keys still in the ignition. She pulled the key to the jeep out of her belt and jumped in.

Hurry. Hurry. She burned rubber again getting the jeep moving.

Hurry. The freeway.

Eric . . .

Just let me get to him. And let it not be too late. That's all I ask, after that I don't care.

Would you give up everything?

The voice didn't seem like a stranger this time, didn't seem menacing. Just curious. And Thea had an answer.

Yes.

If I can just get there, in time, I can send him away. I can tell him some story, make him go somehow. Make him hide. I'll tell the Circle I tricked him or enchanted him into helping; I won't even tell them his name. They can't make me.

Whatever they do to me, he'll be safe. That's all I care about. That's all I'm asking.

But even that was a lot, and she knew it, so she kept her foot mashed down on the gas pedal.

Freeway off ramp. Side road.

She drove crazily fast. The pounding inside her head kept saying hurry, hurry, even as she was careening off curbs.

Desert.

Now the road was bad. It was hard to see; the moon was almost down. The jeep lunged over bumps and lurched into potholes.

Eric, be doing something. Be talking to her, be running. You're so smart, please, please, be smart now. Keep her distracted, keep her hair away from your neck.

How strong was a spirit? Thea didn't know.

Please, I see everything so clearly now. I've been selfish, only thinking of me, what would make me happy. All that 'encased in ice' garbage. I should have been dancing in the street. As long as Eric is all right, I don't care if he lives on Mars, I don't care if I never see him again. As long as he's well I'm happier than anybody has a right to be.

A jolt rattled her teeth. She was off the road now, driving by landmarks. Through forests of dead yuccas that looked like skinny grey Cousin Its.

It's taking so long, it's too long. Hurry. *Hurry*.

She could see red sandstone in front of her. Pillars in the headlights.

That's it! Go, go!

The jeep rocketed over clumps of blackbrush. She could see fire in the depression between the pillars. She drove straight toward it.

Fire – movement – the top of a silhouette . . .

'Eric!'

She was yelling even as she slammed on the brakes. The jeep ground to a shuddering stop a few inches from a misshapen sandstone tower.

'Eric!' She had the backpack in her hand. She tore the door open and jumped out, running.

'Thea! Stay out of here!'

She saw him.

The light of the fire cast an eerie glow onto the already lurid sandstone. Everything seemed red, as if this place were bathed in blood. The roar of the jeep's engine and the roar of the fire merged to sound like the flames of hell.

But Eric was alive and fighting. Fighting *it*.

Thea threw herself at it, even as her brain was registering impressions.

A wraith shape that looked at one second like a woman, and the next second like tattered clouds. Part of it seemed to be coiled around Eric, and he had both hands at his throat. Bits of the pine-needle amulet Thea had made for him were scattered around his feet. Useless.

'Get away from him! I'm the one who set this up!' Thea screamed. She reached Eric and grabbed wildly at the wraith, at the part of it around his throat. Her hands felt Eric's hands, felt cold air.

'No, Thea, watch out—'

She saw the thing come free of Eric, who staggered. She saw it reform, gather, then dive straight for her.

'Thea!' Eric knocked her sideways. Cold air rushed by. She and Eric fell in a heap.

She gasped, 'Eric, go,' even before she got up. She tried to shove at him, looking around for the wraith. 'Go, get out of here! The jeep's running – get in and just *drive*. I'll call you later.'

'Stay back to back,' Eric said breathlessly. 'She's incredibly fast.' He added through his teeth, 'You know I'm not leaving.'

'This is witch stuff, you jerk!' she snarled, standing back to back. 'I don't *want* you. You'll just get in my way!'

It was a valiant effort. She even managed to inject something like hatred into her voice. And Eric wasn't perfect. He turned around, grabbed her by the shoulder, and yelled, '*You know I'm not going, so don't waste any more time!*'

Then he shoved her sideways again and freezing wind streaked by her cheek, leaving her ear numb.

'Sorry,' he said in his normal voice. 'You OK?'

Thea spun and looked behind her. The wraith was bobbing there. It was shaped like a woman made of vapour, with arms and legs only suggested, but with a long tail of hair that whipped around.

'I've got the stuff,' Thea muttered to Eric. Admitting she knew he'd never leave. 'But it'll take a few minutes to do the spell. We'll have to keep out of—'

She was watching the lashing tail, but she wasn't fast enough. There was a sound, something between the snap of a whip and the crackle of electricity, and the tail flashed out. It was around her neck.

At first it just felt cold. Insubstantial but icy, like a scarf of sub-zero wind. But then the wraith gave a jerk and it tightened and it *did* have substance. It felt like metal, like a pipe full of supercooled liquid, like the tentacle of some alien creature with ice for blood. It was choking her.

She couldn't breathe and she couldn't get her fingers under it. It squeezed tighter, hurting her. She could feel her eyes start to bulge.

'Look at me!' Eric yelled. He had a stick that was blazing at one end and he was dancing up and down like a crazy person on the other side of the fire. 'Look! Suzanne! I'm going to get your little sister!' He poked the burning stick at the dummy Lucienne, not at the wood piled around her, but at the actual doll.

'There! There! How do you like that?' He jabbed at the doll. A ring of fire blossomed in the black clothes. 'Confess you're a witch!'

Thea felt something slide away and her neck was free.

She tried to shout a warning to Eric, but all that came out was a croak. He was already diving to one side anyway.

That must be what he's been doing all this time. Dodging.

'Eric, keep it up!'

'OK, but work fast!' He threw himself the other way.

She forced herself to turn her attention from him. Her backpack was at the edge of the circle where she'd dropped it. She grabbed it and dumped the contents out on the ground.

She had to do this right and she had to do it faster than she'd ever worked a spell before.

Oak and ash. She threw them on the central fire, then scooted toward it, dragging the other materials close with a sweep of her arm.

She ripped open a plastic bag and grabbed the quassia chips. They were light, and she had to thrust her hand into the flames to make sure they actually went in the fire. Blessed thistle was powder; she threw it. Mandrake root was solid, she threw it, too.

She had just grabbed the ounce vial when Eric shouted, 'Thea, *duck*.'

She didn't look up to see what she was ducking. She fell flat instantly. It saved her. Icy wind blew her hair almost into the fire.

'Suzanne!' Eric was yelling. 'I've got your brother! Look!'

There were fires at all three stakes now, and Eric was dashing between them, poking at one figure after another.

Thea pulled the plastic cap off the vial with her teeth. She shook it into the fire, her hand in the flames again.

One, two, *three*.

The fire roared up, louder than ever, and pure blue. Thea fell back from it.

'Suzanne! Over here!' Eric's voice was faint beyond the roar.

Tears were running down Thea's face, her nose and eyes stinging from the acrid smell. She fumbled for the last object necessary for the sending-back ... the bag of residue from the bronze bowl. She took a handful in her left hand and dropped it between two charcoaled logs at the edge of the fire.

Then she stood up – and saw that Eric was in trouble.

He'd lost his burning stick. The wraith had him by the throat and it was whirling him around, changing shape every second. His mouth was open, but Thea couldn't hear any sound.

'May I be given the Power of the Words of Hecate!'

She *screamed* it, into the roaring fire, toward the wheeling, changing spirit shape.

And the words came, rolling off her tongue with a power of their own:

'From the heart of the flame ... I send you back! Through the narrow path ... I send you back!'

She put all her own power into the words, too, screaming them with an authority that she'd never felt in herself before. Because the wraith was *fighting*. It didn't want to go anywhere.

'To the airy void ... I send you back! Through the mist of years ... I send you back!'

Eric staggered, was jerked sideways. He seemed to be lifted off his feet by the wraith.

'To beyond the veil ... I send you back! Go speedily, conveniently, and without delay!'

Eric's feet were kicking in the air. This is how Kevin died, Thea realized suddenly and with absolute certainty.

She found herself yelling words she'd never heard before. 'By the power of Earth and Air and Water! By the power of Fire on this night of Hecate! By my own power as a daughter of Hellewise! *Go speedily, conveniently and without delay, you bitch!*'

She had no idea where *that* came from. But the next instant Eric fell. The wraith had dropped him.

It shot toward Thea – but then it stopped as if it had slammed into an invisible brick wall. It was directly over the fire.

Caught.

The blue flames were belching smoke – but sideways. Thea could see the wraith clearly above them. And for the first time, it didn't look like a cloud shape. It looked like a woman.

A girl. Older than Thea, but still in her teens. With long dark hair that floated around her and a pale face and huge sad eyes. Her lips were parted as if she were trying to speak.

Thea stared. She heard herself whisper, 'Suzanne . . .'

The girl held out a pale hand toward her. But at the same moment the fire flared up again. It seemed to turn the girl's hair to fire, too. Dark fire was burning all around her and there was an expression of infinite sadness on her face.

Thea reached out a hand instinctively—

The fire roared—

And there was a flash like lightning.

Suzanne had been drawn to the heart of the flame. And now the lightning formed a cone: the narrow path.

Plastic bags and other debris whipped around the circle as if caught in a whirlwind.

Suzanne and the cone of white lightning disappeared into each other.

To the airy void. Through the mist of years.

The fire flared up above Thea's head, and then sank down. The blue seemed to fall to the bottom. The flames turned yellow, like ordinary fire.

It was as if a curtain had been drawn.

To beyond the veil.

That was where Suzanne was now.

At the edge of the bonfire, where the residue had been, there was a lump of soft clay. Thea knelt and picked it up. She looked into the centre of the flames – and saw a coil of long hair, the colour of mahogany. The ends were starting to blacken and shrink in the fire.

Thea reached in to grab it. She folded the hair over and quickly pressed the clay around it. It was a clumsy job, Blaise would have done much better, but the hair was enclosed. She groped on the ground for the wooden seal, found it, punched it into the clay. Suzanne's symbol, the cabalistic sign for her name, was printed.

It was done.

The amulet was restored, Suzanne was trapped again. She'd stay where she belonged unless somebody else was stupid enough to summon her.

Thea dropped the amulet without looking at it, got up, and staggered around the fire to where Eric was lying. Her vision was strangely grey.

After all this . . . he *has* to be all right . . . oh, please, let him be . . .

He moved when she reached him.

'Eric, we did it. She's gone. *We did it.*'

He grinned faintly. Said in a scratchy voice, 'You don't have to cry.'

She hadn't realized she was.

Eric sat up. He was terminally mussed, his hair wild, his face dirty. He looked wonderful to her.

'We did it,' she whispered again. She reached out to smooth his hair, and her hand stayed there.

He glanced at the fire, then back at her. 'I kind of hated to say those things to her. I mean, no matter how bad she was . . .' He touched Thea's neck, stroking gently. 'Are you OK? I think you've got a bruise.'

'Me? You're the one who really got it.' She put her free hand to his throat, fingers just barely touching. 'But I know what you mean,' she whispered. 'I felt – sorry – for her at the end.'

'Don't cry again. Please. I really hate that,' he whispered, and he put *his* free arm around her.

And then they were just kissing madly. Deliriously. Laughing and kissing and holding each other. She could taste her own tears on his lips, warming with his warmth, and she was trembling like a bird in a thicket.

A few moments later a noise broke in. Thea didn't want

to move, but Eric looked, and then he stiffened.

'Uh, we've got company.'

Thea looked up.

There were cars just outside the sandstone pillars. Parked cars. They must have driven up sometime during the fight with Suzanne, while the roar of the fire blocked out the sound of their engines, while Thea's attention was focused on the wraith trying to kill her.

Because the people were already out of the cars. Grandma Harman, supported by Aunt Ursula. Rhys in his lab coat. Dumpling-shaped Mother Cybele, with her hand on Aradia's arm. Old Bob, Nana Buruku.

Most of the Inner Circle was here.

CHAPTER

16

Thea started to let go of Eric. She could still try to save him.

But *he* wouldn't let go. And her own instincts told her to hold on to him.

They stood up together, holding each other, facing the Inner Circle as a unit.

'Well,' Mother Cybele said, blinking rapidly. 'Aradia brought us here thinking you might need help. But you've taken care of things yourselves. We saw the end, very impressive.'

'I saw it, too,' Aradia said. Her face was turned toward Thea, the faintest trace of a smile on her lips. 'You did a good job, Thea Harman. You're a true Hearth-Woman.'

'Yes, and where did that last invocation come from?' Gran said, shifting her weight to the cane Rhys gave her. 'I've never in my life heard of anybody calling on their own power as a daughter of Hellewise.' She said it in a grumbling way, but Thea had the strange feeling that she was almost pleased.

Thea faced them all, Maiden, Mother, and Crone of the Inner Circle. She was still holding Eric. 'I don't know where it came from,' she said, and was glad to hear that her voice wasn't shaking too badly. 'It just . . . came.'

'And what about you? What's your name, young man?' Gran said.

'Eric Ross.' Thea was proud of the way he said it, quiet and respectful, but not cowed.

Gran looked from him to Thea. And back again.

'You're in this with my granddaughter?'

'He doesn't know anything . . .' Thea began, but of course that was hopeless. And ridiculous.

'I know I love Thea,' Eric said, cutting her off. 'And she loves me. And if there's some rule that says we can't be together, it's a stupid rule.'

He sounded terribly brave and terribly young. Thea felt a wave of dizziness. Her fingers tightened on his until both their hands were shaking from the pressure. She realized for the first time that her right hand was fairly seriously burned.

'Please let him go, Grandma,' she whispered. And then, as Gran stood silent, 'Please . . . I won't ever see him again and he won't ever tell. All he's done is try to help me, try to save lives. *Please* don't punish him for what's my fault.' Warmth pooled in her eyes and spilled over.

'He tried to uphold the law,' Aradia said. 'At least, I think so.'

Thea wasn't sure she'd heard right. Gran didn't seem to be, either. She said, 'How's that?'

'Hellewise said it's forbidden for witches to kill humans, didn't she?' Aradia asked, her face serene. 'Well, that spirit was a witch who'd already killed a human – and who wanted to kill more. And he helped send her back. He helped Thea undo the forbidden spell, and he helped prevent witch law from being broken again.'

Rhys muttered, 'Neatly put,' but Thea couldn't tell whether that meant he agreed or not.

Gran shuffled a step forward, looking at Eric. 'And just what did you do to help, young man?'

'I don't know if I *did* help,' Eric said in his quiet, straightforward way. 'Mainly I just tried to keep her from killing me—'

'When did you light the fires?' Thea asked in an undertone, still clutching his hands.

He glanced at her. One side of his mouth quirked slightly.

'Nine o'clock,' he said.

'Even though I wasn't there.' Thea's voice was just slightly louder now. 'And you knew Suzanne would come and try to get you, and you didn't have any magic to fight her. So why did you do it?'

He looked at her, then at Gran. Then at her. 'You know why. Because otherwise she'd have gone over to the party.'

'And killed more people.' Thea looked at Gran.

Gran was staring at Eric, her dark old eyes very keen. 'So you saved lives.'

'I don't know,' Eric said again, maddeningly honest. 'But I didn't want to take the chance.'

'He saved my life, too,' Thea said. 'Suzanne tried to kill me. And I could never have gotten through the spell to send her back if he hadn't kept her distracted.'

'That's nice, but I'm not sure it's enough,' Old Bob said, running a hand over his stubbly chin. His weathered face was quizzical. 'There's nothing that says upholding one law makes up for breaking another. Especially Night World law. We could get in a mess of trouble fooling with that.'

Gran and Mother Cybele looked at each other. Then Gran turned to Old Bob.

'I changed your diapers – don't tell me you know more about Night World law,' she snapped. 'I'm not about to let a bunch of bloodthirsty vampires dictate to me.' She looked at the others. 'We need to take this somewhere private. Let's go back to my place.'

Somewhere private. Hope kept racing giddily through Thea as the jeep bounced and rattled home.

Eric was driving, and Thea was in the backseat, so they couldn't talk. Aunt Ursula was in the front beside Eric.

Gran's fighting for me. And Aradia, and maybe even Mother Cybele. They don't want me to die. I don't think they even want Eric to die.

But reality kept trying to push the hope away.

What can they do? They can't condone a witch and a human being together. They can't risk war with the rest of the Night World, not even to save me.

There's no solution.

The little caravan pulled up the back alley behind Gran's store.

And then Thea was in the workshop again, in the circle of chairs. Creon and Belfana had been waiting. So had Blaise and Dani, who were both sitting down.

'Are you OK?' Dani began, standing – and then she shut up. She was looking at Eric, her dark, velvety eyes huge. A human in the Circle.

'We put Suzanne back,' Thea said simply. She took Eric's hand again.

The Inner Circle reformed around the two of them, witch and human, standing centred.

'We have a situation,' Gran said. And she explained even though most of them already understood the problem. She did it thoroughly, looking at each of the Circle members in turn. Aradia and Mother Cybele sat on either side of her, occasionally putting in a thoughtful remark.

Thea figured it out in a few minutes. Gran was recruiting each of them, appealing to them – and showing that the Mother and Maiden both agreed with her. She was working them all over to her side.

'And the end result is, we've got these two,' she said at last. 'And we have to decide what to do with them. This is a decision for the Inner Circle, for the daughters and sons of Hellewise. *Not* for the Night World Council,' she added, looking at Old Bob.

He ran a hand through rough grey hair and muttered, 'The Council might not see it just that way,' But he smiled.

'There was a time,' Gran said, 'when witches and humans got along better than they do now. I'm sure anybody who's gone far enough back with their family tree knows that.'

Eric looked at Thea, who shook her head and looked at Blaise.

'She means,' Mother Cybele put in, 'that we used to take human husbands, a long time ago. To make up for the fact that there have never been enough witch men. That was back in the days when there was still the third Circle, Circle Daybreak. The one that tried to teach magic to humans.'

'Until humans started burning us,' Belfana said, her freckled face grave under its coil of deep red hair.

'Well, *this* one isn't likely to burn anybody,' Aunt Ursula said acidly. At that moment, Thea loved her.

'Nobody is arguing that the laws should be changed,' Mother Cybele said, putting her plump fingers together. 'We can't go back to those days, and we all know the danger from humans now. The question is, is there any way to make an exception in this one case?'

'I don't see how,' Rhys said slowly. 'Not without all of us ending up accused of treason.'

'It'll be the Night Wars all over again,' Nana Buruku added. 'Each race of Night People against the others.'

'I don't wish them harm,' Creon said from his wheelchair, his cracked voice barely audible. 'But they can't live in our world, and they can't live in the human world.'

And that, Thea thought, sums it up perfectly. There is no place for us. Not while one of us is witch and the other is human . . .

The idea came in a single flash, like the lightning from the balefire.

So simple. And yet so terrifying.

It might work . . .

But if it did, could I stand it?

Would you give up everything?

Everything, including Gran and Blaise. Dani and Lawai'a and Cousin Celestyn. Uncle Galen, Aunt Gerdeth, Aunt Ursula . . . Selene and Vivienne, everybody at Circle Twilight.

The smell of herbs, lavender mixed with rose petals. The kiss of cool stones in her palm. Every chant, every invocation . . . all the spells she'd learned. The feel of magic flowing through her fingertips. Even the memory of Hellewise . . .

Hellewise in her white shift, in the dark forest . . .

Would you give up everything . . . for peace?

For Eric?

This time the inner voice was her own. She found herself looking at Eric and knowing she already had her answer.

He was so good, so dear. Tender but intense. Smart and brave and honest and insightful . . . and loving.

He loves me. He was willing to die for me.

He'd give up everything.

Eric was watching her, his grey-flecked eyes concerned.

He could tell that something was going on with her.

Thea smiled at him. And was so proud to see that even now, surrounded by people who must seem like figures from some horrible legend to him, he could give her a wry half-smile back.

'I have an idea,' she said to Gran and the Inner Circle. 'The Cup of Lethe.'

There was a silence. People looked at each other. Gran was startled.

'Not just for him,' Thea said. 'For me.'

Long breaths quietly drawn in the silence.

Gran shut her eyes.

'If I drank enough, I'd forget everything,' Thea forged on, talking to all the grave faces. 'Everything about the Night World. I wouldn't be a witch anymore, because I wouldn't remember who I am.'

'You'd become a lost witch,' Aradia said. Her lovely face was calm, not appalled. 'Like the psychics who don't know their heritage. And lost witches can live with humans.'

'And neither of us would remember about the Night World,' Thea said. 'So how could we be breaking any laws?'

'The law would be satisfied,' Aradia said.

Eric's hand tightened on Thea's. 'But—'

She looked at him. 'It's the only way for us to be together.'

He shut his mouth.

This silence was very long.

Then Blaise, who had been standing with crossed arms, watching, said, 'She told *me* they were soulmates.'

For an instant, Thea thought she was saying it spitefully, to harm.

But Gran was turning in surprise. 'Soulmates. That's a

notion I haven't heard in a while.'

'An archaic myth,' Rhys said, shifting in his lab coat.

'Maybe not,' Mother Cybele said softly. 'Maybe the old powers are waking up again. Maybe they're trying to tell us something.'

Gran looked down at the floor. When she looked back at Thea, there were tears in her fierce dark eyes. And for the first time since Thea had known her, those eyes looked truly old.

'If we did let you do this,' she said, 'if we let you renounce your heritage and walk away from us . . . where would you go?'

It was Eric who answered. 'With me,' he said simply. 'My mom and my sister already love her. And my mom knows she's an orphan. If I tell her Thea can't stay here anymore – well, she'd take her in, no questions.'

'I see,' Gran said. Eric hadn't mentioned that his mom already thought Thea was living in an unstable home with an unbalanced old lady, but Thea had the feeling Gran knew.

Another pause, as Gran looked around the Circle. Finally, she nodded and let out a breath. 'I think the girl's given us a way out,' she said. 'Does anybody disagree?'

No one spoke. Most of the faces were pitying. They think it's a fate worse than death, Thea realized.

Blaise said suddenly, 'I'll get the Cup.'

She clashed through the bead curtain.

Good. It's *good* to get it over with, Thea thought. Her heart was pounding wildly. She and Eric were holding hands so tightly that her burned fingers stung.

'It won't hurt,' she whispered to him. 'We'll be sort of confused . . . but it should come back to us . . . except anything about magic.'

'You can transfer into zoology,' he said. 'And go to

Davis.' He was smiling, but his eyes were full.

Dani stepped forward. 'Can I . . . I'd just like to say goodbye.' She got through that much steadily. Then she choked and threw herself into Thea's arms.

Thea hugged back. 'I'm sorry I got you in trouble,' she whispered.

'You didn't, you told them it wasn't my fault. They're not going to do anything to me. But it's going to be so lonely at school without you . . .' Dani stepped away, shaking her head, trying not to cry. 'Blessed be.'

Blaise was back, little bells ringing. She had a pewter chalice in one hand and a bottle in the other.

Just seeing the bottle sent a shiver through Thea. The glass was so dark with age she couldn't tell what colour it had been originally, and so misshapen it was hard to know if it was meant to be round or square. There was wax over the cork and all sorts of seals and ribbons.

Gran broke through the seals, pulled off the ribbons. She tried to twist the cork out of the wax, but Blaise had to help.

Then she tipped the bottle above the cup Blaise held.

Brownish liquid ran out. Gran poured until the cup was half full.

'When you drink this,' Gran said to Thea, 'you'll forget me. You won't know anyone here. But we won't forget you.' She spoke formally, an announcement before the Circle. 'Thea Sophia Harman, let the record show that you are a true daughter of Hellewise.'

She shuffled forward and kissed Thea's cheek.

Thea hugged her, feeling the fragile old body for the last time. 'Goodbye, Gran. I love you.'

Then Blaise came, offering the cup in both hands. She looked wild and beautiful, her hair a cataract of black tumbling around her, her hands pale around the chalice.

'Goodbye,' Thea said, and took it from her.

Blaise smiled.

Now, Thea told herself. Don't hesitate. Don't *think* about it.

She lifted the cup to her lips and drank.

And choked slightly on the first swallow. It was – it tasted like . . .

Her eyes went to Blaise's.

Which were large and grey and luminous. They looked at her steadily. So steadily that it was a warning.

Thea kept drinking.

Tea. Watered-down iced tea. *That* was what the Cup of Lethe tasted like.

That bottle was sealed – she didn't have time – there was wax on the cork . . .

Thea's mind was churning. But she had enough sense to do one thing – she drank a *lot* of whatever was in the cup, so there wouldn't be any left over for the Circle to examine when Eric was done.

And she kept her face blank as Blaise took the chalice from her and gave it to Eric.

Eric drank, looked slightly surprised, and kept drinking.

'Finish it *allll*,' Blaise said. Her eyes were still on Thea's.

And that was when Thea knew for sure.

You did it before, when you were first talking about giving human boys the Cup of Lethe after spilling their blood at the Homecoming dance. You poured it out and stashed it somewhere and put in tea and redid all those seals – of course *you* could reproduce them with moulds. And now . . . and now . . .

As Blaise took the chalice back from Eric, it hit Thea in a wave that almost made her hysterical.

This is never going to work. They're never going to *believe* it. But . . .

Thea took Eric's hand and sank her nails into his palm. She didn't dare say a word to him, didn't dare even look at him. But she was thinking, don't speak, don't do *anything*, just follow my lead.

She made her face as blank as a wax doll.

Eric was just standing there. He didn't know what to expect, but he obviously felt Thea's nails. And he proved how smart he was by not speaking.

'We stand adjourned,' Gran said tersely. 'Blaise, take them out while they're still confused. They should be able to get home on their own.' She turned away without looking at Thea.

'No problem,' Blaise said.

Aradia said, 'I'll go with you.'

CHAPTER

17

They walked out to Eric's jeep. The night air was very cold and there was no moon.

Thea kept her hand on Eric's back, ready to press if he hesitated. But he never did.

At the door of the jeep, Thea looked at Blaise. She was afraid to show any expression. Could Aradia see them? She wanted desperately to give Blaise a last hug.

Aradia said, 'Is there a window from the shop onto this street?'

Thea looked at Blaise. Blaise said, 'No.'

'Then you can say goodbye. After this you're going to have to pretend not to know each other.'

Thea stared at her, then felt a wild choked giggle well up. 'Now I know why you're Maiden,' she said, in a bare whisper. 'But, does anyone else realize?'

'I don't think so. Some may wonder, but I think they'll keep their mouths shut. Say goodbye quick.'

Thea hugged Blaise, couldn't make herself let go. 'Thank you. Oh, Eileithyia, Blaise, I'll miss you.'

'Now *I'm* the last of the Harman line,' Blaise said in a bad imitation of a smirking voice. 'I'll have a bedroom to myself,' she added in more believable tones. 'And I'm going to get Sheena good.'

'Who?'

'That's right, you didn't hear. She was the one who turned us in. She's one of Tobias's little girlfriends, Circle Midnight. It seems he's been spying on us. He told her enough that she understood we were doing forbidden spells, and she told Gran.'

'It doesn't matter now.'

'Are you kidding? I'm getting sent to the Convent. I'm going to *kill* her.' The bells rang as Blaise tossed her head.

Then she tightened her grip on Thea. 'I don't know why you want to be with a human,' she whispered. 'But I hope you keep on wanting it now that you have it.'

'Blaise, when you get back – please don't hurt them anymore. They're people. Really.'

Blaise sighed noncommittally; Thea could feel it. But all she said, almost too softly for Thea to hear, was, 'I'll miss you, sister.'

Then Thea could let go.

When she was in the jeep, Aradia leaned into the open door.

'Two things,' she said rapidly. 'And they're all the help I can give you. Mother Cybele mentioned Circle Daybreak. I've heard rumours that there are witches somewhere who are starting it up again, witches who want to forget the Burning Times, and who don't hold to Night World law. I don't know if it's true. But if it is, maybe you can find it.'

Thea's breath was taken away. The possibility leaped inside her like some unimagined joy.

'And the other thing,' Aradia said, with a rare smile – almost a brief grin. 'Word is that some of your Redfern cousins have started going peculiar. I've even heard that they're talking about finding human soulmates, just like you. You might try and contact *them* and see what the story is.'

Thea's breath came back, and with it, tears. 'Oh, Aradia. Thank you.'

'Good luck, Thea. And Eric. Both of you, wherever you go.'

Eric, who had been sitting quietly behind the wheel, reached out to touch her hand lightly. 'And you, too.' Thea could tell by his voice that he was puzzled and dazed, but he was trying not to show it.

Then they drove away. Thea turned around to watch Blaise getting smaller and smaller. A little wind blew Blaise's hair, and she looked like a dark and mysterious Aphrodite, a goddess who always did what you least expected.

Eric drove fast until they were a good distance from the shop, then pulled to the curb on a tiny residential street. He looked at Thea and said cautiously, 'Am I immune to *this* stuff? Because I'm not forgetting anything. Or is it going to kick in any minute now?'

Thea kissed him.

Then she began to laugh hysterically.

'No. No.'

'You mean we're really safe? You're going to keep your powers?'

'Yes! Yes!'

She had to keep telling him over and over to convince him. But finally he got it and his face changed. Was transformed by his lightning-bolt smile. He squeezed her and shook her and finally jumped out of the jeep and yelled 'All right! Way to go, Blaise! *All right! Yes!*'

'Eric!'

He pounded the jeep.

'Eric, get back in, you idiot! There might be Night

People around.' Then, still laughing uncontrollably with love and gratitude and the relief of tension, she said, 'Come in *here*.' And she held out her arms.

He jumped back in. They fit together perfectly, his arms around her, his breath against her hair.

'I'm so happy,' he said. 'I love you, witch.'

Thea was laughing and crying at once. 'I love you, too.'

He kissed her temple. She kissed his cheek. Then he kissed her mouth and stayed there for a long while. And Thea forgot about laughing, forgot that there was a world outside the two of them.

And then they sat together in the darkness, resting against each other, just breathing. Safe. Connected.

Thea was with someone who knew her, who saw what she saw. Her soulmate. And they were free to be with each other, without being hunted, without fear.

She was filled with joy and tranquility.

And with quiet sadness, too. It wasn't as if this new beginning came free. She still was an exile, cut off from her family. Gran was lost to her. If she saw Blaise, it would have to be in secret. She'd given up a lot. *Almost* everything.

But she didn't regret it. Not with Eric warm and solid in her arms. Not with the Night World saved from civil war, and the threat to the humans here over.

And what now? she wondered.

Strangely, even though there was no clear answer, she didn't feel afraid. She could visualize many futures, and they all seemed equally likely.

Now they would go to Eric's house, and Eric's mother would be puzzled but generous, and Roz would be ferocious but delighted. And next week Thea would go back to school and transfer into honours zoology.

She would get a scholarship to Davis and become a vet

and use her powers to find out what was wrong with sick animals. Or she would find herself interested in wolves or elephants and would become a naturalist and visit faraway places to study them. Or she and Eric would adopt a puppy like Bud and write a book together to help people understand their dogs.

Or she would find Circle Daybreak and meet witches who wanted to forget the Burning Times. And they would be the first to reintroduce humans to magic, and Rosamund would grow up fierce and proud, knowing all the legends of Hellewise.

Or she would find her vampire cousins and see if the soulmate principle was really coming back. And their group would be like a magnet, attracting other young Night People with radical ideas, starting an underground revolution.

Maybe a new generation of Redferns and Harmans were forming alliances with humans. Maybe it was time for hatred to stop.

Maybe the old powers were waking and new times were coming. Maybe the world was about to change.

Only one thing was sure.

There were infinite possibilities.

She held Eric and felt his breathing and was at peace with the night.

NIGHT WORLD
L.J. Smith

The Night World is a secret society of vampires, werewolves, witches and creatures of darkness – a place where it is too dangerous to fall in love . . .

Read the third compelling volume of Night World:
HUNTRESS, BLACK DAWN and WITCH LIGHT

In *Huntress*, Jez Redfern is wild and dangerous, and the leader of a gang of Night World vampires. But Jez discovers a shocking secret, and faces a terrifying choice: she must either remain a deadly crusader of evil, or fight to protect innocent mortals from her former friends . . . But can she resist her instinct for blood?

In *Black Dawn*, Maggie Neely's biggest worry is leading her soccer team to victory – until her brother Miles goes missing. Maggie must find him. Her search leads her to the vampire Delos, to whom she is strangely attracted. But while Delos lives, Miles could be lost forever. Can Maggie bring herself to destroy him? Or will Delos get to Maggie first?

In *Witch Light*, Keller is part shape-shifter, part panther. She is searching for a new Wild Power. But can the dizzy human girl, Iliana, really be it? And then there's the dashing, romantic Galen. Keller has strong feelings for him, but he's destined to be Iliana's soulmate. Can Keller keep away? Or will she break her promise and fall in love?

h HODDER **A stunning new supernatural series . . .**

BEAUTIFUL DEAD

By Eden Maguire

Not alive. Not dead. Somewhere in between lie the Beautiful Dead . . .

Book 1
Jonas

Something strange is happening at Ellerton High. Jonas, Arizona, Summer and Phoenix. All dead within a year.

Jonas Johnson is the first to die, in a motorbike accident. But there are many unanswered questions, and the three deaths that follow are equally mysterious. Grief-stricken, Darina can't escape her heartache, or the visions of her dead boyfriend Phoenix, and the others who died. And all the while, the sound of beating wings echoes inside her head . . .

Are these visions real? Or do the Beautiful Dead only exist in Darina's traumatised imagination?

THE LAST VAMPIRE

These are the tales of the greatest female vampire of them all . . . Alisa Perne – a beautiful teenager, yet she has lived for 5000 years.

All six compelling stories now available as three satisfying bind-up editions

THE LAST VAMPIRE Bind-up 1:
THE LAST VAMPIRE and BLACK BLOOD

Beautiful, strong, dangerous and deadly, Alisa Perne is not your average teenager. For 5000 years she has endured heartbreak, betrayal and near death – enough for several lifetimes. Now Alisa is living in the 21st century, ready to take on an ancient and poweful enemy. She will do whatever it takes to protect herself and her secret. Even if that means destroying the people she loves.

For Alisa, human weakness must be battled against. The Last Vampire will not die.

THE LAST VAMPIRE

These are the tales of the greatest female vampire of them all . . . Alisa Perne – a beautiful teenager, yet she has lived for 5000 years.

All six compelling stories now available as three satisfying bind-up editions

THE LAST VAMPIRE Bind-up 2:
RED DICE and PHANTOM

The US government is in pursuit of Alisa and her partner. Intent on obtaining their vampire DNA. Alisa has no choice but to go on the run. She cannot allow her blood to seep into the public domain – it is way too deadly, too dangerous. Then Alisa makes a discovery that both delights and terrifies her. If all plays out as she hopes she will finally know happiness. If not, she faces untold tragedy and danger. And all the time a powerful force is watching over Alisa. Someone who knows all that ever was, and all that will be . . .

From the bestselling Christopher Pike . . .

THE LAST VAMPIRE

These are the tales of the greatest female vampire of them all . . . Alisa Perne – a beautiful teenager, yet she has lived for 5000 years.

All six compelling stories now available as three satisfying bind-up editions

THE LAST VAMPIRE Bind-up 3:
EVIL THIRST and CREATURES OF FOREVER

Alisa is battling with a heartbreaking dilemma. Her daughter Kalika has disappeared. Alisa knows the great danger Kalika poses to the human world – but can she bring herself to destroy her own flesh and blood? And another threat looms large to Alisa. Someone means to destroy the 5000 year-old vampire, and Alisa's only hope lies in reliving the evil of her monstrous past.

Then she can eliminate it, for ever . . .